Fuel the Fire

Addicted Series

RECOMMENDED READING ORDER

Fuel the Fire

KRISTA RITCHIE
AND
BECCA RITCHIE

BERKLEY ROMANCE
NEW YORK

BERKLEY ROMANCE
Published by Berkley
An imprint of Penguin Random House LLC
penguinrandomhouse.com

Library of Congress Cataloging-in-Publication Data

Names: Ritchie, Krista, author. | Ritchie, Becca, author.
Title: Fuel the fire / Krista Ritchie and Becca Ritchie.
Description: First Berkley Romance Edition. |
New York: Berkley Romance, 2023. | Series: Addicted
Identifiers: LCCN 2023022022 | ISBN 9780593639641 (trade paperback)
Subjects: LCGFT: Romance fiction. | Novels.
Classification: LCC PS3618.I7675 F84 2023 | DDC 813/.6—dc23/eng/20230512
LC record available at https://lccn.loc.gov/2023022022

Fuel the Fire was originally self-published, in different form, in 2015.

First Berkley Romance Edition: December 2023

Printed in the United States of America
1st Printing

Book design by Kristin del Rosario
Interior art: Broken heart on wall © Valentina Shikina / Shutterstock.com

To you, the reader:

When we originally wrote the Addicted series, we were in college with big, lofty dreams and hopes of Lily and Lo's story finding some people. It became so much more than just one romance between childhood friends, thanks to readers who wanted to see more.

It was about sisters, written by two sisters. It was about friendship, and the family you have and also make along the way. Rose's and Daisy's stories—the Calloway Sisters spin-off series—are woven so intrinsically into Lily's novels because we believe that one life does not stop while another goes on a journey. Every novel impacts every character. So the best way to read Lily's story and not miss a thing is by combining her series with the Calloway Sisters series in a ten-book reading order. It's the order we wrote the novels—all three sisters intertwined together.

This is the Addicted series. Ten books. Six friends. Three couples. One epic saga.

We hope these characters bring you as much happiness as they've brought us throughout the years.

As Lily would say, thankyouthankyouthankyou for choosing them and us. Happy reading!

All the love in every universe,
Krista and Becca

Prologue

Connor Cobalt

N ame?" Behind a desk, a woman shuffled through white cards with crimson lanyards attached.

"Richard Connor Cobalt." I gave her an amiable smile.

She procured the corresponding name tag. "Welcome to this year's Model UN, Richard. Good luck." Her last phrase—while nothing more than a meaningless farewell—punctured a part of my head, poking at a nerve.

Good luck.

I liked having control of my fate. And luck meant that I had none. That I'd have to let someone inferior decide *my* outcome. I understood that some judges were biased, most of which I could likely outwit. But climbing over people was my specialty. I wasn't battling a slot machine or a computer.

People were malleable. People were predictable.

I would beat the judges. I would win.

Instead of wearing my irritation, I gave her another relaxed smile and put the lanyard around my neck. She was staring at me like I was a teenage boy trying to play the role of a grown man. It was that look that dug beneath my skin, the expression that said I was small and undeserving because I was only just fifteen.

"You should remember my name," I said.

She laughed hesitantly. "I'll try, but there are a lot of you."

"And yet I'm the only one you'll see win every year."

Her uncertainty only grew, like *did I hear you right? Did you mean what I think you did?*

My eyes barely flickered to her laminated pin and then I gestured absentmindedly to her stack of cards. "The twenty-seventh name tag is out of place. 'Rolland' comes before 'Rose.'" I smiled again. "Good luck, Marianne. You'll need it."

I was a prick.

An asshole.

A conceited, arrogant son of a bitch.

But to me, there was nothing more frustrating, more exasperating, than being deemed unworthy for the pure fact that I was younger than whomever I faced. My thoughts, my ideas never mattered to most adults. To have someone seriously listen to me, as an equal, was nearly impossible. I was simply "a kid"—an intelligent kid but not one whose thoughts superseded theirs.

I would never talk down to an infant the way that people talked down to me, a fifteen-year-old.

I knew that I'd gain respect with age. I had to *wait* on some absurd timeline created by society. *Bullshit*, I thought. Life was bullshit, and the only way for it to not grate at me was to play along.

And so I always did.

She stared at me, open-mouthed and unsure.

I waved her goodbye, and my grin spread across my face as I walked down the lobby hallway, my leather duffel slung on my shoulder.

After I signed in, I headed towards the elevators. The hotel had sectioned off a number of floors for competitors. Faust Boarding School for Young Boys would take the sixth floor with three other preparatory schools.

Fourteen- to eighteen-year-olds already rode up and down the glass elevators in boredom or with actual places to be, like me.

Guys in burnt-orange blazers shuffled off the elevator. I entered and pressed the sixth-floor button, tempted to hit the "close doors" button as well. But I waited, watching two girls approach. The taller one with glossy brown hair had these hellfire eyes that struck me as malevolent, pinpointed and blazing. No matter which direction she turned. Her mouth moved at a rapid pace, gesticulating angrily as she talked.

I couldn't hear her; too much noise interference from people congesting the hotel.

I scrutinized the girls from afar. No name tags, so they hadn't signed in yet. Both wore navy-blue plaid skirts, their white-collared blouses tucked in. I caught sight of the embroidered insignias along the breast pockets: *Dalton Academy.*

I didn't have any preconceived notions of the coed private school. Last year, we beat them. And the year before that, we had no trouble. I assumed this year would be the same.

"No, I'm *not* letting it go. It's utter bullshit, Lydia," the taller girl cursed. They slipped into the elevator, the girl too pissed to realize that she needed to press a button, and I was too curious to interrupt.

"The manager had a point," Lydia said with resignation. She had a slender frame, freckles and one long, red braid.

The other girl placed her hands on her hips, fuming. She choked the elevator with each heavy inhale.

I grazed her from head to toe: black high heels, dark red lipstick, sleek brown pony and tyrannical yellow-green eyes, burning holes into the glass. I was sharing an elevator with a tempestuous, electric storm that I refused to calm. I always wished to be swept into madness, if only for a moment, to truncate the mundane, ordinary moments of my existence.

"His argument was that three *girls* can fit in a king-sized bed, but three *boys* can't. So we have to take the worse room when management booked the same suite twice. Do you see how ridiculous that is?"

"It's true though. Boys are bigger than us." Lydia shrugged.

The elevator doors slid shut and we rose.

"We're sleeping in the suite we were assigned," the girl refuted. "*They* can take the smaller room."

"They won't agree to it," Lydia said.

"You just don't want to argue with them about it," the girl retorted. "If you want to stay quiet, that's fine, but I can't let the Faust boys win. Half of them believe they piss gold, and the other half walk around like they created the earth and sky."

I lowered my head to hide my grin. I was part of the latter half.

She continued, standing taller, "Their heads are so inflated that I will *cheer* when someone decapitates them at the neck."

I could barely hold back from laughing. I stared at the ceiling, my lips curving upwards even more.

I'd never heard a girl like her before.

Never in my life.

I had most of the details I needed to understand the events. Management had double-booked the same suite with Dalton and Faust and now they were telling one of them to move.

Lydia softened her voice. "The Faust boys are intimidating for a reason. Sebastian said they win Outstanding Delegation every year."

"Every year that *we* weren't here," the girl rebutted.

That pushed me to speak. "I don't think we've met." I turned towards them, and the girls shifted their stances, finally acknowledging the third person on the elevator.

They both perused my towering frame. At fifteen, I was six foot and still growing. My wavy brown hair was styled perfectly, my brow was arched in mock contemplation and I wore a black blazer with a crimson tie.

Faust's uniform.

The girl's nose flared, especially as she eyed my name tag, *Faust Boarding School for Young Boys* typed in small script below *Richard Connor Cobalt*.

Lydia paled.

I held out my hand to her first. "Nice to meet you."

She shook it, her palm clammy and her grip limp.

When I turned to the other girl, she crossed her arms over her chest and tapped her heel repeatedly. I waited for her to introduce herself. I wanted to know her name. Badly. I ached to hear it. Any part of it.

I told her, "You're my greatest competition." I hoped she'd soften at the compliment. Whether I spoke true or not, I had no clue yet. She remained tense, and the doors began to slide open on the sixth floor, *my* floor.

She didn't answer me. She pushed past to exit.

Lydia sprinted to catch up to her friend. "Rose," she called out.

I stepped into the hallway with a wider grin, and Rose glanced over her shoulder with a scathing glare, knowing Lydia just unleashed what Rose denied me. I didn't have to check my room card again. I was in 643, one of the balcony suites that overlooked the café and courtyard in the middle of the hotel.

I thought, for a split second, that maybe I was in the double-booked room too. The chance was microscopic, but it wasn't improbable.

As soon as I saw Dillon and Henry waiting at the door marked *643* with another Dalton girl—all of them glowering—I realized that I belonged to this fight too.

"Management gave you a new room," Rose lied to Dillon, passing keycards to the blond-haired sixteen-year-old.

The second I approached, her brows knotted in confusion.

"Dude." Dillon nudged my arm. "They double-booked us with these Dalton girls."

I didn't take my eyes off Rose. "I heard." I grabbed Dillon's keycards and passed them back to Rose.

Realization washed over her face.

This was my suite too. And no one ever took what was mine. Not unless I willingly gave it to them, and I wouldn't just give her this room. I didn't want to cram in the same bed with Dillon and Henry. I wanted the living room, the extra desk, the couch, more quiet space to study.

But so did Rose.

"Just switch with us." Rose tried it this way. "It's the polite thing to do."

"Why?" I asked. "Because you're a girl?"

Her eyes narrowed. "Richard."

"Rose."

She let out a small growl. "What do you want for it?"

My brows lifted. *Be careful, Rose*, was my first thought. I knew she was fourteen, if this was her first year competing, and maybe, just maybe, she was willing to do anything to win.

Maybe she was just like me.

"Let's play a game," I said, dropping my duffel on the ground. "The winner will take the suite. The loser gets the smaller room."

"Smaller room?" I heard Henry huff behind me, realizing that Rose was going to fool him into switching.

"What kind of game?" Her voice was frosted with ice.

"Trivia." It took us another ten minutes to sort out the details. All six of us wrote down categories on slips of paper and put them in Dillon's baseball hat. Only Rose and I would compete. Dillon and Henry knew my IQ was higher than theirs. And both girls, Lydia and Anna, pointed immediately to Rose. Whether they were scared to go against me or whether she was merely smarter than them, I didn't know yet.

"Who's going first?" Dillon asked, holding the hat.

Rose opened her red handbag on the crook of her arm and

acquired a quarter. "We'll flip." She called tails, and I lost to chance. But I wouldn't lose to anything else.

She plucked a paper from the hat. "'Ancient Egypt.'" According to our rules, we had to create questions without using any reference material.

I wondered if she could even do this part.

I waited. And her eyes met mine in a harsher glare. "God of wisdom and learning," she challenged.

My lips twitched into a smile. "Thoth."

She knew I was right, but her shoulders still pulled back, not giving up.

"Is he right?" Dillon asked Henry, who sat on the ground with his laptop propped open.

"Yeah," Henry said into a surprised laugh.

Dillon patted me on the shoulder. "Good job, Cobalt. Keep it up."

Off the same category, I asked her, "Wife of Akhenaten?" I watched her think about it. I could stop here, stump her with little information, ending the game quickly. Or I could test her, to truly see how much she knew.

I wanted to prolong this.

So I added, "Stepmother of Tutankhamun, known for attempts to change polytheistic religion to mono—"

"Nefertiti," she cut me off.

She was right.

It was my turn to pick the next category at random. I read the paper aloud: "'Medical terms.'"

Her chest rose and fell heavily.

I couldn't hide a burgeoning smile. "Rapid breathing," I challenged.

"Tachypnea," she retorted. "Stop smiling."

"Now she doesn't like smiling."

"Not all smiling."

"Just mine, then?" I questioned.

"*Mainly* yours." It was like she was saying, *don't think you're that special.*

I rubbed my lips, trying not to laugh. "And what's mine like?"

She glared. "Like you've already beaten me. Like you're halfway up my skirt. Like you're the ruler of every free nation and every free man. Shall I go on?"

"Please do," I said, amused. "I was wondering what else I rule. Could it be every free animal? Or just the ones in zoos?"

"Oooh," people heckled. More students had gathered around us, not only from Faust and Dalton but from other schools. They packed around the balcony and hallway, having to cram in while we continued this game.

She ignored me and challenged, "An abnormal growth of tissue caused by the uncontrolled and rapid multiplication of cells."

"A tumor."

"Also known as *you*," she retorted.

"Oooh," the crowds jeered again.

I actually laughed. And that merely wound her up all over again. I could practically read her enraged eyes, which said, *Shut up.*

Fifteen minutes passed and both of our questions were becoming more difficult. We drew closer together somehow, only a couple feet separating us as we spewed questions and answers to star constellations, composers, aesthetic theories, philosophy and American history.

She was much smarter than I'd initially thought. Perhaps, even, the smartest competitor I'd encountered in my adolescence. She liked facts, random knowledge, as much as me.

"Your turn, Richard." She said my first name with *spite*, venom seeping into each letter, as though she were slaughtering the syllables. I didn't care to correct her, to tell her that everyone called me Connor. I was taken by her passion, so I wouldn't stop her. Not once.

I looked down at my slip of paper. It was in neat, precise cursive. It had to be her handwriting. *Characters from Shakespeare's Plays.*

She tried to force back a smile.

So she liked Shakespeare. I told her a character: "Sir John Falstaff." Now she had to name the play.

Without a beat, she answered, "*The Merry Wives of Windsor* and *Henry IV, Part 1* and *Part 2*." She was quick to ask me a question. We no longer waited for Henry to confirm answers that we knew were correct. "Ariel?"

"*The Tempest.*" I assumed it must've been her favorite.

She plucked the next paper. "Birthplaces of ancient civilizations."

I tried not to gloat since she was already heated. I was the one who'd written down that category.

She took a deep breath and stared at the ceiling, racking her brain for a trivia fact. "Mesopotamia . . . 1800 to 1686 B.C." Her voice was quieter, more uncertain about this category than the others.

"Old Babylonian," I told her in a hushed voice too. It felt like we were the only two in the hallway for a minute. Our eyes met, and I could see the defeat in hers before I even asked a question. She had no confidence in this subject.

I waited to ask her something. There was a long string of silence except for Henry's fingers hitting the keyboard.

"He's right," Henry exhaled.

Every Faust boy cheered. The Dalton girls and guys whispered among themselves and tried to pump Rose with encouragements.

I didn't want to bring her down as much as I wanted to build her up, but I also liked to win. And I wouldn't lose this game. "Crete, 3000 to 1100 B.C."

After one minute, she frowned and shook her head. "I don't know." Each word sounded wrong from her lips.

"It's Minoan," I announced.

Everyone groaned behind her. Everyone cheered behind me.

I tried to tune them out, leaving just her and me. I craved more time, maybe even alone. I wanted to talk. I wanted to explore her. I wanted so many things in that moment that my brain went five directions at once. I was overwhelmed.

More overwhelmed than I'd ever been.

"Congratulations!" she said, having to raise her voice through the applause and groans. She pushed the keycards into my chest. I thought she'd put up a bigger fight than this. I would've tried a different avenue, an alternate path, to obtain what I wanted.

"That's it?" I asked, dipping my head towards hers so she could hear me.

"You won fairly. But I'll beat you *fairly* this week." She wasn't willing to make a bargain, a barter, something *more*. She wasn't giving up. She just played by the rules, whereas I always searched for loopholes.

Rose wasn't a carbon copy of me, I recognized. She was someone else entirely.

"You'll see a lot more of me," I realized. If she was this smart, I'd see her around the academic circuits. I'd see her even more if I asked her out, but that wasn't nearly as alluring as being her competitor. Not yet, at least.

"Then you'll need to buy me some barf bags." She looked me up and down. I was always physically fit, and I appeared exactly as I dressed: well-off, cultured, proper, rich. An elite boarding school prick.

"Do you always vomit on guys you like," I asked, "or just me?"

She glared. "The more you fish for compliments, the more I want to puke on you."

"So it is just me, then."

She growled.

I grinned.

And our respective friends began pulling us away, towards our different hotel rooms. I never realized how bored I had been with life. How mundane my surroundings looked. How unchallenged I'd become.

I never realized all of these things.

Until I met her.

Eleven Years Later

One

Rose Cobalt

Take directions from your husband, Rose Cobalt.

Who, *who* fated me with this night? *You, Rose.* A sour taste fills my mouth. I am partly to blame, I'll admit. I refused to let him drive. I thought if I was behind the wheel, he'd tell me where we're headed.

Instead, he's given me the barest of directions. I'm driving blindly, at his will.

Take directions from Connor Cobalt, outside of the bedroom. I'd rather drown myself in hot, bubbling magma.

"Turn left at the light," Connor says, his fingers to his lips. I catch his smug smile, illuminated in the blue glow of the dashboard.

I itch to do the opposite, to take a sharp *right*, but wherever we're going, I want to be there as much as him. The endgame—which I am privy to—means more to me than starting a fresh rivalry with my husband. So I suck up my overwhelming pride and whip my Escalade left.

I can feel him gloating. "The more you grin like I'm giving you a quickie in a disgusting public bathroom, the more my ovaries wither and *die*," I tell him. "So just think about all of our future children you're annihilating, Richard."

He outstretches his arm behind my headrest. "I'm so extra-ordinary that my mere grin can make you infertile?"

"I was insulting you," I retort, my eyes flickering to him.

His brow arches with more satisfaction. "It was partially a compliment and partially erroneous."

I scoff. "Erroneous?"

"Illogical, irrational, senseless—"

"I *know* what 'erroneous' means. I just want to cut off your tongue for using it against me." He may be right. It's not a rational statement, but I would hope my ovaries would stand with me and not firmly on his side.

"You forget that I use my tongue for your pleasure—turn right."

I swing the car to the right. "I don't need your tongue," I refute. "I have other means of pleasuring myself." Though masturbating isn't quite as good or substantial, but I'm avoiding another compliment towards a man who finds them in insults.

His fingers drum the headrest. "Are these means battery-operated?"

I shoot him a sharp look, not denying the truth.

His thumb brushes my cheek, and I actually relax some. "Your argument lacks evidence, darling. Turn left after this light."

I roll to a stop, the red light gleaming along the nearly deserted street. It's 10 p.m. on Thanksgiving night, and everyone is eating pie with their families indoors. Not gallivanting across the back roads of Philadelphia on a bizarre mission.

"Where are we going?" I ask for the fourth time.

"A parking lot," he says again.

"I've passed about thirty of them already." I motion to the empty one beside a dimly lit gas station. "Will that one not suffice?"

"A *specific* parking lot," Connor amends. One that he'd had to Google on his phone, the device clutched in his palm. "We're almost there. Do you think your ovaries will survive until then?"

"Do you plan on impregnating me in this parking lot?" I glare, spinning fully towards him while we wait for the green light. He wears a blue button-down and suit jacket, tailored perfectly for his six-foot-four frame. Connor Cobalt is as classy as he is conceited. Both attract me.

Both annoy me.

I'm a paradox. And maybe that's why he loves me.

"I plan on impregnating you seven more times," he declares, "but not tonight." He cups my face, and his thumb brushes my bottom lip in a slow, measured line.

My chest falls shallowly, especially as his eyes flit to my mouth. He wants eight kids. An *empire*. We already have one child together, but there are stipulations that we haven't discussed in full detail yet if we want more. For another time. Another day. We have too many crises to stir another one.

"You're taking too much pleasure in this," I say a bit quieter than I intended. I'm not even sure what I'm referring to: our proposed empire, him controlling our destination or him turning me on?

"You're the one out of breath," Connor says calmly, but I hear the humor behind his voice. After being married for almost two and a half years, I've learned the subtlety in his tones. Either that or he's decided to ease off the façade for me. I like to think it's a little of both.

But I doubt I'll ever know.

"It's green," he announces without breaking my gaze.

I turn my head, and his hand drops. I drive to "wherever the hell he directs me to"—which is my least-favorite destination.

After another five minutes, he tells me to slow down and turn right into a parking lot. I pick my foot off the gas and the car idles.

"Right here." He gestures ahead of us.

I swerve into the empty parking lot and digest my surroundings: the front of a closed fabric store, lights off, the building as dark as the starless sky.

I park my Escalade in the third row and switch off the ignition, my heart thudding against my tight rib cage. The quiet blankets us, the reality of our choices starting to catch up to my head.

Connor watches me, not speaking. Maybe he thinks I'll back out.

I won't.

I understand who and what this is for.

"Let's just do this quick." I unbuckle and swivel around to face him. "Before anyone realizes we're gone." We slipped out of my parent's house after apple pie. I set my six-month-old daughter in my mother's arms and left her there for a couple hours. That was harder than this will be.

I pull my glossy brown hair back into a sleek pony, snapping the band violently before I focus on Connor in the passenger seat. His brows are pinched, lines across his forehead, his enjoyment depleting with mine.

My spine is at a stiff ninety-degree angle, and I struggle to uncross my ankles. "What now?" I ask, though I'm fairly certain I know what happens next.

"You want instructions?" He gives me a pointed look like, *you've been arguing with me for the past hour for giving them.*

My eyes flame. "When it comes to your penis, I would like instructions, yes." I've yet to master blowing him, and the whole ordeal gives me an anxious heat that I almost never wear.

Blowing him in a public parking lot—I never imagined I'd do something so juvenile. But when it comes to protecting the people I love, my list of *don't*s decreases dramatically.

He unclips his seat belt. "Lean against the door and spread your legs open." My eyes grow in surprise.

"What?"

"Lean against the door—"

"I heard you the first time," I retort. "I just . . ." I have to read between his words. *Spread your legs open.* I dazedly shake my head.

Translation: *You're not blowing me, darling.*

He waits for me to accept this switch.

I hesitate, only because I like following the rules. "Connor, they told me to give you oral." If we really wanted, I could even *pretend* to blow him. We just need to act like we're doing it close to the windows.

He slides near me and reaches down, gripping my ankle. He slips off my black, five-inch heels before I can protest. And then he lifts my feet onto the seat, so I'm forced to lean against the door like he previously requested. I need the support anyway, blood rushing through my veins at his strong, assured movements.

With my ankles still in his grasp, he splits my legs apart. I tug down the hem of my pleated black dress, shrouding my lacy black panties from his view—but more importantly, the view of someone outside.

A determined look pulses in his blue eyes, ambition and confidence that's harder and better than a slap on the ass.

He kneels on the seat and reaches beneath my dress, his fingers skimming my panties.

"Connor," I warn. All I can think—if we don't do this right, to their liking, then we're screwing everything on day one.

"Ils jouent notre jeu. On ne joue pas le leur." They play our game. We don't play theirs. He adds in French, *"Ensemble." Together.*

We do this together or not at all.

I'm more in love with him conquering the world by his side than I ever was as his competition. He was ready to be my teammate the minute I graduated prep school, but I put the brakes on that, choosing a different college than him. I wasn't ready to be something more. We stayed rivals. He didn't want to wait for my cap and gown, for our entrance into adulthood, and so when the opportunity arose, he asked me out.

We dated. We married.

We had a baby.

Together, we're a force of nature to be reckoned with. That's not my hubris speaking. It's just the truth.

I nod once, power pouring through me. "*Ensemble.*" *Together.*

He kisses my ankle as he raises my leg, slipping off my panties. I keep yanking at my dress, the side of my ass exposed. Though I'm not sure how much someone can spot through the windows.

Connor sets my panties on the dashboard and then places his hand on mine, shielding more of my body from view. He lifts my left leg over his shoulder, his body hovering over the middle console.

He whispers, "Lean back and shut your eyes."

I do as told; even if I'm not in the bedroom, this is a bedroom activity. And I'd rather not be in control.

I rest against the car door and close my eyes, trying not to think about anyone lurking outside.

Connor grips my hips and scoots me closer to him, so my back is at a better angle, only my shoulders braced against the door handle.

In the quiet moment, a distant car honk sounds closer, and my eyes snap open. I try to straighten and peer out the windshield.

Connor grips my face, rotating my head to him. "Focus on me. Or would you rather suck my cock?"

I glare. "Would *you* like to switch?" I challenge, even though I *in no way* want to be photographed with my head above his pants. Not if there's an alternative.

His head in my crotch. I approve.

"You know what I find mildly irritating?" he asks, his voice calm, collected, but I hear the tightness of his words, as though annoyance, a hidden emotion, fists each syllable.

"Your voice," I rebut.

He withholds a grin. "Answering a question with a question." His clutch is still forceful on my jaw. My body is in his complete possession. "This is how you answer a question, Rose."

I listen closely.

"No," he says, "I do not want to switch places with you. They believe we're their marionettes. We'll show them the strings, but we will *always* move on our own accord." He pauses, his eyes flitting to my mouth again. "But most importantly, you believe my tongue is expendable." His face nears mine, which he grasps, and I breathe so heavily as he whispers, "You're going to remember, Rose, why it's *absolutely* essential."

I feel myself clench.

"Now close your eyes," he commands.

I have no problem listening to him now, blocking out our surroundings—or at least my imagination, which is doing more harm than good.

I shut my eyes again, and as he lowers his head between my legs, his hand travels from my jaw to my neck. He's reaching up and choking me with the right amount of force. *Oh God.* His tongue and mouth kiss my heat—I shudder and grip the leather, the back of my head hitting the glass window, shoulders digging into the handle.

"Please," I cry deeply, feeling him adjust his fingers around my neck, gripping slightly harder so I can't speak. My head lightens . . . *God, yes.*

The sensitivity that his tongue plays with—it's better than any of my toys. It shocks each nerve and flames my core, my skin flushed. I hear only my staggered breaths in the silence of the car.

I open my eyes. Just to see his head disappeared between my legs. One of his hands is up my dress, clutching the side of my ass. And his other long, outstretched arm lies against my body as he steals my oxygen.

That arm builds my arousal as much as everything else, my toes beginning to curl. *Connor* . . .

I hold on to his forearm and touch his large hand that wraps around the majority of my neck. And then his phone buzzes by the gearshift, threatening to tumble beneath the depths of my seat.

He removes his hand off my ass to grab it, but he continues pleasuring me, a second cry in my throat at the way he hits a nerve.

He passes me the phone, reminding me that we're a team here. His fingers loosen on my neck, only a little to reorient my head. I keep the cell low and open his lock screen with his password: 0610.

It's a text message.

Where the hell did you and Rose go?—Loren

I try to stifle a cringe, hating to think about Loren Hale while I'm with Connor like this. Actually, thinking about him at all is almost as low on my to-do list as setting myself on fire. (Setting myself on fire ranks higher.)

Though that's not entirely accurate, seeing as how we're new business partners. I never thought that'd happen. I'm not wholly happy about it, but I'm not disappointed either. Besides Connor, my relationship with Loren is the most complex one I have.

Before I can even tell Connor about the text, another one buzzes.

And this time, I have a hard time reading the words. Connor suddenly fills me with his fingers, and my back arches and my head tips to the side, my eyes tightening shut, too many heightened emotions overtaking me in a hot, electric wave. My body is his in this moment. He could do whatever he wanted to me, and I'd let him, willingly.

"Please," I beg. I used to hate the sound of my voice when I was with him in bed. How weak and wanting it was—but now I love that I can give myself to someone else this way. I'm allowed to be vulnerable too.

He pumps his fingers deeper into me, simultaneously flicking my clit with his tongue. He squeezes my neck, and I reach a blinding climax, my lips parting. No noise escapes, too breathless to create a moan. My hips rise and my muscles constrict. He leaves his fingers inside of me while I pulse around them.

Connor raises his head, watching me catch my breath, his own desire washing over his features. He stares at me like he'd rather fuck me at our house than return to my parents'. If we didn't have responsibilities, like friends and a daughter, then maybe that'd be possible.

But I like the way our life is. Minus a couple large kinks that we need to smooth down before Jane reaches a certain age. Before we decide to have more children.

These are the kind of kinks that have deadlines. If we don't iron them by a certain point, it's over for us. The Cobalt family will just consist of Jane, Connor, and me.

I want Jane to have a sister, more than anything else. The best parts of my childhood consisted of Lily, Daisy, and Poppy. And I can't imagine her growing up without one.

Connor looks at me as though he's reading my innermost thoughts, with reverence and intrigue. I touch his hand around my neck and he laces my fingers with his.

He sits up, kneeling.

I check his phone again.

What the fuck are you doing? Samantha just opened photo albums. We're going to be stuck here for another three fucking hours if you don't come back.—Ryke

"It seems we're wanted."

"We're always wanted," he says, pulling my arm so I straighten up against the seat. His lips linger near my neck. "We're the oldest, smartest and most responsible of our roommates."

I turn my head to call him conceited and maybe note that his ego is choking me more than his hand.

The minute I swing in his direction, he kisses me, not for long, but enough that my insult disappears. He bites my lip gently before he releases.

I swallow, and as I clench between my legs, I suddenly remember something. I am not wearing panties. And I'm sitting on a leather seat. *My* leather seat. And I'm aroused and wet and—I push away from him and snatch my panties off the dashboard. I try to examine the damage I've caused to my beautiful leather seat, and how gross it must be for me to sit here while we drive back.

"You're not that wet, Rose," he says.

I smack his chest. "Shut up—"

He clasps my hand again and lifts me onto his lap so I can see the seat. No stains, but I contemplate whether or not I should have the leather properly—

"I'll have it cleaned tomorrow," Connor tells me, easing my concerns. I nod, and he slips my panties up my legs, dressing me. He reaches over and opens the passenger door before climbing out, setting me on *his* chair. When he walks around the Escalade to the driver's side, his cell vibrates in my palm.

Got the photo. You'll see it tomorrow.—WA

My shoulders relax. "They accepted the switch."

Connor hears me as he shuts the door, the corners of his lips rising. He'd been certain they wouldn't have a problem. His confidence in life and his choices are unparalleled.

He turns the car on with a much wider grin. "'Look like the innocent flower, but be the serpent under it.'"

I tilt my head at him. "*Macbeth*." The quote from Shakespeare is very familiar to me.

He wears that billion-dollar grin again. We won round one of a much larger game tonight. At least that's what it feels like.

At the end of the day, we're still in bed with the media. And no one knows this but Connor and me.

People look to Connor to fix their problems, to solve things greater than them, and usually he says no. If there's no benefit for him, he sees no point to help, to take that risk.

But there was one exception.

I saw it happen. That day. Weeks ago. Connor came into our bedroom and told me that he had to bury an article. He said the only way to do it was to make a deal with the press. Me and him. If we fed a tabloid scandalous photos or a headline every so often, then they'd agree to never print this one defaming editorial.

"Is it about Jane?" I asked, my eyes flaming. I was ready to raise hell at the *Celebrity Crush* offices, to march to New York and stick a finger in the face of a journalist and shout and scream. I even grabbed my purse off my vanity stool.

Connor stopped me, and I read his gaze well enough.

It wasn't about our daughter.

The article was about someone else. He explained how *Celebrity Crush* was going to run a story on Lily and Loren's son, my sister and my brother-in-law. How the tabloid was going to claim their paternity test a forgery, citing Maximoff's deep chocolate-brown hair as evidence of his being Ryke's son. Ryke, as in Loren's half brother.

Lo has light brown hair. His birth mother's hair color. Not dark brown, the shade that Ryke, their father, and now Moffy all share.

The article is a stretch, a false claim. But one that would rock Lily and Loren's world. After fighting for so long, they deserved a win.

Their son deserves to *never* doubt his parentage.

"I have to help Lo," Connor said, his brows cinching at his own words. He knew. He knew that what he was doing was so out of his character. Because here was a man who always weighs opportunity cost. This in no way benefited him. In fact, it cost him.

And for the first time in probably his entire life, he was choosing a price with no reward for himself.

"You know when you asked me to do this with you?" I say softly while he drives back to my childhood house.

He nods once.

"I think I fell in love with you all over again," I admit. This is something I would have chosen. Without a second thought. To protect the people I love. Years ago, Connor would have laughed at those words.

Love. It meant nothing to him.

Now it's guiding his choices.

Two

Connor Cobalt

can already tell that she has bad taste in clothes," Rose declares, our six-month-old daughter sitting upright between her legs. "I put this Chanel clutch in front of her and an ugly straw hat, and she went after the ugly straw hat."

I rub a towel through my hair, just coming out of the shower. On our four-poster bed, Jane wears a straw hat that dips below her big blue eyes, a delighted smile pulling her soft cheeks. I can feel mine rise.

I wondered if I would feel weakened by a child, like a soft-hearted, loving fool—emotions that my mother refused to feel with me. But it wasn't ever the case. I love Jane, and I feel strong enough to move mountains for her, to part waters and dig through stone.

Rose is glaring at me. "I'm glad you find this amusing."

"I find both of you beautiful." I splay the damp towel on a chair. "The only amusing part is that you put our daughter through an experiment to test whether or not she likes Chanel."

"I was curious." Rose bunches her wet hair on her shoulder. She took a shower before me. We've been awake since four this morning.

For one, Jane was wailing and couldn't sleep. It's not unusual, even after six months.

For another, we're both waiting for our late-night activity to surface on the *Celebrity Crush* website. Rose has her laptop propped open beside her, and she refreshes the page every minute.

I step into my black slacks. "She chose the straw hat because of the tassels."

Rose examines the hat on Jane's head, the bright-yellow ribbon and the dangling strand of lime-green frill. "But the Chanel clutch has a gold clasp and it's cuter."

"That's partly an opinion, not a fact, darling."

She shoots me a look and then touches Jane's toes, who giggles and babbles. Jane tries to raise her head at Rose but the hat falls further over her eyes. While I clip my silver watch on my wrist, I observe Rose's smile, a smile that she produces only for Jane.

I cling to the rarities in life, the unusual fragments that open windows into a person's soul. Rose's genuine, *warm* smile is a rarity. It's not a constant. And I wouldn't want it to be. It's a powerful blip that punches me hard. If this happened frequently, it wouldn't have the same effect. It wouldn't be unique anymore.

A child, *our* child, unlatches things inside of us that we've both kept closed. Love, for me. Warmth, for her. I selfishly crave another. I selflessly would ruin my reputation to protect every child of mine.

I call that even.

Rose speaks to Jane in her normal voice. "I knew I didn't toss away this hat for a reason. You can have it, my little gremlin." She kisses her cheek, and Jane almost says something like *ya-ya*.

"What will it take?" I ask, standing at the foot of the bed, enamored with the scene. I don't elaborate since I've asked her this before.

Rose stares off at the comforter while she collects her thoughts.

"A couple kinks need to be smoothed down before we think about having more kids." She always says this. It's a rehearsed line. And she always calls them *kinks* instead of what they really are.

I'm not bringing up our sex tapes. I'll leave that for another time. It's nearly out of my control—I can barely even admit it to myself.

But the other "kink"—we can smooth. Together. "You're afraid that we're denying Jane a choice to be in or out of the media. She's involuntarily going to be in magazines throughout her adolescence because she's too young to say yes or no. And in a perfect world, you'd like to wait for her consent to be thrust into this type of spotlight."

Rose hugs Jane closer to her body. "It's not just up to us, Connor." She grits her teeth. "Last week, I was grocery shopping with Daisy and some asshole with a camera approached me and . . ." Her eyes blaze and her throat bobs as she swallows.

I frown, my stomach roiling at her hanging endnote. "I haven't heard this story."

"Because I can barely repeat it without vomiting."

I sit on the edge of the mattress and place a hand on her bent knee. I don't want to draw illogical conclusions. If he'd touched her, Rose would've sued. Still, my head pounds like it's being flooded with water.

She inhales strongly. "He told me that he bought a house a few miles from our neighborhood, and he said—I quote—'I'm going to be around for every moment of Jane's life. Probably until she leaves for college.' I . . ." She shakes her head. "It's gross, and I can't help but think that we've taken some sort of freedom from her. If this is the world we're bringing children into, I'm not sure it's safe enough to have another."

What I'm about to say next will piss her off. But I have to say it. "There's no way to rewind time and go back to the way things were." Fading into the background, ignoring the media, we all tried it for months. In the end, they just swallowed us more, finding parts of our lives interesting: birthdays, vacations, lunches in Philly, pregnancies, new haircuts, a car wreck. Anything.

"I put us here, then?" she says, taking more blame than I thought she would. "The reality show made us more popular, to the point where people now crave parts of our lives."

"It also helped people see Lily and Lo in a better light. They became *loved*, Rose. Two people who needed affection more than any of us." I don't add that the reality show also bolstered my company's success. That fact is tangled with the notoriety of the sex tapes, both benefiting my diamond business: a branch off of Cobalt Inc.

She fixes Jane's straw hat, deep in thought, her eyes beginning to flame. "I don't see a solution. These cameramen are going to follow Jane to and from kindergarten, elementary school, middle school, and she's going to wonder why strange men are hiding in the bushes, why they're stalking her and why that's okay. What do we tell her?" Rose lets out a defeated laugh and lifts the flap of the straw hat. *"I'm sorry, Jane, it's just the way it is."*

Jane clasps her hands together and makes a sound that could be comparable to *ma-ma* but not quite.

"No," I suddenly say, sliding further onto the bed in front of Rose, Jane between us. "That's not the way it'll be." The future of my family is at stake, and I'm not the type of man to let it drift into an ocean and see which way it floats.

I want many things. The first of which is to protect my girls. Then I want to have more children. Lastly I want my family to feel safe and loved and complete. I have to give Rose peace of mind while shielding our daughter from the media's focus.

But we're already doing that for Moffy, creating gossip and stirring the media, and, in exchange, we're keeping a rumor from surfacing on *Celebrity Crush*'s headlines. It's part of an agreement we have with the tabloid, but we can take matters into our own hands too. "What we're doing now for Moffy, we can do for Jane."

Rose listens intently.

"Jane becomes interesting when nothing else is happening in our lives. She becomes the focus only when we're not."

Rose digests this quickly. "You want to tip them off more, so they'll be distracted from Jane and focus only on the headlines we create?"

I nod. "If we can't leave the spotlight, Rose, we have to redirect it onto us and not our daughter."

Rose pauses, considering this for a moment. "And what if she grows up and reads these false things about her parents, things *we've* created?"

"What if she grows up and reads about herself? You have to pick one, Rose." I reach out and hold her hand, lacing my fingers with hers. I remember when Jonathan Hale told me there was nothing I could do to help Lo. He was resigned to the fact that his son would be slung through the mud again, this time with his grandson. He had no chips to bargain with. But I did. I do.

Lo isn't the only one in the public eye. So I put my celebrity status on the table for Andrea DelaCorte, the new editorial director of *Celebrity Crush*.

Andrea told me that if I wanted the article about Moffy gone, I needed something of equal caliber to replace it.

So I went down on Rose in a public parking lot, contacted *Celebrity Crush*'s photographer for an exclusive picture, and now they're the only tabloid with this story. It's not the only exclusive photo we have to tip them off to. To be even, we have to do a few more.

I can still use that power, the fame that we have, to detract the attention from Jane. We just have to make certain our stories are more newsworthy. And to do that, we may have to create extreme situations—do things out of our nature. Play a different sort of game. An unfamiliar one to Rose, but a very familiar one to me.

Rose lifts Jane onto her lap, removing the straw hat. Her fingers brush Jane's cheek. "You deserve a choice, don't you?"

She's going with my plan.

"We need a time limit to test this," she says. "We can't just keep doing it forever if it's not working."

"Six months," I say. "If we see progress and she's not in the media as often, we'll do this for as long as we need to. And we'll have more children. If we don't see any progress or not enough, we'll stop." I don't finish the rest, but she does.

"And we'll just have Jane."

I have to nod. I have to agree with this. She's been forthcoming about more children so far, and if this is her stipulation, I have to compromise what I want. The next six months will be the most important to me—in my entire life.

I lean forward and kiss her on the lips more forcefully as my hand slips into her hair. Jane babbles between us, and Rose breaks away first, Jane wrapping her fingers around Rose's black robe.

"She'll speak soon," I tell Rose. "Maybe just one whole word."

Rose says, "I hope so."

I lift Jane into my arms, and she giggles happily, her eyes searching for something to clutch. I'm shirtless, without long hair like Rose, but Jane fixates on my watch, trying to grip it between her fingers.

Jane is hyperaware of her surroundings, more so as she grows older. She latches on to specific toys for comfort, cries when her setting has changed or a stranger comes close. She sleeps terribly. But according to my late mother, so did I. Katarina used to say it was the sign of a beautiful mind at constant work.

I hold Jane to my chest while she inspects my watch, her eyes a brighter blue than mine.

"What quote comes to mind when you look at her?" Rose asks me.

I recite the one that pulls at me first. "'We can never give up longing and wishing while we are thoroughly alive.'" My lips rise at Jane. "'There are certain things we feel to be beautiful and good, and we must hunger after them.'"

"George Eliot," she correctly attributes the quote. "*The Mill on the Floss.*"

"Well done. I'd kiss you again, but I'm busy." I unclasp my watch and let Jane hug it close.

"A kiss isn't a suitable reward." She attempts to wear irritation, but her smile appears again and stifles any dark looks. "Stop staring at me like that."

"Stop smiling like that, then," I quip with a grin.

She tries to tighten her lips in a thin line.

I return to Jane. "Your mother apparently doesn't prefer kissing. She likes other unnamed things."

I feel Rose watching me, not listening to my retort. And then she suddenly says, "You love her."

"You say that three times a day, which is the definition of 'redundant.'"

"I just didn't believe you would."

"Neither did I." It's the honest, bitter truth. Loving many people means being selfless, and I usually only do what's in my best interest.

I've always seen children as a greater challenge. Whether or not I loved them never mattered to me. Rose made me realize that love is necessary, even if it's costly. Anyway . . . it'd be impossible not to risk my life for Jane and give up everything I value. I'd do it all.

My thumb brushes Jane's soft cheek and she smiles like the universe has opened. "You're very easy to love."

I kiss her forehead and set her back on the bed with Rose. I stand to put on my charcoal-gray button-down, and Rose yawns into her hand before she refreshes the computer again.

"I'm going to make us coffee," I say.

She nods, too entrapped with the laptop. I can tell the article hasn't appeared, just by her stiff shoulders. She won't relax until it's published.

We've planned a much bigger experiment than whether or not Jane Eleanor Cobalt likes Chanel. The next six months will be a test with a life-changing outcome.

And it begins today.

Three

Connor Cobalt

Right when I start the coffeepot in the spacious, stainless steel kitchen, the basement door clatters against the wall. I expect the six-foot-three, unshaven, foul-mouthed roommate I've been living with—for almost an entire year—to barge through in a brooding tirade.

Instead, I see long brown hair.

I leave the cupboard open, abandoning my pursuit of coffee mugs, and I lean against the granite counter. I watch Daisy stumble through the doorway with glazed, dim eyes. My concern is at mid-peak. Out of ten, I'd give it a four-point-five.

If she nears the knives, it'd shoot to an eight.

But right now, she looks as fine as she can be. Her hair is dyed back to her natural color, and a long scar cuts across her cheek from the Paris riot. This is the first time I've seen Daisy Calloway sleepwalk, but I doubt it's the first time it's happened. These past few months have been unpleasant for Rose's youngest sister.

Daisy sways a little near the leather bar stools. The door is shut to the living room, so I think she'll be stuck in the kitchen with me. I'm impressed that she was able to open the basement door. Her heavy-lidded eyes sink tiredly, trying to open all the way.

"Daisy," I call.

She raises her head but stares past me.

Interesting. I reach behind me and grab two mugs while the coffee brews. "Do you want to know a secret?"

She just continues to stare past me, looking slightly disturbed. I'd find it eerie if mental disorders frightened me, but nothing like this does. Its effect is horrifying on her, but it can't horrify me.

I set both mugs down. "When I was seventeen, I found someone attractive at Faust, my all-boys boarding school." I pause to observe her level of lucidity.

She sways closer to the bar in front of me, the counter separating us, still not aware of her surroundings.

"Theo Balentine was a pawn," I tell her, rubbing my lips in thought. "But an interesting pawn. One that smoked too much pot and quoted too much Thoreau. He was intelligent in his own right, and he didn't hide who he was. I liked that about him."

She wobbles and bumps into a stool. Her green eyes graze me.

"So I fucked him," I say casually. "Literally. Rose caught me coming out of the bathroom with him at a national Model UN conference. I'd just blown him, and Rose didn't seem to care." I smile at the memory. "She knew me well enough that I barely had to explain anything. She accepted me as I was." I drop my hand to the counter. "My time with this guy lasted a month. I grew bored with him."

Daisy seems slightly aware, blinking. But maybe it's just my fear—of her knowing. My pulse seems to speed. Still, I continue, like I need to tell this to someone else. "And then years passed, and somehow he landed a job at Hale Co.: the assistant to the marketing director. Somehow, our brief time together at Faust reached Jonathan Hale's ears. And my life became a fucking mess with rumors and truths that Loren's father could hang over me."

I'm not worried about Jonathan, not really. He's like a barking dog that threatens but knows better than to bite. He won't enact any kind of plot against me. His relationship with his son would be at stake, and that's something Jonathan can't afford to lose.

The coffee maker beeps and Daisy drifts backwards, silent and unblinking. I stay still as though she'll respond soon with harsh words that I'll need to defend. She blinks once, sluggish and unaware.

"Thanks for not judging," I tell her. "I always knew you were one of the good ones." When I return to the pot, I hear bare feet rush up the basement stairs. I tense and begin to pour coffee into a mug.

"Fuck," Ryke curses. Daisy's twenty-six-year-old boyfriend bounds into the kitchen, wearing nothing but gray boxer briefs, which means he jumped out of bed.

It's only six in the morning, so I'm not surprised that he was still sleeping and woke to find Daisy missing.

His narrowed eyes momentarily flit to me. "You're just fucking standing there?" He manages to quietly growl the words.

"I'm not in the business of waking sleepwalkers," I reply calmly. Daisy already has a history of panic attacks, and forcing her out of this type of sleep increases the likelihood of one. I assume Ryke understands this. He's smart enough.

Ryke ignores me and gently rests his hands on her shoulders, steering her away from the bar counter, which she repeatedly knocks into. She guides him more than he's able to guide her, and she wanders further into the kitchen, near the open space where I stand.

She plops down on the hardwood. Ryke crouches just as she keels over into a deeper sleep. He catches her and gently rests her head on the floor before standing.

"You could have done *that*," he tells me.

"I preferred watching you do it. Now I'm completely positive this is a common occurrence."

With festering agitation, he runs his hand through his

disheveled brown hair. "You could have just fucking asked like a normal person." He's still speaking in hushed tones while I choose to talk normally. It's not that I don't care about Daisy. It's just that I don't think changing the volume of my voice will do any more harm than good.

I pour coffee in the second mug. "Where's the fun in that?"

"This is fucking serious."

"*Je le sais, mon ami.*" *I know, my friend.*

He exhales a heavy breath.

It's been hard to build any kind of relationship with Ryke that doesn't include his brother or Rose's sister at the center. Our personalities clash. He's aggressive. I'm calm. He's in your face. I'm out of it. He loves with all of his heart. I love sparingly, moderately or not at all.

I can't understand all of him the way that he can't understand all of me. We rarely open ourselves up past conversations about Lo and Daisy, and so I have no clue how many languages he speaks, if he still talks to his mother, if he's planning on a career outside of rock climbing.

Of all the people in my life, I know the least about him.

It's mildly annoying.

It makes me want to poke at him until he gives me something more, but I'm not entirely in the mood to rouse an agitated beast.

"She needs to see a new therapist," I tell him.

His shoulders lock, but he's not defensive. "She likes her therapist."

"Liking one isn't the same as having an effective one," I reply. "She's not getting any better, and she has too many problems to be complacent." Rose and I hear the same thing from Daisy: *I'm doing okay.* While Ryke says, *she's doing the same.*

Those updates are irritating for people who like details.

Ryke keeps shaking his head, frustrated.

I pass him a coffee, knowing he'll drink it black. He takes it, and I find another mug to fill for Rose.

"It's not that fucking easy," he says. "She needs stability. Not to go through a bunch of random therapists to find one that works." He lets out an angry breath. "And what if she gets a shit therapist like Lily?"

"I never recommended that therapist to Lily. Her parents did." I pause as I realize how I can have more details and help Rose's sister at the same time. "Daisy can see my therapist. I've known Frederick for years, and he's almost as smart as me."

Ryke glances at Daisy, who rolls onto her stomach, still sleeping. "What kind of therapist is he?"

"Frederick is a jack of all trades." I evade the question. "He'll be equipped to handle her problems." He'd take her on as a patient without hesitation. Firstly because she can afford him. Secondly because her case is complex.

Ryke's jaw hardens, his hand tightening on the mug.

"Do you trust me?" I ask him. I want what's best for Daisy. Besides Jonathan Hale, Ryke always questions my motives the most.

"I feel like you're manipulating the fuck out of me, Cobalt."

I am. Partly. I want more information about Daisy, which Frederick may be able to give me. "I want what's best for Rose's sister," I say, only a portion of the truth.

Ryke nods, as though he's trying to believe me. "You'll have to talk to Daisy about it. It's not my decision."

I nod too. Ryke and I always cross paths in the morning, but usually it's when I go to work and he goes rock climbing. We never utter a word to each other. Daisy lying on the floor between our feet has forced us to communicate at 6 a.m.

A string of tense silence lingers in the air.

He sips his coffee.

I sip mine. "I've had better conversations with a stuttering parakeet Frederick used to own, though he wasn't nearly as intelligent as you."

Ryke digests my statement quicker than most. "I'm sure you loved hearing your own fucking words repeated back to you."

My lips rise into my next sip of coffee, remembering the bird's high-pitched squawk and how it took him five minutes to repeat one fucking sentence that I said. "I'm a narcissist, not a masochist." I pause in thought. "Maybe if the parakeet didn't have a stutter."

Ryke laughs under his breath and shakes his head.

So I ask, "Are you nervous about the surgery?" It's not a topic he likes to discuss, especially with me, but I'm curious. In January, he's donating part of his liver to help his father survive. Jonathan Hale destroyed his own liver after decades of alcohol abuse. His son is his best match.

The surgery is a selfless act, since:

a. Ryke doesn't like Jonathan
b. Ryke will have a six-week-long recovery process, and . . .
c. That's only if there aren't complications. I've personally never seen Ryke bedridden or told to lie down.

It seems out of his character.

Ryke shrugs. "I just want to get it fucking over with."

"OhmyGod! OhmyGod!" Lily races into the kitchen from the living room, a black Halway Comics sweatshirt stopping at her thighs. Daisy somehow remains asleep, but Ryke watches her closely, ignoring his brother's wife, who bounds towards us like she's on an urgent mission.

Lily has a tablet in hand, waving it around as if no one notices its presence.

I immediately reach for my phone . . . which I left in my bedroom. I usually always have it on me, but I didn't expect to be in the kitchen this long.

Lily is mainly focused on me, mutually ignoring Ryke, and in seconds, she accidentally rams into his bare chest. When she raises her head, she absorbs his shirtless, toned body, realizing he's only in his underwear. She glances at her own sparse attire.

Really, I'm the only one properly dressed. I'm never surprised.

A deep shade of red blemishes her cheeks. *"OhmyGod."* This time, she sounds mortified. "Why aren't you wearing any clothes?"

"Animals generally don't wear them," I answer first.

Ryke flips me off casually, about the same moment that Daisy shoots up in alarm, incognizant of her new surroundings. Ryke hurriedly squats in front of his girlfriend, hands on her face so she focuses on something familiar.

"Oh, shit." Lily hesitates to rush to her sister's aid, afraid to worsen the situation. I can read her guilt at the sight of Daisy's distress and confusion, the sweat beading her little sister's forehead.

"Dais," Ryke whispers. "You're in our kitchen. Nothing bad fucking happened, I promise."

Daisy blinks repeatedly, trying to listen instead of falling into a panic attack.

I place my palm on Lily's back, directing her to the living room. She almost stumbles over her feet, in a slight fog.

"He'll orient Daisy," I say. "We don't know what happened, but he does." I'd rather Lily believe that someone else is on her side, no one casting blame her way for this small event.

Lily nods a couple times, focusing on the door ahead of us. "That's a good idea." She licks her chapped lips. "We shouldn't overwhelm her."

When we enter the living room, I shut the door behind us, no coffees with me. Living with two other couples has made life far from predictable. I can't complain.

"Umm . . ." Lily puts a couple steps between us. She tugs at the hem of her sweatshirt, her thin legs pressed together, maybe out of habit more than arousal. She's a sex addict, but very rarely has she ever been turned on by me.

I already know she's here about the article, since I've been waiting for it to publish. If Rose and I are going to handle this alone, Lily can't be aware of this fact. "I've already put the *Team Raisy* sticker on my limo," I tell her. She's been on a Raisy crusade for the past year, in support of Ryke's relationship with Daisy, just as we all are. Lo too. The public is more pro-Raisy than it used to be. Daisy getting older has helped.

"It's not about the Raisy ship, but thank you." She nods in appreciation and then pushes the tablet in my chest. "Just to be clear, I was online shopping for Black Friday deals, not actively snooping on the *Celebrity Crush* website. But I think you should see this before Rose does."

I'm positive Rose has already seen the article and reread it a dozen times by now. I wear a blank expression and skim the screen, opened on *People*, who reposted the original article. I click on the link that takes me to *Celebrity Crush*.

The headline: EXCLUSIVE! CONNOR COBALT CAUGHT GOING DOWN ON ROSE CALLOWAY IN PUBLIC.

My jaw muscles twitch. They used her maiden name. I understand she was famous before she married me, but I take pleasure knowing she's Rose Cobalt because she chose it. What they published is inaccurate.

I purposefully let my irritation filter through. Rose and I already discussed what we'd say in defense of the night. I have to seem disgruntled, shocked and briefly alarmed. All the normal sentiments that'd accompany this out-of-character situation.

"You look upset," Lily notes. "Is it real? Not that I'm judging." She raises her hands. "I've been there before, plenty of times, but never photographed . . ." Her eyes light up at the thought that Rose and I have somehow trumped her sexual escapades by a fraction. "This is strange."

"The part where I went down on my wife or where I did it in public?" I ask easily.

Lily's cheeks flush even more. "Uhh . . . both? No, wait. That's not the right answer, is it?"

I smile. "There is no wrong answer. It's an opinion, but I like hearing yours."

She relaxes and points to the tablet. "Have you read it yet?"

I shake my head, focusing on the photograph at first. They captured Rose at her climax, eyes closed, lips parted, and my hand clutching her neck. Her long legs extend out of frame, but you can see my head in between them, her panties on the dashboard. That's all. Shadows and darkness conceal the majority of her features, enough to question the validity of the photo. As Lily just did.

The photographer is credited in small font beneath: *Walter Aimes*.

I read portions of the staff writer's article, passing over the facts and concentrating on the opinions she's constructed.

With four sex tapes already released, it seems like Connor and Rose are trying to top the most notorious, sexual celebrity couple: Loren Hale & Lily Calloway.

Could this be a LiLo-Coballoway feud? It's likely! An inside source of the family told *Celebrity Crush*, "Both sisters have newborn babies, and they're basically fighting over popularity in the media."

As they battle for "favorite" among the fans, we're expecting more scandalous photos, wild nights and shocking events from the Calloway sisters and their men. Keep your eyes peeled!

That's how they're twisting this, then.

"Soooo . . ." Lily draws out the word. "I know this is kind of awkward—"

"I don't find it awkward," I say, passing her tablet back.

She hugs the tablet to her chest and squints at me, possibly trying to narrow her eyes, to no avail. "Is that a nerd star power?"

I understand almost everyone, but Lily and Lo throw out references that I have trouble recognizing. "I don't know fandom references," I remind her.

Her eyes grow big and she looks over her shoulder like someone spoke for her. And then she clears her throat and pulls back her shoulders, appearing half an inch taller. "I didn't mean to say that. What I *meant* to say was, how can you not feel the awkwardness from this?" She raises her tablet. "I'd be embarrassed. Rose may be embarrassed, and I'm worried about her reaction when she reads the article."

"She won't be embarrassed. She'll be pissed," I say. "And I've personally never been embarrassed in my life. I won't start now."

Her lips almost form those same words: *nerd star power.* And they think I'm weird.

"I'm overly confident. Some call that arrogance. I call it four parts charm and six parts self-respect. I'm under the belief, and truth, that I'm superior to everyone and all things around me. Now, how can plankton make a shark embarrassed of itself? The correct answer is: it can't."

Lily squints more, reading into my words.

"Don't fucking call her 'plankton,'" Ryke retorts behind me.

I turn sideways, noticing Ryke's arm wrapped around Daisy as she sips a Ziff River Rush sports drink. "Don't worry, I didn't leave you out," I say. "I called everyone 'plankton,' including you and you."

Ryke looks like he wants to punch me, probably for now calling Daisy a microscopic organism. He should be elated that he's the same organism as his girlfriend.

"Except Rose, right?" Daisy says with a smile, more color to her skin.

I'm about to agree, that Rose is superior with me, when a door bangs upstairs. Muffled voices echo, and I leave Lily's side to reach the staircase. She follows close behind with Ryke and Daisy.

"You think I wanted to see that photo? I wish to God I could forget what I just saw." The edged voice belongs to Lily's husband, Rose's brother-in-law and my best friend.

Loren's subtitle could also be *Rose's sworn enemy*, which is why I skip two stairs as I ascend.

Four

Connor Cobalt

W hat the fuck are they talking about?" Ryke asks no one
in particular.

"Connor . . . uh, did something to Rose," Lily tries
to explain. She points downward, towards her crotch. And when
she sees me glancing over my shoulder, her face reddens. "Not *my*
vagina, just to be clear. You know, her vagina." Lily crinkles her
nose. "In my head, this conversation was a whole lot smoother."

"And clearer," I say.

Ryke keeps shaking his head. "I'm so fucking confused."

"Connor waxed Rose," Daisy guesses with a goofy grin. "Or
you made another baby." She wags her brows.

I arch mine. "Someone's feeling better."

"Indubitably." She bows. Very swiftly, Ryke picks her up and
tosses her body across his shoulder. She laughs, her head hanging
upside down near his ass. "Best view," she muses.

I stop midway when I have a clear visual of Rose and Lo. Both
of them hold their respective children, their eyes heated and their
stances strangely open for two people who hate each other.

I begin to smile. Their bickering is amusing three-quarters of
the time. The one-quarter where one of them drags the other in an
undertow always alarms me.

"Oh, so someone *forced* your eyes to a tabloid page that said, *Connor goes down on Rose*? Was it Moffy? Let me see your five-month-old son put you in a choke hold. I will laugh." If she weren't holding Jane, she would've crossed her arms in triumph. She raises her chin instead.

"What the fuck?" Ryke says below me. Rose and Lo are too entrapped with their conversation to even notice the four of us on the staircase, Ryke and Daisy at the bottom.

"You're so funny," he says dryly. "I bet Connor laughed into your pussy."

Rose fumes, her shoulders rigid and tense. I climb two more stairs, my smile fading. Rose steps towards Lo, but he has another sentence, to try and retract the other. "Rose, I've been *actively* avoiding your sex tapes for years—"

"Which proves my point that you *actively* looked at that photo!"

Lo grips his cell phone in one hand, his other arm supporting his son to his side. "I don't know why you're yelling at me," he retorts. "You're the one who drove three goddamn hours on Thanksgiving just to be eaten out." He cringes at his own words and even mouths, *fuck*. He's trying not to sling verbal insults her way, which I appreciate. But it's what he's good at and what he's been conditioned to do.

Rose jabs a finger towards his face. "I'm yelling because *Celebrity Crush* took a photo of me orgasming and put it on their fucking website. For one second, can you please be sympathetic?"

Lo clenches his teeth, lifting Moffy higher on his waist. He's only in drawstring pants, his cheekbones sharpened, hair shorter on the sides, fuller on the top. His son wears a blue onesie and kicks out for Lily, but she's frozen one stair below mine, not wanting to interrupt Lo and Rose's fight.

"It's hard to be sympathetic when you left to knit a sweater and decided to tell no one your plans. That's fine, you know, none of us were concerned about either of you. No one fucking cared . . ."

I feel my lips pull downward. Rose and I are always diligent about keeping tabs on everyone, and never did it cross my mind that they'd be upset if we snuck out. I thought they'd shrug it off, laugh and joke. When we returned to her parent's house, Lily rushed to Rose and hugged her tightly while Rose stood stiffly in shock.

They all thought we'd been in a car accident.

"We've already explained this," Rose says. "When we left, we thought we'd be gone for five minutes, but each store was closed, and I needed lace for Jane's dress, not *yarn*. I didn't want to go out today with the Black Friday crowds."

"Wait," Ryke says, more to me than to anyone else. He drops Daisy carefully on her feet, and his voice finally captures Rose's and Lo's attention. "You're fucking telling me that you two snuck out and had a quickie in a parking lot last night?"

"Relatively speaking," I say.

Ryke's nose flares. "I called six fucking hospitals, and you two were getting off?" Daisy wraps her arm around his waist in a comforting hug.

Lo gapes. "Jesus Christ, there's a photo of Connor getting off too?"

"No," Rose snaps.

"This has really traveled beyond the point," I announce.

I hear Ryke mutter, "Unbelievable." Normally I'd have another response for him, but since this is a much different scenario, with Rose and me at the center, I let it go.

Lo lifts Moffy to his ear, his son now concentrated on him. The pale-skinned, dark-haired boy touches Lo's jaw and actually presses his lips to his father's cheek. Lo nods in mock realization. "That's right, little man. There are liars among us."

I find it more amusing than worrisome. For now, at least. Jane murmurs something in Rose's arms, the straw hat back on her head, covering thin, wispy brown strands.

"She said you're wrong and I'm right," Rose retorts.

I rub my lips, trying to hide my grin.

"Just say the words, Rose," Lo tells her. "You. Left. To. Get. Off."

I wait for Rose to accept this partial truth as the whole story, but it's not the truth she'd usually tell. *We did it for you* is the one that's sitting on the tip of her tongue. But some things have to be kept secret, for the betterment of Lily and Lo and the simplicity of this entire process. Rose and I don't want four other voices in this ordeal. It's easier constructing plans without them.

Rose inhales sharply, raises her chin again, and says, "Fine. I left to get off. Do you feel better, Loren?"

"Yeah." His amber eyes drift to me now. "If you needed a private location to go down on your wife, I could've directed you to the Calloway girls' clubhouse. Backyard. Perfect place to fuck."

I can't hide my escalating grin. "Then why haven't you ever invited me, darling?"

"My door is always open." The innuendo is clear.

I tilt my head in thought. There was a time where I truly believed Lo wouldn't understand me, would maybe even act different towards me if I told him about my experiences with men. I have a natural, undeniable fear that the relationships I've cultivated will somehow morph into tangled, uncertain strands, made up of cold shoulders and cautious glances from them to me. All because of past hookups and short-lived flings that have no basis on what I do today, now, with my wife and my friends and my child.

I told Loren the truth, not long ago. He's the second person in my life to ever know.

He barely flinched. I doubt he knows this, but how he acts towards me now—like nothing has changed, like our lighthearted jabs have the same exact connotation as I want them to—has made me revere him and respect him even more.

"I'll be sure to knock," I tell Lo.

"I like my bell rung, love."

"Even better."

Lily raises her hand. "I agree with Lo. The clubhouse is a good alternative." She nods repeatedly.

"Me too," Daisy pipes in from the bottom of the staircase.

Lily smiles wider, knowing someone else has been in there before. "When did you . . . with you?" She motions between Ryke and Daisy.

Ryke actually tries to lighten his features for Lily, his scowl almost dissipating. It doesn't work well. "Who else would it fucking be with?"

"I can name a few bastards," Lo says, disgruntled at the thought of Daisy's past boyfriends. But his use of "bastard" causes everyone to look at him, me included. "Not *me*." He cringes. "What is fucking wrong with you people?"

"So we're talking about metaphorical bastards, then," I say easily.

Ryke pinches his eyes. "I fucking hate all of you—except you." He rests a hand on Daisy's head. She leans into him again.

Lo descends the stairs to reach Lily. He says to his brother, "You're just pissy because I brought up Daisy's ex-boyfriends."

Daisy is mouthing something to Lily and then to Rose. The three of us, the guys, are ignoring them.

I chime in, "And if you rewind a little, Ryke, you're the one who asked for the 'other people' she possibly could've slept with. So really, you should be hating yourself right now, but I don't advise that approach."

"No, I'm pretty sure I fucking hate you, Cobalt." I know it's not true by his relaxed tone.

Rose taps her foot. "So we're done here, then?"

Lily takes Moffy from Lo, the baby clinging onto her arm. "I think we are," Lily says.

I ascend the staircase, towards Rose.

"Seriously though," Lo adds. I can feel his gaze on my back. "Next time you both disappear, even to make out—which must be like an annual event for you two—just . . . let us know where you're going, okay?"

I'm not used to that speech being directed at me. Ryke usually gives it to Lo: *be careful, tell us where you're going, don't run off to fuck without saying something.*

I understand their concern. We managed to leave the Calloways' gated neighborhood without being followed by paparazzi, which is rare. They could've tailed us. We could've wrecked. Totaled the car. Died.

Anything's possible, but Rose and I haven't even been able to agree on who should be Jane's godparents and take care of her if something happens to us.

"We'll text next time we're running late," I assure him. Lo nods in thanks, and when I reach Rose, her eyes drill holes in me.

"Don't say it," she whispers. Jane tugs on Rose's dried hair and puts a strand in her mouth. Rose will wash her hair again no matter what now, so she lets Jane play.

I lower my voice. "I wasn't even thinking it. You didn't fail." *At lying to Lo.* I can't add the rest aloud. "But there's always room for improvement, unless you're me."

She rolls her eyes and whispers back, almost in a growl, "I'm sorry, I didn't major in deceit in prep school."

I edge closer to her, Jane between us. "Too bad you weren't a boy. You could've attended Faust and then I could've tutored you."

Her yellow-green eyes flit up and down my body. "And how many pupils would there've been?"

"*Seulement vous,*" I whisper. *Only you.*

I never took anyone under my wing at Faust. Had it not been an all-boys boarding school or had she really been a man in order to attend, I would've taken her, in every way. Even so, I'm glad this was the order of events. I'm glad we had years of being rivals before we became something more. I wouldn't change anything. I adore every piece of my life, how I've lived it, and the only regret I have is not allowing myself to love Rose sooner. Or maybe just not believing I did.

I stroke the back of Rose's neck with my thumb, and she begins to relax more. Jane's head lolls as she dozes off in her mother's arms.

When we participated in the reality show, Rose asked me to play her game. We were supposed to be us—no performing. Even when the producers wanted us to—even when they edited us how they saw fit—we were always supposed to be ourselves.

Now I'm asking Rose to play my game.

To find the loopholes, to take the manipulative, deceitful roads, to do anything to achieve a goal. I'm asking her to lie, bend sideways and fit into cramped boxes. To change to fit someone else's needs.

It's not easy for someone who follows rules, for someone with a strong, fiery personality. I hate asking this of her, but I need Rose on my side.

I can't do this alone.

"Cobalt," Ryke calls.

I turn my head, and from the bottom of the staircase, Ryke stares at me with knotted brows, his jaw hard. Daisy is turned into his chest, her back to us. So he's alone in his thoughts.

Here is a simple fact.

Ryke can't act any other way than how he is.

He's the opposite of me. I can change. So I'm something less, something easier to swallow. Ryke gives himself to you like a bottle of sand or a bag of shrapnel. *Chew and swallow*, he says. *I'll take care of you if you bleed.*

The point is that Ryke can't help Rose and me. He'd make it so fucking obvious that we're staging events for the press. He'd basically wear *I'm in bed with the media* on his forehead.

I need people on my team that will make this easier. Not harder.

He's a shackle, a weight, a cost that I can do without.

So while he stands there, glaring at me like I'm lying, I worry that he's going to ruin something he'd support. He'd do anything for his brother. But he can't do this. It's not in his ability. *Sorry, Ryke.*

I'm benching you.

"Yes?" I say, pulling my face with confusion, even when I feel none.

He hesitates, frowning. "Never mind . . ." He shakes his head and whispers in Daisy's ear. She nods, and they leave the living room and disappear into the kitchen.

Rose watches them exit and says quietly, "He's too smart."

Between the media's involvement with Jane and Moffy, our sex tapes and Ryke, he's the least of my worries. "Just remember, he's not smarter than us."

No one is.

Five

Rose Cobalt

T his is the stupidest thing I've ever done," I realize, in slight horror. I stand firmly in the master bathroom, dressed only in one of Connor's white button-downs and my white panties. I considered doing this stupid, stupid thing in our smaller bathroom upstairs, but I imagined the mess, the smell, and I decided against it. The master has been vacant since Connor and I changed rooms, opting for the second floor to be closer to Jane's nursery and more integrated in the house's happenings.

"You haven't done anything yet," Connor says, casually flipping through the tiny packet of directions. "And it's a far cry from stupid."

I pace back and forth in front of the his-and-hers marble sinks, my hands unintentionally stroking my long brown hair. Bleach, developer, and toner sit next to the faucet, chemicals that I've never contemplated using on my hair, not once. Not even when my mother prodded me for highlights when they were "popular among girls my age" during the early 2000s.

Connor suddenly tosses the directions on the counter.

I freeze. "You read those for two seconds. I swear to God, if you skimmed, I will drop-kick you into shark-infested waters."

"I think you'd fare better if you swore to me and not the air."

He unscrews the top off the powdered bleach, his lips beginning to rise.

I hate that smile. But I love that smile. I growl, fed up with my brain's indecision about a man I love to hate. I hesitate to steal the bleach from him, but he's already mixing the powder with the developer in a plastic bowl.

Instead, I reach out for the instructions, but Connor beats me, snatching the tiny packet and pocketing them in his navy-blue gym pants, shirtless. I refuse to even acknowledge the six—no, *eight*—abs in front of me, which are both desirable and detestable. It's not fair that someone as intelligent as Connor Cobalt is also this fit. It's all purposeful. He works hard to maintain his appearance, to be as put together outside as he is inside.

"I read the directions," he says, holding my gaze. "They're straightforward. They're simple, Rose. There's absolutely no way I can do this incorrectly."

I trust him.

More than anyone in this world, I trust Connor. But . . . "You're not a hairdresser, Richard. Unless I missed the part where Faust taught all the boys how to perm each other." This would be less stressful if I could march into a salon and have a professional treat my hair with delicate, experienced hands. Instead I had to condition my hair for the past three days, in fear that this home treatment would damage hair that I've spent years nurturing like a fucking toddler.

Connor reads my boiling, anxious expression. "How many times have you gone to the salon without paparazzi waiting outside?"

Never. I glare. "I could've had a stylist come to the house."

"And how many times has a stylist tipped off the media?"

Four times. They tipped off my wardrobe for a charity event to *Style Now* . . . and described my sock bun. One of the four also took pictures without my knowledge. I can't trust just anyone, and

I've yet to find a stylist honorable enough to bring into our current situation with *Celebrity Crush*.

When so many people morph into paparazzi with their own cell phones, capturing an exclusive photo is incredibly hard. It's why Andrea covets them. It's why I have to swallow my fear and do this the old-fashioned, hazardous way—all to ensure that Walter Aimes will snap his photo and *Celebrity Crush* will have a beautiful headline about my ugly hair color.

Jane and Moffy are worth more than your hair. I keep mentally repeating the mantra. I accept the situation—that this is about to happen—as soon as he puts on plastic gloves.

"Don't get it on my hands or skin," I remind him, gripping the edge of the counter and facing the sink. The toxic smell is already curdling my stomach, and I know it'll be in my hair and on my scalp soon. It's why I've tasked him with the laborious part of this process.

He steps behind me, much taller since I'm without heels. "I'm well aware of your preferences," he says, plastic bowl in hand. "My name is at the top of it beside the number one."

I watch him through the mirror, my eyes like pools of fire. "You wish."

"I don't wish things that are already true," he says with a bigger grin. I suppose my retort was weak in comparison, falling into his conceited aura too easily. I blame the bleach and his closeness, his chest almost right up against my back.

One more step and I'll feel his pelvis against me. His toned arms always seem larger and more sculpted without a shirt: perfect with a suit on, not too bulky, and perfect with a suit off, not too lean. There is too much *perfect* behind me—it's infuriating.

"Take a step back," I command.

He tilts his head just slightly and raises a brow. "Excuse me?"

"One. Step," I force.

"No," he says definitively, denying me this.

"I can't think clearly when you're this close," I admit. I end up stepping towards the sink counter, my legs and waist pressed up against it.

"You don't have to think at all right now. Close your eyes."

I stubbornly keep my eyes open, glaring in the mirror at him. Off my punctured stare, his desire swims in his deep blues, sexual longing that he often shows me. Without breaking my gaze, he bites off one of his gloves and then slaps my ass. The breath knocks out of me, a pleasured shudder vibrating my stiff limbs. He slips his hand beneath my panties, his large palm soothing the sting.

This time, I willingly close my eyes, letting him take control of me. Some of my anxieties start to dissipate, even as he applies the cold bleach mixture to sections of my hair. He keeps his other hand beneath the button-down I wear and beneath my panties. I like how he clutches my ass, but still, I white-knuckle the counter's edge.

"How does it look?" I ask.

"Like it's not finished," he says. "Count backwards from two hundred and maybe it'll be done by then." I hear the smirk in his voice.

"I dream of murdering your smile," I say.

"Your dream clearly hasn't come true."

I ignore that annoying comment. "I'd cut it to pieces and sell it to the highest bidder."

"So you plan to profit off my body?" He steps forward, so close that his erection melds against me. *Oh God* . . .

"You better be concentrating on my hair and not my ass," I say, too nervous to look at the progress he's made.

"I'm proficient at multitasking," he reminds me. "It's relatively easy for me to concentrate on all of you at once."

I'd say that he's placating me, but I'm certain he's skilled enough to accomplish both. "What part of me would you murder?" My cold tone of voice challenges him to answer.

"I wouldn't murder any part of you," he says, "and I definitely wouldn't sell those parts either." He surprises me. I almost lose my balance, but his hand ascends from my ass to my bare hip, seizing my waist, which has grown just slightly since I had Jane, more shape than I once had.

"Not even my tongue?" I have to annoy him. I annoy myself three times out of six during the day.

"You want me to sell your tongue to another man?" he asks. "So they can have this conversation before me?"

No. I don't want that. I highly doubt another man would entertain these bizarre *would you fall on a sword and bathe in cow's milk?* types of questions that I always throw at Connor. And he always grins, analyzes them and slings them right back at me.

I feel a glop of cold at my neck, and I stiffen—

"You're fine," he assures me quickly. "It's not on your skin."

I swallow hard and inhale sharply. More confidence seeps into me as he holds me tighter around the waist.

"Would you rather make love on goat's blood or cut off my tongue?" I say the words like I'm one second from wielding a knife and enacting these hypotheticals.

I sense him hardening even more. "I'd fuck you on goat's blood. I'd never cut off your tongue."

"Would you share me?" It coils my muscles and stomach, my fingers curling even more around the counter, the idea of me being passed between hands. I only want to be in his clutch, but the concept of being so completely *his*, in the face of other men, stirs forbidden parts of me.

"I've never been good at sharing," he tells me deeply. "Not accomplishments or titles, and I'd certainly never want to share you." I can feel him twisting my hair and clipping the strands on top of my head.

I open my eyes now, the cream evenly applied over every lock, nothing reaching beyond my hairline. The twisted mass of developer and hair weighs heavy on my head, but I keep my neck straight, able to support it fine.

"Thirty minutes," he tells me. "And then I'll wash your hair." He removes his grip from my waist and snaps off the sodden glove in the empty plastic bowl. His arms weave around my body to reach the sink, and he cages me here while he washes his hands. I take note of the time on his watch.

He's still staring at me, like he's not finished playing with me yet.

I'm not done talking. "What about ménage à trois?" I test him, unblinking and hardly wavering from this question.

I wonder if he's imagining this twisted picture of another man together with us. After he shuts off the faucet and dries his hands with a towel, he wraps an arm around my waist, pulling my back against his chest so hard that I ache between my legs and barely maintain my grasp of the counter's edge.

I keep my head away from him, avoiding a mess of bleach. Even so, his voice sounds close to my ear. "This man wouldn't stand a chance in bed with us. I'd never let him near you, not to touch you and never to fuck you." His fingers make their way up the soft flesh of my thighs, cupping me, his thumb teasing me in circular motions against the lace of my panties.

My chest rises and falls heavily. "What if he takes me from the front?" My voice is layered with ice.

Connor swiftly spins me around now, my back digging into the lip of the counter, his hand lifting one of my legs around his waist, his erection in line with my panties. He pushes against me, the force at breakneck speed in my mind, the force so hard that I could beg aloud to be naked with him.

I don't though. My mind orients itself quickly enough. I hang on to his muscular biceps, and his lips near my ear as he whispers, "I'd rotate you." He pushes my ass up, like he wants to fuck me this way, right now, repeatedly. Over and over. "*Comme ça.*" *Like this.*

I'm so unbelievably wet.

I grab his wrist to stop his movement. "Now he can snap off my bra," I combat, able to meet his gaze. "You failed."

Those two words cause his jaw to tic, so subtly that I almost miss it. Without moving, he says, "I'd possess you in bed, Rose, so much that any other man would leave in *misery*." I believe him. "No satisfaction, no release." He grazes me with his eyes, my breasts nearly popping a few buttons with my deep breaths. "Balls aching, dick begging—"

Someone knocks at the door. "If you're playing Scrabble in the bathroom, you two are at a new level of weird," Loren says.

"Drop me," I whisper to Connor, smacking his arm.

He doesn't, not yet. "We'll be ready to head out in an hour," he tells Lo.

We're all going to the nearest rock-climbing gym as a way of celebrating Ryke before he undergoes surgery after Christmas, the holiday already in two weeks. The gym is also where Walter Aimes is supposed to take photos of us, unbeknownst to my sisters and their significant others.

Lo speaks through the wooden door. "Willow is here early to babysit, so we're going now."

My eyes widen in horror. *Now*. My hair. I reach out, subconsciously about to touch my head. Connor rapidly releases my leg and seizes my wrists, right before my palms nearly plant on the goopy, bleachy mess.

My heart is in my throat. "I almost . . ."

"You didn't," he says, his smile dimmed to seriousness. I've become more than a tad bit obsessive-compulsive since my pregnancy and Jane's birth. High-stress situations just puncture little parts of me, and I fixate on things I shouldn't.

"Open up." Loren knocks on the door again. "What is that smell?" He pauses. "Is that bleach?" I hate Loren Hale's nose. I want to murder that too.

Connor mouths to me, *stay calm*.

"I'm always calm," I snap, the statement clearly false. It's by far the worst retort I've used all week.

His lips still curve upwards as he walks backwards to the door. "Your acting needs work, darling."

True.

In seconds, my acting is about to be put to the test again. I'd pray to a higher being to give me strength and success, but I keep hearing Connor's voice in my head, which says: *I'm the only person you should pray to.* His egomania is clouding my judgment and my sanity.

But strangely I'm still glad he's on my team.

I can't do this alone.

Six

Connor Cobalt

Lo puts his hand on the bathroom door, opening it wider to see all of Rose. "Jesus Christ." He scrutinizes her hair and the products on the counter. "Are you having a quarter-life crisis?"

"I wanted a change," Rose snaps in defense. Beneath the white developer-and-bleach mixture, her hair has begun to lighten.

"So you thought blondes have more fun?" Lo walks further into the bathroom with me.

"No," Rose snaps. "I can castrate you equally as a brunette as I can a blonde." She gives him a wry smile.

He returns one. "Your idea of fun is fucked up."

Two more people suddenly emerge in the doorway. Lily pants, out of breath, in leggings and a plain black baggy shirt. Daisy is next, in similar workout clothes, only a shorter top that says *wild at heart* and significantly less wheezing.

Lily holds a stitch in her side. "Are you two almost ready? The bodyguards are waiting and getting kinda grumpy." Before she walks forward, her eyes grow big at Rose's hair. "Whaaa . . ."

Daisy puts her hands to her mouth, eyes growing to saucers.

"She's . . ." Lily can't find the words.

Lo helps her. "Lost her mind."

"She's blonde," Lily manages to say, all on her own.

"Wow," Daisy mutters, still in shock.

Lo pulls Lily into his chest for a hug, and he even kisses her cheek. She's too concentrated on Rose to even notice, which means this is a larger ordeal for the Calloway sisters than I thought it'd be.

"Hair color is temporary," I say. "It can always be changed." I just need this to go smoothly—for the sake of Moffy and Jane.

"But Rose has never dyed her hair before," Daisy explains what I already know.

"Rose," Lily starts, "you said you'd skin a cat before you became blonde."

She rotates, a chill in her eyes. "Maybe I have." Her voice is flat and cold, but it isn't her best acting.

"Okay, you're scaring me," Lily says. "I never thought this would happen." Her voice cracks.

Lo frowns and looks down at his wife. "Are you crying?"

Lily wipes her eyes.

Rose is trying not to cry.

Daisy looks upset.

I didn't predict this. I couldn't have.

"It's just," Lily begins, "you can count on so few things in life, and one of them is Rose's hair."

"Jesus Christ," Lo groans.

"It's true," Daisy nods.

I never knew her hair was so special to her sisters. "She wanted to change it," I tell them. "Can you all be supportive of this?"

Lily frowns in deeper confusion. "You really wanted to change your hair, Rose?"

Daisy keeps shaking her head. "This doesn't feel right, does it?"

Rose takes a sharper breath and pulls back her shoulders, getting in the game. "Call it what you want," she replies, "a quarter-life crisis or a change of scenery—I just felt impulsive and destructive and . . ." Her nose flares. She lifts her chin. "And I did what I wanted. So *there*." If we were alone, I would fuck her.

"'So there'?" Lo gives her another look like her body has been hijacked by fictional creatures. "Didn't you use to brush your hair three hundred times a day?"

"I can still brush my hair even if it's blonde, and the absurd frequency is a rumor that one of you"—she points between Daisy and Lily—"started behind my back."

Lily crinkles her nose. "Might've been me."

Daisy stares up at the ceiling. "Or me."

"And I think we said one hundred brushstrokes, didn't we?" Lily asks Daisy and mouths, *when was this?*

Daisy shrugs and shakes her head. "New Year's?" she whispers.

Rose snaps her fingers repeatedly. "Concentrate."

Lily and Daisy spin back to her sister, both of them standing taller like her minions or soldiers, when in fact they're her adoring, admiring little sisters. I can see, between them, why Rose would want this for Jane. I want it for her too, someday. It's what we're fighting for in the end.

"I am blonde now," Rose says proudly. "Deal with it."

My lips rise.

"Queen Rose has spoken," Lo banters.

"I'm going to wash Rose's hair and then we can head out," I announce to the room.

Lily nods, stealing one more look at Rose before she departs. Daisy follows suit.

Loren reaches the doorway but doesn't leave. Instead, someone else walks in. I rub my mouth, frustration pulling my brows. When I meet Rose's eyes, she's smiling at me, the smug kind of smile that I always have for her. She's gloating at my distress.

I nearly turn towards the counter, my erection worsening. When I need one fucking second, I lose five more. Time is rarely on my side.

Ryke walks further into the bathroom, holding lime-green Nikes by the neon-blue laces. He stops short, jaw unhinging at the sight of Rose. "What the fuck."

Rose crosses her arms, tightening the shirt, which unfortunately pops a few of her buttons, unbeknownst to her. I restrain myself from pinching the bridge of my nose.

I motion between the two of them. "Rose has decided to dye her hair. Of the events we've all shared together, this is really mundane."

"It's fucking weird," Ryke mutters, his gaze lingering on her breasts.

After Rose's warped image of me sharing her with another man, one I don't celebrate at all, I'm not really in the mood for a wandering male gaze. I almost walk in front of her, which would piss her off more than it would help any situation.

Lo smacks the back of his brother's head before I move a muscle.

"Fucking A, let me process this," Ryke says, rubbing beneath his hair.

"Process what?" I ask. "Rose's hair or her breasts? You do know that women have them, right? Or are you just now figuring out basic human anatomy?"

Ryke flips me off.

"Oh, good, he knows where his fingers are," I banter. Rose begins to button her shirt.

"Fuck you," he curses.

"No, fuck you." My facial muscles tighten. Definitely, not in the mood.

Ryke raises his hands now, understanding that I'm not playing around. "Look, I don't fucking care what anyone does to their hair. I just wanted to give these to Rose." He nods to her. "I know you won't rent rock-climbing shoes or wear any kind of footwear that's been previously used, but Daisy had an extra pair. I figure she's your sister, so it might be different. She said you two were about the same size." He still has one of the shoelaces looped on his finger.

They're not rock-climbing shoes, but they're a decent alternative: slender sneakers with what looks like good tread.

Rose's eyes drill a hole in them, like they've offended her. "What are those?"

I answer first. "Sneakers. Tennis shoes. Running shoes. There are a plethora of useless names for them, in my opinion."

When her eyes ping to me, they narrow. And I grin, any sort of annoyance starting to seep into better sentiments that I enjoy.

"*Your* opinions are useless," she retorts.

"And your opinions are biased. Do you want to keep going?"

Lo cuts in, "Please don't."

It takes Rose an extended moment to detach her gaze from mine, fixing it on Ryke. "You can leave those things by the door."

Lo elbows Ryke's arm. "You're a common serf in their kingdom, bro. Don't take it too personally."

Rose frowns. "You know what 'serf' means?"

Lo rolls his eyes. "Jesus, I'm not an idiot. I may've been expelled from college, but I can count to one hundred and multiply and divide too."

"A borderline genius," I quip.

Lo winks. "I knew all this time you were scared I'd beat you."

"You have a way with words," I say honestly. "Most men should be frightened of you." I'm not most men, but this is the truth. Once he has confidence in himself, he should be unstoppable.

Lo digests my statement with a nod, hearing my sincerity.

Ryke brings us back to the point. "You have to wear these, Rose. I'll put them right here, but you can't show up in the car or at the gym with high heels on."

Rose sighs heavily. "What if—"

"No," Ryke forces.

Rose glares. "You suck."

"How old are you?" Lo interjects.

Rose flips him off.

I grin. "I'm the oldest here—"

I can't even finish my statement before Rose interjects, "I'm twenty-six too."

"Yeah, me too." Ryke sets the Nikes by the door.

We all look to Lo, who's just twenty-five. "What?" he snaps. "Do you three have some sort of older kids' club?" Slightly, yes. We talk about Lo and Lily and Daisy all the time. Right now, no one says anything, and he glowers. "I was joking."

"I'll wear the sneakers." Rose diverts the conversation.

"Thank you." Ryke taps the doorframe on his way out.

Lo walks backwards as he begins to leave. "Ten minutes? Will you be ready then?"

I need more than that, but clearly we've lost time. "Fifteen," I amend. "We'll meet you downstairs."

Lo nods, and as he disappears into the master bedroom, I lock the door behind him.

R ose immediately spins towards the sink, drumming her nails on the marble counter. I come up behind her, the pungent bleach watering her eyes. I suspect it's burning her scalp, but she won't complain of pain until she has third-degree burns.

While I tower above her, inspecting her hair with sight alone, she says, "Rape me."

I set a hand on the counter, beside her waist, my confusion pushing me towards her when it should do the opposite. Her eyes are blazing through the mirror. I'm not sure I heard her correctly. I say, "*Parlez clairement.*" *Speak clearly.*

She licks her red lips. "*Rate* me," she says slowly, "on my performance."

That sounds more like Rose. "I give you a B-minus. You struggled with your sisters."

She crosses her arms, popping buttons on her shirt again, no bra, and this time, I notice her nipples hardening. My cock digs closer to her ass. She stiffens, her collarbone protruding.

Her cold voice never changes temperature. "Well, I give you an F." As expected.

She keeps flunking me today—with challenges that I'm certain I'd win, given any circumstance. "Are you trying to incite me, darling?" That's usually my job.

"I speak the truth."

She sounds like me. Those are my words. Swiftly, I spread her legs open with my feet, breaking them apart. She chokes on a pleasured noise, and I grip her ass beneath the button-down, my lips to her ear. "You're plagiarizing me now."

That one comment riles her, and not in the way that I like. She spins on me, forcing her ass out of my clutch. Her back digs into the counter. I cage my arms around her, slyly turning on the faucet.

"So now you have a monopoly on truths?" She rests her palms flat on my bare chest as a warning, enraged. "I *never* plagiarize. You can't copyright facts."

This is all true, ironically. "Why did I fail?" I ask.

She raises her hand to scratch at her hair, and I catch her wrist right before she succeeds. She exhales shortly and says, "You cursed Ryke out for real. You broke character, Connor."

It's not like that directly hurt our ploy. "I was me," I state. That was a real reaction, an emotional one, she's saying.

"You can't be you," she reminds me. "That's the point of this. We play up the dramatics, be fodder for the media, be salacious and scandalous for popularity. We're something else. You taught me this."

You taught me this. She taught me how to be real. I taught her how to be fake.

I wish I could take pride in this part, but I have none. I don't want to discuss it anymore. "Lean over," I say. "Your eyes are watering."

She rotates back around, leaning over and dipping her head into the sink's basin, and without stepping away from her, I put on a new plastic glove, using one hand to wash her hair. I massage her scalp as I rinse the bleach. She tries to close her legs, but I keep my foot between hers, forcing them apart.

Her eyelids flutter open.

"Keep your eyes closed," I command, worried that bleach and water will run into them.

She reluctantly shuts them again. "My neck hurts." She tries shifting her shoulders.

With my free hand, I adjust her, turning her head a fraction, so she isn't staring straight at the sink. "Better?"

"Mmmh." She relaxes into the head message. With the bleach almost gone, I notice the color of her hair isn't blonde—not yet, at least. We needed to let it set longer than we had, and the strands are tawny, the color of rust.

Rose will call it orange.

She's beautiful no matter what color hair, no matter if she had none, but she'll be pissed. I just need her hair to smell good so she won't feel uncomfortable. When the bleach is rinsed, I discard the glove and lather shampoo along her scalp, her body loosening even more.

My cock has been patient enough. With my dry, clean hand, I skim the hem of her panties. And I rip them off.

Her eyes snap open. "Connor."

"Close your eyes."

She does, partially because shampoo begins to slide from her forehead to her nose. I wipe the soap away and continue kneading her scalp, washing off excess shampoo.

I run my fingers between her thighs. "You've been standing here this fucking wet?"

She breathes shallowly. "Connor . . ."

I drive two fingers inside of her, and she reaches out for something to grip for support. I guide her hands to the counter so she can clutch the marble. Her wrists drip with water as I return my hand to her hair.

I lean closer to Rose, my hard cock digging against her ass and my lips brush her ear, my breath low and hot. "You better be ready for something bigger."

She squeezes her eyes tighter closed and reaches for my hand between her thighs. "Wait . . ."

I retract my fingers and guide her hand *back* to the fucking sink. "If you have something important to say, then say it now, otherwise, I'm pushing into you." I clasp the back of her head with more force, causing her throat to bob in arousal.

"Shut off the water," she requests.

I turn the faucet off, so she can concentrate on us and not fear drowning. Then swiftly, I turn her around to face me, her back pressed against the lip of the counter. I grip her face in a strong hand and kiss her lips. *"C'est tout?"* *Anything else?*

She lets out another breath. *"Ne soyez pas gentil."* *Don't be gentle.*

I can't even remember the last time that I was. "I wasn't planning on it." I lower my gym pants and compression shorts, finally free. In assured, hard movements, I lift her left leg high around my waist, her head tilted back and supported by my other hand. Then I grip my shaft and ram all the way into her.

She cries, her back arching off the counter. I keep her body stationary, and I thrust into her with deep, fast strokes, needing to do this quickly.

My body heats with hers. I push harder.

"Fuck," Rose cries, her legs quivering. She has trouble catching her breath, her mouth open. I groan when she pulses against my cock.

I unbutton her shirt, her chest exposed, breasts bigger and fuller than before her pregnancy. It grips my attraction even more, and I kiss her nipple before biting once. She moans and mutters a word that sounds like "yes." I kiss the top of her breast before holding on to her waist, curvier—I thrust deeper.

"Connor," she gasps.

I watch my long, throbbing cock disappear between her legs. Over and over. Inside the woman that I love. Inside the mother of my child. Inside my teammate and equal. A grin pulls at my lips. One more thrust and a blinding sensation washes over me. And her.

She shudders, her pulse quickening. I can almost feel her heart pounding.

"Oh God," she mutters.

I straighten up and arch a brow at her.

She still has her eyes closed.

I slap her ass.

She moans again.

"I need to find a new way to reprimand you. You enjoy this too much." I grip her ass, which I'd love to fuck one day. For another time, I know.

She props her body on her elbows, half of her still in my possession. "Honestly," she breathes, "I'm not sure what I said."

I slowly pull out of her, and she makes a choking sound. I rub her clit. "You thanked God again."

"It's a euphemism."

"It's an annoying euphemism when I'm the one who makes you come."

She licks her lips. "I was going to give you an A-plus for the sex, but I'm dropping your score to a B."

"I don't like your grading methods."

"I don't like your face." Her eyes dance around my features in pure attraction.

"Maybe you should say that without looking like you want me nine inches deep inside of you."

"Maybe it's not you that I want in me."

I raise my brows and stop rubbing her—the statement is such a lie that it's hard to even react negatively. "You've had plenty of other opportunities." And she never took any of them when we were younger. Technically speaking, she waited for me. If I were more moral, I think I'd feel guilty for not returning the favor. But sex wasn't emotional for me.

"What if I had taken those opportunities?" she asks seriously.

I set her foot on the floor. "I'd love you the same, but I'm self-ishly happy you didn't."

"Because now you can have all of me," she states. I've never been deceitful about my narcissism. It's not a front or a mirage. I truly feel entitled to most things, and when I have them, I take good care of them until I grow bored. Then I find something new to play with.

However, I would never grow bored with Rose. So I married her, and in that sense, I am moral. I'm committed to the person I truly love rather than someone I momentarily like.

"Yes, I have all of you," I reply, "but, Rose, I'm married to you. I never weigh my experience against your lack of experience and think you're less than me. You're always, and will *always* be, my equal."

She nods. "I believe you."

I tuck a damp piece of hair behind her ear. She shivers, the strands wet on her shoulders. By training her mind back on her hair, she's more aware that it's dyed. Her eyes are right on mine, gauging my reaction to her new color before she looks.

I'm completely impassive, her hair actually more copper than rust.

"Just tell me," she says, swallowing hard.

I lift her chin with my fingers and whisper, "'A rose by any other name would smell as sweet.'"

She smacks my arm with the heel of her palm, recognizing the quote from Shakespeare's *Romeo and Juliet*.

I can't restrain a grin. "It's a famous euphemism, Rose." I draw her closer to my body, peeking into her open shirt for a millisecond. She tugs the fabric closed with two hands. I'm hugging her with her arms tucked to her chest, which is normal for us.

"It's an annoying, famous euphemism, Richard," she says, her lips almost twitching upwards.

"Is that a smile?"

"No," she says. "It's a hateful frown."

"If we're going to rename all of society's constructs, then I'll be sure to call that sink a table and the ceiling the floor."

"You're infuriating."

"You're gorgeous."

She actually smiles fully, and I hold her cheek, my thumb brushing her red lips.

"Shall we go on?" I whisper deeply. We don't have enough time, unfortunately. I want more with her. Always.

She shakes her head and inhales, more confident. "I can dye it back next week, right?"

"Sooner," I say. "Anytime after the picture, you can go to the salon."

"But *Celebrity Crush* said—"

"Rose," I breathe. "They just want the picture." Andrea suggested one week as a timeframe for Rose's altered appearance. She should be satisfied enough with the world's reaction after one day. It'll be exponentially greater than her sisters' shock.

After one more silent moment, Rose rotates to the mirror, and I keep her in my arms, watching her eyes morph into pinpoints. Her shoulders tighten, and her nose flares.

"It's fucking orange," she curses, about to grab the directions. I let her peruse them this time.

"I did everything correctly except wait longer to let it set," I explain. "We didn't have time, and it was burning your scalp."

"I was fine." She huffs though, knowing she wasn't. She tosses the instructions in the wastebasket and thumbs a strand of her hair. "Stop smiling."

"I'm not smiling," I say easily.

"And I have to wear sneakers. And I have to rock climb." She presses her hand to her forehead. I kiss that hand and then I kiss her temple.

"*Ensemble*," I murmur. *Together.* "My time will come."

This may be hard on her, but it won't be long before one of these scenarios boomerangs back to me.

Seven

Rose Cobalt

Philly Rocks! is a poorly titled gym that contains vertical multicolored inclines with ropes and harnesses and more or less peril and doom. The apt name would be Philly Die! or Philly Misery & Ungodly Things Since I Can't Wear My Five-Inch Heels!

What's worse: I have two sisters stretching beside me, gazes plastered on my orange hair, which I've tied in a high pony. No one has slung an insult my way yet, and I realize my murderous *I will run over you and then go in reverse for good measure* glare has shut their lips. Lo just asked that I wear a hat, quickly attaching his explanation: *the paparazzi will tail us if they see your hair, and we all want to do this in private today.*

If only he knew.

I complied, stuffing my hair beneath one of Connor's baseball hats, but as soon as we entered the gym, I had to remove it. We rented out Philly Rocks!—no kid's birthday party or hovering instructors in sight. Ryke has permission from management to teach us.

Connor already tipped Walter on our whereabouts, so the plan is set and in motion. Surreptitiously I check over my shoulder, at the floor-length gym windows, slightly tinted from the outside. I wonder if he'll have to wait until we leave to snap a photo.

As long as there's not an entire brigade of cameramen outside, Walter will have his exclusive photograph. Rumors about Moffy will stay out of the press. Everything will be fine.

"Earth to Rose." Daisy waves her hand in front of my face.

I wake from my stupor, lounging with my hands behind me. Fuck stretching. "I was just picturing the wall violently swallowed by flames. Who has a match?" I look to Lily.

Lily tries to look stern, her back straightening. "This is about Ryke. We can't burn his place of love."

I snort. "His place of love is between our sister's legs."

Daisy waves her hand again. "I'm sitting right here."

"I know, I fully intended for you to hear that," I say curtly, checking my matte black nails, remembering their beauty, since they'll be chipped by tonight's end.

Daisy ties her brown hair in a messy high bun. "Lily is right though."

"I am?" Lily beams.

"Most definitely." Daisy nudges her arm with a bigger, brighter smile. "The weather has been horrible these past few weeks, and he's been really antsy." Ryke hasn't been able to climb outside, she means.

I sigh. "Fine," I concede. "Maybe this will make up for our awful Christmas presents for him." We spent four hours in the mall, flocked by our bodyguards and tailed by elated fans and cameramen. It was an ordeal, largely from our indecisiveness. We usually buy Ryke rock-climbing gear that he requests for both Christmas and his birthday, but that seemed insensitive this year, considering his surgery is in January.

I bought him a nice electric razor, but I'm sure he already has one, his unshaven jaw clean and never with a gnarly beard. I asked Connor what he bought him and he simply said, "I've had his Christmas gift for a year."

A year.

He refused to clarify that irritating answer.

My phone pings, and as I grab my cell off the carpeted floor, I notice the three guys by the gym wall, talking among themselves. I skim the screen.

Tweet notifications:

@callowayforever: Was that really Connor going down on you? @RoseCCobalt

Yes. We do have sex, even if some people believe we're cold and unfeeling and—like Lo said—make out annually. I refrain from replying back, especially to negative comments. Our publicist basically said: being defensive is the worst opinion you can have. Standing up for yourself with your back arched and claws bared is not allowed on social media, at least not from my end.

It's hard for me.

My finger itches to press "reply," but I move on to the subsequent notification.

@liloloverallday: Do you even love Connor Cobalt? You never act like you do. He deserves someone who wants to kiss him. @RoseCCobalt.

God. This must be in reply to when I turned out of his kiss at the mall. No one heard him quote Plato with the smuggest grin I've ever seen. That didn't deserve a kiss, a hug or a handshake, and he knew it.

@rachelle4beauty: @RoseCCobalt you're such a slut! First the pornos and now public oral. Seriously?

Yes, seriously.

@camibrat8: @RoseCCobalt is not a fucking role model for women. I'm so sick of people calling her that. She's dumb and a disgusting piece of trash.

I try not to ingest any of these words. With a stiff spine, I look at the next tweet.

@_GoodWitchh: eww @RoseCCobalt

I nearly smile at the irony of a "good witch" saying *ew* to me.

My phone vibrates in my palm. Everything okay?—Connor

I raise my head. He's still in a deep conversation with Lo and Ryke halfway across the room, but he took the time to type a message to me.

People aren't amused by our Thanksgiving activity. I press "send" and watch him read the text calmly before typing back. When his fingers stop moving, my cell buzzes.

In case you've forgotten, three-quarters of what people say about us is incorrect, exaggerated or fallible.—Connor

He's right. Though I won't reply with that. I have a perfect memory. I forget nothing.

Then you remember when you were fourteen . . .—Connor

My smile fades, and I notice his lips beginning to curve upwards in triumph. "Don't you say it," I mutter under my breath.

"Are you texting Connor right now?" Lily asks, her head swinging between us.

I can't answer. The next text pops up.

. . . and Faust beat Dalton at Model UN and I went in for a handshake, so you could congratulate me after I defeated you. And you actually did it.—Connor

"They're totally texting," Daisy says with a laugh.

I raise my hand at her while I type: I also remember trying to squeeze your hand hard enough so your fingers would break. I press "send." "This is important . . . " My phone buzzes.

I remember you not succeeding.—Connor

I scoff, open-mouthed. I'm going to kill him. In the kindest way. I tighten my lips, my fingers flying over the keys. I remember you not getting laid tonight. I win. When I look up at Connor, he's still grinning, like he's very, very far from losing what he wants.

Dammit.

When I was fourteen, I thought for sure I would beat him at Model UN, but I wasn't nearly as smart back then. Our rivalry pushed me to work harder. And when I was seventeen, Dalton almost won in a tiebreaker, but partly because I think he was thrown that year.

I caught him coming out of the bathroom with another guy—their body language said more than Connor wanted it to. I don't think he intended for me to see the hidden parts of his life. But a veil opened that day. He said five words to me. Just five.

I don't look at genders.

And after he took in my reaction—a nod and softened eyes—he walked away. I never once asked for more. I understood that he looked at the world in a different way, stripping the complexities and absurdities of society into bare simplicities. To be attracted to someone not because they're male or female but because you feel a connection, in some way, you feel something more.

It made me realize how much there was left to see in Connor, the truths I'd yet to discover. And I wanted another piece of him, another *real* piece.

There was a reason why he hid. What I really learned that day was that the world might not have been ready to accept Connor, and that's a bigger shame than anything.

But I have every real part of him. Every part I love. Even if the world may not understand him, I do.

I see a new text drop down.

You can't remember something that hasn't happened yet.—Connor

Translation: *I win. You lose, Rose.*

The towering rock wall in an array of nauseating primary colors has already sealed my fate long before Connor Cobalt did. I know my weaknesses, and anything that requires the removal of high heels sits at the very top of the list.

Eight

Connor Cobalt

When I pocket my cell, Lo brings his phone to his ear. He places his hand on his head in distress. "What do you mean they backed out?"

I lean my shoulder against the rock wall while Ryke abandons his task of untangling two harnesses, both of us concentrating on his brother.

"We always run commercials on GBA," Lo refutes. "Daniel said the network has the highest percentage of female viewers. We're not putting baby shampoo promos on Fox or ESPN." Lo rubs his eyes and meets Ryke's gaze first.

Ryke mouths, *hang up.*

Lo shakes his head. "I'm fine," he says softly to him.

Their relationship is better than it ever has been. I can see it as well as everyone else. Lo spends more time with Ryke, and his comments towards his brother are never spiteful or biting like they once were.

It took years for two estranged brothers to finally reach common ground, and if I were more empathetic, I think I'd be moved.

Lo groans. "This shouldn't have happened!"

Ryke grinds his teeth, probably thinking that his brother isn't fine, but he's doing well considering the nature of his job. I'm the head of a multibillion-dollar corporation too. For me, it's relatively easy. Sometimes moderately taxing, but rarely hard. For a normal person, it'd be stressful, difficult. For a recovering alcoholic, it might push them over.

Lo paces in front of me, wearing black track pants and a gray V-neck. His hair is in style, but when I first met him in college, the shorter-side cut, longer strands on the top, wasn't popular. He probably deserves credit for its ascent to the masses.

I scan him, his sharpened features and deadly gaze.

He's someone I'd never entertain or associate myself with in college unless he was of use to me. I never really needed him though. I had no reason to use him. Still, my seventeen-year-old self would've said: *Good, you found the rich bastard with connections. You needed him. You used him. Now let him go.*

My twenty-six-year-old self is more aware of what certain people mean to me—beyond endgames and goals and profits. My life is dull without Loren Hale. If I let him go, I'll be searching for someone like him—sharp-tongued, trusting, sensitive and cynical—and I'll realize that Lo exists alone, as a unique individual without a duplicate. I enjoy the darkest parts of him as much as I do the lightest ones, and I won't leave him just to find someone with a better use.

If that hurts me in the end, then I'll deal with the consequences. His friendship is worth it to me.

Lo puts a hand to his forehead. "How many fuckups are going to happen in three hours? . . . That was rhetorical. Put Mark on the goddamn phone."

Ryke scratches his unshaven jaw, trying to stay rooted to the ground. His natural reaction would be to disrupt Lo, giving his brother slack from this job. He's trying a new tactic: being supportive, not treating Lo like a fragile, breakable human being.

It's empowered his brother more than Ryke may realize.

At the end of the day, Ryke can be cautious, but he can't make

Lo feel inferior. It's easy for Lo to look at Ryke and wonder if his older brother would excel in the same position that he'd flounder in. But he's not floundering yet.

Lo turns his head and catches Ryke staring with even more brotherly concern. Mine is hidden.

Lo flips Ryke off while he talks. "Why the hell is our marketing director on vacation?" He shakes his head. "Who's his assistant?"

I stiffen and tensely check my phone again. Rose hasn't replied. Across the room, she has her phone raised above her head while Daisy and Lily try to tackle her to reach the cell and Rose swats them away with her hand.

My lips start to rise.

"Well, get Theo to call GBA and work this out," Lo says, his feet slowing to a stop.

I try not to focus on that name. I haven't talked to Theo in years, and I'd like to keep it that way.

"If the network doesn't answer, then bombard them with messages until they do." Lo pauses, his tone less edged. "I really appreciate it. Let's just hope Theo can solve this before Mark returns." Lo hangs up and nods to me. "Tell me your staff calls you for things they should be solving themselves."

"Every day," I say easily.

The girls rise to their feet and begin to walk over to where we stand. Rose declares, "If you read my texts, then we have to switch phones and I'll be reading yours and yours." She motions to her sisters and then stops a few feet from me. She places her hands victoriously on her hips.

Daisy and Lily look questioningly at each other while Ryke, Lo and I watch them. I'd rather no one read the personal texts I send my wife, but I'm curious enough to make this trade, just as Rose is.

Lily wavers. "I don't have anything to hide."

Lo shrugs beside me. "Why am I going to text her when we're always together?"

Daisy flips her phone in her palm, apparently not eager to relinquish it. "I don't know."

Ryke is rigid, clearly feeling the same as his girlfriend. "Let's just fucking climb." He finally untangles the harnesses and passes one to each of us. I don't want to let go of the conversation that easily, but my wife bristles at the mention of climbing, and I'd rather not prolong this.

Lo sets his harness down and helps Lily, squatting and holding the holes open so she can step into them. Rose has dropped her harness to the floor and unearths a bottle of hand sanitizer from her purse. I watch her squirt a glob onto her palm while I gear up.

Ryke tosses a harness to Daisy. "You want to go first, sweetheart? You can help me demonstrate."

Rose cuts in, "Shouldn't we just watch you climb?" She shifts her weight, perturbed by this event. She wears yoga pants and an old Princeton T-shirt, an outfit I've never seen her in before, and to top off this change, she starts stroking her copper ponytail. As though touch alone will revert it to the natural color.

I near her while Ryke answers, "I get bored by gym rock over real rock. You all climbing while I'm belaying is better. But if you don't want to do it, Rose, you don't have to."

Rose is stubborn and loyal. If her sisters had to walk through fire, she'd be right beside them, bearing the pain. Even with the choice to back out, she wouldn't. Solidarity, comradery—they mean everything to Rose, and through years of catalytic moments, Ryke has become a large part of our family.

So I'm not surprised by Rose's next declaration.

"No, I'll do it." She nods a few times.

Lily lets out what sounds like a cross between a moan and an embarrassed gasp. We all look over, her cheeks fire-engine red. Lo has his hands on the straps of her harness. Obviously he just pulled them tighter, putting pressure between her legs. "I didn't do anything!" she announces, her hands wavering, like she's debating whether or not to cower and cover her face. Lo leans down and whispers in her ear.

This is nothing new.

After tightening my harness, I squat and gather Rose's. This isn't the first time I participated in top-roped climbs at a gym. Ryke, Lo and I have all done this multiple times to change our workout routine. I understand the need for locking carabiners, both twist-lock and screw-gate, and I'm well acquainted with the figure-eight knot and the basics of belaying. Only Lily and Rose have never been climbing before, and they need more instruction than the rest of us.

But Rose isn't going to climb today.

With my back turned to everyone, I break two plastic buckles: one on the waistbelt and one on the left leg loop. When I stand, I pass the harness to Rose.

"It's broken," I tell her.

She frowns, examining the harness. "What? Where?"

"These are snapped." I show her the buckles. And she lets out a deep breath and looks to the ceiling.

"Are you thanking God right now?" I question.

She rattles the harness in my face. "This is what people call fate, Richard."

It's what I would call a greater power. Me. Myself. And I. I'd love to claim this accomplishment aloud, but I can't. She'll stubbornly still climb if I'm the force behind this act. "I call it a broken harness," I tell her.

"What's broken?" Ryke nears, rope in hand that's anchored to the top of the wall.

Rose passes him the harness.

"Yeah, you can't wear this."

Rose almost grows four inches taller with this fact.

"There are more in the back—"

"No," she cuts him off. "Fate has told me that I can't climb. I know it sounds ridiculous, but the broken harness was a sign that I shouldn't do this."

Ryke nods in acceptance. "My friend Sully is superstitious when he climbs."

"How so?" I ask. He rarely talks about Adam Sully, his friend he meets around the world, mostly in South American countries to climb rock faces. I've never seen him before. Ryke keeps that part of his life separate from us.

"He likes to kiss his carabineers before he leaves his fucking house, and he circles his Jeep around the parking lot three times."

I can barely hide a cringe. It seems juvenile and pointless and like something Rose would make me do. And I'd definitely do it for her. "You have strange friends," I tell him.

"I know," Ryke says, straight to my face.

He called me his friend. This is a rare day.

Rose waves to us. "You all can sort this out. I'm going to watch from over there." She struts towards the wooden bench that faces this particular wall, overflowing with confidence again. Through her sudden joy, she risks a few glances around the tinted windows, searching for Walter Aimes, the photographer who's been out of sight and supposed to snap the exclusive photo of Rose's hair.

The rest of us migrate closer to the wall to watch Ryke and Daisy demonstrate for Lily. My phone buzzes and I check my message.

How much sleep did you receive last night? Do you have less energy than yesterday, more or the same?—Frederick

This text wasn't meant for me. I briefly look up at Daisy, who's already ascending the wall, halfway up.

Clearly you slept poorly last night. I send the message to my therapist, who's been in contact with Daisy. She had her first session last week and seemed to like him.

"Is that supposed to be easy?" Lily asks, watching Daisy reach the top to ring the bell. Lily shakes her head back and forth and recoils into Lo's chest.

"You'll be able to do it, love." Lo kisses her on the cheek.

Another incoming text vibrates my cell.

Pretend you didn't see that.—Frederick

I type back: Only if you give me her answers to the questions.

No. I already did you a favor by taking your cat.—Frederick

My grin vanishes. We couldn't keep Sadie around newborn babies when she has jealous tendencies and likes to claw, so I temporarily gave her to Frederick.

I type: I did you a favor by referring Daisy to you. I talked about Rose's little sister during sessions with Frederick more than a few times, and his interest was piqued. He likes complex personalities and disorders. Frederick isn't one hundred percent altruistic. He's driven by knowledge. It's why I like him as a friend, even if I pay for his company.

By your account, we're even. I don't owe you anything. And you shouldn't be making deals with me, Connor. We've been through this before.—Frederick

I'm not allowed to manipulate my therapist, even when it's incredibly enticing, according to his rules. I respect that, but it doesn't mean I haven't tried to go around it. We'll talk later. I send the message and he replies even faster.

Monday.—Frederick

I pocket my cell just as Lily approaches the wall. Daisy has already descended and gives her sister an encouraging thumbs-up. Lily spins around, walking backwards, and points a threatening finger at all of us. It's mild in comparison to the ones I'm used to. "Don't laugh at me. I have very poor upper-body strength."

"No one's going to fucking laugh at you," Ryke tells her.

She takes a deep breath and hoists herself up to the first rock, grabbing on to it. Her shoes fit onto the one about two feet off the ground. It's the next move that proves difficult. She has to use her upper body to lift herself higher. She struggles, her fingertips pinched over the new rock, but her shoe is too far from the purple foothold. Each time she tries to lift herself, she barely rises a couple inches.

After four failed attempts, Lo walks over and puts his hands on her ass and pushes her up with complete ease.

"Lo— OhmyGod," she slurs, louder than she probably intended. But it works. She reaches the higher rock, her foot now supported and her body another two feet from the floor.

Lo can't help her anymore.

"Uhhh . . ." Lily looks around, eyes wide, knowing she can't make it past this point. Her legs begin to quake with her arms, and I remember that she's afraid of heights.

Brrrrring! A ringing noise emits from Daisy's cell. She holds it up. "Congrats, you rang the bell, Lil!" she calls out to her.

Lily blows out a breath of relief. "Okay . . . now how do I get down?"

"Just like Daisy did," Ryke explains. "Jump and I'll support your weight."

"You're only four feet off the ground," I remind her. "That's shorter than your husband, if you need reference."

"She knows what four feet looks like, Richard," Rose says from the bench.

"And I promise it looks higher from up here," Lily says, taking another breath. She closes her eyes and jumps backwards. When she lands on the ground, she dramatically falls to her knees and kisses the padding.

We all stare at her as she rises to her feet.

Her elbows flush. "I've always wanted to do that," she says with a nod before running into Lo's arms. He embraces her without question, his hands even lowering to her bottom, and he squeezes like no one is watching.

We spend the next half hour taking turns on the wall. Daisy

wants to race up it, so I time her on my watch. Rose even comes over to see me climb. Normally I'd give her a hard time about staring at my ass, but she's been alternating between cleaning her hands with sanitizer and rubbing her hair.

When we finish, Daisy and Lily flock to their older sister, noticing her distress. I'd like to talk to her alone, but Rose enjoys being in the company of her sisters, so I don't steal time from them.

Daisy nudges Rose's hip with hers. "Hey, wanna trade phones?"

"Dais," Ryke calls out to her with caution in his voice.

"I don't want to see the dick pics you've sent my sister, so don't have a coronary," Rose interjects, combing her fingers anxiously through her pony.

"Fucking hilarious," he says under his breath.

The three girls walk towards the locker rooms, out of earshot, and Lo, Ryke and I stay behind to gather the equipment.

Nine

Connor Cobalt

As the girls leave the main area by the rock wall, I study Ryke's uneasy expression, and my brow arches.

He gives me a side-eye. "Don't look at me like that."

"You sext?" I ask. Rose was joking before, but it could be a valid theory.

"She's my fucking girlfriend." He throws the sixth harness onto a pile and hands me one of the long ropes to roll.

I just can't imagine his dirty messages any more than he can probably imagine my text conversations with Rose.

Lo leans against the wall beside us, making no effort to help. "People can hack into that shit, you know."

"It's not like I've sent full-frontal nudes."

I chime in, "That statement implies that you've sent nudes before."

Ryke runs his hands through his hair. "No one fucking asked you to insert yourself in this conversation, Cobalt."

I can't even take offense to the weak rebuttal. First off, I technically started the conversation by asking him if he sexts. And secondly, his relationship with Lo never makes me feel inferior or jealous. I never weigh meaningful relationships against each other the way Ryke does. I weigh profit and benefits.

"Those of us with IQs in the .01 percentile have an invitation to all conversations," I tell him. "I know you're not privy to this, so don't be upset. There are geniuses. There are rational people. There are idiots. And then there's you."

Ryke lets out a laugh beneath his breath. "I'd like to know how you weren't beat to shit in prep school." Before I respond, he adds, "And I'm being serious this time. If you said that where I went to school, guys would've gotten in your face." Misplaced concern begins to wash his features. It may be the first time he's questioned this part of my past.

I start winding the rope around my arm to avoid tangling. Lo scratches his neck, standing off the rock wall and nearing his brother's side. They now face me.

This is new.

"Ryke and I were talking the other day . . ." Lo searches for the right words but has to turn to his older brother to finish. That's rare too.

I frown.

"You were barely fucking hurt in the Paris riot," Ryke says. "Why?"

Lo adds, "I saw you duck punches like it was nothing."

Unlike Ryke, I have no problem explaining the deeper parts of my history. He becomes brick-walled the further anyone digs into his past, but I only shut down if it costs my reputation or if someone is searching for an emotional response from me. Facts are easy. Simple.

I tie off the rope and throw it into a basket with the others. "I'm very flattered by your concern for me, but I was never bullied. I was"—I can't restrain my grin—"well-liked by most at Faust and hated by almost no one. I needed some people, and so I was painstakingly nice to them. I'd never speak to certain guys the way that I speak to both of you."

"Thanks for that," Ryke mutters, but his shoulders are more

relaxed. He was worried that my past was as tortured as his little brother's. It's not. Lo had more against him than I ever did. He believed he was worthless because his father told him that every day, and he had to find his self-confidence, which had been ripped from him.

I never lost mine.

I look between them: Ryke with his disheveled hair and brooding scowl; Lo with his sharpened jawline and daggered amber eyes. I'm a misfit when I hang around them—polished, hair actually combed—but the irony is that their insides are probably warmer than mine.

"As for the fighting," I explain, "I took fencing, tae kwon do, and jujitsu as recreational activities while I was at Faust."

"Let me guess," Lo banters, "chess club was full."

"Not full," I say. "Too easy."

Lo's phone buzzes, and he glances at the screen. "I have to take this." He walks over to the empty receptionist counter.

Ryke hangs by my side. I remember that he had trouble finding Daisy a Christmas present at the mall. He claimed he's never had to buy a girl so many gifts, and it's becoming harder, especially since she has everything she wants already.

"Does Daisy like silk?" I ask.

Ryke's jaw hardens, his brows cinching in irritation and warning. You'd think I asked if she liked it in the ass. "For you to give to her," I clarify. "Lingerie."

His darkened glare basically says: *don't ever repeat that.*

"You're a pleasure."

"Yeah? I don't talk about your wife's fetishes."

I tilt my head again. "Daisy has a silk fetish?" I can barely keep my composure, my lips rising.

"Fuck off," Ryke says. "And aren't you supposed to be celebrating me today?"

"I left my excitement in my limo," I tell him. "Maybe you can go fetch it for me."

"How about no backhanded compliments or fucking insults?" Ryke squats to collect the six harnesses. "Or is that asking too much?"

"It's asking a lot," I tell him honestly.

Ryke finishes organizing the equipment, and we both watch Lo, who stands by the receptionist desk. He gesticulates wildly with his hands as he talks on the phone.

"He's doing okay, right?" Ryke suddenly asks.

Cobalt Inc. is a five-minute drive from Hale Co., and I see him more during a workweek than Ryke does. I'd know whether he was coping with the stress. "I think he's doing well. Better than I predicted." I'm happy that I was wrong. I thought he wouldn't be able to handle the first week.

Lo isn't the same person I met in college. He's so much stronger than that guy.

Ryke turns his back to Lo and angles towards me, seriousness in his strict demeanor. "If something happens to me . . ." He clears his throat. "You'll take care of them?"

He means Lo and Daisy. He's waiting for me to agree. "Living donors almost never die during transplant surgery." He shouldn't worry about this.

"Connor," he says, "I don't want your fucking facts. I just want you to say that you'll . . ." He shakes his head, running his hands through his thick hair like it's a frustrating request—at least requesting this from *me*. "Fuck this." He straightens up, his gaze drifting to the tinted gym window, the parking lot empty except for Rose's Escalade.

For some reason, I keep envisioning a flock of teenagers with signs that say *Marry Me, Ryke Meadows!* He's popular among the younger girls since Daisy is only nineteen. But only Walter Aimes, the *Celebrity Crush* photographer, should know where we are right now, today. Otherwise, Rose dyed her hair for nothing.

I suddenly say, "I'll make you a promise. And I always keep my promises."

Ryke turns back to me. "Yeah?"

I nod. "You die *climbing*, and I'll take care of them. We both know that you're not going to die during that surgery and you're not going to die any other way than by your own pursuits." The longer he free-solo climbs, the shorter his life span. His longevity is in his hands, and for Ryke to believe it's in anyone else's is simply bullshit.

If he's so afraid of leaving the people he loves, then maybe he should start rethinking his hobbies.

"You're such a pain in my ass," he says lightly, heading towards the locker rooms where the girls are.

I follow beside him. "Impossible," I say, "I've never been near your ass."

He flips me off—the usual response. Our friendship may be odd, but at least I can call it one.

Ten

Rose Cobalt

A distant ring fills my drowsy mind, and the constant, pulsing noise grows as I begin to wake from a dead sleep. I squint in the darkened room, the blue glow of the clock blinking 3:42 a.m. on my nightstand. My phone simultaneously vibrates and rings against the wood.

I numbly reach out for it, turning on my side. Connor's arm slides off my waist. Who the hell is calling me this early? I want to murder them, but I'm too tired to think of clever ways to enact my revenge.

"Rose?" Connor whispers, waking too. He props his elbow on the pillow and runs a hand through his unkempt hair.

I unlock my phone and answer before I distinguish the words on the screen. "Hello?" I say softly, yawning into my arm. I tug the sheet closer to my chest, my nipples nearly peeking from my black silk cami. It's not like the person on the phone line can see, but I'm too delirious to take stock in this.

"Rose, what have you done?"

Oh God. Someone kill me. "Mother," I say icily, pressing two fingers to my forehead and tightening my eyes shut. I open them after a deep breath.

Connor relaxes against the headboard and collects his phone off the other end table.

"You dyed your hair," she fumes, irate with this news. "You *dyed* your hair *orange* without telling me. You didn't even consult the publicists before you went out in public. Did you do this yourself?"

"Where are you reading this?" I dazedly lift my body up next to Connor and peer over his shoulder. He scrolls through the *Celebrity Crush* website.

"Online," she practically spits. "Did you hear me?"

I bite my tongue and slowly say, "I heard you, Mother."

Connor clicks into an article, posted five minutes ago with the headline: ROSE CALLOWAY'S NEW HAIR COLOR! [EXCLUSIVE PHOTOS]. My chest begins to unbind. Five clear photos show me exiting Philly Rocks! with my sisters, Connor, Ryke and Lo. Walter Aimes zoomed in on my hair, styled in a high pony. Nothing special except that it looks like a fox died on my head.

"I don't know what you want me to say," I tell her. "And what are you still doing awake?" I feel old, asking my mother this. Connor watches me intently and I whisper to him, "Am I old?"

His lips pull upwards. "No, darling. We're still young."

"Good," I say, putting the phone back to my ear. My mother is answering me in a spew of heated syllables that I don't want to digest at almost four in the morning. It'll keep me up all night with an upset stomach.

I catch the tail end. ". . . Tori has an opening tomorrow. I already texted her, and she said she can take you at noon."

"You texted your hairdresser in the middle of the night?" *Let the woman sleep.*

"We're friends," she says like it's nothing, slightly cooling down. "Will you make it to her?"

"Fine," I agree. "Noon, Tori, I'll skip my work lunch." If *Celebrity Crush* weren't a victory tonight, I might've fought her on this.

I wave to Connor to return to sleep, but he catches my hand midair and laces his fingers with mine. I'm about to say goodbye to my mom when she adds, "I'm sorry about the house, Rose. I meant to call you earlier. Your father and I thought they'd take your bid."

My back straightens off the headboard. "What?" I immediately put the phone on speaker. "The Realtor never called me."

"Are you sure?"

"Positive."

"That's really unprofessional of them," my mother begins to fume again without giving me more details. I am swatting the air like I'm attacking the perpetrators who stole this house beneath me. I've been trying to buy the mansion down the street since early November. It's diagonal from us, and it has the perfect amount of bedrooms and baths for either one of my sisters or myself when our families grow larger.

I'm aware that we all can't live in this house together forever. There will be a time where we have to split up, and I'm hoping that separation won't be miles and miles away.

Down the street seemed more ideal.

"Where'd you hear this?" Connor suddenly asks, his brows furrowing in confusion. We put in the bid together. It was a lot of money, and I didn't think anyone would buy it out from under us.

My mother's voice turns high-pitched and freakishly cheerful. "Connor, how are you doing tonight? Do you approve of Rose's hair color?"

My scathing look could burn holes in a man, and yet Connor doesn't even bat an eye. He's sleeping in the same bed as a volcano that would very much like to sear and scald everything around me, including him, and he's okay with it. What is wrong with my husband?

He's at ease as he says, "I'm doing well, Samantha. I also don't seek Rose's approval for changes to my body, so I never expect her to seek approval from me."

Good answer.

My mother pauses. "But her hair is hideous."

"Mother!" I shout.

"If I can't tell you the truth, then who can?" she rebuts.

I mouth to Connor through gritted teeth, *get her away from me*.

He's trying not to laugh. This is not a laughing matter. He asks casually again, "Who gave you this information about the house? Did the Realtor contact you?"

"Olivia Barnes did. She heard from Linda, who heard from Tammy that a wealthy friend was settling back into Philly. She said that Rose knows him."

A wealthy friend.

Back in Philly.

I know him.

My mouth falls. "Sebastian."

Connor practically rolls his eyes at the idea. It makes the most sense. Sebastian was my best friend in prep school, and the only one that went to Princeton with me. We had a falling-out our senior year when he tried to ruin my relationship with Connor and help Lily cheat on exams.

I haven't spoken to him in three and a half years.

"I'll call Mrs. Ross in the morning and see if it's him," my mother says. "He was recently hired by Patrick Nubell for their public relations team." Nubell Cookies is located in Philadelphia.

I fling the light-blue comforter off my body. "I hope he chokes on a Nubell Cookie and vomits all over himself."

"Rose," my mother says sternly.

I stand from the bed, grabbing my silk robe off a gray Queen Anne chair. "I'm not letting him get away with this. He probably heard that I wanted that house, and so he outbid us on purpose."

"Olivia said the man's attorney already filed the paperwork and closed the deal. There's nothing you can do."

"I don't care what Olivia Barnes told you." I put my arms

through the holes of my robe. I feel disastrous. Like a tornado ripping through a city, shattering glass left and right. "I'm not waiting for you to call him in the morning."

"We'll talk to you tomorrow, Samantha." Connor quickly hangs up the phone as I tie my robe and march to the door. He runs ahead of me, dressed only in navy drawstring pants, and he blocks my exit by outstretching his arms. He has too many inches on me. He is towering like he can thwart my mission. No. He's in my way. I need through.

"Move," I force.

"Think rationally."

"Don't condescend to me." I push him in the chest.

He hardly flinches.

"Richard," I grit.

"Rose," he retorts. "He just signed the papers. He hasn't moved in yet. You're going to knock at an empty house."

"Then let me knock at an empty house, and *then* I will drive to his parents' house and knock on *that* door. He's either here or there. I know it."

"How?" Connor questions, his deep blue eyes focused only on me. "How could you possibly know this, Rose?"

"Because I feel it." I hear my voice and how unreasonable I sound, but my gut is telling me to storm down the street. Right now. I have to confront him.

"We both wanted that house, but this isn't an end all. There are other neighborhoods—"

I duck below his arm. He catches me around the waist, his lips to my ear. *"C'est le milieu de la nuit." It's the middle of the night.*

"Perfect. I'll have the satisfaction of waking up his traitorous ass." I try to escape his hold.

He grips my forearms, pinning my back to his chest. "It's winter. You're wearing silk."

"My rage is keeping me warm enough, thank you." I tear out

of his arms, mostly because he finally lets me go, recognizing that I need this, maybe. I have to see him.

I race down the hallway with a hurried stride. Connor follows. I don't want to hear about other neighborhoods, twenty miles away. I had a long-term plan. We *all* had a long-term plan. We thought of this together, right after Halloween. And Sebastian ruined our future out of spite.

We've fought to stay in this gated neighborhood, to make it safe, and there are only ten houses here, only four on this particular street. The chance of another entering the market in the next five to ten years is slim.

That's what this backstabbing Realtor told us.

"There is a cold place in hell for traitors."

Connor keeps up with my pace, passing doors along the hallway. I wait for him to make a jab at "hell" for not existing in his beliefs, but instead, he says, "You're going to regret this."

I hope not. "If you try to stop me, I'll put an ice pick between your eyes." Guilt plumes in my twisted heart for this comment, which isn't unlike others I've said. I have no idea why that is, but I don't let my mind rest to contemplate the nooks and crannies.

"Your dramatic threats don't scare me," he says, "so try again."

I don't try again. I fly down the stairs in a tirade, steam blowing out of my ears. I just keep thinking about the Realtor and Sebastian, their faces on a bright-red target. I propel darts at them in quick, violent succession. My mind is a grim, haunted place. This level of fury almost frightens me, my arms shaking. I think I'm scared more than I am angry.

Scared of losing all that we've built together. Scared of destroyed plans that I need to keep sane.

I swallow a rock, slipping on Lily's flip-flops by the front door, two sizes too small. My heels hang off the back. I type the security code, failing multiple times to hit the right buttons.

"Are you sure fate isn't telling you to turn around?" Connor mocks, leaning his shoulder against the door and observing my hostility with a mixture of concern and arrogance.

The security system beeps and blinks green. "See." I point at the machine.

"I see that it took you seven tries to do something that usually takes you one."

I raise my hand at his face and then swing open the door. The winter chill steals my breath for a second, but I march on ahead, the house in sight but a decent five-minute trek. Land sits across from our home, a nice view, and then diagonally is the closest mansion: gray stone with white trim around the windows, circular hedges framing the long driveway.

It's gorgeous.

"You're shaking," Connor says, worry edging his normally calm voice.

"In fury."

A gust of wind blows, a larger chill snaking down my neck. I shiver, wondering if the universe is against me or on my side tonight. I can't tell anymore.

Connor reaches out and clasps my hand. I'm afraid that he's going to draw me towards our house, but instead, he cocoons my hand between his, rubbing them back and forth. The friction warms my skin.

The full moon casts more light than the street lamps, and in a matter of minutes, we hike up the driveway and climb the stone steps.

Connor scans our surroundings. "I don't see a car."

"It could be in the garage." I debate on pounding my fist against the black door, using the silver eagle knocker or ringing the bell. I decide on the loudest option and push the buzzer repeatedly, the bell audible through the thick wood.

Seconds pass, my heart thrashing, and then a light floods through the window. "He's home," I announce.

Connor immediately draws me behind his back, and before I can refute, heavy footsteps sound and the door swings open.

Blood rushes out of my head, color draining from my face. Dread and other mixed, panicked and incensed emotions whirl through me at breakneck speed.

That's not Sebastian.

It's someone much worse.

Eleven

Rose Cobalt

was going to invite you over tomorrow for some wine, but you both are too eager to see me, aren't you?" Scott Van Wright rests his bare shoulder against the doorframe, dressed only in white Ralph Lauren pajama pants. Even skimming his features—a douchebag smile, dishwater-blond hair parted to the side and thin stubble along his jaw and upper lip—bores cavernous holes in my stomach and then fills them with acid.

My mind eats his words and spits them out. I charge him, ready to tear out his heart and curb-stomp the organ until justice is finally, *finally* served.

The second I pass Connor, he snags me around the waist, yanking me into his chest and holding me tightly, so I can't rush into Scott's house and unleash my pent-up rage.

"Better find a leash for her," Scott says, not even moving a muscle. "In fact, you're already halfway there." His eyes flit to my bare neck, subtly hinting at the diamond collar that I sometimes wear in bed, only when Connor and I have sex. It's a large reminder that he tricked me during the reality show. The executive producer of *Princesses of Philly*, Scott Van Wright, owns countless sex tapes of ours and sells them every so often to porn distributors for profit.

There was no way we could win that lawsuit, so Connor used the exposure and publicity for his company's benefit, and I've been trying to fool myself into believing we won—that my private life, for everyone to see, has no effect on my mental state. I've stampeded the horror of what happened for two and a half years, the very last time I saw Scott, and meeting him face-to-face tonight surges every little bit of pain.

"I hope you die," I sneer through clenched teeth, my eyes burning and welling with malevolent hate. I have no dramatic death planned for him. I don't care how; I just want him gone, out of my life, my face, my world—nowhere near my sisters, my daughter and my home.

Scott mockingly winces. "And I thought we were old friends, Rose."

Connor snakes an arm around my collarbone, pressing me closer to his body, less like a cage and more like I'm a part of him, like we share the same wrath, even if mine is more outwardly apparent.

In a terrifyingly calm voice, Connor says, "This is the part where I tell you to speak like an intelligible human being, minus the bullshit. And this is the part where you explain how you can't—that you're incapable of speaking on the same comprehendible level as us because you enjoy theatrics. Because you would rather piss in circles and drum at your fucking chest than reach the higher place where we stand, towering above you."

Scott's douchebag smile begins to fade.

Connor says, "Now that I've cut out five minutes of pointless conversation, tell me why the fuck you're here."

"You're still the same." Scott crosses his arms but stays leaned against the doorframe. I notice the cardboard boxes piled behind him near a grand staircase and black banister.

"Except now I'm twenty-six years smarter than you." Connor isn't even partially amused. I can feel his fingers pressing harder along my shoulder as he holds me close.

The talk of ages reminds me that Scott is thirty-one now. He wears an expression of distaste, as though Connor stuffed something foul in his mouth. I bet I share the same contorted look. Stomaching Scott's presence revolts every part of me. I'm not sure how much longer I can stand here without lunging forward and clawing off his face.

"Bullshit aside," Scott says, "I'm not fond of either of you." He nods to Connor. "You're the biggest prick I've *ever* met, and I've had the pleasure of meeting hundreds of distinguished people." His disgusting eyes land on me. "And you're the most stuck-up rich bitch I've ever had to pretend to be in love with." Before I can sling an insult, he adds, "But I'm not here to fight you. I'm here to work *with you*."

My nose flares. "I wouldn't work with you if it was the key to saving my life." I'd die. I would without a doubt die before I placed Scott anywhere on my team.

He ignores my statement. "Things have changed since *Princesses of Philly*." He hesitates for a moment, choosing his words carefully. His gaze flits to the stone steps. The winter chill wraps me tighter than Connor's arms, the hairs rising on my neck.

I wonder if he means the sex tapes or if he's referring to my daughter.

"Not enough that we'd ever need you," Connor tells him. "So explain to me why you need *us*." We're in the driver's seat, then. I place my hand on Connor's, the one that rests on my shoulder, his arm across my collar.

"Don't kid yourself," he says. "I could sell another sex tape and get one-point-five million right now."

"That's it?" Connor's brows rise. "That's not even a fraction of what this mansion costs. And didn't you buy a forty-million-dollar yacht?"

Scott's lips stretch in a stiff smile. "I have expensive tastes."

He needs more money, more than selling our sex tapes can give him, clearly.

"Thankfully I'm not fronting the cash for this house. GBA is."

My stomach curdles. Global Broadcasting Association has the rights to anything we ever film on network television. They aired *Princesses of Philly* in a coveted prime-time slot with high ratings, and ever since my sister and I were pregnant, they've repeatedly called Lily, Loren, Connor and me—to air a new season.

With our children.

"We can both win here. I sign you on for *Princesses of Philly*, assign you with a brand-new executive producer, and GBA gives me a high-ranked position at the network. I never have to see you."

"You want us to launch your career?" I sneer. GBA is stooping so low, digging at dirt and chucking it in our faces, just for more ratings. They used to be the number one network with the female demographic, but when our reality show went off the air, ABC beat them the subsequent quarters.

"There's no benefit for us," Connor tells him.

"I'll sell the rights to the sex tapes back to you," Scott says. My heart skips. "GBA is offering me something long-term that I need to sustain my lifestyle. The tapes aren't lucrative past the number I have."

"And how many do you have left?" Connor questions, on a very logical path while I continue to mentally draw devil horns over Scott and shake violently.

As much as I want those sex tapes back in our possession, I'd never trade them at my daughter's expense. I won't expose Jane to invasive cameras for an indefinite amount of time.

"That's for me to know," Scott says, straightening up in the middle of the doorframe. "I'm going to be in your way until you agree to this. I want your daughter on camera and whatever other little brats you squeeze out."

I lunge forward, and Connor grips me tighter. I begin to yell, my throat raw. I scream profanities and curses, my voice bloodied with serious threats. "You will *never* have her!"

Connor pulls me down to the third stair to leave, but I hang on to the iron banister, not ready. "You son of a bitch," I cry. "You can take my fucking life, but you can't take away hers!"

Scott watches without flinching, my heart pouring onto the stone when I wanted, so badly, to crush his, right here.

"Rose," Connor whispers in the pit of my ear.

"No," I choke. He has to know that we won't stand for this any longer—that we'll destroy him someway, somehow, before he ruins all that we've built. He's chaos, and I want him gone.

"Connor!" Loren yells. He races up the circular driveway, his legs pumping quickly, Ryke by his side, both only in drawstring pants, not wasting time with clothes. Behind them in the distance, the second floor of our house glows, the windows illuminated. Even with these volatile emotions mauling my head, I deduce that the brothers heard us leave and from the window spotted us at the neighbor's house across the street.

Then they chased after us when my screams split the night.

Scott lets out a weak laugh. "Where's the other two: the whore and the hot one?" He extends his arms. "Might as well make this a reunion."

"Go fuck yourself," Ryke growls before I can unleash hell. I try rushing the steps, but Connor pulls me down to where the two guys stand.

Scott laughs again and rolls his eyes at the sky. "I'm not looking forward to dealing with you again, trust me."

I suddenly feel a long woolen coat on my shoulders, Ryke placing it there. He brought my coat out to me? I stick my arms through the holes as though he's given me battle armor. "Let's go," I say, heatedly stepping forward, not backwards.

Connor pulls me into his chest again. "Not tonight, Rose."

Hot, pissed-off tears cloud my vision. "We can't let him stay here, Connor."

"Wait—this shitty fuck is living here?" Lo points a threatening finger at Scott.

He smiles a gross smile. "Hello, neighbor."

Ryke breathes heavily and shakes his head at Connor. "I said I would put in money if you needed to outbid the seller."

"We didn't even know they closed the deal," Connor says. "GBA bought it out from under us."

"GBA?" Lo stands eerily rigid, staring at the cement for a long moment.

I wrap my hands around the railing, still searing holes all along Scott's California tan.

"It's simple," Scott tells the two brothers. "GBA wants a season two of *Princesses of Philly*, this time revolving around your kids. They need you, and you've spent years avoiding their phone calls. Now they're prepared to take greater actions. I'm just one of them."

In a slow wave, Lo's dark, malicious eyes lift off the driveway and pin murderously on Scott. "I get it. GBA has decided to break every goddamn contract they have with Hale Co. because they didn't get what they want. That's it, isn't it? You're all planning to make our lives harder until I put my kid under a larger spotlight."

Scott doesn't deny their low tactics. "GBA will work with Hale Co. again when filming for the show begins."

"You motherfucker!" Ryke storms the stairs, and Connor releases me to push him back. Ryke points hostilely over Connor's shoulder. "Stay out of my brother's fucking life, you sack of shit!"

I approve of Ryke's methods, even if Connor shoots me a commanding look to stand down, to return home with him. In this moment, I choose to align myself with the antagonistic, volatile people that share the same heat in my blood.

Scott cocks his head at Ryke. "Would you rather I toyed with your life? The network would love to put you back on air. The statutory *rapist*." Lies. Gross, repulsive lies.

Ryke lunges, and Connor pushes him forcefully off the stone steps for the umpteenth time. I begin to remove my flip-flops.

Lo barrels forward, beside me now. Connor has trouble containing the three of us. He decides to bar Ryke from the four stairs and let Loren and me go.

My ragged, heavy breath smokes the cold air, and I chuck each flip-flop at Scott's head. He blocks one with his forearm, but the second rubber sole connects with his cheek. He nearly laughs when he rests his putrid eyes on my body.

"You look at me," Lo grits, clamping his teeth, his jaw a razor blade.

Scott peels his eyes off my face and onto Lo. "I have a bottle of Jameson—"

"It's your loss, coming here," Lo cuts him short. "By the end of this, the four of us are going to bury you so quickly, you're going to beg for a goddamn shovel." He rises one more stair, his face in line with Scott's. "And no one will dig out a worthless piece of shit like you."

Loren Hale just declared war.

He doesn't wait for Scott to flinch. He steps down and puts his hand on my shoulder, forcing me to turn around with him.

"Wait," I begin.

"No," Connor and Lo say in unison.

I glare, my legs trembling again. I could ball my hands into fists. "I'm not finished, Richard."

"You've all said more than enough tonight." Connor's jaw muscles constrict, his shoulders stiff. He's pissed—not at me, but he's having trouble imprisoning his anger. I realize he's bottling it in order to restrain the three of us.

Ryke walks backwards slowly. Like me, he struggles to allow Scott to stand there so smugly.

"Tell Daisy I said hi." Scott pokes at another sensitive place for Ryke and *me*. I fling around, barefooted on the dirty driveway, with furious eyes. Connor holds me around the waist. Lo has his hand on Ryke's shoulder.

Scott says, "I bet she would've fucked me if I came on to her stronger."

Ryke is quiet, the darkest expression sweeping his face.

"No? You don't think so?" Scott smiles again. "You might not know this, but Trent, a great friend of mine from L.A., came to New York to photograph some models. I believe Daisy just turned eighteen around then. Trent fucked her. Right in the ass."

I'm going to maul him dead. I swear to God, he's going to die by my raging hands.

"Fuck you, you fucking *fuck*!" Ryke yells, thrashing against Connor's stronghold.

Scott finally closes the door, his self-satisfied smile the last view I see. The injustice of it all bleeds my brain front to back.

"He deserves to die," I say, hot tears building again. "He deserves to go to jail and rot."

Lo glances between the two houses. "Then let's try to put him there."

Connor releases Ryke again, who ends up kicking a floodlight on our walk back.

"As much as I despise Scott," Connor says, "murder isn't going on my résumé."

"I meant jail," Lo says.

"I meant murder," I cut in. I doubt I could go through with a crime of any kind, but I've never been one to think small. My mind pushes extremes while Connor stays in the limitations of reality. It's why he's not screaming until his voice dies. He finds it pointless and detrimental to his own self. He knew that yelling at Scott would do no real good, so he kept his mouth shut.

The three exceedingly tall men stare down at me, and I just now feel the dried tear streaks, iced as the wind hits me. I wasn't crying because I was sad. I was crying because I felt violated all over again, and this time, Jane was thrown into the mix.

"Imagine a world," I tell them, "where our children grow up without any privacy, surrounded by people like him."

"That won't be our world," Lo says adamantly.

I wait for Connor to agree. When he doesn't, I stop in the middle of the road, a lamppost bathing us in orange light. I face my husband, halfway to our house. "You're not going to say anything?" Tears sting. I skim his masculine features and spot the blunt, no-nonsense look that denounces any fantastical, illogical concepts that we all construct to pacify ourselves.

I wish he would lie tonight. I wish he would make me feel like we have a chance instead of serving me the honest, bitter truth on a gold platter.

"I don't make promises that I can't keep," he reminds me. "Our children will meet terrible human beings, just as everyone does. I *can't* change the world for anyone, not even myself."

His confession is brutal, and it hits the three of us hard. We all step back once, Ryke scratches his unshaven jaw. I inhale sharply, and Lo stares haunted at the starless sky.

"So we must assimilate," I retort, "and blend in and *pretend* to be okay." My chin quivers in disgust. "I hate your world."

"It's the world we fucking live in," he says coldly. "It's not *my* world. It's everyone's."

Ryke begins to shake his head. "I can't have a fucking kid," he's realizing.

Lo's breath plumes, his cheeks red from the chill. "Don't say that shit. You want a family."

Ryke lets out a low laugh. "I'm never bringing a child into this,

Lo. I fucking can't . . ." He rubs his mouth and curses under his breath again.

It's the same conclusion I've drawn. I can't have more children if we can't keep them safe.

Connor's deep-blue eyes ping from each of us, all spread in an uneven circle. "We can't protect our children from every evil in the world, but what we can do is protect them from a specific group of people."

"The media," Lo answers.

Connor nods. His gaze lands on me, silently reminding me of our plan to enact this. Our six-month test.

I blame no one for my choices, but I still believe our kids deserve to be treated like human beings and not monkeys in a glass cage. They shouldn't lose their basic human rights when they can't even speak for themselves.

Cameramen can follow us, but they don't need to follow them. They don't have to.

Connor breaks the silence. "Let me remind the three of you how this works." He points to Ryke. "You go to jail, Scott wins." He looks to me. "You scream at him, he smiles, he wins." I swallow this sour taste as he turns to Lo. "You sign on to a second season, he wins."

"We do nothing just like last time," Lo says evenly, "and he wins."

"Let me figure it out," Connor tells us. "I'll take care of Scott, but for now, don't give him what he wants. He likes inciting all of you, and tonight was practically his wet dream, so please just calm down." Connor rubs his lips and drops his hand. "You do know what Lily calls the three of you, right?"

We stare between each other, confused. I would've known if she had a nickname for us. She's *my* sister.

"She mutters it under her breath," Connor says off our silence. "The hot-tempered triad."

My lips twitch upwards. Ryke actually laughs, which causes Lo to laugh. My little sister can be clever without realizing.

And then Connor makes this declaration: "Scott isn't winning this time. I promise."

I inhale strongly, and I'm mixed with a strange blend of fear and confidence.

I promise.

Translation: *only one of us will be left standing.*

Twelve

Connor Cobalt

Are you the reason why Rose dyed her hair back to brunette?" a cameraman asks me as I approach a Manhattan high-rise, a coffee in my left hand. With the other, I hold Jane beneath her bottom, her arm on my shoulder and eyes curiously searching the men surrounding us.

I take note that of three photographers and one cameraman, they've only asked about Rose's hair color from last week, nothing about Jane.

I sip my coffee, heading straight to the revolving door.

He rephrases the question. "Did you like Rose's new color or do you prefer her as a brunette?"

"She could be bald, and I'd still be attracted to her." Flashes blink right before I enter the revolving door, and Jane murmurs a collection of sounds, her big blue eyes widening at me. Before Rose left for work, she laid out Jane's outfit: a gray-and-blue-checkered dress, ivory Dior tights, and a gray headband, her short brown hair just brushing her ears.

We impart our sophisticated sensibilities on her since she's too young to choose for herself, but when she's older, she'll pick what she likes best.

I watch her eyes, often noticing the light behind them that

neither Rose nor I possess. The laughter, the innocence that I have trouble believing once existed in me. I can't remember ever being joyful as a child. I was calculated. I was straightforward and honest.

I wasn't light. I was the gray haze after a puff of a cigar.

Before I slip into the elevator, I toss my coffee in the trash and press the thirtieth floor. The quiet cloaks us for a moment, and Jane smiles into a laugh, clapping her hands together. Children laugh for no reason at all. They laugh because they're alive and they're in your arms.

It's senseless, but this senseless moment pounds against my heart more than a sound fact.

"We're going up, Jane," I tell her, pointing at the ceiling.

She giggles and looks up, her headband sliding back. I adjust it, and she pats her head. She says a word that's very close to "da-da" and points up too. When she swings her head to me, I cover my eyes with my free hand.

"Where's Jane?"

She gasps, and I remove my hand, her face breaking into the fullest, purest smile. She claps at my reappearance. I hide my eyes once more, and her gasp pulls my lips higher. "Where's Jane?"

I drop my hand. "There she is."

Jane giggles and touches her cheeks, discovering her own overwhelming smile that accompanies joy. I kiss her forehead, and she tries to speak but ends up babbling certain syllables and sounds again.

"One day, Jane," I whisper, "you'll surpass me in all ways. I hope you do." I think about more children, a fog of a future. "I hope you all do."

The elevator beeps.

"Now, let's see Frederick. He has some information I need about your aunt Daisy. How does that sound?"

Jane points at the ceiling and tries to form the word that I once said.

"Up," I repeat, always in my usual voice. "We're going straight now, Jane." I point at the hallway. "Straight ahead."

Her eyes blink in confusion.

"In time," I smile. "You'll understand in time."

Frederick collapses in the leather seat adjacent to the couch, a coffee mug in hand. He dyes the gray strands of his hair by his temples, only in his early forties, his jaw square and his nose proportionate to the rest of his features, a born-and-bred New Englander. He could've sailed on the *Mayflower* with Christopher Jones and jumped into a time machine to reach present day, if you're a believer of the ridiculous.

The purple shadows beneath Frederick's eyes suggest lack of sleep, and the textbooks and file folders towered on his desk suggest the source.

"Stop analyzing me, Connor. I'm not the patient. I'm your therapist." He sips his coffee.

On the leather cushion next to me, Jane plays with a children's book, textures and audio buttons keeping her fixated.

"Then maybe you shouldn't present yourself like you've had two hours of sleep, Rick," I advise. I distinguish the book titles from here, most about PTSD and depression. "Her case is that difficult for you?"

"It's complicated—" He catches himself, stopping short. "We're not discussing Daisy."

He hasn't cracked yet, but his exhaustion gives me an advantage this afternoon.

"What's new with you?" he asks, resting his ankle on his thigh, and leans back.

I usually tell Frederick everything. He's ethically obligated to keep my secrets, but saying Scott's name aloud creates permanence that's hard to consume without a grimace. He's across the street from my wife and daughter and four other people that belong in the epicenter of *my* world.

Frederick fills the brief silence. "Jonathan Hale called me again today. He still wants a list of who you've been intimate with, and he wants my notes and professional opinion on what you are."

I tilt my head with a fragment of irritation. "What I am?" My lips rise. "The greatest mind the universe will never understand, smarter than ninety-nine-point-nine percent of the world's population, unabashedly arrogant and grossly tired of Jonathan's punitive measures to undermine me." I nod to Frederick. "That's what I am."

"You may not think your sexuality is important," Frederick tells me, gathering that fact from all that I've said, "but he does—people do—and it's something you have to accept."

"I accept it," I say calmly, tugging down Jane's dress, which has bunched at her waist.

"Bullshit," he calls me out. "You don't talk like you just did without feeling passionate about something, Connor."

"What should I do, then, in your *professional* opinion? Should I go to Jonathan and have a one-on-one conversation, splitting my heart open to a man that I find manipulative in his own right? You think he'll revere me, Rick? You think he'll understand me?"

"You've already made up your mind," he says, listening to the tone of my voice. "And I wouldn't suggest going to Jonathan for anything. Of what you've told me, it sounds like he'd use the information against you. I just don't understand why he's so hell-bent on exposing your past relationships."

I do. "He's afraid that I have emotional control over his son, something that he used to have. He's just threatened by my friendship with Loren, and now that his son is running his company, he's worried I'll have more sway with Hale Co. than he will." And Jonathan wants more evidence to blackmail me with so I'll stop being a force in Loren's life.

Even if I'm a positive force.

But I hold more cards than Jonathan, so whatever blackmail he wants to throw my way, it's a useless ploy. Jonathan Hale may have money, but he is beneath me, a human invertebrate. He doesn't even control Hale Co. anymore, which makes me further and further out of his league.

I'm too connected to the people he cares about—Loren Hale and Greg Calloway—for him to make a move against me. It's suicide. And Jonathan Hale is all about self-preservation.

Frederick takes another sip of coffee. "So you were quiet when I asked you before, so I'm going to ask you again. What's new? And it has to be easier to talk about than this."

I roll up the sleeves of my white button-down, heat blowing through a vent above my head. I still try to construct that five-letter name aloud.

Frederick sits up, resting his forearms on his thighs as he cups his mug. He watches Jane attempt to flip a page in her book, but the thick page slips from her weak clutch. She turns her head and looks to me for help. I lean forward and flip the page for her. She mumbles.

"You're welcome," I say with a growing smile.

She lets out a high-pitched giggle and returns to her book.

"She's advanced for her age," Frederick notes.

"Marginally. She's probably a month ahead, but Lo's son tries to keep up with her. I think he may walk first." I've been observing their milestones—speech, dexterity, cognizance, mobility—and when Jane first rolled onto her stomach, along the living room rug, Moffy watched and followed suit. I've seen him attempt to stand, as she does. He has more power in his movements, and he's one month younger.

I'm proud of that baby, and he's not even mine.

"Did something happen with the press?" Frederick asks. When he begins blindly guessing, he shows his cards. He's nervous for me, drawing conclusions around the worst possibilities since I won't talk.

"Scott Van Wright moved in across the street." I detach myself from these words and present him the facts of GBA's involvement and pressure to renew the reality show.

When I finish, Frederick sits back like I've slammed him hard. He's quiet for a full minute, processing everything.

"And?" I ask, needing his guidance. He's nearly as smart as me, and I wouldn't come here weekly if I didn't need reminders of things sitting at the back of my brain, the emotions that I stuff in drawers and the facts I set aside.

"I think you know what you feel," he says.

I'm incredibly numb. "I feel nothing right now."

"You're a narcissist," Frederick reminds me. "It's hard for you to believe you've failed, in any way, and so you make yourself believe you've succeeded."

"I did succeed," I say. "My company—"

"How is Rose?" Frederick asks.

I shut down again, my body unbending. I thought Rose could handle the sex tapes if we benefited from them, but throughout the years, I've seen how the mere mention of them weakens her resolve. I forgot that she's not like me. "What I want doesn't go without consequence. I couldn't dissolve the sex tapes, so I profited off of them in another way."

"And so did Scott," Frederick says. "He's the only person who has ever duped you in your entire life, Connor, and now he's back."

"I'm rethinking these meetings, Rick. I don't pay you to tell me things I already know."

"You pay me to remind you that you're not inhuman and that you have feelings."

I rub my lips and look at Jane for a moment, and she presses a button beside a picture of a cow. *Mooo!* She lifts the book to her ear at the noise, and it falls from her clutch, thudding to the cushion. Still, she smiles.

I want her innocence intact as long as it should be. The thought of Scott even nearing her boils my blood, and the thought of anyone threatening her well-being—it's inconceivable.

"I can't shout. I can't scream," I tell Frederick. "I can't beat at my chest and expect Scott to vanish."

Rose nearly lost her voice after yelling at Scott that night. She also spent an hour scrubbing the soles of her feet in the bathroom—from walking barefoot on the road. She only stopped when I drew a bath for her and poured her a glass of wine.

I have to play this smart.

I run my finger over a scratch on the leather armrest. "I love nearly every game I play, even the recent ones with Rose." The *Celebrity Crush* articles have their allure, especially when we can control the setting and the place and time. "But Scott is like swatting at a mosquito. He's an annoyance, brainless but unyielding, and I receive no satisfaction from this game—I hate every fucking part of it."

"You could pay him more than GBA is willing to give him—"

"No," I cut him off. "That's not even an option. Whatever I do, there will be *no* benefit for Scott. When I win, I'm not letting him win too."

I imagine Jane, five years old and meeting Scott Van Wright as he swings back around, collecting more money, blackmailing us for more and more.

"I have to detach him from my family."

"Just take it slowly," Frederick advises, scrutinizing my features the way I did to him earlier. "You're a new father, the head of a giant corporation, not to mention dealing with Jonathan Hale, and now Scott, and you're already in bed with the media."

"First-world problems," I quip.

He hops over that. "How is your relationship with the media going for Jane's sake, by the way?"

"It's still too early to tell." I think back at how no one asked me about Jane when I entered this building. "But when there are other relevant stories, the cameras usually stay on me. When we do nothing during the week, they fixate on the children, grappling for something."

"It's risky," Frederick says.

My lips rise. "Everything is a risk."

"So you're going to poke the beast?" His voice is even-tempered, which lets me believe that he thinks it's a decent idea; otherwise he'd be chastising me like, *are you sure about this, Connor?*

Irritation still grips my voice. "It's better to poke the beast and let it eat me than wait for it to eat my child."

Off my annoyance, he switches topics. "Are you sleeping well?"

I glance at the textbooks on his desk again. "Five hours a night, the usual." I can run off that easily. "How many hours does Daisy sleep?"

"About the same." His face hardens when he realizes his slip. "No." He points a finger at me and rises from his seat, heading to the desk.

"I won't tell anyone what you tell me."

He ignores me, cleaning the file folders off his desk and stacking them in black metal drawers.

"I could help you," I offer. "She's a complex case, and it might be in her benefit to have two minds on the project instead of one."

Frederick stiffens.

I'm getting somewhere. "It's not uncommon for colleagues to discuss a patient's case."

"You're not my colleague," Frederick retorts.

"Only because I find this whole field boring, and to be honest, I'm overqualified for your job." And then I add, "I could've withheld what happened with Scott and offered you a deal, to trade that for information about Daisy, but I did the noble thing. And right now, you're telling me the noble thing has no rewards." *Then maybe I should revert to immoral tactics.*

Frederick hesitates for a second before he concedes. "I want to put her on medication . . . but I can't pick the right one if I'm not absolutely positive of all her symptoms and what they're pointing me to. She's been given pills that treat only a portion of what's wrong with her, and they exacerbate her other issues . . ." He rests both hands on his desk and shakes his head. "I can't tell, with absolute certainty, if she's manic-depressive or not." He can't discern whether her highs are really highs.

"Having been around her for years, I can tell you that her bursts of energy are fronts. It's not real, Frederick. It's a façade. She's not bipolar."

Frederick isn't so sure.

I realize that he's not far into her case yet. He's stuck at the beginning. I rise, lifting Jane in my arms. "Don't watch her bounce around on television," I advise. "Don't look at her smiling in magazines. Daisy would rather trick herself into believing she's okay than ruin the rest of our time worrying that she's not."

"And how do you know this?" he asks while I head to the door.

"I've mastered the art of hiding emotions." She's good, but she's not better than me.

Thirteen

Connor Cobalt

A marble chess set rests on our bed between us. Charcoal and ivory kings, queens, rooks, bishops, knights and pawns line each side in correct order, the pieces like battlements and soldiers in combat.

Playing with Rose always seems like warfare. We never bring out board games to pass time. We play with stakes, so the loss feels like a loss and the win feels like a win. We play to achieve something greater.

Tonight is no different. If our pieces are captured, we have to remove an article of clothing or tell a truth.

I plan to have her naked.

She plans to have me stripped bare in other ways.

Three pawns removed, and I'm shirtless and she's spilled two useless truths about middle school dances. Obviously neither of us is obtaining what we desire.

I press my fingers to my lips, watching her shift on the bed. She knots the strap of her black silk robe tighter around her waist, hiding white lace lingerie that she only wears when she wants to tease me.

It's working.

I imagine the lacy, see-through material, her nipples partially visible, her hips full, ass round, accentuating her curves and her femininity. If I didn't like games this much, I'd have her on her back by now.

The crystal chandelier rattles above us, the light dimming on its own. This isn't the first time it's happened.

She looks up, the crystals clinking together. "Why does he have to fuck my little sister on the roof?"

"The same reason why you prefer my hands around your throat when I fuck you and the same reason why I enjoy it." I pause. "And dogs need to be let outside from time to time."

She lifts the robe higher near her collar before returning to the chess set, further hiding her bare skin.

"New rules," I suddenly say.

Her fiery yellow-green eyes flit to me, as if I have no power to change what's already been established. *Think again, Rose.*

"You take one of my pieces," I say, "and I tell you a truth."

Her lips purse, but her shoulders loosen. "Let me guess, if you take one of mine, I *have* to automatically remove an article of clothing. No choice at all."

I smile as her eyes heat. "I won't have a choice either," I remind her. "This way, we both get what we want. You naked. Me exposed. We're both winners."

She lets out a short, dry laugh. "There's only ever one winner, Connor."

"Not if you're playing on a team."

"Chess isn't a team game," she says under her breath, already softening to the idea. Her eyes flit to my abs and the definition in my biceps. "What if I want you naked?" A tense silence coils my muscles, and her eyes flit up to me with deadly power, poisonous and beautiful all at once.

"I'll be happy to do that without a game."

Her shoulders lock, and she rolls her eyes at the sight of my wide grin.

"Darling," I add. "We're both bored playing this. Either we

change up the rules or I'm finding a new game. And I'm not sure you'll like it." I want to wind her silk strap around my fist and yank off her robe. *Patience*. I do have patience. More than most men. It's what makes me better than them.

Her cheeks heat. "Fine." She steals a glance at the baby monitor on the nightstand. "I need to check on Jane in a little anyway. We can do this quick."

"Quick" isn't a word I like when it comes to my wife. Every moment with Rose, I would extend for infinite measures of time. Even the hostile, torrid moments where she tries to light the world, and me, on fire. I love them all.

Since she's already agreed to the new rules, I don't argue with her about the speed of the game. I return my attention to the chessboard, her knees perilously close to the ivory pieces as she splays her legs to the side. I sit across from Rose with my elbow resting on one bent knee, fingers to my jaw in contemplation.

I've strategized ten moves ahead, but I deduce—based on the other times we've played—that she's five ahead of me. We're both adept at chess, but neither of us ever competed. "Grandmaster" is one title I never sought or wanted.

Most of my skills arise from my boarding school. I spent almost half my life at Faust, my mother having sent me there for third grade through twelfth. I was seven when I unpacked my suitcase and my mom patted my shoulder in goodbye.

I'll see you when you need me, she said. *But if you're the boy I know you to be, then you won't need me at all.* She didn't want me to be attached to her, and so I never was.

That boarding school became my mother and my father. I refer to Faust more than I refer to Katarina, more than I ever speak of my absent father. The institution taught me how to survive. It gave me more knowledge, but a place can't hug you or love you.

And I remember most days at Faust like vivid dreams set in gray scale. It only bled in color when I met Rose for the very first time.

Chess was common. About fifteen of us would congregate in an upperclassman's room, cigarettes lit and the windows cracked in ten-below winters. We'd begin a clandestine tournament, drinking shots for every piece captured, doubled if someone checked. Moves had to be made in under ten seconds or you'd drink again.

We looked like drunken, privileged geniuses—high off being smart enough to play a game most don't understand. And we were bored enough to spin it into something more exhilarating, juvenile and fun.

Parts of me will never change.

I slide my rook towards her side. She cages her excitement behind suspicion, staring at my vulnerable pawn. I press my fingers to my jaw again. "At Faust, we had a ten-second rule when we played chess," I tell her.

"That must be where the rumor comes from." Her eyes still pin to the charcoal pawn.

She's baiting me with her words, and I feed into it. "What rumor?"

"The one about Faust boys only lasting ten seconds in bed." She moves her bishop, seizing my sacrificial pawn.

My brows rise, just slightly. "And I've been able to disprove that rumor numerous times with you."

She raises her hand to silence me. "This is not the time for you to boast about your sexual talents."

My lips curve upwards at that particular word: "talents."

She points at me and suddenly kneels for height advantage, while I stay in the same relaxed position. "Don't even think it."

"Talent?" I say aloud.

She growls beneath her breath. "I didn't compliment you."

"'Talent' is a compliment by definition."

"It *wasn't* one."

"Let's consult Merriam-Webster, then." Before she protests, I type into my phone's search engine and the answer pulls my cheeks into a much larger grin.

"Richard," she warns, hating that she mistakenly complimented me. I love it, only because it angers her this much.

"'A special ability that allows someone to do something well,'" I read the definition. "That was a compliment."

Her eyes flame.

I stare at my screen with more humor in my features. "Also, 'people who are sexually attractive.'"

She scoffs. "It doesn't say that."

I flash her my phone, and she snatches it out of my hands, her eyes like lasers, scorching the screen as she reads.

"Rose Calloway Cobalt finds me sexually attractive," I say. "If only you'd called me talented when you were fourteen."

She stiffens but keeps her gaze on the phone that she cups between two hands. "And what would you have done if I had?"

I wait for her to look up at me. When she does, I see our history laid flat like an ancient world map. "I would've called you talented right back."

Her collarbone juts out as she inhales deeply.

My grin spreads, the one that she calls conceited. It instantaneously makes her aware of how infatuated she looks. She ices over and chucks a nearby pillow at me, narrowly missing the chessboard.

I laugh and she pelts me with another, beaded one.

"That better not be the truth you owe me."

"What was wrong with that one?" I ask.

"It wasn't real."

"It was real," I say.

"You told me that you didn't find me attractive until you were seventeen."

My smile fades. The real truth: I found Rose fascinating from our very first encounter, but if I admit that, then I'm admitting to the concept of love at first sight. The whole notion is ridiculous, fallible—one hundred percent unbelievable. So I had to have been seventeen when I was first drawn to Rose. Anything else is just fantasy.

"Tell me something real," Rose prods. "And it better be fucking good."

I don't necessarily know what she wants. *Something from the heart.* I hear her voice as I think it. My heart may be anatomically the same as hers, but it's different. I will always be different.

"I love your eyes," I tell her.

She glowers. "I already know your strange obsession with my eyes. That's nothing new. You're *cheating*." She emphasizes the word, believing it'll rile me the way that it does her.

I stay complacent and pass an ivory pawn between my fingers, one that I'd collected fifteen minutes ago. And I think about a truth. *Something from the heart.* "The first time I had sex," I begin, "I lasted much longer than ten seconds. I was good at it."

"Calling yourself a sex god is a personal evaluation, not a truth, and you've already told me some of this before."

"How about the part where I hated it?"

She goes rigid, her hands flat on her thighs.

"I hated my first time," I say again, just as calmly. "There are monumental stages in life that most people eventually take. We talk. We walk. We feel. We cry." I pause. "We *love*. We fuck. And sooner or later, we die." I lick my lips and let out a soft laugh. "Sex was a stage. It was practical. It was what I was supposed to do, but it held no meaning. It wasn't exciting. Physically, I felt pleasure. Mentally, it was lackluster. I couldn't figure out how to make it better than it was. I couldn't figure out what to do differently to turn something ordinary into something that would blind me. Not at fifteen. And so I hated it."

Her mind reels. I can see it spinning in her distant gaze. "You left out emotionally," she whispers.

"Sex was never emotional for me, at least not until I had sex with you."

Rose scrutinizes me, as though wondering if I'm speaking honestly or telling her what she wants to hear. But that's, without a doubt, the honest truth.

"What else?" she asks, wanting me to spill more *feelings*, not just facts. I understand that now.

"My turn." I shut down her question and return to the chessboard.

She crosses her arms, her hot gaze directed on my actions. I shift a pawn to align my pieces, rejecting a more obvious route. Rose plays chess aggressively, more than most. Two moves later and I capture her rook. She sighs in frustration, brows knotted as she traces the board, as if she can rewind time and alter her last move.

"Your robe, darling." I gesture to her clothing, which I desperately want removed.

She lets out another heavy sigh. It took years for her to be comfortable around me. She's conquered those insecurities, so anytime she huffs, it's because she's stubborn, prideful, and therefore struggles submitting to me, even if it fills her with pleasure.

Rose, rather indignantly, pulls at the belt of her silk robe. Maybe she's purposefully being rough and less sensual and slow, so I won't get off. Having an erection would be another bonus for me. She shoves the fabric off her shoulders, and her hostility throbs my cock, much more than anything else would.

The robe falls to the mattress, pooling at her thighs. I almost have to readjust my bent knee, my muscles constricting at the sight of her white lingerie, one piece, like an indecent bathing suit. The lace forms delicate roses along her hip bones, the wire bodice architecting her hourglass frame. A tiny white bow sits between her full breasts, pushed up in two cups, see-through, her nipples already hardened.

Her chest falls heavier than before, the diamond droplet necklace needing to be replaced with leather. My arms ache to pull her into my chest, hard and rough and so quick that every movement afterwards will belong to me.

She clears her throat, scolding me for looking this long.

Rose is so many layers of beautiful that even I'd have trouble touching each one.

"You have me in my underwear. Congratulations." She bends to the chess set, her cleavage nearly spilling out towards me.

My fingers tighten on my kneecap. I attempt to control the urge to shove the board aside and split her legs open, just take her rough without another pause.

"Your pawn is dead," she announces. "Give me a truth."

I frown and pry my gaze off her breasts. She pinches my pawn, her red nail polish stirring my cock again. *Patience.*

I extend my leg out more, my muscles cramped. "I was good at sex because I watched porn. I found it useful."

"You and every other teenager," she snaps. "That's not a truth, it's a fact." Her focus quickly returns to the board, too quickly. She's avoiding a topic we both often skirt around. *Porn.* The sex tapes.

My conversation with Frederick shoots to the front of my brain, about how much those tapes have affected Rose. About my inability to claim them as a failure. Scott may have the sex tapes, but I have a multibillion-dollar business and a new diamond franchise.

In my point of view, I won.

In Rose's, I'm beginning to realize she feels like it's a loss.

"Make your move," she tells me.

"What about my truth?"

Her eyes flit to mine and back to the board. "I don't care anymore."

I care. I care if she's hurt. I care if she's sad or if she's in pain. I care more about Rose than I ever thought I'd care about another human being.

She motions to the board. "Continue on so I can crush you."

I latch onto her gaze. "About the sex tapes—"

"Move your piece," she cuts me off abruptly, "or you forfeit your turn."

"That's not how this game works," I reply. "I tell you a truth." Maybe if I give her something bigger, she'll be more open about those tapes with me. "I started experimenting when I was nineteen, bondage and handcuffs. I pushed it too far for my own personal taste, just to see what I liked, sometimes. I never had a person instruct me. I just deduced what got me off more than anything else."

"What about the other person?" she asks.

"They enjoyed it. I wouldn't try anything on someone who didn't. I'm in the game of pleasing people, even when I'm dissatisfied, remember?"

She rolls her eyes.

I smile. "I don't like when women call me 'sir.' I won't ever call you a slut. What I love most is the control, especially over someone who's headstrong."

"Funny," she says icily, but she clears her throat again, this time in arousal.

"How was that?" I ask her, wondering if my truth was up to par.

She nods. "Decent." Her eyes soften as if to say it was much more than that. "Your turn."

I skim the board and go for the stupid, less calculated move. I purposely capture her bishop. My own motives usurp winning the game. Her panties, clipped to the bodice to form a one-piece. I want those off first. I imagine her sitting on the bed, nothing between the silky blue comforter and her flesh.

By her hip bones, she unfastens the clips, and then begins to peel off the *top*. "Your panties first," I demand.

She freezes. "That's not how this game works," she repeats my earlier words.

I shake my head as she sashays the straps down her elbows, off her arms, and then lifts the lace lingerie over her head.

"You're being obstinate," I say calmly. "It's going to cost you tonight."

She swallows hard, probably picturing how I'll punish her. And when she tosses the bodice aside, she immediately presses her arms over her breasts.

I barely catch a glimpse of her hard nipples before they disappear from sight. There was more to see when she was wearing the top.

I tilt my head. "Is there something wrong with your breasts?"

Her eyes flash hot.

I talk swiftly before she berates me. "It's either that or you're uncomfortable being naked in front of me, but that hasn't been the case for years. So what's wrong?" *She's just being stubborn.* I know the truth. So does she.

"I hate you," she says, dropping her arms.

"I didn't ask for a lie to accommodate removing your clothes, but it's nice of you to offer me something more."

"There's no way you can lose, is there?" she questions abruptly. "You will always twist things so it seems like you win."

Her question makes it hard to enjoy the view of her partially naked. "*Je ne peux jamais perdre.*" *I can never lose.*

She raises a hand at my face to silence me again. "We'll see about that." Without another delay, Rose goes for the winning move, unlike me. She plucks my queen off the board, her knight in striking distance of my king. It surprises me—for how much she doesn't want me to talk about our sex tapes, she'll risk it for the game.

She raises her chin. "Check."

"Truthfully," I say, my eyes fixing on hers, "I could live with the sex tapes for the rest of my life and never feel an ounce of pain from their existence. And all this time, you've made me believe that you could too, but I can see that's not true."

She gapes. "It is."

"Rose," I say her name like *you know the truth like me*, "that night we confronted Scott, you showed your cards." She screamed like the sex tapes had happened yesterday, like they still hurt above all we've been through. "And maybe I knew, all this time, but I just wanted to believe you were like me."

She shivers.

I reach across the board to take her in my arms, but she pushes my bare chest with one hand and points at me to stay still.

"Are you calling me weak?"

"No," I say. "I'm calling you human. Your reaction is the normal one."

"You're calling me *normal*." Her eyes flame, but her features almost shatter like I took a gavel to glass.

"It's not a bad thing," I say.

"From you, it's an insult."

I can't believe I'm having trouble speaking. I try to find the right words quickly. "You are my equal," I say this slowly so the words sink in.

"If you could kill me, knowing that I'd be replaced with the same features but with your exact personality, would you do it?" she questions.

"No," I answer without a beat. "It would be pointless to date someone just like me. I would know every move, every desire, everything. I adore the way you polarize me."

She relaxes more and nods. "I believe you." She tries to exhale. After a much longer pause, she says, "And I didn't realize how much the sex tapes had still hurt me until that night either." Rose tucks a strand of hair behind her ear. "I hate them more in context with Scott than anything. I had no say in whether or not people could jack off to my body, and *he* did."

"You just want justice," I realize. "Now that he's returned, it should be easier to trap him."

"What are we supposed to tell Jane?" she asks, veering off course and asking me to follow.

I try to trace the paths of her mind. Jane, in relation to the sex tapes. "We tell her not to watch them, and that we had no intention of them ever being online because we had no idea we were being filmed in our bedroom. We tell her the truth." I fist the ivory pawn without realizing, an indention in my palm.

"And that'll make it okay?" Rose asks, her voice nearly cracking. "What happens when she's ten or twelve or fifteen and another tape is released and all of her friends see it? What if she's mocked and ridiculed and she doesn't have our strength to face it? It's *not* going to be okay, Connor."

"I'm going to do whatever it takes," I declare. I've always fought for the things I've desired. I've never sat idly and waited for my dreams to happen. I'll find the avenue to obtain the rights to the rest of the sex tapes. It's more necessary now than it was before.

I want this control back before Jane grows up. The previously released tapes, we can't change, but maybe by the time she's older, they'll fall deep into oblivion.

"Says the man who never loses," she whispers, her lips rising a fraction.

Mine match hers. "My turn." I watch her shoulders drop from their inflexible state, more unworried and unburdened. She peruses the board with a quick glance, seeming secure with the outcome of this game: a win for her, a loss for me.

The smart move: I shift my king out of harm's way.

The foolish one: I capture her measly pawn.

Her breath hitches when my fingers grasp her marble chess piece and I eye her last article of clothing.

Fourteen

Rose Cobalt

He did that on purpose.

It was an idiotic move that left his king vulnerable.

"Checkmate," I say under my breath. His gaze trails over my body, devouring every curve. It's not the look of someone who just lost a game. "You *lost*." I emphasize this point so he feels the sting of defeat.

"I have what I wanted," he says. "As do you." A grin envelops his face. "Like I said, we're both winners." Connor leans forward and seizes my ankle. With a firm, swift grasp, he pulls me closer to his body, my back thudding to the mattress and my ass bulldozing the chessboard, pieces spilling around my body, my elbow digging into a knight.

My panties now in reach, Connor rips the fabric with a harsh tug, the lace biting into my flesh. The force pinpricks my nerves, a strong pulse between my legs. He pulls again, this time freeing the fabric completely.

I glare. "Those were expensive."

His lips brush my ear, nibbling, biting. *"Et c'est inestimable."* *And this is priceless.* He clutches my face and kisses me, forcibly, strongly—his dominance bridging my body closer to him. I lose breath when his tongue parts my lips, when he pulls my whole frame off the chessboard and up into his body. My fingernails dig into his muscular back for support.

His assuredness, his overwhelming confidence, drowns me beneath passion, my head sunk below a seemingly calm, motionless river. I don't fight to reach the surface.

While he kisses me, he shoves the chessboard off the mattress, the entire set clattering to the ground. I open my eyes at the violent noise, and I notice the charcoal king still in his grip. He lifts me higher on the bed, setting my head on a light gray pillow.

He kneels over me, my panties still in hand too.

I fixate on my ripped underwear. "There was an easier way to do that." I try to control my ragged breath.

He tenderly brushes my hair off my face and then unclasps my necklace, setting the delicate strand aside on the nightstand. It's a ploy.

Connor Cobalt is many things in bed—tender is rarely one of them.

"If I wanted your opinion about removing these"—he dangles my torn panties on one finger—"I would've asked for it."

I attempt to lock my legs, my heat clenching, but he uses his knees to keep them wide, wide open. "How considerate of you," I reply with empty spite. My natural reaction is to be combative, even if I don't mean it half the time.

He lowers his head to me, his teeth nipping my bottom lip, and very deeply, he whispers French into the pit of my ear. I struggle to translate the velvety words, blood rushing out of my head. He squeezes my ass, his palm large, masculine, and then he slaps me. A noise catches in my throat.

"You like that," he states, bringing his hand to my cheek. I expect him to manhandle me, but instead, he *softly* caresses my skin. "Too bad you've been obstinate tonight."

I narrow my eyes. "I'm only obstinate so your ego doesn't mushroom and asphyxiate every living thing, including me."

He grins, further confirming that his ego is uncontrollable, untamable and on the verge of smothering *me*. I wish that Connor didn't arouse me, but then I'm happy to be aroused by him. God, why can't I just hate him without loving him? It'd be so much easier.

I'm one second from contesting him with more words, but he's faster. He balls my panties and stuffs them in my mouth. My neck burns at the new situation, and my toes curl, craving his hard body against mine, his rough, vigorous movements, pounding inside of me.

He climbs off the bed.

Motherfucker.

I'm close to spitting out the panties and following suit. As soon as I sit up, Connor reaches over and presses a hand on my collarbone, pushing my back flat against the mattress.

"Stay here," he commands. He kicks the marble chessboard towards the chair, the pieces rolling onto the hardwood and off the rug. Scattered. In disarray. My heart palpitates, a dirty chill snaking down my neck. I hate the mess, like a sudden infestation of beetles and cockroaches. My need to exterminate, to feel clean, kicks in.

"Stare at the chandelier," he instructs, sensing my trouble.

I plant my gaze on the chandelier, only a couple crystals swaying from the air conditioner. My mind nose-dives when something cold touches my belly. I glance down and see the charcoal king above my belly button.

He's not . . .

Connor, dressed only in navy lounge pants, makes his way across the room. "When I return, if I see that you've moved the king from its exact place, you'll be in serious trouble, Rose."

Lovely. A test. One I'm sure I'll pass. He's probably headed to the closet to grab the handcuffs and the leather collar.

He pauses by our dresser, to assess me, his harsher gaze

swallowing every inch of my body. My breath deepens, and my ribs collapse and expand, threatening to knock over the king. *Fuck*. I focus on that stupid little king and try to force it still with willpower alone.

It stops trembling.

"One more thing before I go." His gaze sweeps me again. "Spread your legs open."

I don't move.

"*Now.*" His severe tone simultaneously goads me to unfreeze my muscles but then freeze them all over again, out of spite.

I pocket this bit of stubbornness and carefully spread my legs, watching the king remain motionless with my precision.

"Further."

I ache to spit out the panties and retort something *obstinate* at him. I must take too long, or maybe Connor craves touch, because he walks over, clasps my leg and finishes the distance to his liking. They're spread as far as I'm physically capable, and now I'm exposed and soaked.

I actually moan into the damn fabric of my underwear. I really want him inside of me, hard and fast and never-ending. He'd accomplish this to perfection too. But he resituates the king, which has rolled off my stomach, and then steps away from the bed again.

His demeanor changes, refusing me one ounce of attention. He walks . . . towards the bedroom *door*.

He's leaving. My voice is muffled through the fabric when I try to yell his name. The king teeters, and I focus, unable to speak or move.

He doesn't turn around. He unlocks the door and disappears into the hallway, shutting it behind him. There is no lock on the other side, which means anyone can slip in . . .

Spit out the panties without moving. And tear off his head. That is my first goal. I could cheat, and he'd never know. I could spit out the fabric and place the chess piece back in the same spot if it rolls off. He's given me control of my hands and legs, but *cheating* . . .

I wouldn't be able to marvel in my success, knowing I'd achieved it through a shortcut.

Very carefully, I reach up with my hands and remove the panties, my gaze trained on this enemy charcoal king. *I will destroy you.*

When the panties are beside me, no longer barring me from speech, I use my voice. "Connor! CONNOR!"

I hear no movement outside, and I notice the array of chess pieces on the floor again. I swallow and look back at the chandelier. Maybe this is all to help curb my OCD—or maybe that's just part of his goal. I don't like it.

I am completely naked with my legs spread wide open. A chess piece on my belly. And I need to know what's happening outside. I need to see him. What if something is wrong with Jane? What if that's why he left?

I can't just sit here and *wait*.

My mind is on a turntable.

Screw him five ways to hell. I swat the king off my stomach and climb off the bed. *Don't look at the ground.* I swallow again and grab my black robe, slipping it on and marching to the door.

I swing it open, expecting to find an empty hallway and light bathing the nursery where Connor has traitorously gone without me. When I turn my head right, I spot Connor leaning against the wall. He checks his watch.

"You're just standing there?" I gape. My blood simmers, my chest rising in rage.

"You lasted one minute."

I slap his arm, and he grips my wrist, tugging my body into his so quickly. He's pulling me up on my tiptoes, my face closer to his but not quite equal.

My heart thrashes. "You were timing me?"

"You didn't listen to me." His other hand grazes the bareness of my thigh, sliding higher, maybe to see if I put on panties. My breath hitches as his fingers skim my clit.

"I didn't . . ." *Speak properly, Rose.* "I didn't know how long you'd be gone. You just left me there." I growl the last three words. I worry that he'll forget about me—that something will pull him away and he'll leave me tied up or in a compromising position for someone else to find. This isn't the first time I've had trouble being left alone while he checks on Jane.

He clasps my jaw with one strong hand, his thumb skimming my bottom lip. *"Je reviendrai toujours à toi." I will always return to you.*

I blink, my fury dissipating. *I will always return to you.*

This was the point of his test, I realize. He kisses me, his fingers sliding through my hair, to the back of my head. I melt some, slowly beginning to believe and trust him to not forget about me.

Fifteen

Rose Cobalt

She loves that stuffed animal. Do *not* lose it," I instruct Ryke for the tenth time. In the living room, Jane lies at his feet, whacking the pink-frilled blanket with a rattle toy. Her favorite stuffed lion is always in her sight, and when she loses it, she screams horrifically, as though the world is ending.

Moffy is crawling towards Jane from his array of toys. Ryke scoops him around the waist and the little boy laughs, dressed in a Spider-Man onesie. He tries to touch his uncle's scruff.

Ryke is more comfortable with his nephew since Lily and Lo don't have a printed list of rules for handling their kid. He told me that last week when I asked why he never visits Jane in her nursery but he's constantly in Moffy's.

I tap my high heel, the threatening noise dying on the rug.

Ryke suddenly *tosses* Maximoff in the air, the baby out of his hands. Wide, hot and frantic laser beams shoot out of my eyes. Ryke catches him around the waist upon descent, and Moffy laughs again in delight.

My mouth is permanently unhinged. I think I just had a myocardial infarction.

"Ryke," I almost shout his name. Jane will not live past tomorrow with him.

"Yeah, I got it. The lion is fucking important." He sets down Moffy, and the baby beelines for Jane again.

"I swear to everything that's holy, if her first word is 'fuck,' I'm going to strangle you in your sleep."

Ryke sighs heavily, glancing between the babies and me. "We've been over this. If you don't want me cursing around your baby, then don't fucking let me babysit."

That's not an option. When Jane and Moffy were first born, Lily and I took time off work to be with our babies, but now that they're a little older, we have to return to our companies.

Halway Comics has launched a brand-new superhero through a twelve-issue event. Lo, through his own keen eye and passion, discovered the writer and the artist. Even though the company now has a marketing team, Lily is in charge of merchandising the new superhero throughout Superheroes & Scones: cardboard cutouts, sweatshirts, lunch boxes, watches, action figures and more.

It's a critical time for them. This superhero could launch their brand into the stratosphere of Marvel and DC and Image Comics. Or it could fail.

I've also lent control of my boutique, Calloway Couture, to trusted employees while I focus on Calloway Couture Babies with Loren, the fashion line now owned by Hale Co. The only company at a stasis is Cobalt Inc.—which has reached a high profit margin and needs no further growth or expansion right now.

Our "no nanny" policy is still in place. We take turns working from home to watch the kids. Ryke and Daisy offer to babysit sometimes, and I wish my little sister could be here to help her boyfriend and to restrain him from tossing children and things into the air.

She's in New York City for a therapy appointment with Frederick.

Maybe I can wait for her to come home . . .

I glance at my cell.

"Janie will be fine with me," Ryke tries to assure me. He sits on the rug in front of both babies, and they crawl onto his ankles with jubilant smiles. Connor and I argue about her godparents—the same way that Lily and Lo have trouble choosing. They won't tell us who they're leaning towards, and we haven't announced who we are either.

I always lean towards Lily, my closest sister.

But Connor trusts Ryke. He tells me all the time that Ryke is more suited to take care of handfuls of children. Lo can't handle eight kids, if we have that many. Ryke could.

I recall Connor's confidence in Ryke. I hone in on the fact that he'd be willing to leave Jane with him forever if we *died*.

Okay, Ryke. I'm trusting you with my daughter. No lists this time. I desperately try not to think about him throwing her in the air like a football.

"Don't be a hero," I say, my tone icy. "If you think something is wrong, just call me."

"You're on speed dial, Rose."

I nod once, and my heels finally unglue from the rug. It takes an incredible amount of force to slowly walk away and out the door.

should have stayed home.

The singular thought crosses my mind when the chief quality and product integrity officer of Hale Co. decides to ramble about branding for Calloway Couture Babies instead of focusing on his particular field of interest.

Being with Jane is less of a headache and a million times more pleasant than this.

"The board of executives is going to make the final call on what to name the brand," James reminds me for the tenth time.

"You should let go of this so we can move forward. We're working on a timeline."

"I'm aware of the timeline." CCB will be in stores this summer, and until then, I need to sort through labels, advertising, merchandising and appeasing the person with the most sway: the head of this company.

Loren Hale.

I'd rather focus solely on designs, but I love the control Loren has granted me. He designated me the head of the baby clothes division. This isn't just a fashion line. It's a subsidiary company of a huge corporation, something I've never been entirely a part of.

I spent years in college struggling to sell my designs to big corporations like H&M, succeeding only a fraction of the time and ultimately letting the dream fall to the wayside. The stress and uncertainty were driving me insane, and it didn't hold the same value it once did.

Now that I finally have the opportunity to see my clothes permanently in department stores, I won't compromise all of my artistic beliefs.

James continues talking, and I hold up a hand, stopping him midsentence.

"I've heard everything you're telling me from the chief marketing officer." Albeit on the phone while he's away on vacation. "So if the next words aren't an original idea or thought, I'm going to cut off your tongue."

The ash-blond man, twice my age, goes silent. He pushes his thin, silver-rimmed glasses further up his nose.

I drum my nails on my desk. "I like you, James."

"Could have fooled me, Mrs. Cobalt." He lets out an unsure, uncomfortable laugh.

My expression never softens. "You're in my office, sitting in one of my chairs." I motion to where his ass resides, five feet from my mahogany desk. "But if you keep coming in here just to reiterate that the company wants to put HC on the tags and not CCB, you're not going to make it past my doorway again."

I hate being the bitch boss. It's a cliché that I most naturally fit into. My cold personality aside, I struggle to handle my employees and these businessmen any other way. They all look at me as a twenty-six-year-old *girl*, seated here from nepotism and notoriety. I can't trounce the judgment without time and a track record, showing I deserve this position because I'm intelligent, hardworking and damn good at creating clothes—even miniature-sized ones for little monsters.

He shifts uneasily in his chair. *Good.* A small twinge of guilt flares, foreign and very, *very* unwelcome.

"Anything else?" I ask, clutching my pen like a knife, my fingertips whitening. I feel like an Amazonian warrior, ready to assail an enemy at first glance. The only problem: poor James is not my enemy. He's on my team, but it doesn't feel that way.

"Nothing as of right now," James mutters before standing. I watch him dash to the door, ready to leave my office. I bet the first thing he'll do is gossip about me. How nasty of a bitch I am. How my husband probably isn't satisfying me at home.

Those were yesterday's comments I overheard in the break room, right beside the microwave and Fizzle vending machine.

Today's gossip will be more colorful, I'm sure.

When James leaves, I spot a feminine body outside, fist raised. She lowers it and procures a congenial smile, red hair splayed over her shoulder. Hannah is the only female I interact with on a daily basis, and it's usually perfunctory comments or the frequent *Loren Hale would like to see you in his office.*

I'm trying to grow used to Loren having an assistant, one with long, treadmill-toned legs and breasts that bounce as she walks. If I didn't know my brother-in-law's level of devotion to Lily and his type of girl—twiggy with minimal curves—I might be a tad worried for my sister.

James slides past Hannah, not attempting to hide the quick glance at her breasts. I grip the pen harder, imagining stabbing the point into his neck. Not that I'd actually do it.

If Hannah notices his loitering gaze, she doesn't let on. She rests her hip bone on the doorframe, dressed in a cute green blouse and high-waisted pencil skirt. Her pumps are too short for my personal taste though.

"Loren Hale would like to see you in his office," she tells me.

I don't restrain a dramatic eye roll. "For the millionth time, he can just call me instead of wasting *your* time."

"I'm his assistant. It's my job," she says with a forced smile. We rarely talk, but I've never been the approachable type. The few friends I had in prep school most likely flocked to me for status. Or maybe they stuck around because they could rely on me: the responsible, loyal friend. I'd pick up a forgotten textbook from Sebastian's locker at midnight, calling a custodian to let me in, and spend another ten minutes delivering it to his house. Just so he could cram for a test.

I was that friend.

When I graduated, most vanished, off to Harvard, Georgetown, University of Pennsylvania and Yale. I chose Princeton.

I had multiple friends in college, but after my family was thrust into the media, they either wanted nothing to do with my deplorable, fame-hungry family, or they started calling me daily like we painted each other's toenails every night.

I had to choose between being alone or having fake friends.

So I chose my sisters.

And Connor, I suppose.

In the public, there are girls who love me—the ones who ravage gossip magazines, finding me an inspiration. I wish these girls surrounded me. The women here, the ones in corporate America, view fame as vanity, as a disgusting flaw in our country.

Hannah regards me this way right now. With quiet curiosity and contempt.

It's a shame. We're both outnumbered by men—shouldn't we band together now? After years, I still struggle with people's perceptions of me. Sometimes, I do really wish I could change them, but then again, I wouldn't even know where to begin.

I follow Hannah down the hall, walking by her side. "So what's your dream position at this company?" I ask, making small talk at least. Maybe we can be friends. It's a gross, emotional thought. One I want to whisk away. I've tried making friends. It never works. They either come to me by fate or I remain friendless.

I have twenty-six years of experience in the matter.

She gives me a side-eye. *You should have left this up to Fate, Rose.* "I have a great-paying job. I don't want to be anywhere else." We stop at Loren's office door, the walls all glass with a grand view of Philadelphia.

"I didn't mean that as an insult. There's no shame in being a secretary." I stand my ground firmly, even if my skin has begun to shrivel.

Her eyes blink with more heat. "I'm an *executive assistant*," she lashes. "And not everyone can sleep their way to the top."

My back bristles. I don't know why I hate fighting with women more than men. If there's an equally distasteful girl, throwing venom my way, I should attack just the same as I would a guy. Equality for all, right?

I hesitate, but not long enough to go unnoticed. "You can't talk to me like that," I snap—so much for being friends.

Her shoulders pull back and she elongates her neck, about an inch taller than me. "I don't work for you."

I'm half shocked that she just uttered those words. The other half of me ices over.

"I was asking if you had any dreams, which I see the only one you have is to be fired after two weeks of work." Out of the corner of my vision, I see Loren standing from behind his desk, his suit-and-tie wardrobe not as jarring as the corporate atmosphere he's placed in. Thank God he kept his personal style intact: skinny black tie, black button-down, black slacks.

Translation: *he's still Loren Hale.*

Loren's concern gathers as he watches me square off with his secre—*assistant.* I try to rewire this word in my brain.

I add, "And I don't know what makes you think I fucked my way here—"

She actually cuts me off. "How about your sex tapes. They're what made you famous, right? Everyone knows you only landed this job because you have fans. Otherwise Hale Co. would've chosen another, more *qualified* designer."

I'm going to rip her hair out.

Lo opens his glass door and slides right between us before my brain can theorize any other dramatic conclusions to this argument.

"Ladies," he says, apparent edge to his voice, the usual. His amber eyes dart between Hannah and me. "What's going on?"

"She insulted my job," Hannah says swiftly, speaking before I can. It's like she's tattling to Dad. Fuck this. I push past Loren and march into his open office.

I pass his coffee table, the purple orchid, the array of leather couches and chairs, and near his silver desk. I claim the prime black leather chair at the head, gaining a perfect view of Hannah spouting all the gory details of our fight.

I can't hear anything from inside the glass walls, but she gesticulates wildly, pointing to me.

Lo never follows her nonthreatening finger. He nods and nods, remaining silent. It's odd, seeing him in a leadership position, even odder seeing him fill it so well.

When Hannah stops speaking, Lo says a few words, just a few, and she shrinks. Her face falls and skin pales. Then his lips move again, in quick succession, precise and definitive. He has that look in his eyes, one only Loren Hale can summon. The one that says, *I have the power to slaughter everything you've ever fucking loved.*

My glares are histrionic and oftentimes not taken as a real threat.

His are serious.

Moments later, Hannah steps back and leaves while Lo rotates and enters his office.

"Get out of my chair," he snaps.

I uncharacteristically prop my high-heeled feet on the glass surface. My peplum black dress is tight enough on my ass that I shouldn't be flashing him. "You did this to my desk yesterday," I say, "so it's only fair."

He stops midway into the office, crossing his arms. "You called her a secretary." He breaks into a smile, not even a dry one. "Honestly I thought she was going to say you threatened to burn her hair off. Did someone steal your broomstick this morning?"

"I shoved it up your ass, don't you remember? Or are you still trying to forget?" I mime a tear streak down my cheek.

There it is. He flashes me that dry half smile. "Your husband pulled it out for me. He likes my ass."

I roll my eyes. "I gag at your friendship." It's too sweet for me. The *compliments* they bounce back and forth. Ugh.

"I gag at your underwear."

My eyes widen and flame. *No.* He cannot see up my dress. He only raises his brows at me. "Loren," I growl. I drop my feet to the ground, just to be safe.

He never lets me know whether or not he actually saw anything. I bet he's bluffing, but I don't test it.

I glance at the hallway, at an executive sipping a coffee with a file folder in hand. He briefly looks this way before concentrating on his destination, most likely his own office. I ask Lo, "Did you fire her?" A pang of guilt presses against my chest.

"No. I told her that she has to get thicker skin, and if she doesn't respect you, then I will fire her."

I swallow a rock and nod once. "So why have you called me in here like a lowly servant?"

He drags out the chair in front of the desk, but he stays standing, just holding the back frame. "Besides to give you a taste of what Connor and you make us feel every day, I need to talk to you about the marketing division here. Hale Co. wants the promotional campaign to begin well before the summer release."

A knock sounds on his glass door. I careen my head past his shoulder. My stomach drops.

Loren turns. "Which is why," he says to me, "I need you to work close with the assistant to the CMO."

I knew Theodore Balentine worked at Hale Co.

I knew he was one of Mark's marketing assistants.

Had I ever believed I would come face-to-face with my husband's ex-boyfriend?

In all honesty, I'd thought fate would be kinder to me.

Sixteen

Rose Cobalt

Around two months after we began dating, I asked Connor about his past relationships. I hoped to pocket his insecurities like ammo since he never showed any. I could use them against him, if need be. He often prodded me the same way. Whereas I stayed padlocked for much longer, he answered my questions even if, deep down, I didn't really want their answers.

The facts drill my brain.

Eight years ago at a Model UN conference, I spotted Connor exiting the bathroom, another guy right behind him, sans blazer or name tag.

Connor wiped his bottom lip, their hair equally disheveled, indecent, the way people look after a quickie.

Connor had blown him, I deduced.

What I didn't know until years later: Theo Balentine and Connor were dating. Not openly. Hence the rendezvous in the hotel restroom. And this was different from Caroline Haverford, his ex-girlfriend. Connor called his time with her "eleven months and twenty-two days of vapidity and boredom."

He called his time with Theo "fun."

Jealousy should slither down my spine like a snake making

route to my heart. Or rage. I am fire where my husband is water. It's only natural I should burn in the face of his ex.

But I don't feel those things.

I feel triumphant. I've kept what Theo couldn't.

Connor is mine.

When Theo enters the room fully, I draw in a breath. I've seen him numerous times. He was always a part of the academic tournaments at Faust and later in college, but this is the first time I'm seeing him with the knowledge that his bathroom hookup wasn't a onetime event.

He's taller than I remember, paler, the bags beneath his eyes darker. He resembles a sinister villain, aquiline nose and ratty brown hair, and his posture suggests a creature that lurks in shadowed corners.

He enters Loren's office with curved shoulders, hunched and uncomfortable with his height, hands stuffed in his pockets. He shuffles forward, eyes flitting to Lo as though he'd like to self-eject from this room . . . the one that contains *me*.

He wears a prim and proper suit, dark-colored and tailored for his frame. I hone in on his hair, wondering if he purposefully left his locks unkempt. Maybe he heard he'd be seeing me, so he ditched his comb to appear laid-back and pliable, friendlier. It's something Connor would do, seeming as nonthreatening as possible to other men.

But I forget Connor is one of a kind. A manipulator and a genius.

Theo is mortal in comparison.

I scoot forward to the desk, openly giving Theo another once-over, like I'm the automated, full-body security scanner at an airport. *I'm not afraid of you or intimidated.* His eyes find me, the color of storm clouds. Fate is telling me something.

I willfully ignore this ominous sign and straighten my back.

Lo releases his grip from the chair and angles his body, giving me a better view of Theo and vice versa. An awkward, strained tension lingers in the quiet.

I swivel my chair a fraction to Loren. "Why can't I speak to Mark? Or is he too busy to call the president of Hale Co.'s new billion-dollar subsidiary company?" I don't add that Mark has ignored nine of my ten calls. I'd rather he look like an incompetent fool than me look like a reject.

Theo rocks forward on his feet and answers before Lo. "That would be because he's too busy sipping cocktails on his yacht." He shrugs like it's nothing. "Mark has a family and kids and grand-kids and apparently it's been his youngest one's birthday for thirty-five days." He glances hesitantly at Loren, worried like he's said too much in front of Hale Co.'s CEO. "I'd work just as hard if he were gone three hundred days out of the year. I really don't mind pulling the all-nighters. I'm single, so . . ." He cringes a second, scratching at his head and looking quickly to me, then to the floor.

What the hell. Fun? How is he fun?

He's accidentally handing me personal information, making mistakes left and right. Someone just dropped a sad little guppy into my ocean and it's swimming past my razor-sharp jaws. Unless he's manipulating me into believing he's weaker than he is . . .

I rest my hands flat on the desk. "So those dark circles under your eyes aren't from weed?"

I asked Connor for three facts about Theo in case I ran into him at Hale Co. I wanted artillery, and without falter, he gave it to me, zero emotion attached.

1. Theo used to smoke copious amounts of weed at Faust, hot-boxing his dorm room after disassembling the fire alarm.
2. Theo loved poetry and art. He never had passion for the corporate world, but his parents pushed him towards it.
3. Theo liked to be bottom.

I was not excited to learn the third fact, but I pocketed it anyway for later use. Connor wouldn't hand me meaningless information. He'd open a wardrobe of ammunition—of swords and pistols and arrows—and ask me which one I needed.

At the mention of drugs, Theo tries to flatten his ragged hair. "I don't do that . . ." He clears his throat, coughing into his fist. "It was a . . . Faust thing." He lets out a tense breath and turns to Lo, maybe to see if he just drove his job into the ground.

Lo only stares at me. "You know him too?" He was aware that Theo knew Connor from boarding school and that's it.

"Only a little." Bringing up Theo's relationship with Connor will get him fired on the spot. Loren's protectiveness towards me circles around like an eclipse. It's always there, waiting to darken the skies.

Theo watches me carefully, cautious and knowing. I hold the string to his fate, sheers practically glinting in my grasp. His storm cloud eyes are benign, a tornado that never touches down but lingers uncertainly before vacuuming into the sky.

He's the guppy.

I swivel back to Lo. "We knew each other through Model UN and quiz bowl." I don't cut Theo's string. I angle towards him again. "You were their literature trump card."

He nods, his shoulders falling. "And poetry."

"Huh," Lo says, almost bored by the knowledge. His cell rings, and he checks it, making his way to the door. "Theo can take care of whatever you need, Rose. I'll be back in a half hour." He puts the phone to his ear, exiting the office and disappearing down the hall for privacy.

The call is either from his father or Lily. Maybe Ryke.

Theo scratches his head again in thought. Then he gestures to me. "I can take care of any *marketing* needs. Anything else, you can call your assistant." That was rather assertive. He pauses and rocks on his loafers. "I graduated summa cum laude from Yale." He nods a couple times, scanning the office to avoid my gaze.

Yale. Ugh.

Why couldn't he have stayed there and not entered my stratosphere?

And I graduated summa cum laude from *Princeton*, which is like running through quicksand with fifty-pound shackles. In comparison, Yale is like being thrown into a pool with a lifeguard. Connor's college is easier than both, but he didn't attend the University of Pennsylvania for academics. He went for the people. It had the Ivy League badge of pride, but most importantly, housed large quantities of trust-fund babies that he needed to meet. People like Patrick Nubell of Nubell Cookies. Or Loren Hale. And my sister.

After a long moment of silence, Theo points to the chair. "Should I?"

"By all means." I wave him on with a saccharine smile.

He drags the chair closer to the desk. I stiffen some, not having predicted this. I pluck a pen out of a Hale Co. mug, rolling it between my fingers. Connor used to tell me little things about Faust, only after we started dating. He said that all the boys talked about prep school girls from Dalton, Pavawich and Vorwell. He said that rumors circulated about me since he often sought me out during academic conferences.

He said that some were false. Others were true. He only believed in the ones that I verified.

I just hoped that these rumors never extended to Yale after my adolescence. That would be disastrously sad.

After Theo sits, he rubs his clammy palms on his pants.

How many rumors does he believe in? I bet he's already shaped who I am from office and tabloid gossip, the reality show and whatever remnants I left during childhood.

"Do I make you nervous?" I ask outright.

He laughs once. "Yeah." He nods, more to himself. "Kind of. You're . . . you." I'm not one hundred percent positive the context of his answer.

"I don't know what that means." I try to emulate Connor, keeping my voice even and unreadable, but I end up snapping the words.

He opens his mouth and then closes it slowly, rethinking. He still evades my eyes.

"Don't hold back," I tell him. "If I wanted you out of this office, I would've told Loren about your relationship with my husband."

Theo strokes the armrests a couple times, contemplating. "Thank you for that. This job . . . it wasn't easy to come by. Hale Co. runs on nepotism, and what I have in intelligence, I lack in connections." He pauses, finally staring straight at me. The tornado's funnel lowers beneath the cloud line. "Connor used to say it's as bad as having a 1.0 GPA."

"He insulted you." No surprise there.

"He insults everyone, but you probably know that." He clears his throat again.

"Stop doing that." My skin crawls at the noise. "Unless you're a cat."

"Excuse me?" He frowns.

I roll my eyes. He is not my husband, not even marginally. "You sound like you're coughing up a hairball, Theo."

Color drains a little from his cheeks, and he shifts, setting his ankle on his knee. "I'm sorry."

"Don't hold back," I remind him. "Why do I make you nervous?"

"You . . ." He rakes my face, absorbing my fiery glare. "You were the talk of Faust for a while." He pauses too long.

I wave him on.

He nods again. "We never considered Dalton a threat at Model

UN, not until you appeared on their team. You almost beat us, and the guys couldn't stop talking about this girl." His gaze drifts as he pools his memories. "The heiress to the Fizzle empire had more knowledge than five of us combined. Back then everyone expected you to be dimwitted. You were a girl." Fuck yes, I am a girl. "You dressed like it took you five hours to get ready." I do love fashion. "And you were rich." That too.

I shake my head. "It's tragic that it took *me* for all of you to learn that girls can be feminine *and* smart." Had I known this, I think I would've broken into Faust and taped portraits of women who've inspired me all over their hallways. Coco Chanel among them.

"I agree," he says.

"So you're nervous because I'm a confident woman."

He hesitates as if there's more. "There were rumors about you." When he rubs his neck, his sleeve slides up, revealing a tattoo on the inside of his wrist, maybe the start of a larger design.

"Like what?"

"You stabbed a doll with scissors and wrote on its forehead." He squints to recall the words. "Something like . . . *I won't take care of this unless . . . something.*"

I remember. "I won't care for an inanimate object unless the boys do it too," I tell him.

"So it's true?"

"That one is. I don't know the other rumors you've all conjured about me." I'm sure some are overdramatic, even for me.

He looks to the ceiling, as though it'll help him think. "There was one that you were addicted to cocaine. You seemed a little . . ." He pauses briefly off my glower. ". . . high-strung."

"That's ridiculous." I can't simply be this way? I have to have a cocaine addiction?

He nods. "And then the rumor that your father set you up in an arranged marriage when you were little."

"What?" I balk. Connor never told me that.

"You didn't really date. At least that's what we heard from Dalton guys, so it just kind of spread."

I frown. "No one thought that I could've been a lesbian?" This seems like the less theatrical conclusion.

"You always wore high heels," he says.

I grit my teeth. There are just too many stereotypes to weed through. "I could've been a proud lesbian wearing high heels," I retort. "For being so smart, all of you are annoyingly stupid." So I was too feminine to be a lesbian in their eyes—another stereotype to chew on.

"I didn't believe any of that," he says. "I don't think anyone who really used their brains did, but most rumors are usually unsubstantiated and cruel."

He's not awful.

"This was so long ago," he says, sitting up in the chair. "It's all just prep school stuff."

"Yale—"

"Is different," he cuts me off with a slight grimace. "The people that cared enough to know you by name saw you as a trustfund baby, being handed your father's soda company. It was a . . . different atmosphere. Faust guys didn't give a shit where you originated but where you ended up. If it took you one step to reach the top or someone else five hundred, it was all the same to us."

I bounce back and forth between loathing Faust boys and loving them. I'm accustomed to this love-hate conundrum since I'm married to one.

He licks his dry lips, the silence winding more uncomfortable tension. "Are we going to talk about the brand?"

"In a second." I'm not going to squander this time with him, even if my ribs constrict around my lungs the longer we share each other's company. "What was Connor like at Faust?"

I've never had this information from an unbiased source. I'd love even a small childhood secret. Since Connor has no siblings, the guys he grew up with at Faust are as close to brothers as I'll ever come by. Unfortunately, Theo is the first I've encountered outside of a college event, or else I'd have chosen another before him.

Theo meets my inquisitive eyes. "I watched maybe one episode of *Princesses of Philly*, and Connor patronized almost every single person in the span of ten minutes. No one seemed to care."

Connor was edited poorly, but not all of it was fake. That probably wasn't.

"At Faust, he was a lot like that," Theo says, "and he was popular. It wasn't because he was connected and rich as hell, but yeah, he was all of those things too. Connor was just someone you wanted around because he said things everyone was afraid to say. He knew when to be quiet and when to speak, and when he spoke he was the *only* one who could get away with calling you inferior and have you smiling afterwards. He was the only one who could say these things without being hated." He shrugs. "At the end of the day, he was just likable."

Likable.

If he was so likable, how did it take me so long to like him? *You loved me, Rose*, I hear his voice in my head.

I click my pen, mulling this over. "You realize that he was manipulating all of you?"

Theo nods. "Yeah. He would tell us as much. We always joked that he was the type of person who'd explain how he was going to stab you in the front before he actually shoved the knife in . . . and you'd let him. Of course. In some circumstances, he'd probably even pass you the knife so you could shove it in your own chest, and you would."

They would let Connor hypothetically kill them. God. If he could hear this right now, I think his ego would literally engulf the planetary system.

What interests me most—Theo never said anything about blackmail. Connor's tactics are apparent, visible enough that the person recognizes what's happening, but they do it anyway.

That power is frightening, and if Connor saw revenge as anything other than fruitless, I'd be terrified every time someone slighted him.

I veer back on topic. "So you're Mark's assistant. Do you share his opinions about the labels?"

He takes a deep breath. "I'm at a crossroads here. I could tell you that it's a stupid idea to have HC on the label. That people associate Hale Co. with diapers, baby products, and oils. High-end clients aren't going to buy clothes with the same labels as the things their babies shit in. But if I tell you that, then I'm disagreeing with *my* boss. You may have power, but Mark is the one who can fire me."

I click my pen again, thinking. Theo does agree with me, but he cares too much about his job to budge on my side.

"What if I could guarantee your job?" I offer. I'm sure if I talked to Loren I could shift Theo's job title, securing him on my team rather than Mark's. I need another voice in my corner, even if it's as subdued as Theo's. It's something more.

A wave of pity overtakes Theo's face. I grip my pen harder. *Don't look at me like that.* I try to translate these words into a fiercer glare.

"It won't matter. You're going to lose, Rose." Sincerity blankets his voice. "Everyone knows that CCB should be on the labels. But that's not why you're going to be outvoted. You're dead center in a corporation that has been run by a misogynist for thirty-plus years. They'll fall on their swords before they let a twenty-six-year-old woman win."

I can't believe this, even if, deep down I know it's true. Jonathan Hale may never speak ill of me because I'm his best friend's daughter, but I've heard him say heinous things about women before. However, Jonathan isn't running this company anymore. "Loren—"

"Has sway, but most of the board regards him as young and inexperienced. He needs time to build relationships before being able to win over the majority. You two . . . you're standing in the minority right now. Two against fourteen. It's a losing battle."

"How do you know all of this?" I ask. He's just an assistant.

"I hear things," he tells me. "People tend to forget I'm in the room. It's a useful quality."

He is a shadow. In his eyes and in his life.

It's a losing battle. I can't roll over and quit. The board wants me to shut up and use my face as a marketing ploy, taking advantage of my celebrity status. There are blogs dedicated to what I wear every single day and even the outfits I choose for Jane. Paparazzi photographs help us on this account; ironic that the invasiveness grows our businesses but puts our children and privacy at risk. There's a safe line somewhere between the two, and we're all still trying to discover it.

I retrieve a blank piece of paper from Loren's desk drawer. I won't be a voiceless tool for any of these people. Loren hired me knowing exactly who I am, and if the rest of the board won't accept me, respect me, or agree with me, then I need to go about this a new way.

The solution rests at the edge of my brain. I tap the paper with my pen.

What.

Can.

I.

Do?

I shut my eyes for a moment.

"Are you okay?" Theo asks. I hear the leather squeak beneath his ass as he shifts.

I raise a finger. *One second.* Calloway Couture Babies: CCB. Hale Co: HC. There has to be a middle ground . . .

My eyes snap open, and I quickly pull the paper closer to me and begin drawing. Theo cranes his neck, trying to see my illustration over a stack of file folders.

I finish in a couple more seconds and spin the paper to face him. I push the folders closer to Lo's desktop computer. Theo peers at the simple sketch: the letters *HC* inset within the center of the letter *B* of CCB.

His expression remains unreadable, and my pulse races. I notice his eyes flickering to a pen in the mug.

"You have art skills?" I ask, plucking a pen out for him. I set it down on the paper. "Make this prettier." I'm good at drawing. I have sketchbooks upon sketchbooks of numerous designs, but I'm not too proud anymore to pass a task to someone else.

He straightens up, more eager to add his vision to mine, and he begins to extenuate the letters with longer lines, cursive, resembling brushstrokes. He places the *HC* lower, lining it up with the bar of the *B*. When he finishes, he rotates the paper to face me.

It's beautiful. He somehow made a few letters look elegant and whimsical.

"I need you to give this to Mark," I instruct. If Mark approves, he'll pitch it to the rest of the board. "Tell him exactly what you told me—no one wants to buy clothes with the same label their babies shit in—and tell him that you hate me. That you'd never let me have my label, but this"—I gesture to the paper—"will be the best of both worlds. A middle finger to me, but a success for the brand."

Theo rocks back, my words slamming against him. "You have to still outwardly hate it."

I'm not the best actress. Being in bed with the media has proved that enough, but I'd still try my hardest. "I will throw one hell of a tantrum." I pull back my shoulders. "How dare they stick HC into *my* label. And now there's five fucking letters? You all said that three letters was too many, so your resolution is to add two more? This is the worst idea I've ever heard. Whoever thought of it should *burn*."

He puts his fingers to his lips, a smile peeking through. "This is crazy," he says and then laughs. "Now I know . . ." He shakes his head in realization.

My shoulders lower some. "Know what?"

His stormy grays land on me. "Why he married you."

I stiffen. "He loves me," I say on instinct. I believe every sylla-ble. I never question it for a second, but I see the pity in his eyes again. He's disbelieving . . . maybe that Connor can love anyone. But the joke is on Theodore Balentine. Connor is more than what he was. He learned to accept love into his life and to live by it, and *that* makes him a different man. It makes him a better one.

"You shift the pieces to suit yourself," he explains. "Not many people can do that, and not many people want to play that game. I'm sure he values that aspect in you."

The only person I'm questioning is Theo. Is he really as weak as he appears? If he's aware that there's a game at all—that people manipulate and deceive, that some of us choose to be snakes be-neath the grass—then maybe he's slithering too.

My bones harden, wary and cautious.

I think I'm mindfucking myself.

Or he's mindfucking me.

Theo stands, the paper in his grasp. "I'll give this to Mark and slander your name in the same breath, if that's what you want."

"It is." My veins run cold.

He nods, and I watch him head to the glass door. He opens it, practically one foot outside before he pauses and turns his head to me.

"I want you to know," he says, "that as uncomfortable as this all is . . . I hope we can be friends in the future."

A rock lodges in my throat. Is he manipulating me? Why does

it feel like he is? Maybe because it takes more than just words for me to trust people anymore. *Friends*. Those are hard to come by, even harder to believe are real.

"I'm not sure you possess the right qualities to ever be my friend," I tell him, my voice colder than warm. All I want is loyalty, and part of me is as watchful of him as I'd be of a tornado's funnel swirling in the sky.

He draws in a short breath, nods once and exits the office.

I barely relax. My hands shake suddenly, and I busy my nerves by organizing Lo's cluttered desk, alphabetizing his file folders in a neater stack. I try not to zero in on a certain memory, one that amplifies this situation, but it floods the hollow spaces of my mind.

My senior year of college, sometime after spring break in Cancún, Connor and I played Scrabble on my bed—our eyes bloodshot but neither of us could sleep. I didn't want to be alone either, so I didn't ask him to leave. We played the board game throughout the night. Lily's sex addiction had just been publicized a week prior, and our lives were changing faster than we could seize them.

Connor had less to lose from the onslaught of cameras, from the intrusiveness and bad press, but he had to make phone calls every day. I was trying to save my fashion company. He was trying to protect something else. At the time, I wasn't sure who the calls were to or what they were about.

I remember forming a mediocre word with the wooden letters: *star*. Too frazzled and spent to think well.

"How come you haven't asked me?" Connor wondered, vaguely interested in his tiles. He focused solely on me.

"Your riddles are even more infuriating without sleep." I was waiting for him to retort, *you love my riddles.*

Instead, he stayed serious. Not even a silhouette of a grin. "You're not curious as to who I've been talking to?"

It had crossed my mind more than a few times. "It's not my

business," I told him honestly. "Unless you're cheating . . ." My eyes seared.

"No," he said. "I would never cheat on you, Rose."

I didn't want to pry into personal parts of his life without his consent, just as I expected the same in return. We'd only been together for eight months, and it'd be a lie to say that I understood him completely. I only understood the real parts that he let me see.

He continued to ignore the board game. I couldn't read his features. In hindsight, I think he was nervous to bring up a subject that we never discussed in depth.

I mentioned, "We haven't even dated for an entire year. If it doesn't affect me, you're not obligated to tell me anything, Connor." I wanted to know, but I wouldn't force anything out of him. Not if it was personal. Not if it was so soul-bearing. I'd wait, just as I would've waited for Lily to open up about her sex addiction, even if it took her years to share with me.

He rested his forearm on his bent knee. "When we're married, it could affect you."

I snorted. "You're delusional if you think I'd *ever* marry you, Richard."

He almost grinned, but the truth weighed heavy on him. "Then in years, when we're still together, it could still affect you."

I swallowed hard.

"I want to tell you who I called. In case you're ever pulled into this, I want to be completely, entirely, back-breakingly honest with you, Rose."

I was scared. "Okay . . ."

He flipped a wooden tile between his fingers, mentally forming the precise words before he spoke them. "I've been locating all of my exes."

My chest caved, but I let him talk before jumping to irrational conclusions.

"Only the guys I've been with," he said in a short breath. His eyes flickered up to me, to gauge my reaction. I nodded, encouraging him to continue. "I paid them off, and they've signed nondisclosure agreements. I couldn't take the risk of any of them outing me to the media. It could make things more complicated with our relationship, and it could harm . . ." His reputation. Cobalt Inc. He wasn't sure. I wasn't sure. Connor barely expressed this part of his life with me back then, and he wasn't ready to announce anything to the whole world. Not with unknown consequences hanging over his head.

So he did damage control and swept his past into dark corners.

I was glad he told me—that he'd even trust me with this information. It said more than enough. I would've supported his choices. "Okay," I said more confidently.

He still hesitated. "One of them wouldn't sign, no matter how much money I offered and no matter what I said."

I froze. "Who?"

"Theodore Balentine."

I remembered him. "What does he want?"

"Nothing," Connor told me. "He said that he morally couldn't do this to me. He didn't want to slam me into a closet, even if I was the one shutting the door." Connor shook his head repeatedly. He was pissed that a string was going to be left untied. "I just have to trust that he won't say anything to the press."

"If morality is his reasoning, he won't."

"People change," Connor said, leaving me with those two haunting words before he returned to the board.

I have no idea if Theo has changed since then. It's very likely corporate America has had some impact on him.

So even if I just acted like his boss . . . he silently holds all of the power.

Seventeen

Connor Cobalt

Rose carries Jane on the crook of her hip around the kitchen, gathering a tray of mugs. The early start of Christmas morning is quiet, with everyone still asleep at 8 a.m. and no time planned to wake. I enjoy this more than spending all day and night at my mother-in-law's house, which was reserved for Christmas Eve.

I finish pouring pureed peaches into a pink bowl with a small spoon.

"There are three things you can never go without, Jane," Rose says, setting six mugs along the wooden tray. "A great pair of heels, an outfit to your liking and coffee. Or if you prefer hot tea, that will work too."

"Amending your own declaration already?" With the bowl in hand, I block Rose's path to the coffeepot.

"If I could, I would've amended your personality on the first date."

I smile. "And then you would've downgraded me. You should be happy you don't have that power."

"I'm happy that I have the power to do this." She covers my mouth with her hand, and my lips lift beneath it. "Stop grinning." I don't, and she lowers her hand with a growl.

"Clearly your power is limited, darling."

Jane giggles, dissolving the heat in Rose's eyes faster than usual. "That's right," Rose says, "your daddy likes to boast. It's his worst trait."

"That's debatable."

Rose snorts beneath her breath and then brings Jane over to her high chair by the breakfast table. Of course I follow. Jane babbles a few syllables, reaching out for the bowl in my hands. She kicks her little legs. I set the bowl down, and she curiously observes the pureed peaches first, as she usually does. We'll spoon-feed her after she grows comfortable with what she's eating.

Rose spins around to me, much shorter in just slippers and no heels. She crosses her arms over her silk robe. I take the opportunity to hold her around the waist, drawing her closer to my chest.

She asks, "What English monarch was born near London but her mother near Madrid?" Her eyes flit to my lips. "If you answer wrong, I won't be speaking to you for the rest of the day."

The way she declares these rules almost hardens my cock. The stakes are relatively high for me. Unanswered texts, dropped calls and refusals to banter back—it's a particular torture that would only derive from Rose. Anyone else, I think I'd be fine ignoring.

I go quiet for a moment, passing through my knowledge quickly.

"You have thirty seconds." She raises her chin, her eyes still on my lips.

Do you want me to answer or to kiss you hard, Rose? I rub my own lips, her lingering stare pooling my desire.

"Ten seconds."

The answer hits the front of my brain. "Mary Tudor."

She nods once. "Congratulat—"

I kiss her hard, pulling her into my body with force, and her arms uncoil, palms flat on my chest—and she breaks us apart with a push.

She breathes shallowly. "Richard." She's not finished toying with me. I'll try to wait, only because I'm curious what else she has in store. I take note of how my hand is in hers. Rose doesn't seem to notice, and I won't enlighten her to the fact. I always want her hand in mine.

"Yes?" I ask.

She looks to Jane once. Our daughter sticks a finger in the peaches and then puts it in her mouth, tasting the food in measured steps. Rose walks to the bar counter and obtains a thin napkin that I never spotted.

Then she shoves it in my face.

I can't hide an overwhelming grin. There are three names scrawled neatly on the napkin: *Snow White. Ariel. Rapunzel.* I lower her hand. "I have an impeccable memory, and I clearly remember giving you three Disney princes to choose from years ago, and you argued about it."

She waves her hand. "Then I grant you the right to argue, but you still have to answer like I did."

There is a wrong answer in this Fuck, Marry, Kill game. There's always one that will make us question each other more than usual. When I test her, I have an idea of her answer, and if she chooses something different, my mind goes into a tailspin with intrigue, craving to understand why.

She places a pen in my hand, not wanting me to say the words aloud. We never do. This game is written in text or on paper. These rules haven't been amended in years.

I stumble on Rapunzel's name. Daisy's hair used to be extremely long and blonde, and in the media, journalists compared her to the fairy-tale character too often.

Rose knows this.

But Ariel? I calculate my choices quickly, and next to each name in this precise order, I write: *Marry. Kill. Fuck.*

I pass her the napkin, her eyes pierced as she reads. "Why are you fucking Rapunzel?" She looks horrified at that notion.

"Because I don't want to fuck a mermaid."

"She grows legs."

"You're describing the maturation of a *frog*." A tadpole starts with a tail and internal gills and then begins to form legs, but I don't need to explain this to Rose. "And still—surprising to absolutely no one—I'm not fucking an amphibian."

She snorts into laughter, her hand trying to cover her mouth to hide its existence as it escalates.

I begin to laugh too, and I lace my fingers with Rose's, dropping her hand to our sides so I can see her full smile.

Jane giggles behind us. "Mama!" In unison, we both swing our heads towards our daughter. She's raising her tiny bowl of peaches above her head. "Up!"

Her first words.

The bowl slips from her grasp, clattering on the floor, mashed peaches spilled. I gauge Rose's reaction to the mess. Her free hand is pressed to her lips. "Did you hear her?" she asks me, eyes flooded with emotion.

My smile widens. I'm more overwhelmed that their love for each other has trumped Rose's innate tic, which spikes at the sight of chaos. I hug Rose to my side. "I heard, darling."

I'm not even minutely religious, but today, Christmas morning, with my girls enveloped in happiness, feels as spiritual as I've ever come to in life.

Eighteen

Rose Cobalt

"Moffy descends upon the box with a strong, baby grip and a devilish twinkle in his eye," Daisy narrates beside the eight-foot tree, decorated in elegant gold bows and shimmering ornaments.

She braces a vintage video camera while bells clink on her socks with each bounce around the spacious living room, filled with Christmas spirit: stockings along the mantel, snow falling behind the windows, gifts stacked beneath the tree—wrapped both carefully (me) and haphazardly (Loren)—and the smell of vanilla coffee and cookies sweetening the air.

Loren probably believes that I love traditions and festivities because it's another day I can decorate our home, another day to boss people around and orchestrate everything to my liking. I'm a perfectionist, but seeing a leaning gingerbread house and a poorly constructed snowman is fine with me. Parties have always meant something else. Every person I love will be together. My sisters, most importantly.

The other details are just extra.

"Devilish?" Lily's eyes widen in horror. "He doesn't look devilish." On the soft cream-colored rug, Lily peers down at her baby nestled between her legs. Moffy eagerly grabs onto the red-wrapped box, unknowing of its purpose.

Loren sits next to his wife and helps his son tear the paper. Almost everyone is dressed in some sort of holiday pajama. Moffy and Jane in Christmas onesies. Daisy with striped leggings and a white tank that says: *Elf you gonna love me!* Lily in a gray snowflake-printed onesie with pom-poms and a hood. Lo and Ryke in respective red and green flannel pants. Me: all-black pajama set. *But* I do have stylish red ornament earrings.

Connor is the only one not participating. Out of principle, he said. He's in gray cotton pants, and I don't press him to change. I love him, weird quirks and all.

"Moffy looks adorable," Lo confirms. "The devilish baby is sitting on the devil's lap."

And of course, he turns to me.

On the couch, I protectively hold Jane closer, Connor's arm around my shoulders. "You do realize this is being recorded, Loren?" I grimace into a smile. "So now your niece will see how much of a dick you are."

"And now she'll hear her mom's foul mouth," Lo retorts and then slow claps.

Ryke joins the clapping, sprawled on the love seat with the thickest, messiest hair, as though he's just rolled out of bed. Daisy handed him a Santa hat earlier, but he's too lazy to put it on, the red velvet cap still on his chest.

He finally catches my hot gaze and raises his hands in defense. "I'm in support of foul fucking language."

Daisy hops over a present, almost dropping the video camera—everyone may be too sick from the jumpy footage to watch anyway. "I can edit it . . ." Daisy starts, but then stops at my glare.

"I don't want Jane's first Christmas *edited*." I would really like the video to be level too, but I don't mention it. I'm not that rude.

Daisy mock gasps. "Who suggested such a thing? They should be fined with a dozen chocolate chip cookies."

Without budging from his lounged position, Ryke gestures for her to near him. "I can give you something better, Calloway." I try not to read far into his blatant sexual innuendo. Their flirting has the same boundaries as their personalities. They both rip through danger zones and *No Trespassing* signs.

Daisy whips her head to him. "Cake?"

"Better than fucking cake."

She feigns confusion. "There is no such thing."

He flips her off and then gestures to her again. She skips over to him, careful to avoid crushing the many assortments of presents.

Seeing them together reminds me that Ryke's surgery is a little over a week away, the day after Connor's birthday. With the horrendous weather—cold, rain and snow—Ryke has had almost no opportunity to climb since he went to the gym. Which wasn't really his preference for climbing anyway.

When Daisy reaches Ryke, he clasps her hips and lifts her shirt a fraction, kissing the small of her back. She glows, her smile illuminating her features. I've never seen Daisy as radiant as she is in Ryke's presence. I just truly hope it can last, even without him.

"Hey, Santa," Daisy grins, slowly spinning around.

He raises her shirt again and kisses below her belly button, which is cute but also a bit inappropriate due to the setting. I'm so used to groping from Loren and Lily (which is a thousand kinds of *shield your eyes*) that Ryke kissing my little sister's body is tame in comparison.

I live in a weird world, and I wouldn't trade this atmosphere for any other.

"All right," Lo cuts in from the floor. "No Christmas flirting." Moffy has unwrapped a plastic Spider-Man action figure, meant for infants his age. "And can we all not refer to *Ryke* as Santa Claus? I don't want to confuse my kid."

"I agree with Lo," Lily says with an adamant nod. "You're not Santa." She also cups her hands over Lo's ear, whispering to him. I'm almost positive it has to do with him banning *all* Christmas flirting.

"Fuck all of you," Ryke says lightheartedly before putting his head *up* my sister's shirt and kissing her . . . ugh, you know what— I *don't* want to know what his lips are touching.

Connor leans closer, passing me our joint crossword, folded from this morning's newspaper. Since his right arm is behind my shoulders, he filled it out with his left hand, annoyingly ambidextrous. Like he needs another *talent* in his arsenal. My eyes glaze over the square boxes, the descriptions scratched out and the title written in his neat handwriting: *Fornication.*

Instead of doing a normal crossword, we just fill the boxes with words pertaining to our chosen category. *Fornication.* I swear Connor is trying to make me aroused or incensed.

He filled in ten boxes with the word "acrophilia."

Also known as the fetish of fucking someone in high altitudes. Like in the mountains or on rooftops. Also known as Ryke Meadows.

I shoot Connor a quick glare, but he's tickling Jane's foot, putting her on his lap while I concentrate. I want to use the word "fellatio," but the only eight boxes available use the *p* from "acrophilia," which screws up everything. There is no damn *p* in "fellatio."

I could go with "testicles," nine letters somewhere else, but I don't think that fits the category well enough.

"About this fictional character . . ." Connor begins.

Lo interjects, "They're going to believe in Santa Claus and the Tooth Fairy and the Easter Bunny and everything else that you think is a crock of shit."

We've never had this conversation, not outright, but there have been numerous moments where it *almost* surfaced.

I hold my pen on the newspaper too long, an inkblot bleeding into the thin sheet and almost staining my pajamas.

Ryke is out of Daisy's shirt, and she sits on his lap, his arms wrapped snugly around her waist. She powers off the camera.

I snap my fingers at her. "Keep it on. *Unedited*, remember?" I've had too many people edit my life. My children won't see the edited version either.

Daisy switches the camera on. "I don't understand why Jane can't know the truth while Moffy knows the kid version." In my youngest sister's head, there is a happily ever after for everyone. And my black heart understands, too well, that happiness *for all* is a cruel myth.

Lo crumples the red wrapping in a ball. "Because Jane will ruin it for him."

"And for every other fucking child in kindergarten," Ryke adds. He nods to Connor and me. "Your daughter will literally be *that* kid who fucks up Christmas."

This issue hasn't been important to me, not enough to disagree with Connor, so my opinions aren't as strong as everyone else's.

"And what was your childhood Christmas experience exactly, Ryke?" Connor asks. "How was Santa so special to you?"

Ryke shrugs. "The way it is for every kid."

His answer is too vague to appease Connor. "Describe it for me."

Ryke sighs in frustration. "I don't know." He shakes his head in deeper thought.

Jane drops her stuffed lion at Connor's feet and tries to climb down his legs to reach the toy. I bend forward to collect it, passing the animal to her. She clings to it with such fervor that my black heart nearly softens. I stroke her head. *I love every little piece of you.*

"Eloquent," Connor says.

Ryke combs his hand through his wild hair. "Wasn't Christmas just your mom and you?"

"I'm assuming it was for you," Connor says. Both he and Ryke were raised by single mothers. I thought they'd find common ground through this tiny similarity, but it hardly strengthened their uneven, slightly bent relationship. I know Connor trusts Ryke. I know Ryke trusts Connor. Analyzing anything beyond that gives me an unwelcome, pulsing migraine.

"Yeah," Ryke says, "so when I saw a present from Santa underneath the tree, I got fucking excited. It felt like . . ." He struggles for the precise words.

"Like someone else cared about you," Connor finishes.

Silence heavies the room, Ryke not denying this fact.

Lo frowns, as though realizing the true loneliness of his brother during holidays. Loren spent Christmas with us, the Calloways, and his father. My grandmother, with her chewy, stale fruitcake and god-awful hyena cackle, adored Loren and always bought him gifts.

One year, I may have broken his Game Boy after he compared me to Angelica from *Rugrats*, and then he shaved my Furby, proving that he is just as much Angelica as me.

"It was like that for you too, then?" Ryke questions, wondering why Connor is so anti-Santa when they seemingly share this bond. Connor was just being a vague asshole, so Ryke would spill more truths. I know, for a fact, that the first time he had Christmas was at Faust. Even then, it's not the same as spending it with your family.

Connor says, "I never celebrated holidays with my mother. She found them pointless. I understand that fictional creatures can make you feel better, but we shouldn't have to construct a lie just for that emotion. Jane will be comforted with the knowledge that Santa *isn't* real and everyone else is living in fantasy." He values the power that his mother gave him, able to see the world from the "real" viewpoint.

Loren sighs now. "Come on, man. Being a kid means getting to *believe* in the impossible. It means believing that fairies exist, along with spells and magic, and that on your eleventh birthday you'll receive a letter from Hogwarts. It means thinking your presents arrived from a workshop in the North Pole and not the store down the street. And Connor . . ." Lo's face twists at a thought. "I'm really sorry your mom took that shit from you. If you'd had even a semblance of it growing up, you would realize how special it is. Don't take that away from Jane."

I balk at the idea of taking something from Jane, anything at all. Naturally I want to give her everything and more—all the things that I never had. Like a sympathetic mother, not a controlling, overbearing one.

I look at Connor while he mulls over Loren's speech. "You know," I say, "we can see who figures out the truth first: Moffy or Jane." This may entice him to keep the charade for Jane, so she can believe in magic too.

Lily crinkles her nose. "That's evil."

"Well, it is coming from the devil," Lo says, breaking some of the tension. He flashes a half smile at the video camera. "And Jane, if you're watching this when you're older, just know it comes from a place of love." He can barely say that with a straight face.

I clap. "You're so convincing that my heart is starting to thaw."

"You have a heart?" Lo quips.

"Did someone gift me something sharp for Christmas?" I ask, a threatening gleam in my eye.

Lo shoots everyone a look like *whoever gave her a weapon is goddamn crazy.* Then he lands back on me. "Stay away from my balls."

"You have balls?" I snap, not as good at sarcasm as him.

"You're mixing your dreams with reality. You haven't cut them off yet."

Ryke pulls Daisy closer to his chest, watching everything

through the video camera screen with her. "This is the most fucked-up baby's first Christmas video," he mutters.

"Okay," Connor suddenly says, a hush falling upon the room. Jane prattles a few soft syllables and looks up at her dad. He tells her, "*Tu seras magnifiquement naïve.*" *You will be beautifully naïve.* I know that he's at peace with this concept when his lips rise in a genuine smile. Lo must've convinced him.

Daisy whispers to Ryke, "Is this good?"

He can translate for everyone, but instead of reiterating word by word, he nods. "Yeah. He's going to let them believe."

"Thanks, man," Lo says, his son sounding out noises while he whacks the action figure on the rug.

Connor nods. "I think you all still have my presents left to unwrap."

Daisy stands to hand them out, passing the video camera to Ryke. While she works on finding his gifts beneath the tree, I return to the crossword and find twelve boxes, horizontal and using the *p* from a two-box word: "DP."

A nearly perfect word comes to mind, but it's slightly tainted by its definition—which may cause Connor to arch a *what the fuck?* brow.

"Stumped?" he asks, staring over my shoulder at the giant inkblot beside *Fornication* and no progress on my end.

"No," I snap. Stumped. I'll stump *him.* I lick my bottom lip and neatly write the letters: *s-c-o-p-t-o-p-h-i-l-i-a.* "Scoptophilia."

A fetish for looking at erotic photography or watching sexual acts. Like through mirrors. Or with sex tapes.

He reads my new answer as I pass him the paper and collect Jane off his lap, hugging her with two inflexible, solid arms. My little gremlin hardly cares that I suck at hugging—she still smiles. I couldn't love her any more than I do. My heart is full.

When I steal a glance at Connor, both of his brows are raised in confusion and intrigue. We've never watched those tapes together.

Hell, we could barely *talk* about them until Scott returned. They've been this toxic stain in our relationship that we've covered with a rug instead of removed with bleach.

We've finally begun scrubbing at it.

His fingers brush my neck, questioning in the electric stroke. My hairs prickle, and we lock eyes. I can't say whether or not I'd want to watch them—if they'd just stir something worse. I can't know because we've never tried.

I hear Lily whisper something to Lo like *mind reading*—which is ridiculous, albeit a cute thought. Connor can't read my mind, but maybe he can read my wants and desires and insecurities. Anyone who knows me well enough can, and Connor, of everyone, understands me the most.

"Here you go." Daisy plops a package beside me, a heavy square object perfectly wrapped in light-blue paper. We peel our gazes off each other.

Connor skims the crossword. "You should all open them at the same time." He's already filling in the crossword. Really?

Daisy hands the last present to Ryke, and we all begin to tear at the smooth, crisp creases. I open presents like I plan to save the wrapping paper for later, but every year, someone (Loren Hale) throws away my stack of neatly folded pieces. It's extremely rude. His defense is always: *I'm saving you from becoming a hoarder.*

So I'm the slowest to reach the present.

Everyone is already shouting exclamations.

"What the fuck?" Ryke says. He hasn't unwrapped the present all the way, so I can't see.

Lo laughs and looks to Connor. "If you hated it, love, you could've just told me." Moffy's empty bouncer is in my damn view of Lo's gift.

"Huh?" Lily holds her hefty set of The Chronicles of Narnia.

I gape. No, he didn't. That was the present Lily gave him last year for Christmas. He asked all of us to give him presents that we enjoyed. We chose books as the overall theme.

"You regifted?" I ask him in distaste.

Loren must have A Song of Ice and Fire beside him, a stack of five books. Daisy is holding *The Iron King* by Julie Kagawa, a young adult fairy novel, I believe.

I haven't even finished peeling off the paper of mine, but I'm certain a vintage copy of Shakespeare's *The Tempest,* my present to Connor last year, lies beneath.

"Open them," Connor says, unconcerned. He spins his pen in his left hand.

When I finally unearth *The Tempest,* I flip open the cover. Sticky notes lie inside the margins. Dozens of them, his neat scrawl in blue ink. I thumb through the pages, my heart racing. He annotated it.

Shakespeare's words: *I would not wish any companion in the world but you.*

Connor's annotation: *Nothing is truer.*

His lips to my ear, he whispers, "'Hear my soul speak.'" I feel his grin against my cheek.

Those four words are on this page too. He didn't highlight them, but he drew an arrow to the line on top of a yellow sticky note.

It's beautiful. My favorite play with his real thoughts combined.

My eyes lift from my book to Loren and Lily. They flip through them keenly, smiles expanding with each new page turned. I notice writing along the margin of the paper instead of sticky notes like mine.

"Yours is vintage," Connor explains. "I didn't want to write on the pages." He knows me well.

"Thank you," I breathe. Right then, Jane tugs on my hair. My head knocks into Connor's from the sudden momentum. *This is a sign.*

He recovers before I do, and he places his hand on my forehead, which took the impact and wells with pain.

"This is what happens when I say something nice to you," I tell Connor, the pressure of his hand stopping my forehead from throbbing. "The universe rebels."

"You just equated our daughter to the entire universe, and *I'm* the conceited one?" He laughs once, inspecting the bump on my head. "You're okay. Do you need ice?"

"Yes, for your ego."

"My ego isn't bruised. You must've really hit your head hard if you think it can be." He winks. He *winks*—I huff, glare and poke him with a finger, hoping my manicured nail digs into him.

He smiles more. "Yes?"

"Wait, what the hell did he get you?" Lo's loud, edged voice cuts into my hot streak, his question directed to his older brother.

I now just notice the small, leather-bound journal in Ryke's hands. Ryke really cheated last year. Connor wanted to learn more about everyone by reading our favorites, and Ryke handed him a blank journal—basically saying *fuck you* in a present.

I have no idea what Connor did to that journal. No one does but Ryke, and he barely flips through it. "It's just the same thing I gave him." Ryke clears his throat some, which means that Connor did write in it—but instead of sharing, he slides the journal into the back of his pants, like one would a handgun.

"Right where I love my gifts." Connor smiles.

Ryke flips him off, putting his middle finger in *front* of the video camera lens.

"Your kids are going to love that someday," Lo says.

Ryke gives him a look. "What kids?"

Daisy tucks a piece of hair behind her ear and then stands. "Anyone need coffee refills?" She collects her mug and mine.

"I'll come with you," Lily says, climbing to her feet and carrying Moffy. She disappears into the kitchen with Daisy, leaving me with the three guys.

Connor passes me the crossword. *"C'est à votre tour."* *Your turn.*

"Dude," Ryke snaps at his brother, propping the camera on the armrest. "I'd chuck a fucking pillow at you right now, but I don't want to hit your kid."

"Pillow fighting this early?" Connor banters.

He can't slice through the frothing intensity. "I said *someday*," Lo retorts. "Don't get so bent out of shape over it."

Ryke rubs his eyes wearily. "Sorry. It's just everything—the surgery, I don't fucking know." He has to be nervous, regardless if the success rate is high or not. Once he comes out of surgery, the waiting game finished, he'll be better. I have faith that he will be.

"You're not dying," Lo says adamantly. "Okay? You can't die."

"We all die sooner or later," Connor muses.

I swat him with the newspaper, which is not as satisfying as poking him with my nail. He simply arches a brow. I scowl and return to the crossword.

The new word on the paper: "Osculate."

I . . .

I don't know this word. I hesitate to reach for my phone and do a quick dictionary search in front of Connor. "Osculate." I bet it's slang for anal or maybe some kinky position that I've never heard of before.

Osculate, my brain repeats the word. Curiosity prevails and I procure my phone, bringing up a dictionary app. Out of my peripheral, Connor wears the most conceited, self-satisfied grin. He knows I'm confused.

"It better not mean anal," I say tensely under my breath. I don't think I'm ready for him to put *anything* in my ass.

"You'll see."

I almost recoil at his words. It's worse than anal sex. What's worse than that?

The definition pops on screen: 1. [mathematics] a curve or surface touching another curve or surface, having a common tangent point of contact.

What?

2. a kiss

I freeze. *A kiss.*

"The Latin word for 'kiss' is '*osculum*,'" he explains and then kisses the top of Jane's head, his lips pulling higher, eyes right on me.

I do something out of the ordinary, unlike me, my heart blazing with fire. When he raises his head, I make the first move and kiss *him* on the lips, his surprise touching me for a split moment, not long enough for me to waver. His shock vanishes as he nips my lip and then kisses *me* harder, stronger—

Jane pulls my hair again, abruptly separating us. I try to remove her grasp and distract her with the lion, my neck heating at Connor's silence.

"Say something," I whisper to him.

He cups my face, lifting my gaze to his. His thumb strokes my cheek, his eyes soulfully blue. "I know I've married the right person when words turn you on as much as they do me."

I read deeper into that, as I should.

Translation: *I could only ever be with you, Rose.*

Nineteen

Rose Cobalt

While I clean up the wrapping paper after presents, I notice Lily suspiciously sneak upstairs, cautiously checking over her shoulder to see if anyone is watching her. Somehow she misses my beady, narrowed eyes.

I've been preoccupied this past week staging two scenes with Connor for *Celebrity Crush*—one of which was Connor kissing me against a brick wall right outside of Lucky's Diner.

We almost never kiss in public, so it was a front-page headline.

I worry I've been out of the loop concerning my sisters. Connor, dressed in khakis and a navy sweater, barely bats an eye as he passes Lily on the stairs, finished putting Jane in her crib for a nap.

"That wasn't weird to you?" I ask him.

He doesn't glance back at her. "Your sister is always weird to me," he says. "She speaks in fragments and uses words like 'OTP' and 'shipper.'" Before my spine arches in defense, he adds, "I like weird. It's better than normal."

I drop the trash bag. "Well, I think she's up to something." *And I plan to find out what.* I march towards the staircase, realizing that he's not following. I look back at his hands stuffed casually in his pockets. He's acting suspicious too. "Are you joining me?"

"To investigate your sister based on her weirdness? I don't think so."

I point at him. "You're going to wish you had."

"I sincerely doubt that, darling."

I choke on an irritated laugh and then perform a signature hair flip. I stomp up the stairs, determination fueling my forceful stride. I feel Connor watching me, waiting for me to leave before he does. His caginess puts me on guard. Like I really need two Christmas mysteries.

I decide to stalk my sister first, trusting Connor more since I'm fucking him and he better believe my vagina will cast out his dick for a hint of betrayal.

Once I reach the top of the stairs, I immediately spot Lily standing outside *my* bedroom door, biting her nails.

She turns her head to the crack of the door and whisper-hisses, "Hurry up."

If I had high heels on, she'd have heard me. This is a clear case of fate. I'd shove this in Connor's face, but of course he's not here. I encroach her space quickly, and she jumps, almost falling against the wall. She rights herself before she does.

"Rose!"

"Who's in my room? Is it Loren?" I ask, edging past her easily and ramming the door open with my foot. Lily tries to grab on to my arm, but I am a one-woman bulldozer, steamrolling everything in my wake.

No one is in my room, but someone haphazardly threw my pillows on the bed, my vanity drawer left half-opened. A velvet blanket has been misplaced from the chaise to a nearby ottoman . . . also not in its proper spot by my Queen Anne chair.

I beeline for the bathroom.

"Rose," Lily calls, struggling to keep up with my vigorous pace. "I need you to take me to the doctor's. I'm not feeling well."

"Nice try, Lily," I say. I am on the hunt.

"I told you this would never fucking work! Rose can sniff out a predator a mile away!" Loren shouts from the hallway, which means someone else is in my bathroom . . . or my closet. I veer towards my closet instead.

"I'm not a predator," Lily tells him, drawing away from me and towards her husband.

"Of course not, love." His voice softens for my sister.

I swing open the closet door. Ryke, of all people, is crouched beside my extensive rack of heels, searching behind them. I clear my throat, and he stands, not even trying to hide the fact that he has been digging through my belongings.

"What are you doing?" I place my hands on my hips.

He scratches his unshaven jaw. "I was looking for something."

My brain circumnavigates to the sex tapes, to the diamond collar. "My sex toys?"

"Fuck no." He grimaces, eyeing the exit behind me like he plans to leave without offering me a single answer.

I lock the door, imprisoning us both, and I even stand guard. "Spill."

He saunters forward, only a foot from me, and he tries to reach behind me for the knob. "Move, Rose."

"You're the one who's been snooping in *my* personal things."

"Is someone going to help me here?!" he calls to his allies on the other side.

Lily jimmies the knob. "It's locked!"

Ryke looks down at me again. He won't physically push me aside. I've never seen him manhandle a woman unless it's playfully or flirtatiously. This falls into neither category.

"You give me the truth," I say, "and I open the door. It's not so hard, is it?"

"I was looking for your husband's cocaine stash," he says bluntly. "Is that what you wanted to fucking hear?"

No.

Shock, from being caught, washes over me before I can shroud a trace of it. The other *Celebrity Crush* article this week centered on Connor dropping a little baggie of white powder, being photographed picking it up. It was powdered sugar, but Walter took a wide shot, the substance up for interpretation.

Ryke reads my uneasy features. "For fuck's sake, Rose, are you doing it with him too?"

"No. And he only did it once," I lie, spinning on my heels and trying to unlock the door quickly. I fumble with even turning the knob, Ryke putting pressure on me as he hovers close, his stance carrying too much doubt.

"Are you sure it was just once?" he asks.

"Yes, I saw him."

"What if he has a fucking problem, Rose?"

I finally free myself from the closet with Ryke. "You've *all* tried it before. He doesn't need your concern. He's twenty-six."

"I don't care if he's fifty-five," Ryke retorts. "We're fucking worried. You both are acting unusual—"

"We are not." I begin to clean my disorderly room, fixing the pillows so they're not turned sideways, shutting the crooked nightstand drawer. Lily and Lo linger in the doorway, his hand slipping down her pajama pants.

I'm not even joking.

Rooms. There are rooms for these things (and *not* my room), but when it comes to teasing Lily, Loren rarely cares about the location.

"You dyed your hair orange for a day," Ryke says. "That's not fucking strange to you?"

"*Blonde,*" I say. "It was supposed to be blonde."

That *Celebrity Crush* article about my hair was horrendous. They said that I was trying to be like Daisy, grasping at my youth since I've had a child. Some people cited it as a mental break. I change my hair color *once*, and I'm losing my mind. Daisy can change her hair color every other week and she's expressing herself.

It's unjust.

"Connor went down on you in a fucking parking lot."

I stop midway to my curtains, which are creased incorrectly. I rotate to face him and our chests collide. I refuse to step back first, and unfortunately, he stands his ground too, his features darkening like *what the fuck is going on?*

"And you go down on my littlest, most precious sister on our *roof*." I point a finger at his chest, hoping he'll take *one* step back. He does not. "I could've castrated you for even waving your dick around her, you know. You're *my* age." I bring up old news to thwart the current event.

His jaw hardens. "Thank you for not castrating me." I wait for him to say *I like fucking your sister* just to piss me off, but I forget that he's not Loren. "And you're right—it shouldn't be strange that you're doing things that the rest of us do or have tried once. I guess none of us thought you two would be so . . ." His brows pinch, unable to find the word.

"Wild," I answer for him.

"Yeah."

I return my course to the curtains. I think I did really well, even *without* Connor's assistance. "I thought you don't read tabloid articles." I wonder how he read this headline. "And you rarely believe anything inside of them. Unless you really have been in a three-way relationship with Lily and your brother?"

"Fuck *no*." He follows me to the curtains. "Daisy saw the article first, and she asked me if I knew that Connor did cocaine. I asked Loren, who asked Lily, and we were all just confused. Look, I didn't want to fucking believe it, but some photographs can't be taken out of context. I couldn't spin this any other way."

"He was picking up drugs for a friend. How about that one, Ryke?" I stop by the window, straightening the chic, light-blue fabric that matches my bedspread.

"Is that true?"

"No," I say, "but you could've just asked us."

"Addicts lie," Lily chimes in from the doorway, her face flushed from Loren's groping. He's just holding her around the waist now and whispering in her ear.

I smooth a crease in the curtain. "The only thing Connor is addicted to is his own monstrous ego." I glance at the window for a brief second, movement outside causing me to do a double take. *Is that . . . ?* I edge closer until my legs touch the wall.

"Guys!" Daisy calls, bounding into my bedroom with wet hair. Ryke rotates abruptly, his body tensing, but Daisy is fast approaching, unharmed. She squeezes past Lily and Lo. "After I finished taking a shower," she exclaims quickly, "I looked out the window and I saw—"

"What is he doing?" My eyes sear holes through the window. In freshly plowed snow, Connor treks along the street, wearing a black winter coat, a blue-wrapped present in hand.

Loren knocks into my shoulder, trying to peer down below. "Did he say something to you?" *No.* Lily worms her way between us, her nose nearly touching the glass. There's not room for all five of us, not until Ryke lifts Daisy onto his shoulders, his body squished on my right.

Connor veers towards the gorgeous stone house with manicured hedges and circular driveway. Scott's house. "He better be gifting Scott rat poison," I announce. Why wouldn't he ask me to join him? I recall last time—where I couldn't bottle my emotions. Where all of us went off the hinges. All of us but him.

"I bet it's roadkill," Lo guesses. "Maybe a dead armadillo." That's something that Lo would've done to frighten Scott.

I can't picture Connor mimicking Loren's actions. I draw another blank. He's hiking up the driveway to Scott's front door.

Daisy has both palms to the glass. "I bet it's a *fuck you* cupcake."

Ryke holds her legs affectionately and stares up at her. "Cute, Calloway."

Their exchange pulls my mind to that night again, when Scott planted vicious seeds of misery in our heads. "Daisy," I begin, "did you ever sleep with someone named Trent?" I question how much bullshit Scott was spewing our way.

Daisy opens her mouth and closes it, uneasy since she's sitting on Ryke's shoulders.

Ryke glowers at me. Their relationship is ultimately the most private of everyone's in the house. I don't know how much they tell each other or what they share. "You can't ask her that, Rose."

"She's my *sister*," I refute.

"And she's my fucking girlfriend," he retorts. "You don't need to know who she's slept with." He knows the truth. He knows the truth *before* me. That's so backwards.

Where is the sisterly loyalty? I try to swat away the reality: that we're all just a little bit closer to our men than we are each other. *This was always going to happen, Rose.* I know, but I thought we had more time still.

"It was a really long time ago, and I don't remember a lot," Daisy finally answers. "So hey, I figure it barely counts, right?"

"What do you mean, you don't remember?" I'm ready to shed my protective armor and fling it on my sister. Loren and Lily have pried their gazes off the window and onto Daisy too. Ryke is the only one who seems caught up.

"I drank a lot of champagne. It was after a modeling thing. It really doesn't matter." She shrugs this off, her gaze drifting back to outside. "Hey, he's at the house!"

Her distraction works. Across the street, Connor rings the bell.

Seconds pass before Scott opens the door. I can't discern small details, but I catch Scott's trademark smile, smug and pompous. After a quick exchange, I expect Connor to shove the present in his chest and leave.

Instead, Scott swings the door wider, welcoming Connor inside. He nods and disappears within the confines of that house, the door shutting closed.

"What the hell," Lo says, stunned.

"Connor is probably threatening him." Lily nods a couple times.

"In his fucking house?" Ryke shakes his head. "He's not that stupid."

He's making a deal, I conclude. Our doorbell chimes throughout the house, splitting my thoughts. I didn't see anyone traipse up our driveway. Every noise, every new change, pricks my neck, setting my mood to *cautious* and *severely alarmed*.

Twenty

Rose Cobalt

I dart away from the window first, rushing to answer the door.

I'm not the only one.

It's a stampede to downstairs, with Lo lifting Lily in a piggy-back, pushing ahead of me. I walk quickly, close to his heels. Ryke still carries Daisy on his shoulders behind us, moving at a lacka-daisical pace.

"Did someone call Mom?" Daisy asks, her fingers combing through Ryke's thick hair.

"No," we all say. That would be a horrible surprise—to open the door in a quick rush, finding our mother on the other side. I love her, but she already spent Christmas Eve criticizing my gift choices for Jane.

After storming down the steps, Lo stumbles over a decorative three-foot Santa Claus, causing Lily to drop off his back and try to beat me there. I've already passed her, speeding through the foyer.

I clasp the knob, partially out of breath. Just as I open the door, the person presses the buzzer one more time.

The young guy solidifies when he meets my hot gaze, and he stuffs his fists into his black hoodie, a blue Dalton Academy beanie shrouding his brown hair. I know *exactly* who this seventeen-year-old is.

"Uh . . ." His eyes flicker to Lily. She tries to squeeze through to greet him with open arms. I crack the door so my body wedges into the space, not allowing her exit.

"Rose," she complains.

"I got here first," I tell her but keep an intimidating glare on him.

Garrison clears his throat, nervous. "We haven't met." He out-stretches his gloved hand.

"Yes, we have." I don't shake his hand, the ten-degree chill numbing my fingers on the door's edge. "You and your friends sprayed red punch on my *infant* daughter and me with a water gun." Before Halloween, we had a long-standing feud with the teenage neighbors. It ended with all of them being charged with burglary, all but Garrison, who chose not to break into our house like his friends.

His character, in my mind, is tarnished until I see otherwise, but he works as a cashier at Superheroes & Scones, thanks to Lily's kindness and Lo's empathy for broken, spiteful teenagers.

"It was stupid . . . I'm sorry . . ." He chews his chapped lip for a second. "Hey, is Willow here? I know she's a distant cousin, or whatever . . ."

He means Loren's half sister, but Willow has to lie about her connections to her brother the same way that Ryke once did. No one can know that Willow's mom is actually Lo's birth mom. I learned that Lo's mom was underage, only *sixteen*, when she was pregnant with Loren.

Jonathan Hale would have gone to jail for statutory rape, and he's had his two sons and this woman cover for him for decades. Willow could live free of this humongous lie, only by returning to her hometown of Maine and staying with her mother. By choosing to be in Philadelphia and be a part of her half brother's life, she has to tell everyone that she's a distant cousin to the Hales.

No one is more upset over this than Ryke—since he had to lie about his familial relationships as a teenager too.

"She's coming around at two!" Lily answers in the background.

"Lily," I snap, opening the door just a tad. I remember Lily saying that Willow wanted to stop by later, to not interrupt. I'd like to think we're inclusive when it comes to blood, but she only knows us from the media. It's why she's chosen to live in an apartment and not in our house. I would probably insist she live here, but Lily and Lo aren't as pushy as me.

Lily gives me a stern look that is especially comical from my loving sister. "Willow and Garrison are coworkers."

Lo puts a hand on the door, prying it out of my grip. It hits the wall and now he can see all of Garrison. Thankfully he shoots the guy a dark glare. "A coworker doesn't show up on Christmas morning looking for another coworker."

Garrison scrapes the icy stoop with his boot. "Does this mat say *welcome* under here? I can't read it with all the snow."

"He's funny," I say icily.

"You're scary, no offense." He coughs into his glove and checks over his shoulder. "You're going to make me invite myself in, aren't you?"

"Yes."

His eyes ping from each of us, his breath smoking the air. "I just . . . I wanted to tell her that I'm . . ." He lets out a weak laugh, his eyes reddening. I notice an unlit cigarette between his left-hand fingers. "Never mind, it's fucking stupid . . ." He turns to leave.

I snatch his hoodie, drawing him back.

"What the fuck?" He spins around and gives me a familiar look that says, *I don't even understand you. You're kind of insane. What the fuck?*

"Are you asking her to prom?" I question. "Because this is the most pathetic proposal I've ever seen. You need flowers, first of all."

"I'm not asking her to prom." His voice shakes some, his nose red from the cold. "I came to tell her that I'm leaving, and I guess to tell you too." He nods to Lily and then briefly glances at Loren, not holding his gaze for long.

"What do you mean?" Lily asks.

That's when I see Connor in the distance, trekking back to our house. I snatch my coat off the hook and slip on a pair of nearby boots: *Daisy's*, nearly the same size as me, thankfully.

"My parents handed me my only Christmas present this morning: a white envelope," he says bitterly. "I . . . *they* are withdrawing me from Dalton and sending me to this boarding school for 'proper guidance' to finish my senior year."

I pass Garrison on the landing, my hand freezing as I grip the railing, careful not to slip on the icy steps.

"Where is it?" Lily asks.

I head down the driveway, Garrison's voice drifting in the background. "Upstate New York," he says, "Faust Boarding School for Young Boys."

A chill nips my spine. I approach Connor at a hurried speed, meeting him at the mailbox, where he has his hands in his coat pockets, unsurprised by my sudden appearance. He stands tall, unconcerned and unafraid of everything, despite just having spoken to that detestable rodent.

"You went into the lion's den," I say, my throat raw from more than just the cold.

Connor shakes his head. "We're the lions, Rose. Our den is right behind you."

My nose flares. He's saying that we're stronger and better than Scott, but I can't move past *this*. "What deal did you just make?" *This*—we did not agree upon. We did not discuss. We did not—

"None."

He pops my thoughts. "You gave him roadkill."

His lips rise in a humored grin. "I'm not Lo."

I should know what he did. He's my husband, but I can't see the answer that's literally standing right in front of me. Snow begins to fall again, dusting our hair with flakes and wetting my nose and cheeks. I have to ask outright.

"What'd you do?"

"I gave him a bottle of expensive wine."

My brows tighten. "You drugged him?"

His grin widens. "Rose, darling, come back to Earth."

I perch my hands on my hips, eyes narrowed. "You just *gave* him a bottle of wine? What are you, friends now . . ." My face falls. "No, Connor." This is what he does. He fakes friendships and then slices them at the knees when he has no more use for them. "He'll never believe you're his friend."

He holds my cold hand. "Scott isn't smart. He's self-righteous and irritating. He *can* be manipulated. I never had the chance to do this before, not in the constraints of the reality show, but I do now."

"And you can just *bear* to make nice to him?" Hot tears try to well, and I'm impassioned and disgusted by the mere idea.

Connor's hand rises to my face, his blue eyes assured but calm, so calm to my fervor. I want him to crack, to unleash his fury and appease my insides that begin to roil, but he can't . . . or else we lose.

"My skin is crawling." I shake. He probably shared fake laughter with Scott and even complimented him.

"Then you know how mine feels." He seems so put-together, but it's all inside—the things I can't see, deep down, his disgust at having to befriend him.

"Can you stomach this?" I ask.

He nods once. "It's our best chance." And then he recites, "'The worst is not. So long as we can say, *this is the worst.*'"

"*King Lear.*" *Shakespeare*. I try to push him off. "You just quoted a tragedy, Richard."

He refuses to let me go, holding me closer. "I need you," he suddenly says.

I freeze. "What?"

His gaze bores down on me. "I need you to keep looking at me like you're going to burn a hole through my heart, and I need you to tell me that you love the real me. Every day, I need you, Rose. That's how I'm going to stomach this."

Without hesitation, I say, "*Bien sûr.*" *Of course.*

I can't remember another moment where we've both been so unsure about the future. It's as though we're standing, hand in hand, at the edge of an obscured forest, riddled with iron traps and predators and prey. I only cling to one certainty.

We're entering this tragedy together.

Twenty-one

Connor Cobalt

lie in bed past 11 a.m., light streaming through the windows. January 3, of all days, I try to sleep past the morning to cut out a chunk of time. I did this last year, and the day seemed somewhat shorter.

I roll onto my side, Rose already gone. My fingers graze the blankets, absent of a second warm body. My eyes lift a fraction, and I flinch.

Lily is perched on the vanity stool beside the door, wearing a white, furry *Star Wars* Wampa hat, jeans and a Superheroes & Scones T-shirt in blue block letters. This may be one of the only days she's been dressed before me. She raises a hand and gives me a sheepish smile. "Hi."

I sit and fix my tousled hair. She's up to something. "What are you doing, Lily?" I grip the comforter, about to climb out of bed.

"Waitwaitwait!" she slurs, panicked. "Rose said you have underwear on, but I just need to confirm before you get up." So Rose is a part of this. Lily rambles, "It's not so much about my sex addiction, but just respecting my sister's husband on his birthday." She nods resolutely—and then flushes. "Not that I wouldn't respect you on any other day."

"I understand, Lily." I smile, half forced from the mention of my twenty-seventh birthday, the word instantly deteriorating my mood. "Thank you, and don't worry, I'm clothed." In underwear *and* navy flannel pants.

She lets out a breath while I stand, and then she springs to her feet, blocking the door.

My brows rise. "Are you holding me hostage?"

"You can take a shower," she says, not denying the fact that she's keeping an eye on me. "In fact, you should probably wear something nice today." She keeps nodding. Then she adds, "Just . . . no one wants a repeat of last year."

Last January 3, they all decided to throw me a surprise party. I surprised them by flying to Ontario for the day and returning home the next morning. No one was pleased but me, and I thought they learned their lesson.

I have no problem celebrating someone else's birthday. If it holds meaning to them, that's fine, but my birthday holds no meaning to me. My age has always been a restraint. It bars me from advancing as fast as I'm capable. I could've driven at twelve. I could've been an informed voter at thirteen. I could've outwitted professors at fifteen. I don't like celebrating my age—this irritating, unbending nuisance that parallels with time.

Lily claps her hands. "So take a shower—not with me, of course. You know, by yourself. Just you. I'll be right here. In this bedroom, not anywhere near your nakedness." She's fire-engine red.

It's hard to not laugh. I head to the bathroom, already concocting an escape route. I'll just leave out the back door and through the garage. "Where's Jane?" I ask.

"With Rose."

Maybe she's planning to drop her off at her mother's house. "Where are we going tonight?" I try asking straight out.

Lily opens her mouth and then shuts it. I watch as she squints at me, attempting to narrow her eyes. "You're asking too many questions."

I swing open the bathroom door. "What happens if I leave this house?"

"Wait, are you planning on leaving already?" She shifts nervously on her feet like she has to pee. "You can't leave yet, and if you do, I'll have no choice but to use physical force." It's comical coming from the girl wearing a fuzzy hat that has a face and horns. "And I may also have to call for *backup*."

Backup?

The minute she emphasizes the word, the door blows open and Ryke and Loren saunter into my bedroom, both dressed casually in jeans and T-shirts. The handcuffs are unmistakable in Ryke's clutch.

I still stand halfway between the bathroom and my bedroom, bottling my aggravation. "If you want me to cuff you to my bed, all you have to do is ask."

"Hilarious," Ryke says, "but these aren't for me."

Lo is half distracted by his wife, tugging the flaps of her Wampa cap and kissing her cheek. She whispers rapidly to him, accidentally gesturing to me, more obvious than stealthy.

"You're early, darling," I quip, pulling Lo's attention to me. "I never cuff you before noon."

He smiles. "Today is different, love."

I shake my head. "No, today is the same as any other day unless the three of you try to make it something more."

"Here's the deal," Lo says. "You're going to take a shower, get dressed and no Jedi mind-tricking anyone." He looks to Lily at that last request and she nods in approval.

"You're not going to tell me what Rose has planned, are you?"

"Not a chance." If he were closer, I'm sure he would've patted my shoulder. His phone rings before he checks the caller ID. "It's my marketing assistant." *Theo.* "Ryke, will you—"

"I have him," Ryke says. "Take the call." Lo leaves with Lily, and I fixate on Ryke's silver handcuffs again.

"Are you planning on handcuffing me to the shower?"

Ryke stares unflinchingly at me. "If I fucking have to."

Wonderful.

I restrain the urge to roll my eyes—which is something I almost never do. I slip into the bathroom and start shedding my clothes, leaving the door wide open. I could stay in here for a while, but Ryke purposefully foils my plan, entering the bathroom with me.

He hops onto the counter, opening and closing the latches on the handcuffs with a key. "Don't take longer than thirty fucking minutes. I don't want to be in here any more than you want me in here."

Ryke is the muscle, the only one who can physically keep me in Philadelphia, which is why he has now replaced Lily as my unofficial guard.

I'm on house arrest.

On a day where I usually flee the country alone.

I step out of my boxer briefs and near the glass shower. "I wasn't aware that dogs can tell time."

"Fuck you," he says, his words harsher than usual. It can't be for the small joke.

"Normal people don't curse out their friends on their birthday," I mention before slipping into the shower, warm water beating down on my tense body.

He speaks loud enough that I hear him. "And normal people don't manipulate their friends on Christmas!"

This. "I'm not normal!" I shout through the gushing water, running my hands along my wet hair.

Through the fogged glass, I can make out Ryke's silhouette, head shaking. "You made me think that you had the same relationship with your mom that I had with mine, just so I would fucking tell you about my childhood."

He asked me: *Wasn't Christmas just your mom and you?*

I replied: *I'm assuming it was for you.* I never said yes. I never said no. I never answered his question until he answered mine. "All you had to do was read deeper into my words," I explain, raising my voice without shouting now. "And you would've realized that I never agreed with you." I scrub shampoo into my hair.

"Sometimes I feel like you purposefully make it hard for me to trust you."

It's not my intention, though I know it's a consequence of prodding in someone's life. We're both quiet while I finish taking a shower. After shutting off the water, I wrap a towel around my waist and step out. I head to my sink where Ryke still sits.

"I'm not telling you how many pages I can read," he says, briefly looking up from the handcuffs to meet my eyes. He's talking about his Christmas present. In his blank journal that he gave me last year, I wrote passages to him in several different languages.

I squirt a line of toothpaste on my toothbrush. "I didn't think you would." I wrote truthful, honest messages about him, things that I admire, but he won't be able to read the ones that he can't understand, not without an online translator at least.

I brush my teeth.

"You confuse the fuck out of me," he says under his breath. He thinks I had an ulterior motive with the journal. I had none.

I rinse my mouth and spit out water. "Says the guy who makes everyone think he's stupid when he's smart." He speaks different languages. He votes in every election. I bet he can quote authors. I bet he understands references that Rose and I use. He shrouds these parts of himself, as if they're reminders of how he was raised. As the "yes kid" who did what his mother asked of him.

Study hard for me. Yes, Mom.

Be athletic for me. Yes, Mom.

Run track for me. Yes, Mom.

Learn French for me. Yes, Mom.

Stay quiet for me. Yes, Mom.

Lie for me. Yes, Mom.

Tell no one about me. Yes, Mom.

The yes kid has no opinions of his own. The yes kid has no voice.

I'm not sure when Ryke finally spoke freely, but it's clear he hates returning to that place. I can still see remnants of it in him when he struggles to open up. He's used to being silent about specific parts of his life.

"I don't make anyone think anything," he retorts. "I just don't give a fuck about trying to prove them wrong."

"You are who you are." I set my toothbrush back in the holder. "At least you have five people that can put up with you."

He flips me off and then raises the handcuffs like *it's time, Cobalt.*

I blink twice. "You're not serious."

"Lo said to think of it as birthday punishment." He hops off the counter, one inch shorter than me.

"And why am I being punished exactly?" I head into my closet, picking out black slacks and a white button-down.

"I don't fucking know," he says from within my bedroom. "Maybe for being an arrogant prick seven days a week." I step into my pants and begin to button my shirt as he adds, "Or how about for making a birthday celebration harder than it has to be."

While I finish buttoning my shirt, I slip back into my room again. Ryke physically blocks the door. I try to plan an escape. I can't run faster than Ryke. He was the captain of his track team in college. I'm not stupid enough to try.

Then again, I'd rather try to leave than do nothing and be handcuffed. "You're punishing me for being me," I tell him.

He holds my concentrated gaze. "At least you have five people that can put up with you."

Five people who love me so much that they want to celebrate a mundane, pointless day in my honor. I grab my phone off my dresser and call Daisy, my cell to my ear.

"You have to follow me to the kitchen," Ryke says. "If you fucking bolt, I have no problem tackling you."

My brow quirks, and the phone line clicks.

"Hello there, birthday boy," Daisy greets like she's in the same room as me. She has to be in the basement or in the kitchen.

"Do you mind entertaining your boyfriend for ten or fifteen minutes?"

Ryke shakes his head at me, silently saying, *that's not going to work.*

On the phone, Daisy sighs. "I wish I could, but Rose made me promise not to help you today. She almost made it a blood oath pact . . . so she'd be really upset if I chose you over her. Sisters before misters."

"Where is Rose?" I ask.

"What was that?" She feigns confusion. "You're breaking up." And then someone else's voice creates a static noise in the receiver. *Lily.* "Sorry, Connor, I can't hear you!" Daisy hangs up before I do.

I pocket my cell, and Ryke opens the door, gesturing for me to follow him. I realize that if I want to leave this house, there's no other alternative than physically overpowering Ryke.

Without another word, I walk behind him along the hallway. As we descend the steps, I decide it's better to make a quick exit through the back door and not the front.

He leads me into the kitchen anyway, and the minute he tries to reach for me, to handcuff me to the fucking kitchen *chair*, I sprint to the back door.

"Connor!" Ryke yells, chasing after me. Right as my hand reaches the knob, he seizes my bicep and pulls me backwards.

I spin out of the hold easily and twist his arm behind his back, my lips close to his ear. *"Tu perdras cette lutte, mon ami." You will lose this fight, my friend.*

And then his elbow rams into my stomach, the force knocking

the wind out of me. I cough roughly, enough to where he slips from my grasp. I hear the *click* before I feel the cold metal on my wrist. I jerk my arm, but I've been restrained to a rung on the kitchen chair. I can move enough to find a paper clip and unlock the handcuff, but not with Ryke Meadows as a bodyguard.

My jaw muscles tense more than usual. I thought his heart was too soft to inflict physical pain on me.

Ryke rests his elbows on the bar counter, lounging. *"Veux-tu dire la lutte que tu viens de perdre?"* You mean the fight that you just lost?

He replied back in French. This is rare. If I'm going to be stuck in this gigantic kitchen to a six-person round table, I might as well make the best of it. So I switch to Italian.

"Conosco un segreto sulla tua fidanzata di cui nessuno è al corrente, nemmeno tu." I know a secret about your girlfriend, and no one else knows it, not even you. It sounds mocking and slightly childish, but I'm in a strange mood.

His face darkens, concern hitting him. *"Stai mentendo."* You're lying.

He knows Italian.

I can't restrain my grin. I switch to German. *"Ich lüge zu meinem Nutzen. Natürlich."* I'm lying for my benefit. Of course.

His spine straightens, worry still present in his narrowed eyes. "Connor, I'm not fucking playing around anymore."

"You don't know German," I realize.

His nose flares, and he shakes his head. "No. I don't know German."

Rose and I prefer French, but I grasp this certainty: a language Ryke won't understand if we need privacy. Though her German isn't great either.

Unlike Rose, I had a penchant for linguistics at Faust. I liked words, the roots, the structure, the foundation. It's almost like math, and uncovering one language made another easier to learn.

"Connor—"

"I lied about Daisy," I say. "I don't really know anything more than you do."

He rolls his eyes. "I'm going to let this go. Only because I hit you on your birthday."

"Special privileges?" I can barely feign excitement, and I try to lift my arm, only for the chair to scrape the floor and the cuff to rattle. I notice the boxed cake mix on the counter beside a tub of chocolate icing and bottles of sprinkles. The sentiments are nice, but no one needs to make today about me. It's unnecessary. "Can I at least have a paper and a pen?"

Ryke gives me a strange look. "What the fuck for?"

"I'm writing a love letter to my wife," I say flatly. He still wears that look. "As a former journalism major, I assume that you understand the concept of *writing*. It's the process by which you scrawl your name or, in your case, profanities, onto a surface, in this case, paper. You do know what paper is?"

"Fuck off."

The echo of heels sound along the hardwood from the living room, and Rose emerges through the doorway, shutting it behind her. I sweep her features instantly.

She wears a black floral kimono and a simple black cotton dress, one she'll sometimes put on when she does her makeup. Her hair is sleeked back in an elegant pony, her lips stained deep red and eye shadow too smoky for a casual event.

She's in the process of dressing up for something. The moment she sees me, a smile plays at her lips.

Twenty-two

Connor Cobalt

This isn't funny, darling." My voice sounds complacent but serious.

She walks further into the kitchen. "What's funny is that your jet is scheduled for Hong Kong in . . ." She checks the oven clock. "Three hours."

"He wants paper and a pen to write you a letter," Ryke says, already heading for the basement door. "Can you fucking text me when you need me to come back?"

She nods, but her eyes stay on me. I watch her procure a pen and paper without question, and she slides both to me and sits across the table.

I take a seat in the chair I'm attached to. "You can join me in Hong Kong," I tell her, "if you promise not to say the b-word. Or better yet . . ." I scoot closer to the table. "I can put something in your mouth so it won't even be possible."

Her cheeks flush, and my desire pumps blood to my cock.

What I'd give for our positions to be reversed. I raise my wrist, the one still cuffed to the rung. "Unlock me and we can make it a date."

Rose leans back in her chair, her ankles and arms crossed. "I can't. I have plans tonight and you running away like Cinderella will ruin them."

"Isn't it customary for me to receive things that I want on my birthday?" *What I don't want: to go downtown with Rose or to go on some romantic getaway trip on* this *day.*

"It is," she agrees. "But you never take stock in birthday traditions." She presses her red lips together, smoothing out the lipstick.

I click the pen. "Don't move until I'm finished with this," I order. "You can do that at least?"

She scowls, her eyes narrowing. "I can do a lot of things, Richard. Like scoop out your eyeballs with a spoon or sew your lips together with my needle and thread."

"The latter would dissatisfy both of us, so I don't suggest it."

She watches me write on the paper. "Jane is down for a nap . . ." Her voice is distant with curiosity. "The irony is that we're both stubborn on our birthdays, just for different reasons."

She loves her birthday like a narcissist would—like *I* should. And I adore giving her my full, unbridled attention on August 5, pampering her every need.

I pass her the paper and pen. I scrawled three names: *Connor Cobalt on his birthday, Connor Cobalt working at his office, Connor Cobalt beating you at chess.*

Her glare could kill.

My arousal spikes, my cock throbbing, and I shift my legs to try and impede an erection.

"What if I don't answer?" she asks defiantly. Her eyes flicker to my lips.

"I'll spank you in the middle of this fucking kitchen."

Red heats her neck, but her yellow-green eyes pierce me more. I think, for a moment, that she wants to attempt this. She'd like me to take her across the table and play with her, but she hesitates, sliding into her head. She tries to tuck a flyaway hair that doesn't exist and resumes her concentration on the paper.

I go to stand. The chair legs clatter as I extend my arm. Dammit. She has to spot the irritation and frustration tightening my face, because she writes faster.

I pick up the wooden chair with one hand and move closer to Rose. I drop it roughly beside her. She jumps, shooting me a third glare. I stay standing, towering above her frame. Her chest rises and falls heavily, and she sets the pen down when she's finished.

"Done," she announces.

I read the answers over her shoulder. *KILL. KILL. KILL.*

Rose rarely cheats. I bend down slightly and clasp her waist before kicking the chair out from under her. She gasps, but I swiftly push her body over the table, my pelvis digging into her ass. Her ragged breath breaks any silence.

I outstretch her hands with one of mine, my cuffed palm planted firmly on her ass. I crave to thrust against her, ceaseless and hard motions, until we're both coming.

"Connor," she warns, her eyes darting around the kitchen.

I place the pen in her grip so she can rewrite her answer, my lips low to her ear. *"Pas de triche." No cheating.* I spank her hard, and she shudders, her fingers whitening around the pen.

She licks her bottom lip, her mouth partially open as she collects herself. I try to reach forward to clasp her face and turn it to me, to kiss her, but my hand is still caged. I take the moment to suck the nape of her neck, very slowly, and her body trembles in want of more. I lift my lips to her ear, deeply irritated by this fucking handcuff.

I'm not used to any restraint. "Where's the key?" I ask her.

She cranes her head over her shoulder to look at me. "I'm not unlocking you, Richard."

I lean forward, my dick grinding into her ass, and with her head turned, I kiss her forcefully, until a moan breaches her throat and seems to echo down mine. I part just enough to say, "You'd rather I break the chair?"

Fire swirls in her gaze. "You're not breaking my chair."

"*Our* chair," I correct. We own seventy-five percent of the furniture in this house together. I chose this table since I won a round of Scrabble. She chose the kitchen appliances by beating me at Trivial Pursuit. Games solve our differences when we're both unwilling to concede.

Her eyes ping between the chair and the handcuffs. I wonder what she cares about more: the material item or her plans tonight.

I expect her to protect the chair, but instead, she turns her head back to the paper, focusing again. She won't unlock the handcuffs, even at the cost of our furniture.

My phone buzzes in my pocket. I stay in the same position and try to answer it, but my wrist jerks to a stop at my waist. *I'm breaking this fucking chair.* I have to remove my hand that lies on top of Rose's left one and pass the phone between my palms. I catch the caller ID and my muscles tense.

SCOTT

Unfortunately, I have to answer the phone. "Hey, man," I say, the casual greeting like salt on my tongue. Rose taps her pen on the paper, still mulling over her answers.

"Happy birthday," Scott says, cordially enough. I spent three mind-numbing hours at his house last night. I learned three things.

1. He drinks excessively; his favorite: pale ale.
2. He name-drops every five minutes, and he warms easily to compliments like: *I can't believe you know him. I would literally die to meet that guy.*
3. He may not trust me one hundred percent yet, but he needs me. That's more leverage than anything Scott has.

"Thanks, thanks," I say, aching to grip Rose's ponytail and tilt her head back towards me. *But this goddamn fucking chair.*

"So I'm about to go into a meeting with the executive from GBA, do you have any updates for me?"

Updates. "Lily is thinking about the second season more than Rose," I lie. None of us will ever do it, but I have to dangle him for a little while longer, so I can have more time to build trust between us. "She'll take time."

Rose whips her head to me and mouths, *Scott?*

I mouth, *answer the question.* This Fuck, Marry, Kill shouldn't be this hard. She hasn't even written one new response.

She sighs heavily before resuming her focus.

"How about you just force her to do it?" Scott says with an annoying laugh attached. "She's your wife. You know what'll work?"

My fingers press harder into the phone's casing. "What's that?" I hear my even-tempered voice, but I grind my teeth.

"Backhand her when she says no." He takes a short pause . . . and then he laughs at his own repulsive joke.

I hold Rose protectively at the waist. I bring on the shortest laugh I can muster without sounding sarcastic or mocking. "I'll keep that in mind," I say lightly. "Good luck." If anyone knows me at all, they can tell I'm being fake by those two words.

Good luck.

"Same to you." I let him hang up first.

"What did he say?" Rose asks.

"He's meeting with GBA right now. It's not important." I pocket my phone and then rub her neck, leaning forward, hard against her ass again.

She sets down her pen. "Finished."

I rest my hand back on her outstretched one, keeping her breasts flat against the table. "Let's see, Miss Highest Honors."

Above *Connor Cobalt working at his office*, she wrote: *Kill.*

She crossed out *Connor Cobalt beating you at chess* and re-wrote: *Connor Cobalt playing chess with you—Marry.*

Slightly cheating, but not quite. I'll accept the amendment, but if our positions were reversed, she'd never let me make one like that.

And then, last—*Connor Cobalt on his birthday*, she wrote *FUCK* in all capital letters. I harden almost instantly, and I grip one of the rungs of the chair and slam it on the ground. Rose flinches, but I hold her jaw with my free hand, keeping her head straight ahead so she can't watch the decimation of her fucking chair.

It takes two more contacts with the floor before the legs break, and then one strong tug later, the rung detaches from the wooden frame. The other cuff slides off of the rung, and I'm freer than I was.

I pull her ponytail, and a gasp escapes her lips. I kiss her again, my other hand slipping up her inner thigh.

I part her lips with my tongue, tasting her, toying with her, and then I release her hair and push her face back onto the table.

"Connor," she warns, but her eyes stay attached to me, not wandering around the room. She tries standing up, but I force her chest back down, a firm hand between her shoulder blades.

Her palm peels off the table, and she attempts to remove mine from between her legs. I slap her away and then I spank her ass.

She cries into a soft moan, and then she says, "Wait . . . wait, Connor."

You'll like this, Rose.

I stroke the soft flesh of her thigh again, and she reaches for that hand *again*. I slap her away and spank her ass. She chokes on a noise. "Connor, *wait* . . . you have to wait . . ."

I lean forward, my erection digging into her, and I can feel her leg muscles flex in arousal. "You want me to fuck you," I whisper in the pit of her ear. "I want to fuck you. We both win, Rose."

She breathes shallowly. "Connor . . ." I'm close to her pussy. "No!" This time, she squeezes my wrist, but the panic in her voice already hits me. I immediately take my weight off my wife, and I gently rotate Rose. I cup her face with tender care, rapidly skimming her entire body for any kind of sign.

She places two palms on my chest, her eyes fluttering like I've already fucked her hard. I barely even played with her.

"Rose?" I murmur.

She licks her lips. "I have plans. You can't ruin them." That's what this is about? She oddly keeps tugging down her cotton dress, hiding whatever she has on beneath.

I lift one of her hands, about to kiss her palm, but she retracts it and raises her chin, collecting her bearings.

"Just wait until tonight," she snaps.

I take her hand again and put it on my crotch, a rock-hard erection aching to fit between her legs. "I can't wait around, so I'm either coming inside your pussy, in your mouth or in the shower. Would you like to pick?"

She cautiously checks over her shoulder and then whispers, "Go into the pantry."

Since she's reluctant to give blow jobs, struggling always to take me entirely in her mouth, I figure she's succumbed to sex but wants to do it in a more private setting. I lead the way to the walk-in pantry. She shuts the door behind us and switches on the light.

I focus so much on her penetrating gaze that I miss the tiny key between her fingers and her unlatching the free handcuff. My mind catches up the minute she locks the cuff to a wire shelf.

She leaves.

"Rose!" I yell.

She returns very quickly. "I had to set down the key," she says, sidling closer. She unbuttons my pants.

"I need my hand—"

"You only need one. I'm blowing you."

I can't hide my surprise. "What?"

She glares. "I know I'm not good at it, but you're not fucking me right now. And you're not rubbing one out on your birthday." She drops to her knees, tugging my pants to my ankles. Her eyes soften a fraction. "I need your help."

I'd rather help her than just watch. "I always guide you, Rose."

She nods, pulling down my boxer briefs. The length of my shaft intimidates her in this position. I clasp her wrist and bring her hand to the base.

"This would be easier if you didn't cuff me," I say.

"Then it's a challenge. It should be more fun for you," she retorts.

Being tied up isn't the kind of challenge I like. "Not more fun, more aggravating."

She squeezes my dick with more force, and a grunt scratches my throat. She says, "I want to be with you on your birthday for once."

"I would've taken you to Hong Kong. Open your mouth." I rest my hand on the back of her head, planning to control the movements.

She stares up at me. "No, you wouldn't have."

Maybe she's right. I never even considered bringing her with me before.

"I'm going to show you why you should love today."

"Starting with a blow job?" I question. It's not the most uncommon thing between us, but it's not frequent either.

Her yellow-green eyes drill a hole straight through me, and then she opens her mouth.

Twenty-three

Rose Cobalt

> If you don't hurry, Connor is going to rip the shelf out of the fucking wall. —Ryke

After the blow job that made Connor momentarily satisfied and made me infinitely more aroused, I had to leave him handcuffed in the pantry. If I'd let him loose, he would flee, and he'd miss out on a night he'd actually appreciate.

"Did he escape?" Lily asks. "You're glaring at the phone." In my bedroom, she sets down two dinner plates of sea bass and squash on an elegant tablecloth.

Daisy darts around her, lighting candles. "Ryke wouldn't let him escape." She sticks up for her boyfriend. He's been very helpful in corralling my husband.

Connor isn't a fan of surprises, but this is a low-key one. Just him. Just me. If he hates this, then so be it, but at least I tried *something*.

I would have prepared a more extravagant event—anything outside of this house—if I'd thought he'd like it. From previous attempts at making birthday plans, I know he wouldn't. And despite the handcuffs, the rest of the day is about *his* enjoyment.

I dim the lights on the wall. "He's still locked up." I text Ryke, send him here in three minutes. My veins pump full of adrenaline, slightly worried that this may all backfire. "I think that's it," I tell Daisy and Lily.

My sisters canvass the area: the intimate dinner for two, the sultry lighting, Connor's favorite classic rock songs playing on low volume in the background. I'm wearing possibly the most elegant dress I've ever designed, something suited for the Oscars and not just a late-night dinner in my bedroom.

But some events deserve the most expensive wine, the crème brûlée dessert, and that rare one-time-only dress meant to be un-zipped slowly.

My gown accentuates my hourglass figure, the fabric almost completely sheer in a deep merlot hue with floral appliqué and shimmering crystal embroidery. With long, sheer sleeves, the dress fills two needs of mine: sophisticated but entirely sensual. Parts of my body are exposed through the fabric like I'm standing in a misted shower, the illusion of being naked but still covered.

"He's going to love it," Lily says with an assured nod, her furry hat still on her head. She can tell I'm nervous.

I imagine war if he's put off or dissatisfied by my efforts. I may grab a candlestick as a weapon. "Let's hope so, because I didn't buy another fire extinguisher." I tighten my ponytail. Somehow a hay bale caught on fire during Halloween. I surprisingly had no part in its destruction.

"I'll fill some buckets of water downstairs," Daisy offers. She gives me a wink. "Just in case." I love my little sisters, my muscles almost uncoiling. I shouldn't be anxious about this. I feel like I'm fourteen again, preparing to annihilate Connor at Model UN, crammed in that tiny hotel room and flipping through flash cards. I had the worst stomach pains, more at the idea of seeing him again than at the idea of losing to him.

Upon years of reflection, I question whether they're my form of butterflies, my body willfully rejecting anything so sweet and lovey-dovey.

If so, then I'm the recipient of nauseous butterflies that make me want to hurl. I've been married for two and a half years—you'd think they'd die already.

My phone buzzes in my palm.

He's coming up.—Ryke

"You two need to go—thank you, but shoo." I wave them off, especially as Lily tries to bound over for a goodbye hug. I recoil at the thought of one.

"Just a little hug?" Lily asks, pushing her fingers together as if I don't know what "little" means.

Daisy sidles next to Lily. "I'll be Rose's stand-in hugger." She wraps her arms around Lily's scrawny frame and squeezes so much more than I ever would. It's a terrific hug, which is why I don't torture anyone with my stiff ones.

Lily squeezes Daisy back with equal sisterly affection. "That's such a good hug, Rose," Lily smiles. I give them five more seconds before I physically tear them apart, a hand on each of their shoulders, and steer them to the door. Their smiles are welcome *outside* my room.

They leave just in time, racing down the hallway to Lily's bedroom and disappearing out of sight. Connor is the only one who ascends the stairs. I shut the door before he sees my outfit, and my eyes flit over the room. Candles lit on the dresser and table, his favorite winter food from his favorite restaurant. His favorite music. And then me, his favorite person.

Everything is perfect.

For some reason, I've already concluded that he'll hate it, so when he opens the door, I am scorching as hot as the flames behind me.

He sweeps my features and my body in a long, inexpressive wave, and my legs harden to cement. I force my feet to move nearer, and then I reach over his side and shove the door closed. All the while he stares down at me, my heels not equalizing our height difference.

I raise my chin, an inch or so separating our bodies. His hand slides to my hip, his firm grasp sending shock waves and pulses below. "You're wrong," I tell him strongly.

"Am I?" he questions.

I nod once, refusing to concede on this matter. "I'm not celebrating your age, Connor. January third is a day where I celebrate you existing for another year. I don't care if you're seventeen or if you're eighty. You're here, and I'm . . ." The compliment is *right* on the tip of my tongue. It tastes foreign but not foul.

His lips begin to lift in a grin. "Go ahead, Rose." His enjoyment usually riles me to do otherwise, but today is different. He needs to see that.

"I'm *grateful*," I say, "to have you in my life, and if you hate all of this, then I will *never* try again. You can spend every single birthday after this one alone in another country, and I'll let you leave without hassle." I can't read his stoic features, not as much as I'd like to. I think maybe the intimate dinner hasn't persuaded him, so I push myself to do something else out of my nature. I reach for the zipper at my shoulder blades, attempting to undress.

He seizes my wrist to stop me, and his deep-blue eyes possess me first, filled with serenity and finality. He zips the dress back to my collar. My heart pounds, my blood simmering, and I watch him walk around me to the table. Still standing, he begins to pour wine into the glasses.

He's purposefully quiet, leaving me to guess his iron-locked thoughts. If he despised this, he'd be gone by now, so I cling to this fact and pull back my shoulders with more confidence. I strut deeper into our regal light-blue-and-gray bedroom, taking a seat on my vanity stool.

He's not interested in the food. That much I've gathered.

I find myself tapping my heel on the floorboards while he sips his wine. He watches my eyes narrow to pinpoints.

"If your silence is *my* punishment for handcuffing you," I say, "then you should know that it's more of a prize. Your voice bleeds my ears."

His lips curve upwards. "*Vous êtes ravissante.*" *You are exquisite.* His serious tone clenches my heart, his eyes sweeping my sheer gown once more, to show that he's talking about more than my previous exaggeration. Then Connor picks up the second wine-glass. "And I've spent the past three hours in a pantry with only Ryke as company, so I've had plenty of time to decide what your punishment will be. The silent treatment isn't nearly satisfying enough to be a part of it."

"If I hadn't tied you up, you would've left," I refute.

He doesn't deny this. He stands in front of me, sipping his wine and holding out the second glass. I reach out to take it, but he draws it to his chest again.

I scowl at his juvenile tactic.

He grins more, and then he scans the room for the third time, his mind seemingly reeling, but I see the smile behind his eyes. "Say something nice about me, and I'll give you the wine."

I think he's testing to see how far this "compliment" situation will go on his birthday. I fully meant to be kinder to him today, for the sake of celebrating him. But it's difficult to compliment a man whose ego outsizes the room. "You're not a horrible lover," I start, even forcing a tight smile.

He drinks *my* wine. Ugh. "You can do better than that, Miss *Highest* Honors."

I cross my ankles. He uses his foot to spread them open, my knees parted. My chest expands in a deep inhale, his dominance so apparent and unyielding. "You're tall," I say.

He drinks more from my glass, consuming about half. I love and hate that burgeoning, conceited grin. I love and hate his good looks: polished in black slacks and a white button-down, his wavy brown hair styled, his skin smooth with charming eyes and a self-satisfied mouth.

"I'm waiting." He swishes the wine, cupping both glasses, but he focuses just on mine.

"Your dick is huge." I press my lips together.

He laughs once. "That's a fact, darling. It's not what I want from you." He swigs another fourth of my wine.

I let out a breath. "You're demanding when you want to be." He almost raises the glass to his lips again, but I speak quickly. "And you're so brilliant and attractive; it becomes maddening"—my heart pumps faster—"that someone like you exists, and that you should be here in *our* bedroom, that we should share a bedroom at all—it's unreal and the most fulfilling life I could ever think to dream." I whisper, "I'm tragically in love with you, and I wouldn't want it any other way."

He clasps my hand and lifts me to my feet. I watch him pour his wine into my glass, filling it entirely before passing it to me. He sets his empty glass on the vanity behind me, the silence winding more and more tension. I take a small sip, my body already warm and flushed.

His hand rests on my lower back. I hold his gaze, imagining we're alone in a ballroom together, dressed accordingly, prepared to conquer the world. He asks, "And how does time act on my birthday?"

Time.

"It's malleable," I breathe. There is no carriage ready to morph into a pumpkin at midnight. I'd push tonight into the morning.

My words seem to move him, his lips meeting mine first. He kisses me slowly, then more forcefully, lasting a brief moment that sets my pulse on fire. He rotates me to the vanity and pries the wine from my fingers. He sets the glass on the floorboards, out of reach. "Put your palms flat on the surface," he orders.

I push some of my Chanel perfume bottles aside and then place my palms on the wood, my back still straight.

He leaves for a second, his warmth edging further away from me. Through my vanity mirror, I see him slip into the closet. When he returns, he carries more than a few items: a belt, a diamond collar, a tie, and, of course, handcuffs. Of everything, the belt worries me the most. He's never hit me with one, and it's not a particular fantasy of mine.

We have small floggers, but if he uses them, it's to tease me, never to whip me. I have a threshold of pain that stays at pain and never verges into pleasure.

He knows this, but the belt still causes alarm. "Connor," I say, "I don't want to be whipped."

His legs knock into the backs of mine, pushing me further against the wooden edge. The force slides the stool underneath the vanity. "I know, Rose." He kisses the nape of my neck once—no, twice, my pulse thrumming for more.

Then he sets the diamond collar beside my flattened palm and instead hooks the *belt* around my neck, tight but not suffocating me. He wraps the end around his fist, the visual more stimulating than I thought it'd be, my leg muscles constricting and heart skipping every other beat.

"Your punishment," he says in the pit of my ear. And then I feel the soft fabric of his tie around my eyes. He knots it behind my head. I'm blind to his movements, but I *feel* him slowly, so slowly, unzip my gown, cold pricking my bare back.

He shifts the fabric off my shoulders, uncovering my arms. I can sense my breasts being fully exposed, my nipples hardening as his large, masculine hands travel across my skin. I may not have a bra on, but I do wear panties. They're something I've never worn before. I meant to one time, but I chickened out and changed before he saw.

I thought tonight would be perfect since there is no way in hell

I'd ever wear them again. But now I can't even see his reaction with this stupid blindfold.

I lift it above my eyes as he pinches one of my nipples. Connor catches me through the mirror, and he spanks me, so hard that I careen forward, my hip bones digging into the wooden edge. A gasp tickles my throat, and I think I'm sufficiently soaked now.

He tugs the tie down. "Don't touch this."

"I'll wear it in a second," I refute, about to pull it back up to my head. *I have to see your reaction to my panties, goddammit.*

His brows furrow, curious now as to my odd demands. While he's thinking, he unbuttons his shirt, and I absorb every little curve of his defined muscles. He sheds his shirt and rewraps the belt around his fist. His gaze suddenly trains on my ass. He knows he has to finish undressing me.

And then my vision darkens once more, the tie covering my eyes. "Connor—"

"If you want to negotiate, you need to give me something in return. That's how deals are made."

He has to be so technical. Though, I usually am too. He tugs my dress further down my waist, basically telling me I have five seconds to put in an offer. "If you remove this blindfold, I'll . . . let you hit me with the belt." I cringe as soon as the words escape.

"No," he rejects my offer. I'm sure he wants me to shut up . . .

"You can gag me with the tie."

"Okay," he agrees, but he never removes the tie. Instead, he yanks my gown to my ankles. I swear his entire body tenses against me, and I instantly pull the blindfold to my forehead, witnessing his expression through the mirror.

Connor rubs his lips as though to hide a grin, but it's overtaking his face, consuming his features and escalating with each second. I wear simple boy-short black panties, but the ass says: *I LOVE CONNOR COBALT!*

There's even a lipstick print beside his name.

It's the biggest ego stroke. "Stop smiling," I say, out of instinct. I huff. "I mean . . . smile, laugh, make fun—" He suddenly tightens the tie around my mouth until I'm biting it.

His lips skim my cheek. "Do you see me making fun of you?"

I shake my head, and I feel his hand cup my ass. *Oh God.* His fingers snake across my panties, right between my legs. My feet try and fail to constrict in my rigid heels.

"Step out of your dress," he commands, his gaze planted on my ass. His growing desire stirs mine even more. He squeezes the right part of me before spanking again. "Move, Rose."

I choke on a breath before I step out of the fabric. He doesn't just chuck the gown aside. He picks it up as if it's another one of my limbs (it might as well be), and he carefully sets it on a nearby chair. Then he bends down and removes both of my heels, which brace my feet a certain way. My orgasms are always more heightened without them.

And then he handcuffs my wrists together. "You want to see how fucking hard I am, Rose?" he asks. *Yes.* My chest collapses and lifts aggressively. He removes his black pants and his boxer briefs, his cock so rigid that I can practically feel the fullness before he even pushes in.

I'm so wet that his fingers stroke my clit beneath my panties for one minute, and I already clench over and over. His name and my cries are muffled through the tie. While my head spins, he pulls me back by the hips. My forearms hit the wood, more bent over, and he spreads my legs open so my ass is in his possession, the typeface on my panties in his view.

He leans his body forward while tugging back at the belt. The leather digs into my windpipe, causing my eyes to flutter. His erection presses against me, and I ache for him to thrust inside.

His warm breath hits my ear. "I'm going to fuck my name on your ass." He plans to keep my panties on as much as possible. He brushes aside the fabric, just enough on the bottom to where he can slip in . . . and he does. Slowly. So slowly that the pressure mounts like a spark eating a fuse line.

I moan and may accidentally say the word "God" more than once, but it comes out garbled with the tie. *Connor.* I catch the arousal in his face from the mirror, his focus on my ass, and his arms clutching me with this neediness that I desire in bed. I want to be wanted, and this man completely, utterly wants me.

Before he rocks and creates that friction, he lowers his head to my cheek again. "Since time is malleable, this will last until I've watched you come so many times that you pass out."

I moan again, the blood rushing out of my head. He thrusts hard. I cry, trying to grip the vanity for support. My fingernails scrape the wood. He thrusts again, and I'm already on the verge of coming. I'm so full of him that I can barely even move.

He bites my shoulder blade, the sensations driving me insane. He slaps me. He chokes me with the leather. He pulls my hair. He plays with every intimate part of me, thrusting against my ass, my love *written* across it for him to see.

I come, practically screaming into the tie, my teeth clenched down on it. He's so quick, lifting me onto the vanity and ripping off my panties. He spreads my legs open and fucks me again, my wrists cuffed. His lips are above mine, and he lowers to them to kiss me. Rocking inside, further, deeper. The momentum and pulsing builds me higher once again. When he's not kissing me, he whispers French between deep, pleasured grunts, some murmured rapidly in the pit of my ear.

I can't translate any of it, my mind on a whirlwind.

We switch positions again, so he has access to my ass, and I kneel on the stool, forearms back on the wooden surface. He stands behind me, gripping my ass as he pounds. My whole body is paradoxically numb and on fire. He removes the tie from my mouth and then spanks me again and again, the sting mounting on top of all the others.

"How long . . ." I choke. I can't do this for much longer. The intensity keeps heightening.

His teeth nip my ear. "Until you pass out."

I pulse and clench, my muscles cinching everywhere. "Connor!"

He groans at my aroused cry, but he's not even close to being finished. As my eyelids struggle to rise, he taps my cheek, not quite a slap, but enough to wake me up. My lips swell beneath his. I kiss him, and I fall into his possession once more.

M y ass hurts from being spanked. I'm so exhausted and spent. That is all I think when Connor effortlessly carries me to our bathroom. I can barely hold on to him, but he adjusts me so my head rests against his bare chest.

Connor sets me in the tub, already filled with warm water. My sore muscles ooze and begin to uncoil. I think I even let out an audible sigh. I open my eyes just enough to see him. He kneels beside the tub, his lips reddened from kissing and his skin coated in a thin layer of sweat.

He strokes my hair back, gentle and caring. "How do you feel?"

I wonder what time it is and when I passed out. "How do you think I feel?" I know answering a question with a question annoys him, but it slipped. And technically his birthday has literally come and then gone; no more regurgitation of compliments at his will.

He grins, recognizing this too.

I bring my knee up, and my muscles scream in protest. I wince, and he leans over the tub and massages my thigh beneath the water.

"*Tenez-moi,*" I whisper. *Hold me.*

Already naked, he climbs into the large tub and sinks beside me. He wraps his arm around my shoulder and he pulls me onto him, until I'm half draped across his body. I rest my cheek against his collarbone, listening to his pulse slow in relaxation with mine.

After a few minutes of quiet, Connor taking care of my aches and pains with a softer hand, he says, "Thank you."

Thank you. I try to translate its deeper meaning, but my mind has been spun around and fucked for too long. I fight to keep my eyes open. "It must've been the best sex you've ever had." For me, it was in our top five.

"It wasn't about the sex," he says, so faintly that I almost miss it.

"What, then?"

"You tried harder yesterday to please me more than you ever have, and . . ." He pauses in realization. "I've never wanted to miss out on rare moments in life, and every year with you, on my birthday, I've been escaping one." He adds softly, "This was perfect."

I begin to smile, clutching onto him more. "You truly believe that?"

He nods, the sincerity washing over his face, and then he kisses my forehead, leaving a warm imprint even after his lips withdraw. My eyes are nearly shut as he whispers, "And Rose?"

"Yes?" I breathe.

"I'm tragically in love with you too."

Twenty-four

Rose Cobalt

We don't have time for this," I say pointedly, a phrase that flexes his muscles in annoyance. I straddle Connor Cobalt on my vanity stool, more in control and more unsure than I like to be. His semi-hard cock digs into my crotch, letting me know one of us is having fun.

He checks his watch. "We have thirty minutes."

I inhale a breath of confidence and then scoot closer to him. His fingers splay in my hair, holding my head steady while my lips descend to his neck. His large hand practically engulfs the back of my head. His firm grip reminds me that he has *some* control here. It's not all on me.

This lights my core, but it doesn't numb the fact that my tongue is on his skin. I kiss him gently, not sure what else to do.

I've never really kissed Connor here, not like how I need to right now.

My tongue laps at his nape with uncertainty. He massages my scalp, as though to say, *come on, darling,* in a caring yet fierce manner. If he could give himself a hickey, I'm sure he'd prefer that over me being hesitant and uncomfortable.

"Harder," he demands. He fists a chunk of my hair and pulls. The pressure steals my breath for a moment.

I lift my lips off his skin, and a frustrated noise—like a dying hyena—breaches my throat. "This is a stupid idea," I complain. "Teenagers give each other hickies. Stupid, idiotic, hormone-induced teenagers."

I just feel so silly and uncertain each time I kiss his neck, my confidence depleting like some fiend is vacuuming it right from my soul. I hate feeling this way, so I usually avoid the tasks that put me in this position.

Sucking on his neck until it reddens and bruises is definitely one of them.

"You just called Daisy stupid," he tells me with the arch of one brow. She's nineteen. A teenager. And like all of my sisters, she has absolutely no problem giving Ryke giant "pleasurable" welts.

I scowl. "Stop twisting my words. My *teeth* are near your neck."

"Do you plan to bite me?" he asks seriously. "Go ahead, Rose." He knows I won't, so his smile grows and my eyes narrow. I want nothing more than to wipe his grin off his face. You know what . . .

I press my hand against his mouth; at least I don't have to look at it. And then I *feel* his lips rise in a smile beneath my palm, but I don't retract my hand.

"You should just give me a hickey," I say. "Between the two of us, you're obviously more hormonal." I shift on his lap, referring to his erection that presses up against me. I don't mention how it's starting to affect me, the pulse between my legs beating in sync with my heart.

He lets out a ragged noise, one he tries to contain. His hands settle low on my ass, where my black dress rises, my bare flesh exposed. I drop my hand off his mouth, needing to hear his response.

"Your argument lacks evidence, darling," he tells me, his palm dipping down my inner thigh. I snatch his wrist before he touches my lace panties to deduce how wet I am.

I am wet, okay. But I'd rather him not smirk in satisfaction. *I am satisfied by the appearance of his erection. Let me gloat.*

His brow arches again, more combatively.

"We don't have time for you to gather evidence and cross-examine witnesses and consult a jury," I refute. We're supposed to be at the hospital soon.

Three days ago, Ryke underwent the liver transplant surgery with his father. Before Ryke was rolled away, he hardly spoke. He just said a few *I love you*s to my littlest sister, and I heard him say one to his brother.

We all took off work and stayed in the waiting room. Hours later, we learned that everything had gone smoothly between the donor and the recipient, and we could finally see Ryke. He was groggy and nauseous from the anesthesia, but he was alive and healthy, still saying "fuck" every sentence or so.

Since cameramen have practically set up camp outside of the hospital, eager for photos of the five of us entering and exiting, Connor and I devised a strategy to stir more media attention off Jane and Moffy and onto us.

A simple task: Get Connor photographed with red welts on his neck.

Only problem: I have to put them there.

"Let's use makeup," I offer suddenly. It's the perfect solution. I almost swing my leg off his lap, but his hands tighten on my hips.

"The media may not care if it's real," he says, "but people online will be able to dissect the photos and discover a farce."

My lips draw into a flat line, my pulse about to follow. How do I do this with confidence and without feeling like a sloppy, horny teenager?

Connor's deep-blue eyes fill mine, and then in a swift movement, he lifts me up in his arms, my legs around his waist as he stands. I think he may drop me to my feet, call it quits, but instead, he hooks his ankle to the vanity stool, dragging it halfway across the room. He stops right in front of our ornate full-length mirror.

Fuck me.

This is even worse.

My eyes sear his skull, branding exclamation points across his brain. He sits on the stool with me on his lap, as though we've been here all along. He takes my chin in his large hand. "I'm going to do you first," he says. "Watch and learn." Those last words should sound condescending, but they don't. He's being serious.

And I realize Connor is tutoring me.

He ties my hair into a pony, holding my gaze for a moment. I think I would've allowed him to teach me as a teenager too, even though we were competitors. I'm not sure I would've listened all that much or been a very compliant student, but I would've tried.

His thumb skims my bottom lip before he leans into my neck and kisses the soft flesh. I focus on the mirror, able to watch his lips close over my skin, his tongue gliding before sucking *hard*. An uncontrollable moan escapes me, a sharp breath attached. His fingers squeeze the base of my neck, and his teeth nip at my skin.

My body throbs just watching.

He moves as though he's meant to give pleasure, never unsure, not silly or inept at the task. He's a man emblazoned with confidence and power that I want to mimic and then surpass.

I absorb every little action, every lift of his head. I count the seconds he sucks and the moment his teeth bore into my skin. My eyelids flutter as his hand lowers and pinches one of my nipples.

I slap his thigh. "I'm trying to concentrate."

He grins into the next kiss.

It lasts for a few more minutes before he raises his head. He rubs my neck with his thumb, the spot reddening. "You'll need to put makeup on to hide this," he tells me.

I nod. This was just a demonstration, and he's been very adamant about dolling out equal tasks to stir the media. *It's my turn*, he told me with resolution.

His eyes set on my lips. "Let's see how good of a student you are, Miss Highest Honors." He caresses my cheek with the stroke of his thumb, and my lips part with a heady breath. He slips his thumb into my mouth, and I feel his cock grow underneath me. It pours confidence through my bones.

When his thumb leaves my lips, wet and glistening, I scoot forward, grinding on him, and then I press my mouth to his neck.

Every move he made, I repeat, trying to outperform him. I press my hand on the back of his neck, clutching him, and my fingers dig into his skin. I graze my teeth along his nape, tugging at his flesh.

He watches my precise movements in the mirror. I only stumble once, when he shifts my panties, his hand on its own mission between our bodies.

"Keep going," he commands.

His fingers fill me first, and my thighs tighten around him. Then I feel something larger replace his fingers, something harder . . . I gasp into his neck as he pushes his erection into me.

He holds the back of my head, forcing me stationary at his neck.

"Rose," he says sternly.

"You're the one who went off topic, Richard—" I cry as he rocks *up*, gripping my hips. How long have I been sucking his neck? Numbers flash through my head with curse words and more exclamation points.

Fuck me.

"Harder," I choke.

"Rose," he snaps, his movements ceasing.

I'm a terrific multitasker, so this theoretically should be within my capabilities. We have little time before we need to leave, and he's attempting to kill two birds with one stone. However, my mind keeps shutting off in favor of an incoming climax. "We don't have time," I suddenly say, my voice raspy.

His jaw tics in irritation. He guides my head back to his neck. "Do what you feel, not just what you saw." I listen and suck again, my body warm and pulsing. I find myself rocking against him since he's motionless, *needing* that friction between my legs. I never question or hesitate this time.

And then he clasps my hips again, so strongly that I stop rocking, and he moves his pelvis up and down, his cock sliding in and out in hard, deep waves. *Fuck.*

I kiss him to the pulse of this fiery, vigorous rhythm. Both of us connect on another level, one meant only for two people who love winning together.

But the cautious side of me will always fear for the day where we both lose.

Twenty-five

Connor Cobalt

I ride up the hospital elevator with Lo. The three girls drove separately so they could drop Jane and Moffy off at Poppy's house. None of us even considered bringing a seven-month-old and an eight-month-old into a hospital, and thankfully Rose's older sister has no issue babysitting for a couple hours.

"Read his order to me," Lo says, digging through the Lucky's Diner take-out bag.

I scroll through the group text between Lo, Ryke and me.

Chili fries, jalapeño poppers and a Philly steak with onions, mushrooms, peppers and cheddar cheese.—Ryke

Also if they still have quiche, get a slice of that too.—Ryke

Plus extra mustard . . . and get me a Reuben. I can save it for tomorrow if I'm still in this fucking hellhole.—Ryke

I read his requests aloud. ". . . quiche, extra mustard, and a Reuben," I finish, slipping my phone into my khaki pants pocket. Ryke eats more than the hospital provides him, so we're trying to rectify this. He'd use food as an incentive to stand up and sprint down the street to a local diner, splitting open his stitches.

However, we can't remedy his other need. To climb mountains, to work out, to run.

"Fuck," Lo curses, pulling out a wrapped sandwich to peer deeper in the bag. "Did you say extra mustard?"

"Yes." I remember specifically telling the cashier for more.

"There's none." His jaw sharpens, and he chucks the sandwich back in, rolling the top of the paper bag in frustration.

"He won't notice." The elevator rises slowly.

Lo looks younger today, in jeans and a black V-neck. "Maybe." His eyes drift to me, landing on my neck, noticing the hickeys for the fifth time. I wait for his cringe to appear again.

There it is.

His brows knot and face scrunches. "I keep imagining this robotic succubus latching onto you, because the Rose I know"—he shakes his head in disbelief—"would *never* give anyone a hickey, husband or not." Worry flashes in his amber eyes as if he's thinking for a brief second that I might've cheated on my wife.

In his mind, he can't see me with anyone other than her, but he's having trouble drawing a realistic conclusion. So he paired me with a robot.

"I can be persuasive," I remind him.

"You know, I'd never even seen Rose kiss someone in public until you."

"She likes her privacy." We've lost almost all of it, but what we outwardly project for the tabloids isn't entirely real. What we do alone in our bedroom is, and still, we've lost some of those moments through the sex tapes. It's complicated, but I knew this life would be.

Lo motions to my neck. "Then she's going to chop off your balls for not covering that shit." Cameramen bombarded us when we entered the hospital, so it's clear to him that it'll be in some tabloid. Regardless of a hickey, there would be articles about us, but it's important that they're spun around us, not the kids.

Without our interference, they could say: *Where are Jane and*

Moffy? Are Rose and Lily neglecting their children? Why aren't they seen anywhere?

It doesn't always work, but that's why this is a test. "I'll protect my balls. Don't worry, darling." I wink.

He laughs, more lighthearted. We exit the elevator and walk down the hallway, already signed in. I find his room quickly, and when I swing open the door, we catch Ryke in a compromising position.

"Bro!" Lo shouts, pushing ahead of me.

Ryke is on the concrete floor doing push-ups, his bare ass peeking out of his flimsy blue hospital gown. "Fuck off," Ryke grunts as he lowers his body weight, his arms flexed as he raises himself back up.

"Frankly, I'm not surprised," I chime in. "I thought we would've had to check the pound on day two. Mooning the room isn't even that bad."

Ryke shoots me a glare on his next rep, his IV stand on wheels beside him. "Remember that time you were cuffed beside the canned fruit and hamburger buns?"

I almost wear my irritation. "It's amusing you mention *buns*." I glance once at his ass for reference.

Ryke doesn't give a shit. In fact, he does a one-handed push-up and flashes me the middle finger with the other.

He continues to do whatever he wants to do. Per the usual.

I walk deeper into the hospital room and sit on the stiff chair beside the bed. The privacy curtains shroud the second empty bed. The other patient, a gallbladder removal, left yesterday afternoon— so he's not subjecting someone else to his nude workout.

Lo squats in front of his brother and waves the Lucky's bag. "I'm going to toss this out of the goddamn window if you don't stop."

Ryke instantly snatches the bag as he stands to his feet.

Lo pats his brother on the shoulder. "Cute socks."

I laugh into a grin. Ryke has to wear white compression stockings to help with blood flow, but I'm sure his constant trips out of bed help his circulation enough.

"Fuck you," Ryke says lightly. He sits on the edge of his bed, already scouring the bag's contents.

Lo takes a seat next to him. "Really though, were you coherent when the doctor said you could damage your spleen and need a second operation?"

Ryke pops a fry into his mouth. "I was coherent, and I also heard him tell me that they didn't damage any of my fucking organs during surgery." He pulls out a wad of napkins from the bag. "I can't hurt my spleen on my own. The surgeons would've had to majorly fuck up three days ago, and they didn't."

I lean back. "An infection is still entirely possible."

Lo nods a couple times.

Ryke glares once at me before eating another fry. "I'm fucking fine. I should be out of here tonight—"

"No." Lo cuts him off with a darkened look. "You're supposed to be in here for at least six days." They've never been in this role reversal: Ryke being the invalid. Loren being the healthy one. Neither is doing well by the switch.

To alleviate the tension (what I do best), I say, "There is a pair of communal handcuffs floating around our house somewhere. I'd be happy to pay it forward and cuff you to your bed."

Ryke unwraps his Philly cheesesteak. "How about—fuck off."

Well, I tried. He's never been cooperative when subjects circumnavigate around him. He's just used to dealing with his personal life in private and his weaknesses by himself. I can understand that, but he has people that care about him now.

He's not alone anymore.

Lo scratches the back of his neck. "You haven't been running, have you?"

Ryke eats his sandwich, staying quiet.

Lo stares faraway at the ground, shaking his head a few times and cracking his knuckles. Ryke meets my gaze once, and I raise my brows at him like *you have to talk about it*. He can't shut Lo out, not after all of the strides they've made in their relationship.

Ryke takes a swig from his water bottle. "I tried to run once, and the nurses stopped me."

"Good," Lo snaps.

Ryke digs deeper in the Lucky's bag. "Did you forget the mustard?"

Lo turns to me with an expression that I read as *what were you saying back in that elevator? Oh, wait, you were wrong.*

I pass over the mustard inaccuracy. "How exactly did the nurses stop you?" I wonder, trying to picture this act.

"They said stop and I fucking stopped."

"Did they pat your head and say *good boy* too?"

Lo laughs.

Ryke glowers.

"What kind of treat did they give you? A belly rub?"

Lo chimes in, "Did that feel good, bro?"

Ryke throws a greasy fry covered in chili at me and then at Loren. It stains my navy sweater. I'm not necessarily happy about it, but I knew it was the risk of teasing him. Ryke is fond of projectiles, and food lies in his vicinity.

He checks the closed door over his shoulder, his body tensing in seriousness. "How has Daisy been sleeping at night? I've asked her a few times, but she just tells me not to worry."

Lo looks to me, unsure of how to answer. Daisy has trouble sleeping alone from her PTSD, and the first night, Rose checked on her at three in the morning. All the lights were on in Daisy's bedroom down in the basement. Rose said that she was wide-awake, alarmed by the smallest noises, so Rose has been sleeping in her bed to keep her company.

Last night, both Lo and I rushed in at two in the morning to her terrified screams. Rose struggled to calm her little sister down, and Daisy was adamant that a man was peering through her window.

We checked, and no one was outside.

"Rose said that Daisy tosses and turns a lot." I offer this information, wary to give the rest. I think Daisy is part of the reason he wants to leave by tonight. "They're on their way here, so you'll see her."

Ryke looks sick to his stomach. He actually stops eating, his sandwich on his lap. "Could Rose tell how long she slept?"

"Maybe four hours." *Or less.* "The more she sees Frederick, the better he'll be able to discern what type of medication she needs to sleep."

Ryke nods a couple times, and someone knocks before the door blows open. I expect the girls, but it's actually two nurses dressed in white scrubs: an older woman with glasses around her neck and a younger, blonde girl—possibly a nursing student.

"What's all of this now?" the older woman asks, scrutinizing the assortment of greasy food.

"Sustenance," Lo says with a dry half smile.

"Right," the older nurse snorts, still trying to determine whether she should collect the food as contraband.

The young nurse focuses solely on Ryke with a curious gaze that I've seen often from fans. She plucks his chart off the end of the bed and flips through the papers. "His digestion has been doing well, no problems with his intestines, so the extra food should be fine."

"No shit," Lo jokes to his brother. "I wouldn't be surprised if this combination gives you the runs." He gestures to the chili and the cheesesteak. Ryke shoves his brother's arm playfully.

I'm waiting for the older nurse to yell at the student about confidentiality and not being allowed to share his condition in front of visitors. The older nurse never says a word, pumping up Ryke's pain meds through the IV.

"All right, you can keep the food," the older nurse says. "Maybe we can have you boys sign some things for us too? I have a niece who is obsessed with *Princesses of Philly*."

Lo takes control. "No problem," he says. "The girls will probably be happy to sign stuff too."

"Really?" Her face lights up. "That's so sweet of you."

I almost laugh, but instead cover it with an amiable smile. "Sweet" isn't a word I'd use to describe Loren.

The younger nurse sets the chart back at the edge of the bed. "Do you think the show will ever get a second season?"

Before Ryke and Loren say no, I beat them and tell her, "We're actually considering it."

Her smile stretches her face, one she can't contain. I can tell that she's biting the inside of her cheeks to try. "That'd be really amazing."

Ryke and Loren look a little pissed and frustrated, understanding that we have to keep a level of mystery. Scott needs to think we're still mulling over a season two, and sending a definitive *no* out into the world, even by a small rumor, will make gaining his trust harder for me.

"Before I go, do you need anything else Ryke?" the young nurse asks. "Have you been in pain at all?"

He meets her gaze, and I've been around Ryke long enough to read his level of interest in a girl. Since he's been serious with Daisy, he's never seemed to think twice about someone else.

"I'm fucking fantastic, which is why I need to get out of here tonight." He's not reciprocating anything with her, not even accidentally throwing mixed signals. His thoughts are with his girl-friend.

"You know that's not possible," she says. The older nurse

passes my chair and then exits, as though she's been paged somewhere else.

"That's what I've been telling him." Lo twists his wedding band. It's an anxious habit, a giveaway that says he's craving a drink.

Ryke follows my gaze and notices the sign from his brother. He sighs heavily. "I'll be out of here in two more days, then?"

"That's possible." She nods. "We just need to keep watching your vitals. If you take it easy but keep walking *gently* around, you'll be out of here in no time."

Ryke wraps his sandwich back and places it in the bag. "I'll do that, then." He's letting go of this fight for his brother. Strangely, his love for Lo may be what helps him stop from getting an infection.

If my mother were alive and could see this, I'd show it to her as evidence: love benefiting someone's health. It's tangible enough that she might've accepted it, as I do now.

When the nurse leaves, Lo says, "She seemed like your type." I hear the warning in his voice.

Lo can't read Ryke as well as I can, which is why they need to communicate through words to avoid fighting. That's not easy for either of them, but thankfully they've grown better at expressing themselves to each other.

Ryke sets the bag of food aside on a tray table. "Who?"

"You didn't notice the blonde nurse?"

"So you think because you've seen me date—what—*three* blondes, that's my thing?" Ryke asks, swaying a little from the pain meds. This is amusing.

I rest my ankle on my thigh, watching my current entertainment for today. "He's right," I tell Lo. "I could give you the percentage of women he's dated according to hair color, and the blonde ratio is small. I'd do the math in my head, but honestly, I don't care enough."

Ryke rolls his eyes and they somehow land on my neck. "What the fuck is that?"

"I think your species calls it *woof woof.*"

Lo bursts out laughing.

Ryke is too doped up to join in.

"It's a hickey," I say. "And yes, Rose gave it to me. And yes, I forgot to cover it up before I left."

"So the tabloids caught you?" He shakes his head slowly. "You forgot? *You.*" He points at me.

Lo snorts with another laugh attached.

"I know it's incredibly hard to believe." Because it's not true. "But I was running late. Time essentially bested me." Which has happened before. His pain medication may be on my side today.

He seems mildly disbelieving still. "The whole thing is fucking weird."

Lo nods in agreement. "Didn't Daisy get caught with a hickey once?"

"But that was . . ." He's about to say, *that was Daisy. This is about Rose and Connor.* He grimaces at his own words. It's not fair to say that Rose can't do something that other women can, simply because she's set a precedent for being uptight and high-strung.

Truthfully though, it's the reality. Once you change your nature, people question.

Ryke lets it go, resting an arm on his brother's shoulder. "You know what my type is?" And he wears a drugged smile, his lips slowly lifting at the edges. "Daisy Calloway."

I've known that all along.

Some attraction is easier to spot than others. Theirs may be so outwardly apparent, but Rose's attraction to me and mine with her is faint to most. It's making these articles more popular for the press to pick up and run.

Ryke's smile slowly wanes, her name bringing concern for these past few days again. He runs a hand through his thick hair. "I hate being away."

"Yeah, but shit happens, right?" Lo says. "You have to let her figure out how to deal with some nights on her own." He pauses. "You have two more days here. At least you're not away for three goddamn months."

The air thins a little. When Loren went to rehab, he left Lily for three months, around the time when she was struggling with her own addiction.

Ryke stares at the floor. "You know what's funny?" he says, his voice deep and raw. "When I was looking after Lily while you were away, I gave her such a hard fucking time." He makes a growling noise. "If anyone did that to Dais . . ." He shakes his head. "I'm such a fucking asshole."

Lo puts his hand on his shoulder. "Welcome to the goddamn club."

"I'll happily decline my membership," I tell both of them.

Ryke rolls his eyes and Lo just laughs.

The tension breaks, but in the back of my head, I wonder how long it'll be until one of my friends finds out what Rose and I have been doing with the media, who it'll be, and how many voices will begin to complicate our world.

Twenty-six

Rose Cobalt

I peruse a wall display of dildos and vibrators, my shoulders stiff as I indiscreetly look outside the store windows for the umpteenth time. *Take the photograph, Walter.* My cell never buzzes in confirmation, so I have to meander around the shelves longer.

I snatch a leather whip off a dominatrix display and twirl it around, feeling a little destructive today. This isn't my first time in an adult store. In college, I went a few times, when there weren't cameramen chasing me and the only people who really cared about my business were nosy women in my mother's social circle.

Online shopping may be more discreet, but I like being informed about my product choices. The employees here know more than I do about sex toys. Growing up, I never had mental blocks at the idea of masturbating, but I always froze at being intimate with someone else.

"Cool . . . yeah, man. Just give Lily and Lo space. The more you crowd around them, the less likely they are to do it. I'll talk to them for you, okay?" It sounds nothing like my husband, but yet, that's his voice. He crests the corner at the end of my aisle with his cell braced to his ear.

I twirl my whip with a hotter stare. I imagine Scott on the other line with Connor, and little minions with pitchforks dance across my brain. I recognize that Connor is partially putting on this charade for me. He could live with the sex tapes. I'm the one who can't.

I'm thankful to have someone like Connor, who'd be willing to do whatever it takes so that I don't have to. I can't fake it as well as him. If I come into contact with Scott again, I'd maul his face off.

I snap the whip, and it cracks in the air.

Connor's brow arches, but agitation coats his face at whatever Scott is saying. I can see it surface as he rubs his lips. He plasters on a cheerful, congenial voice. "Golf on Saturday works for me, just don't go too hard. I haven't played in a year." His eyes rise to mine.

I mouth, *ew.*

He grins. "See you then." He hangs up.

"What two kings sit on the thrones of England and France at the beginning of *A Tale of Two Cities*?" I ask him. "You have one minute." I crack the whip again.

His lips keep lifting upwards, his usual arrogance returning. Normally I'd scoff at it, but I do love this part of him, definitely after his fake conversation. I'm happy to see the real sides emerge.

"George III and Louis XVI," he answers correctly.

"Congratulations, you've saved yourself from a twenty-four-hour silent treatment." I inspect the length of the whip and accidentally glance at the store windows again.

Connor approaches me, his hand slipping to the small of my back. In one sensual, seamless action, he kisses me and nips my bottom lip between his teeth. It would be amazing—if I didn't descend into my head. I go rigid and spot the cashier watching us from the register, the shelves too low to hide us.

"Relax," Connor whispers. PDA is hard for me. I understand it's laughable that I struggle to kiss my husband in public when sex tapes of us are online, but I can block some of that out.

This is right now. Physically all me. Here.

"The store is nearly empty." He can read my little insecurities. Connor called ahead and asked the manager to clear out the customers in exchange for their store being featured in *Celebrity Crush* tomorrow.

It worked, and we had to take off lunch on a Friday afternoon to avoid suspicion from Ryke, Lily, Loren and Daisy. Our bodyguards cover the door, so it's clear that no one will interrupt us.

I toss my silky brown hair off my shoulder and inspect the whip again, a little dazed. "Do you prefer me this way?" I ask him. "Have you always wanted me to be outwardly affectionate?"

Connor tilts my chin, and his deep-blue eyes barrel into me with sincerity. "No," he says. "I love you the way you are. I don't want to change you, but—"

"I know." I nod. He doesn't have to say anymore. This is the last incriminating photo that we need to set up for Walter Aimes and *Celebrity Crush*. We're done with exclusive pictures after this, our debt paid. Now the tabloid won't post the story about doubting Moffy's paternity test.

But it doesn't completely end for us.

We still plan to bolster the media by acting out. More PDA. More random baggie drops of powdered sugar. It's been working, keeping the articles focused on our relationship rather than our children.

"I want Jane to have a sister," I whisper. I'd step outside of my comfort zone a million times over just to give my daughter more in life. This has to work.

Connor draws me to his chest, holding me close. *"J'en suis sûr." I'm sure she will.*

Both of our phones buzz. Walter took the photograph?

Move closer to the rack on the right side. I don't have a good angle.—WA

Ugh. Connor easily clasps my hand and guides me. All the

while I drag the whip across the floor. I'll buy it, just for dirtying the thing, but in no way is Connor using it on me.

We stop by the giant wall of multicolored dildos and vibrators. Some luxury brands, others much cheaper.

"Find anything you like?" Connor asks, partially serious.

I've *never* been in a sex store with him. "I like this," I lie, in a cold voice, waving the whip near his ass.

He steals it from me, and I glare.

"That was mine, Richard."

"And now it's mine," he teases. Then he snaps the whip, the *crack* much louder, echoing like a gunshot. The hairs on my arms rise, my legs turned to gelatin. He carries a whip like he's the king of the fucking underworld.

"So now you're a thief," I refute, having to clear my throat once. He shouldn't be this attractive in a sex store, and what's more infuriating—he knows he is.

"If we weren't married, then yes, I'd be considered a thief." He turns back to the wall of toys.

I scowl. He always has to one-up me. I'll beat him, make him uncomfortable for once. Game on. I scan the wall and remove the largest of the dildos, big and fat, also a shade of blue. Its girth alone looks insanely miserable. My vagina quivers in warning like *hell no.*

I check the tag: *horse cock.*

I swear I'm not lying.

I rotate to Connor. He's not the least bit flustered.

"For you," I say with a tight smile. I'm joking, I think. I swallow hard as his smile fades, staring impassively at me. In the back of my brain, I wonder if this is something he misses. Not obscenely large dicks, but just them in general. I add, "If you need—"

"Rose." He cuts me off. He glances once at the cashier before lowering his voice to me. "Do you remember when I told you that I used to have sex for two different reasons?"

"For manipulation and for pleasure," I say beneath my breath.

He leans close, his lips skimming my cheek before he whispers a secret. "When I was on bottom, it was *always* for manipulation." He cups my jaw. "I'm not missing anything with you."

I inhale strongly. Translation: *you fill all of my needs.*

Of all the places to have a heart-to-heart . . . it's incredibly disgusting this had to be the location. I set the dildo back, already planning on bathing in a tub of bleach and sanitizer when I return home.

"Sex doesn't make you uncomfortable," I say. I realize I'm fighting a losing battle by trying to unnerve him here.

"Not even for a second." He's so comfortable in his own skin that almost nothing can shake him. I thought I was that way too, but I've been tested too much. I have limitations and things that make me tick.

"I have something I need to show you," he tells me.

My mind spins as I follow beside him, edging closer just to steal back the whip. He gives in, releasing his firm clutch on the leather. I feel powerful with it in hand, but I don't want to actually use it on anyone.

"Please tell me you're guiding me to hand sanitizer."

"I'll take a shower with you when we get home," he tells me. I never thought I'd be married to this man, let alone hear him offering showers with me so casually. Two years have already flown by, and the girl who was worried that she *had* to be dominant in bed (or at least every guy expected it of her) has all but vanished.

I gasp and pause by a rack of edible underwear, made from black licorice. I pick up the thong from the display since the others are in boxes, and I hold it with one finger, snuffing out the image of other dirty hands touching it too.

"You can only have sex with me if I wear this. Mind you, you have to eat it," I say flatly, watching his grin return. "*Or* you have to have sex on top of a grave. Choose."

Most guys wouldn't mind edible panties, but Connor hates licorice. Black licorice tops the list. Still, the other option has worse consequences.

Without hesitation, he says, "I'd fuck you on top of a grave."

I glower, my eyes piercing his forehead. I expected a different answer, forgetting he doesn't always choose what I would. "That's disrespectful and heinous on so many levels." I imagine what kind of horrible karma would haunt me for desecrating a grave.

I set the panties back and fix my hair over one shoulder, freezing. I touched *that* and then my *hair. Don't concentrate on it, Rose.*

"Disrespectful to whom?" Connor asks, leaning a shoulder on the wall. "The dead are dead. They don't care because they physically lack the mental capacity *to* care."

My lips press in a line. I can't say the word "ghosts" as validation. He will use it against me in a thousand acidic ways. I try to drop this conversation, nearing him. I fist his sweater with both hands, a collared button-down underneath the navy fabric, preppy and sophisticated.

And I stare up at him with flaming eyes, my four-inch heels not tall enough to meet him perfectly, but they help. I recite the quote in my most heated voice, "'Cowards die many times before their deaths; the valiant never taste of death but once.'"

He looks aroused, his eyes consuming me. "Shakespeare," he answers correctly. "*Julius Caesar.*" He takes my face in his hand, turning my head so he has access to my ear, the forceful movements speed my pulse. "Why would you quote your least favorite of his plays?" He's intrigued. And turned on.

The power I wield sets me on fire. "It seemed timely," I breathe. "We're discussing death." I smooth my hands over his sweater and then push him once, an inch separating us. "And just so you know, we would be *crushed* by karma and fate and ghosts if we had sex on someone's grave."

So I mentioned ghosts. I don't care. He may not believe, but I do. And in this particular scenario, he's fucking *me* on that grave.

He laughs, his teeth showing from his wide grin.

"Don't use your conceited smile and tell me they're not real. It's called faith, and you have none."

"I have faith," he says. "In myself." I let out a snort. He continues on, "And in you." Fine. "And our friends. In the people I can read and see and understand. I don't have faith in the intangible and the invisible." He rests his hand on the small of my back, restarting our earlier walk to the left side of the store, a little closer to the window, in fact.

His gaze lingers on a shelf, right beside a mannequin dressed in a leather thong and studded bra. The mannequin isn't his focus.

My eyes follow his.

No.

"*No*," I say with the shake of my head. "I'd rather be buried alive with snakes. Or better yet . . ." My imagination runs its course. "You can bury me and then fuck on my grave and I'll come back and haunt *you*."

His brows knot. "Who's killing you in this scenario?"

"Myself. Poison. Maybe a knife to the heart. Or drowning. The options are endless."

"You're not Juliet, and you're not Ophelia." He's basically saying that I'm not living in a Shakespearean play. "And just so *you* know, Rose, hyperboles about killing yourself are now my least favorite."

"You can kill me, then." I tap my heel a couple times. "How about by fire?"

He stares hard at me, no trace of that amused grin.

I straighten, confidence bracing my back like a fortress. "You're the one who brought me here to make a point." I motion to the shelf beside us. "How did you think I was going to take it?"

"I thought you were going to threaten my cock," he says, "not your own life."

My defenses break down. I suppose this is a new one for me. I am all about survival, and the occasional self-sacrifice for the ones I love, not throwing myself onto the burning coals for no real reason. Oh God, was that me throwing a tantrum? Like a weird *hyperbole* tantrum?

No.

I am twenty-six.

I am a strong, independent woman.

But when you visit a sex shop with your husband and he guides you to the anal plug section, you're allowed to say whatever the hell you want.

Anal sex has never been a priority of mine. I've been curious but uninterested. It's a conundrum that I know intrigues Connor.

I let out a breath. "I know every girl is different with anal." I think about my sisters, facts that he already knows, so I don't mind sharing as evidence to my feelings. "Lily *loves* it. Daisy hates it, and Poppy has never tried it. That doesn't make me the Goldilocks of anal sex. It may not be *just right* for me."

He tries to stifle a smile, his lips aching to curve. My blood scorches through my veins. I *almost* grab a plug off the shelf and throw it at his head. I stop myself, remembering there is a cameraman outside.

That would be a terrible picture to land on the front of *Celebrity Crush*. The headline: ROSE COBALT ASSAULTS HER HUSBAND WITH A SEX TOY!!!

"If you laugh," I threaten, "I'm going to rip out your tongue, barbecue it, and then feed it to whatever woodland creature stumbles into our backyard."

He smiles but doesn't produce a laugh. "I appreciate that you directed this hyperbole at me." He leans a shoulder on the wall again. "As for your analogy . . ." He rubs his lips, almost laughing.

I point a warning finger at him. "Give me your tongue."

"Later tonight, darling," he banters. "And statistically speaking, you have the same probability of loving it, hating it, and it being *just right* as anyone else. You just have to try first."

Try.

That's the intimidating part.

I've never wanted to do it, but I can tell he does. I know I might like it. Lily raves too much for me to think it's completely terrible.

A text dings on Connor's cell and then mine.

Got the photo. Thanks.—WA

It's over.

I'm surprised by the incoming disappointment, the drop of my shoulders. Remove the uncleanliness of this event and it was fun. I learned some things about him, and he learned things about me. Even though we're married, exploring each other never really ends.

"Rate me," I say to him, wondering how my acting went.

"C-plus."

I roll my eyes.

"Stop looking over your shoulders and at the windows." Thankfully we won't be feeding anything directly to *Celebrity Crush* anymore. I like that we have more control on what happens.

I snap my whip. It comes perilously close to touching him, a complete accident, and my heart lurches. I drop the thing, but he's irrefutably stoic, unwavering. He picks up the whip and draws me close again.

"And what's my grade?" he asks.

I say what I always do. "F."

"Without bias," he amends.

I'm unable to concede. He can't beat me. "An unbiased F."

He kisses the tip of my nose. It's light and nowhere near as rough as I'd want. He knows this.

"Don't ever do that again." I cringe.

"Be honest."

I scoff. "Fine. I'd give you a B. Are you happy, Richard?"

"Immensely." This time when he kisses me, he grabs the back of my head, his lips parting mine with a breathless wave. *We're in public*, I remember, just once.

It freezes me. He doesn't reduce my grade by a letter, but I would.

Right now, I deserve an ugly D.

Twenty-seven

Rose Cobalt

G et over to Hale Co. *now*." Theo's normally meek voice has turned acidic, burning my ears, the cell pressed way too close. I'm in no mood to be taking orders from anyone, especially at 10 a.m. on a Saturday. But his sudden change in demeanor puts me on guard.

I retract the phone, narrowing my eyes at the air. "I think you're forgetting who the boss is in this relationship."

Just as I say this, Connor exits the bathroom, leaning against the doorframe in nothing but a towel. Beads of water roll down his chest and abs. We had a late morning since Jane kept us up most of the night, wailing and shrieking and being a terror in general. I would still throw myself in front of a speeding vehicle for her, but hopefully that situation won't ever arise.

Connor motions to my phone and mouths, *Theo?*

I nod, pressing the speaker button.

Theo says, "Look, I'm exhausted. The board finally approved what you wanted last night, and this morning it's all about to go to shit."

They signed off on the new CCB labels. It's a win I can't celebrate yet. My head is reeling. "What do you mean?" I find myself touching my sapphire necklace, just like my mom would finger her pearls. I stop immediately, a gross taste in my mouth. *You're not like her, Rose.* I smooth my airy black skirt and roll up the sleeves of my white sweater, hot all of a sudden.

"You and Connor were photographed inside an adult store. It's front-page news this morning on all the tabloids. One of the older board members wants to switch his vote. He's already called an assistant to go into your office and shred the contract on your desk." I don't ask how he's heard this. *He's a shadow*, I remember. He hears things. "I thought you had a good idea, Rose. I really did. It would have worked, but no matter if you seem to still hate this new design, he'd rather not have 'Calloway' attached to the product at all."

My throat bobs. "This isn't anything new," I snap. "I have sex tapes. How does walking into an adult store change my public perception?"

"Your sex tapes aren't really a hot topic right now. You being a new mom and your fashion style—that's why the board believes women admire you and why you have a lot of fans. He's worried this photo will begin to jeopardize your current image."

He thinks I'll lose my fans.

Well, if my fans love me for *me*, then they'll stick around after this photo. This isn't even incriminating, but they're saying it is for someone who designs baby clothes.

Theo continues, "All the other board members are keeping their votes the same. He's more conservative, and unfortunately . . . he's the swing vote."

Translation: *you're fucked, Rose.*

But Theo called me for a reason. He thinks I still have time to fix this problem. Maybe if we sign the contract before his assistant destroys it, the man will concede. Loren will tell him that it's done and to move on.

This is how we win.

"Don't you live five minutes from Hale Co.?" I ask hurriedly.

"Get to the office and email me that contract." I pause, needing to add a larger threat. "If you don't make it there before the other assistant, you're fired."

"I'll sincerely try my best." His sincerity causes a wave of guilt to slam into me. *No.* I am a warrior that must take casualties.

We both hang up.

Connor stares at me, his brows raised as I scroll the *Celebrity Crush* website on my phone. "He's sickeningly nice," I tell Connor. "I honestly thought it was a ploy." Maybe I still do.

"It could be," Connor tells me. I don't hear the concern in his voice, and I wonder if he's pacifying me. In one breath being honest and in the other trying not to worry me.

I need a road map to people's true intentions. It's all way too confusing.

My cell phone screen blinks with answers.

The first headline: [EXCLUSIVE PHOTOS] CONNOR COBALT & ROSE CALLOWAY SPOTTED AT A SEX SHOP! LOOK WHAT THEY BOUGHT!

In addition to a picture of me dangling licorice panties, Walter Aimes snapped photos of Connor checking out. The photographer said he was done taking pictures before this, but clearly not. Maybe he hoped we'd do something out of the ordinary.

Thankfully Connor only bought a bullet vibrator rather than the anal plugs, which he'll purchase later. He mentioned that bit of information when we left the store. To prepare me, I'm sure.

I dazedly sit on the edge of our bed, and Connor sinks down beside me. He reads the article over my shoulder.

"Thanks," I say, "for buying the vibrator." Like hell did I want the world to know that we're going to have anal sex. We may have lost the majority of our privacy, but there are a few things I'd like to keep between us.

Connor rubs the back of my neck. *"Bien sûr."* *Of course.*

I log on to Twitter and check my notifications, curious to see how the world is handling this news.

@CeleryHair: @RoseCCobalt Waiting for your sex toy line to come out. Obvs that photo is research. Amirite?

@PoPhilly4Life: @RoseCCobalt You're a goddess. Seriously love that you don't give a shit about being caught shoppin 4 sexy things with your bae 😍

@LilyHaleLOVE2: @RoseCCobalt You should ask Lils for some sex toy advice. Seems like she knows whats what. Just sayin.

@LindsayL453: @RoseCCobalt You're a fame whore and a slut. Worse than all your sisters combined.

I loved that last tweet. If I can take any of the heat off Lily and Daisy, I'll gladly withstand the flames.

I send out a tweet: there's no fear in pleasure #Coballoway

The hashtag is the name that fans use to designate Connor and me. It's just easier than saying "Rose plus Connor," and I like how it sounds.

I scroll through my feed and notice a flirty Twitter conversation from Ryke and Daisy, tweeted yesterday.

@daisyonmeadows: You know whose scar is as big as my scar now? *wink wink* @meadowsryke

His scar from surgery. And her scar from the Paris riot.

I'm used to these types of conversations between them since we've been on Twitter for a while now.

@meadowsryke: @daisyonmeadows mine is bigger

@daisyonmeadows: @meadowsryke prove it;)

I imagine their texts are ten times dirtier than this. I check

Instagram quickly, noticing that Connor posted a photo this morning.

We always post pictures of each other, so I'm not surprised that he uploaded one of me in bed, the sheet covering my lips and only my smoldering eyes exposed. He took that right after he quoted Steinbeck. I ended up glaring like this, and he immortalized the moment.

Among thousands of comments, most are positive. I glance at a few negative ones:

Your wife looks like she wants to kill you.

I would hate to wake up to that in the morning #crazychick

That's when you take an ax to bed!!!

They've added a variety of knife and devil emojis that Loren would find funny.

"People will always speculate," Connor tells me, rising off the bed and stealing my attention. I'm reminded of Connor's own tactics of manipulation. Ones I never used.

"If you were in my position, would you have slept with the board member?"

He runs a hand through his damp hair, smoothing it back. "No," he says resolutely. He opens a dresser drawer. "I don't do that anymore." Because we're together.

"Before I was in the picture," I rephrase.

He pauses. "It would have depended on the circumstance and the variables in the equation. I never jumped into bed blindly." So he's saying *maybe*. It would have to be the path with the highest benefit in order for him to choose it, and he's telling me that sex isn't always the answer.

"Was it easy?" I ask.

"Yes." His voice is even-tempered, his expression even more so. He removes his towel, giving me a view of his toned ass before he puts on navy boxer briefs.

I watch him walk to the closet, and he disappears inside. I follow him there, rolling down the sleeves of my sweater.

"How was it easy?" I question, wanting answers all of a sudden. "I can't imagine you willfully getting on your knees and blowing someone without it being difficult."

My husband loves control, thrives on it. I can't picture him stripped of his dominance during sex. Even when I had him handcuffed on his birthday, he was still incredibly alpha.

Connor steps into a pair of khaki pants. "Dropping to your knees doesn't take much effort."

"I'm not talking about the physical act." But he knows this. He's just stalling.

He finishes putting on his pants and turns to me. "I know what you want me to say. That it took this huge emotional toll on me. That inside I'm *wounded*." Antipathy drips from the last word.

"I don't want you to say that," I reply softly.

"Then what do you want?"

"The truth," I shoot back, hostility suddenly spiking my voice. "Just the truth."

He nods. "Truthfully," he says, "it was easy, Rose. And I know you can't fathom that because it would never be easy for you. But that's because I didn't marry myself." He reminds me, "If I wanted to be with someone a little more like me, then we would never be together."

My shoulders sink as I realize he's right. I can't wrap my head around emotionless sex. I can't pick apart my feelings to accurately understand. I probably never will, and I have to be okay with that.

"Thank you," I say honestly. We didn't need any games this time. I just simply asked and he offered. It wasn't as fun, but it was nice.

My phone rings on the bed. I rush out of the closet to answer it. The minute I put it on speaker, Theo says, "It should be in your inbox. You need to sign and email it back to me while I'm at the office. As quickly as you can." He hangs up without another word.

From my phone, I check my email and then send the contract to the printer. Quickly, I walk to the office on the first floor, pluck the contract from the machine and sign my name in the appropriate places. After highlighting the lines where Loren needs to sign, I switch my mission to tracking him down.

Once I have his signature, I can scan and email them back to Theo, and I've won.

I ascend the stairs to the second floor. My quick steps slow when I near Loren and Lily's room. Muffled moaning sounds filter through the hallway. "Yes . . . yesyesyes!!"

No. No, no, *no*.

Twenty-eight

Rose Cobalt

L ily gasps and repeats Lo's name in orgasmic succession. I refuse to let their crazy sex drive ruin my goals.

Without a single knock, I surge into their darkened room, deep-red curtains pulled shut, and I force my eyes onto the target. I try not to engrain Loren's position on top of my sister, midthrust, her legs spread open around him.

I'll need to bleach my eyes after this.

His bare ass is in complete view, the champagne-colored blankets bunched at the edge of the bed.

"What the fuck?! ROSE!" Loren screams angrily. Lily lets out an embarrassed yelp and starts slapping Lo to climb off her.

I charge ahead, pretending like they're fully clothed and not in the middle of screwing. Yes, I would scoop out his eyeballs and burn them if he did this to me. But I have no time to waste, and they literally could be fucking for the next four hours. I'm not waiting for them to finish.

I extend my arm with the contract and hold out a pen. "Sign, please."

Lo's entire face sharpens, shooting me the signature Hale death glare, which tries to slash my resolve. I don't cower, not even for a second. This means too much to me.

"Get the fuck out," he sneers. "Ride on your broom back to where you came from."

I swat his bare shoulder with the contract. "*Sign.* This isn't a joke. I have minutes, maybe seconds, before I lose this." The desperation must be clear in my voice. His broiling anger turns down a notch, his amber eyes shifting off me and back onto his wife.

Lily has frozen underneath him, her hands pressed to her face as though she can hide. Loren finally moves off my sister, and she shrieks, "LO!"

He tosses a nearby red suede blanket on her, covering her from sight, and then he sits up and faces me. Still entirely naked. He's trying to force me out of his room by sheer embarrassment, on my part. I suck in a sharp breath.

I'm not caving.

I lock eyes with him, never looking down at his genitalia. I will not call his penis by any other name than proper scientific terms.

He snatches the documents from me and flips through the papers. "Jesus Christ, how many pages are there?"

"Ten," I say. "Just sign where I highlighted."

He shoots me a look like I need to find my missing brain cells. "I'm not going to sign something that I haven't read. In fact, I need to call my lawyer to look over these too."

That will take forever. "It's a standard contract," I explain.

"Shouldn't you have learned from your last mistake?" He means when I didn't have a lawyer look over the contracts that Scott gave us for the reality show, and in effect, he legally owns sex tapes of me.

This is different. "It's been in the works for months. I've even helped Daniel draft these. *Please* don't be responsible right now."

He gapes. "Do you hear yourself? Who the fuck body-snatched you in the middle of the night?" He shakes his head. "I don't know why I'm surprised after all the weird things you've been doing. Like yesterday?" He gives me another *what the fuck?* look.

I go rigid. "You saw the article?" *Already?*

"Ummmm." Lily starts to say something, but her voice is stifled beneath the blanket. Gradually she pulls the suede fabric down. Her eyes emerge and then her nose, slowly her mouth. I'm staring at her like *hurry up*. And Lo looks at Lily like he's seconds from fucking her again.

"There are online stores that sell those things," Lily tells me. "You don't have to go out publicly to buy them."

"I'm not ashamed," I say, a little too forcefully . . . It implies that Lily is—and I didn't mean . . .

She reddens. "You shouldn't be." She nods as though breathing in this reality that she wants to own too. I didn't want to make her feel bad for shopping online. That's a great alternative.

Lily clears her throat. "But I just meant that the more Connor and you do these things in public, the more the media has been asking us about you two. We always thought you liked your relationship out of focus. Even while we were filming *Princesses of Philly*, it was more about Lo and me."

I feel like an asshole. "Connor and I are dealing with the attention as best we can."

She squints at me now, confused and suspicious. "I thought you'd be more upset."

"I *was* upset. Ten minutes ago. Now I'm trying to take care of business." I snap my fingers at Lo, but he's still reading page one.

Lily's eyes flicker to his crotch, and she squirms a little.

He ends up grabbing a pillow and placing it on his lap. He flips the page, glaring at the legal jargon. As much as we grate on each other, I can admit that Lo isn't dumb. He's cautious with his businesses. He seeks help in aspects that he's weak in, which, according to my husband, makes a great leader.

I check their bedside clock. It's almost eleven. "Why are you two just now having sex?" I ask. I'd think they would've started and finished hours ago.

"Because your demon baby kept our baby awake last night," Lo retorts. "Which in turn meant we were too exhausted to have sex. And now *you're* interrupting us. Like mother, like daughter." He flashes a bitter smile.

I shouldn't have asked. I cross my arms. "Sorry, Lily. Not sorry, *Loren*." I'm about to wave him to continue reading when a white and furry *thing* bounds through the doorway and into the room. It pushes past me and bolts for the mattress.

"Goddammit," Loren curses, trying to gently push the Siberian husky away from the bed. The dog nudges his bare legs, tail wagging, and then the animal jumps on the bed and lies next to Lily. I take a couple steps back. I do not fear dogs, but I prefer smaller pets. Ones that I can pick up. She's only eight months old, and she already weighs thirty-five pounds.

The husky nuzzles Lily's arm until she responds. Then Lily scratches her thick white fur. My sister immediately smiles, the dog a professional at gaining this type of elated response from people.

She is the antithesis of Connor's cat, and yet it's made me miss Sadie even more. Now that a shedding, slobbering *dog* is roaming around our household, sacrificing our cat seems unnecessary.

Last week, Ryke bought the Siberian husky for Daisy's twentieth birthday. Connor and Loren like to joke about how Ryke and Daisy are now parents too, their husky around the same age as our babies. But we're all well aware of the underlying truth.

This is a certified service dog for Daisy's PTSD and panic attacks. Frederick suggested one as part of a plan to help Daisy, and she talked to Ryke about it, expressing enough interest that he surprised her with one. I'd never seen my sister so happy.

"What's the command we're supposed to use?" Lily asks me while Lo tries to focus on the contract.

"Go see Daisy," I say. As soon as the words leave my lips, the pure white husky springs off the bed, her bright blue eyes directed on the doorway.

"Oh my God! I'm *so* freaking sorry!" Daisy rushes into the room. "Coconut!" The dog circles Daisy's feet. "She's still trying to acclimate to the house."

"Shit," Lo swears, setting the papers back on the bed as he searches for his underwear. It's somewhat interesting that he reacts differently between my intrusion and Daisy's, actually feeling exposed, even with the pillow. What's *not* okay is the contract he's abandoned.

"Loren," I snap.

"Give me a minute," he says with an edge, clearly flustered.

Daisy cringes and turns sideways to shield her eyes. "I'm *really* sorry, guys." She sets a hand on her dog's head who finally heels next to her. "Coconut, be chill." That name is going to be shortened a million horrendous ways except for mine.

"Coco, don't drag snow into the house again." Then I shoo her off with my hand.

"Queen Rose, already giving the dog chores," Lo quips. It wasn't a *chore*. It was an order. You know what—if he has time to say things like that to me, then he has time to read a few pages and sign his name.

I'm about to say so when Ryke *runs* into the room, fast. He bumps my shoulder on his way to Daisy.

"Fuck," he curses, slowing to a stop.

I wonder if his stitches . . . "You shouldn't be running, Ryke," I say.

He's heard this phrase so many times since being home from the hospital that he just simply ignores it now. "You didn't hurt me," he says.

"Of course I didn't; *you* ran into *me*." That sounded so bitchy.

The concern in his face pumps guilt into my bloodstream. "Did I hurt you?" he asks, eyes flitting across my body. He's not his brother. It's ten times easier saying mean things to Loren, and I forget to tone down my hostility for him.

"I'm fine," I assure him, and then I turn to Loren. "Can you please hurry?"

He's still trying to find his underwear by sliding his hand across the mattress, Lily nothing more than a lump under the blankets, hiding from Ryke.

This is a clusterfuck.

Loren lets out a frustrated noise, and I head to his dresser, opening the top drawer and tossing him the first pair of underwear I see.

He doesn't even look slightly appreciative. Now clothed, he searches for Lily beneath the comforter instead of the contracts. He gets a pass. My sister ranks above *all* material things.

"What the fuck is going on?" Ryke asks, really confused.

Connor's voice sounds beside the doorframe. "You all interrupted Lo and Lily having sex, clearly."

"I'm *so* sorry," Daisy says for the fifteenth time—at least it seems like that many.

"Stop saying that," Lo tells her.

Daisy is now kneeling next to Coco, the dog nuzzled against her body. The animal is trained for much more than just providing comfort. Hopefully she'll help Daisy with her nightly troubles and panic.

"I thought the dog already earned her certificate," Connor says. "Why is she running into rooms?"

"She still has to adjust to the house and the people in it," Ryke explains. "Huskies like to explore. I didn't buy a fucking Lab because I thought Daisy would like this breed better."

Daisy looks up at Ryke with the sincerest type of love in her eyes. He knows my sister well.

Ryke adds, "Two more weeks of training at the house and she'll be used to everything."

"You can't train Nutcake here," Loren says. "You're supposed to be taking it easy."

"Number one," Ryke begins, "don't confuse the fucking dog. We've been through this—it's either Coconut or Nutty. Nothing else."

I set my hands on my hips. "I put in a proposal for Coco, and I specifically remember gaining two votes." I point at Daisy and my husband.

"Everyone could only vote once," Daisy says with apologetic eyes. "They counted my vote with Lily's for Coconut, and then Ryke and Loren went with Nutty."

Did everyone fail second-grade math? Hello? "I still have *two* votes. We are two people." I gesture from my chest to Connor's, who walks closer to me in the bedroom, his arm slipping around my waist.

"Your husband changed his vote," Lo says with a dry smile.

Connor looks hardly scared by my withering glare. He should be scared. He sleeps with me.

"Tell me you sided with my sisters at least," I say.

"If I told you that, it'd be a lie."

My mouth falls and then I swat his arm off me.

He's actually grinning. "This wasn't a husband-wife, husband-wife, boyfriend-girlfriend kind of vote." I know what he means. All the guys voted together, and I was the dissention among the girls. Fine.

"And number two," Ryke continues to his brother, "I've been taking it easy for practically two months. I'm not a fucking invalid."

He hasn't been taking it easy. He runs every morning, and I've even caught him lifting weights in our basement gym when he's not supposed to be. He's bored and restless and reminds me far too much of my youngest sister.

His itch to climb can't be scratched for another month or so, and it's what really bothers him. Daisy told me that no other activity really seems to fill his need to rock climb.

Connor breaks the brief silence. "I think it's about time we had a certified, potty-trained dog in this house." Both Ryke and Loren's shoulders slacken almost instantly, and then Ryke flips off Connor, a smile almost attached too.

"Leeaaafff." The mumbled word comes from underneath the comforter.

"Lil wants you all to leave. As do I," Loren says.

"Not yet." I snatch the contract and set it back in Lo's hands.

"Sorry," Daisy says again, on her way out with Coco . . . nut. I internally cringe.

"Daisy." Lo shakes his head at her apology, which shouldn't exist in his eyes. I actually love that he's reinforcing this with her, as Ryke always does. She apologizes for almost everything, just a gut reaction from being raised by our controlling mother.

Daisy nods. "Sor—okay . . ." She ushers her husky out of the door, and Ryke follows close behind.

I clear my throat.

"Give me a minute," Loren says, trying to find his spot in the contract.

"I gave you *ten*. This means a lot to me—please." I hate my own voice. I'm begging him now.

He scratches his neck. "I can't just sign this without a lawyer." He stands from the bed, about to retrieve his cell on the dresser. Loren has no faith in me since the last time I dealt with a contract.

"Let me read it," Connor suggests, leaving my side to look over the papers in Lo's grasp.

Loren pauses and then nods, passing them to his best friend. He trusts Connor, and maybe if I hadn't royally screwed up once before, he would've trusted me too. A breath is caged in my lungs while I wait for the verdict, hoping that we'll solve this soon.

Connor reads ten times faster than Lo, flipping the pages while completely inexpressive. His eyes flit to me once, on the fifth page, but I can't discern his thoughts, good or bad. To Lo, he explains,

"This is specifically just to ensure the name of the brand as Calloway Couture Babies and not Hale Co. Babies, with the main label as CCB and an HC inset."

"Yeah, I got that much, thanks," he says bitterly. Lily peeks beneath the blanket and mouths something to him. He mouths words back, and I tune them out, more focused on Connor's poker face.

A minute later he hands the contract back to Loren. "It's standard, no vague phrasing. Personally I'd sign it without another set of eyes, but it's up to you."

Lo hesitates, thumbs through the pages *again*.

I'm going to have to beg more. "Please," I say. "We have minutes, maybe less." My fashion career has fluctuated so much that every success has been paired with an irksome failure. I want to see my designs in stores with my name on them with my vision. I don't want to lie and endorse something that I don't believe in, that I barely had a hand in creating.

I need this win.

Loren returns to the bed, and my heart sinks. He digs in the blankets—I think to find Lily. But he avoids the lump that's clearly his wife. A second later, he procures the missing pen.

He's going to sign it.

He turns to the correct page. "Next time, send me a text message first, or *knock*." I barely process his words, watching him scrawl his name. It reminds me that Lo has *always* been on my side with this new venture in Hale Co. Whatever I want, he's tried to give me.

So when he passes me the contract, I say, "Thank you." My voice much softer than usual. It even surprises me. He rocks back in shock but ends up nodding.

I waste not a second more. I walk quickly out, down the hallway, and descend the stairs. I turn a sharp corner and enter the office. While I scan the contract and email it off, I call Theo. "It's sent," I say before he has a chance to speak.

"I see it. I can't talk long, but it looks good to me. I'll see you on Monday . . . hopefully with a job."

"Of course." That cloud of guilt looms over me for even threatening his job. We hang up at the same time, but I don't exhale a sigh of relief.

It takes me a couple seconds to detect the source of my unease. While a dog traipses around our house, the little orange tabby cat we've deserted roams the apartment of Connor's therapist. I have no idea if he even cleans her litter regularly or if he forgets to feed her.

I can't look at that dog without being reminded of what we did, and so I make a quick decision. I'm driving to Manhattan today.

And I'm taking Sadie back.

Twenty-nine

Rose Cobalt

I bounce Jane on my hip, and I knock on the office door, eye level with a bronze nameplate: *Dr. Frederick Cothrell*. As soon as the door swings open, my glare already zeroes in on the target. With my heels on, Frederick is the same height as me. I notice his sideburns graying since the last I saw him face-to-face; time clearly passed quickly. Exhaustion also pulls wrinkles by his eyes.

"Rose." He's not even a little surprised. Frederick widens the door, welcoming me inside.

"I need her," I say without clarifying more. I follow him into the room, and I kick the door closed with my ankle, securing Jane on my waist.

Frederick slumps down on his leather chair, motioning for me to take a seat on the patients' couch across from him. *No thank you.*

"I'm not your patient. I'm only here for my cat."

His smile seems genuine. At least more genuine than the ones Connor plasters on for people. "It's Connor's cat," he reminds me.

I suck in a breath. Sadie may have been his cat, but through the years, she's warmed to me. *I'm* the one who cares enough to want her home. For this reason, she's just as much mine as she is his.

"It's time for her to come home." I hug Jane a bit tighter, resting a hand on my daughter's head. Jane babbles and then audibly enough says "hi" to Frederick. She even waves. I'd set her down, but we won't be here long.

Frederick waves back at Jane. "She can walk now?" The way he questions, I feel as though he already knows the answer is yes. I wonder if Connor described the event to Frederick, how Jane kept trying to push herself to her feet, only to fall. We were all in the living room for a Saturday-night movie, *Harriet the Spy* (Daisy's pick), paused on the television.

Moffy kept trying to stand too, both babies attempting to walk towards each other. They weren't racing but just eager to join their cousin on the other side of the rug. Daisy grabbed the video camera as Moffy proudly stood first and walked. An hour later, Jane mimicked his steps.

I can't picture Connor reiterating this scene to Frederick, not the pure emotion that I saw behind his eyes that night. Maybe he just gave Frederick the facts, and his therapist deduced my husband's feelings all on his own. That seems more likely.

"I need the cat." I bypass his question. Where is she? I scan the Manhattan high-rise, my head swiveling right and left. Jane reaches for my dangling diamond earring and tugs hard. "*Ow. Fuck*," I curse.

Jane's bottom lip quivers, a cry rising.

"Not you," I say quickly, attempting to soften my tight voice. "Well, yes, you. Don't pull on Mommy's jewelry." I stroke her brown hair, removing her black headband. "All right, little gremlin." I despise when babies cry, but when my own daughter starts, it's like a razor blade through every one of my internal organs.

Her eyes well with tears, but her lips close, her wail vanishing. She sniffs, and I even wipe beneath her nose. What I do for this one. I kiss her smooth cheek and whisper, "*Tu es forte, ma farouche petite fille.*" *You are strong, my fierce little girl.*

Even with the tears, she's still strong. Strength comes in all different sizes and packages and molds. Lily is proof enough.

"And you were afraid you wouldn't be maternal," Frederick says like he knows me. His tone is friendly, which makes it hard to be upset.

"Have you met my mother?" I ask him, my voice shaking at the thought. Of course I was scared. I didn't know how to raise a human being. I didn't know if I could do a better job than what she'd done with us, and that terrified me.

And so I thought thirty-five would be an appropriate age. By then, I'd have accomplished all that I needed to. A child wouldn't keep me from any goals or any trips or any*thing*. Maybe at thirty-five, I'd find that warmth that children need. It was a plan.

A ruined plan. Destroyed by fate.

Jane was an accident of epic proportions. I was on birth control, and yet I was still very much pregnant. I love Connor, and I'd begun imagining a family with him in the *faraway* future. For that future to be so soon—I was terrified.

People are constantly evolving and learning, and through those nine months and Jane's emergence into the world, I discovered more about myself. I was afraid to raise a boy. Some days I was afraid to raise a daughter. Mostly I was afraid to raise anything at all. When I held her for the very first time, when my fingers touched hers and hers closed around mine, as though recognizing who I was—every anxiety I harbored began to fade.

I created this beautiful person with a brilliant, one-of-a-kind man. There was no conceivable way I could fear holding her or loving her or giving her everything in my absolute power. So I may not be the picture-perfect representation of a mother. I may not be *warm*, and my hugs may hurt more than comfort, but I love this girl so terribly, just as I love myself.

Anyone who tells me I'm doing a piss-poor job or that she deserves better than me—*fuck you*.

"I've met Samantha Calloway before," Frederick says. "She wanted to see her daughter's therapist."

I would give my mother brownie points if not for the fact that she favors all of her daughters over Lily, still never having met Lily's therapist and it's been years. Maybe she's afraid though.

Our mother is partially the source of Lily's problems. She's not really the source of Daisy's.

"And?" I question.

"Samantha is not like you," Frederick tells me, leaning back in his chair.

I want to call him out for pacifying me, but I can't see why he would comfort me in this moment. I'm here to take a cat that's been living with him. If anything, he should want to shoo me away, not console me.

"It's the truth," he says, off my expression.

I shift uncomfortably, not liking how well he can read me, how well he knows me from Connor's sessions. "Just bring Sadie here tomorrow by noon. I'll pick her up."

He shakes his head. "Connor told me not to return her, even if you drove here asking."

"I'm not *asking*," I say. "I'm threatening."

"He also said that you'd threaten bodily harm to me, and that I should be aware you're fond of hyperboles and exaggerations."

I'm going to *kill* my husband.

I tighten my eyes closed. Yes, that is a fucking exaggeration. When I open them, I hope to see Frederick waving a white flag. He's still calm, waiting to escort me to the door when I'm ready to leave.

He adds, "Sadie may not get along with the babies or with the husky."

"She deserves a chance."

He presses his finger to his jaw in contemplation. "Why do you want her back, Rose?" This is the second question that I'm positive he already knows the answer to.

I abandoned Sadie.

I gave up on her, and I never do that.

"She's a lot like me, you know," I say. Sadie and I—we share the same qualities. We're both aggressive and standoffish; we strike without thinking and we struggle to let people see our soft sides.

"Connor let her go because she was expendable to him," Frederick explains. "You're not."

Translation: *he won't abandon you.* The sentiment is nice, but Connor and I are different. He can throw away things when they have no more use to him. I can't.

"What if she's not expendable in my life?" I ask. "Can I have her back then?"

He shakes his head, silent.

My nose flares, and then Jane reaches up for my earring again. I pull my head away, and she lets out a bigger wail, one far more horrifying than simply being told *no*. I touch her bottom, sensing a wet diaper. "I'll be back for Sadie." On my way out, I point at him. "Also, your loyalty to my husband, while admirable, is completely infuriating."

He smiles as I leave through the door.

Thirty

Rose Cobalt

finish off my second lime-green appletini. Drunk Rose is coming out to play tonight, and I've kept her firmly at bay for—well, I can't even *recall* the last time I drank past my limits.

Tonight is different.

In a New York City Irish pub, a band plays a loud rock song, the noise bleeding into the brick walls and vibrating my brain. As soon as we arrived, the small establishment became congested with green-clothed bodies, and now we struggle to move about.

Connor has his hand on my lower back, and I realize he's directing me through the throngs of rowdy people who wear plastic beaded necklaces, four-leaf-clover face paint and glittery green headbands.

His palm descends to my ass, and I heat. *It's the liquor.* He tucks me closer to his side, to avoid an incoming drunken male. His assured, protective gaze hits me once, and I clench. *It's his fucking dominance. It's him.*

His lips brush my ear. "You're blushing."

"I am not," I snap.

He just grins and keeps guiding me through the masses. PDA with my husband is on the itinerary for St. Patrick's Day. Liquid courage will help, so public intoxication is also mandatory for me.

I'm sure the tabloids will love Drunk Rose. I love her in moderation, and I suppose she's due to come out.

It's also the first time Jane will be staying overnight with my mother. The anxiety from that alone makes me want to drink. I put the glass to my lips. It's empty. Right . . .

With the crammed bar in sight, it clicks that he's leading me there. As we pass a train of guys in sparkly green top hats, each one pinches Connor's arm or shoulder. He hardly flinches or even acknowledges that he's being touched.

"Connor Cobalt, why aren't you wearing green?!" someone shouts, recognizing us. It sounds more like a fan than any journalist.

Connor is in charcoal pants, a navy long-sleeve shirt over a white button-down and gray tie. He straddles casual and formal, oozing confidence even without green—and his wavy brown hair has never seen a better day than today. *Shut up, Drunk Rose.*

I swear, if I start complimenting him out loud, tonight is ending without *any* public fondling. I will march to the hotel and stop before I betray myself. *No ego stroking.* That is an order.

I tug at the hem of my dark-green cocktail dress, the beaded embroidery and color making me feel like poison ivy.

I approve.

Someone else pinches Connor's arm. I shoot them a withering glare, and they shrink a little. *Yeah, that's right. Shoo.* I lean into Connor . . . *almost* teetering in my high heels. "What are you paying your bodyguard for?"

His large hand seems to envelop my hip. "To protect my life," he replies, his lips near my ear. I imagine him nipping it, just a little, and then pulling me harder, closer. I heat all over again. "And I hardly think pinches are endangering it."

"That's because you haven't been pinched by *me* yet," I refute icily, topping off the statement with a sip of . . . nothing. Seriously, can I not remember that my drink is empty? *Pull yourself together until drink four.*

He laughs once at my threat, his lips rising in more amusement. "Darling, I think I can outlive your attacks." Casually, so imperceptibly, his teeth graze my ear, and he bites my lobe before whispering, "I'm indestructible." He squeezes my ass, just one time.

Cameras flash everywhere, some from phones, others from outside the glass windows, night upon us at 1 a.m.—and the paparazzi have never been hungrier. Daisy, Ryke, Lily, Loren, Sam and Poppy are scattered throughout the small pub too, so I can see why paparazzi would be rabid tonight.

We reach the wooden bar, but we have to wait for the bartender to serve us. I spin on Connor, his gaze traveling across my body in a long, sensual wave. His desire mixed with confidence mixed with dominance is more intoxicating than my appletini.

I pinch his ribs as hard as I'm able.

He grins.

I glare, wanting only to extinguish that grin that says *I can never lose.* "I want a divorce," I tell him pointedly. His lips continue to rise. Well, that didn't go as planned.

"A WHAT?!" Lily shouts over the music, pushing closer to us with wide eyes. Loren swings his arm over his wife's shoulders.

"A divorce," I repeat, setting my empty martini glass on the bar.

Connor faces me and hijacks my gaze, compelling me to *not* look away.

"Is this another one of your weird nerd battles?" Loren asks.

Connor never wavers from me. "Under what grounds, darling?"

"Annoyance. You're annoying me."

His conceited smile only grows. This is *not* how normal people work. I insult them, they glare. I insult them, they put up a fight. Instead, Connor wears that aroused expression that says *I'm going to spin you around and fuck you hard against the bar.*

"Like that," I say, blood rushing between my legs. "That

annoys me." *And turns me on.* I can't make up my mind, but I think one may trump the other soon.

His grin dims, only because the bartender leans across to ask for our order. While he gets me another cocktail, I clasp Lily's wrist and say to her, "I'm glad you're here!" Her presence will surely drop the temperature of Connor's movements and public groping.

I'm honestly not sure how much I can handle. My mind may implode with stop signs and dead ends if large groups of people start watching, and I'm afraid it might trigger my OCD later.

I really wish I weren't so anxious, since his mere *hair* has my body pulsing. Sexual appetite? Check. Mental blockers? Check.

Lily stands on her tiptoes to be closer. "Me too!" she shouts. "Do you mind holding on to my purse while I dance with Lo?"

I'd plead with her to stay with me, but she's already set desirous eyes on her husband, who's talking to my husband. I was the one who encouraged her to bring a purse anyway, and my reasons for wanting her close are slightly selfish in nature.

"Fine." I accept her purple clutch and hold it with my gold one.

"Thankyouthankyou!" she slurs together and bounces over to Loren. He pats Connor's shoulder in goodbye and then lifts Lily into a piggyback, heading towards the band.

Connor rotates to me again, and as the alcohol kicks in, I realize it's becoming harder to meet his self-possessed gaze head-on. It's like I'm no longer immune to his charm. *Fuck that.* I pull back my shoulders, refusing to be hypnotized by his poise.

I'm poised too, goddammit.

I teeter in my heels.

He nears me, his clutch firm on my hips, pulling me into his body.

I hold on to his forearm for support. "That was unnecessary, Richard. I wasn't going to *fall*." I cringe at that word. Fall. I don't fall.

His lips brush my ear again. "You do remember what tonight is about, Rose?"

Yes. His hands need to be *all* over me. I confirm with one nod, and his gaze soaks into mine, carefully ensuring that I'm okay with this.

I am.

This is our plan.

I like plans.

"Why aren't you wearing green?!" the bartender asks Connor, sliding over my appletini and slicing into our conversation. I gratefully take the drink.

Connor has a shadow of irritation in his eyes, only perceptible by me, most likely. He answers the bartender very casually. "I make my own luck, so really St. Patrick's Day should be celebrating me." He pauses. "And I prefer *blue*."

I press my lips tightly together, trying not to smile even though my lips want to rise so badly. The bartender lets out a humored laugh. I don't pay attention to the rest of their exchange, a cell vibrating my palm.

It's coming from Lily's purse. I procure her phone, too curious not to, and maybe if I weren't tipsy, I'd be more respectful. At least, I think I would.

A text illuminates the screen.

Look how adorable—Mom

I unlock Lily's phone with her password (Moffy's birthday), and then I see the photo my mother attached to her message. Moffy is cuddled in a blue blanket, sleeping on my mother's lap.

What? I check my phone—no updates about Jane. I'm happy that my mother and Lily have rekindled parts of their relationship, but I would've liked *something* about Jane.

"What's wrong?" Connor asks, rubbing the small of my back. He looks between the two phones in my possession.

"It's just hard leaving her there overnight," I admit. I do have a little guilt about not being with her for this long, but my mother urged us to go out. She wanted "grandma" time. I never thought she'd be this enthusiastic about grandmotherly roles. She wasn't when Poppy's daughter was born, but maybe the empty nest is still eating at her since Daisy moved out.

"Jane will be okay," Connor assures me. "If you want to go back to Phila—"

"No," I cut him off. If I return home and mess up our plans, I fail. I need to let go sometimes. "I'm perfect." I make a point of sipping my appletini, and he watches with the most impassive, stoic expression—blank and unreadable and therefore slightly frightening.

Connor cups my face, his eyes dancing around my features, and when his thumb skims my bottom lip, I turn my head, spotting any onlookers. I catch the bartender peeking over, along with *hordes* of people, camera phones still angled towards us . . . though most are directed at Lily and Loren dancing.

Connor pinches my chin, turning my head back towards him. "*Concentre-toi sur moi.*" *Concentrate on me.* His tone is partially comforting, partially as strong as his grasp. He'd never push me into the deep end if he thought I'd drown.

My pulse speeds. "Are you going to kiss me?" I question, hearing the anxiety in my voice. I hate that sound. I chug the rest of my appletini.

He strokes my head, all my hair pulled into a tight, sleek pony. "Get out of your mind, Rose," he coos.

It's not that easy for me, not with so many eyes on us. I set my empty glass on the counter, and he flags down the bartender again. I realize I'm still *clutching* onto Connor's forearm like if I let go, I'll fall.

This isn't exactly normal for me. *Be the fucking shark, Rose.*

I will be. I'll snap my jaws over every human here.

"Rose." That's not Connor. Ryke sidles next to me while Daisy slips in front of my body, settling on a nearby vacant stool. Four-leaf-clover sunglasses shroud her eyes and she's dressed in a graphic tee that says, *Shake your Shamrocks*. Since her back is to me, I can't spot a smile.

I face Ryke.

His jaw is scruffier, making him appear older. He spent the past week camping with Daisy and their Siberian husky in the mountains—still no approval from his doctors to rock climb. Daisy thought camping would help ease the wait.

"What?" I ask, ice frosting the word. At least my bite hasn't disappeared yet. I *almost* pick up my empty glass and take a sip. I remember not to be a drunken fool this time.

Connor detaches from me, except for his fingers that just barely hook around mine. He leans over the counter to speak to the bartender, the persistent music drowning their conversation.

Ryke places a hand on my shoulder and leans closer to me, all so he doesn't have to raise his voice. "Do you have any Advil or Midol?" he asks.

My back straightens, and my eyes flit to my sister. She has her feet on the stool, legs tucked to her chest, sitting in a fetal position. When she swings her head to me, she paints on a bright, all-consuming smile. I almost believe her, but silently, I hear her saying, *I don't want to be the reason you have a bad time.*

"How bad are her cramps?" I ask, opening my clutch first. Lipstick, compact mirror, mini perfume, powder, mints, safety pins . . .

"Enough that she has to sit down." He runs a hand through his hair, watching me dig around my clutch, which is two sizes larger than Lily's. All of my items are packed neatly in pockets and little wallets.

. . . mini sewing kit, bobby pins, stain-removing pen, small brush, driver's license, debit and credit cards, superglue (God forbid my high heel should break) and—

"Advil," I say, handing him a mini tube of pain reliever.

He pops open the bottle. "It's empty."

"What?" I snatch it back and shake . . . to find nothing inside. "Lily might have some." I unclasp her clutch to find her ID, cash, her phone, and condoms floating around.

At least she carries protection.

"Nothing?" Ryke says off my frown. "Fuck." He groans and looks back at Daisy.

"I'll be fine!" she shouts. "It's really okay!" She playfully twirls her green glittery glasses before placing them back on.

He's not buying it, and neither am I.

"Find Poppy," I tell him, my stomach flip-flopping at the thought of being so unhelpful that I have to pass this task off. "She'll have something on her."

He nods, more hopeful. "Keep an eye on Dais for me?"

"Of course." While he squeezes through the masses to search for Poppy, I'm about to fully detach from Connor and join Daisy.

In unison, Connor not only holds more of my hand but Lily's phone buzzes. My head swirls from the alcohol, distracted by the cell enough to click into Lily's texts.

Lil. How long does it take to pee?—Lo

I thought they were dancing? The alcohol must be fucking with my sense of time. It's already 2 a.m.

I whip my head from side to side and finally spot Loren outside the girls' bathroom door, one that has stalls so he doesn't burst through or bang on the wood.

I curiously scroll through my sister's old text conversation with Lo. Sober Rose would *never* do such a disloyal act unless it helped Lily, but morality has all but flitted away.

Their most recent discussion:

Moffy just said poop! We've been saying poop too much, Lo.—Lily

I soften and my frozen joints thaw. My little sister is precious, and luckily, her son's first word wasn't "poop." It was "boo." They've been playing peekaboo a lot with him.

I keep reading the texts.

At least he didn't say shit.—Lo

I roll my eyes, and a new message pings, my drunken gaze landing on every word without permission.

Please just reply so I know you're okay.—Lo

I'm sure Lily is fine, and if Loren didn't irk me so much, I might reply with that. With my free hand, I type out this message with quick, sloppy fingers: Green appletini.

It's as random as I feel.

I press "send" and watch his face scrunch in confusion. He texts back rapidly.

???—Lo

I snort under my breath, a roguish smile rising. Go fuck a cactus, I type and press "send" . . . only to reread the message and realize I sent: Gig fuck a castings.

Really, Rose?

Lo wastes no time, pushing through the bathroom door. Camera flashes go off again, brightening the back area of the pub. In maybe a minute, he exits with Lily by his side, and I watch his daggered eyes pierce and search the room.

They set on *me*. Lily probably told him that I have her phone. He raises his hand in the air and gives me the middle finger.

I raise mine—and I accidentally drop Lily's cell. Nothing is going according to plan. I bend down to collect it. *Don't be broken*, I chant with an angry growl.

I discover a perfectly intact phone and return it safely to her clutch, all of which I place on the bar next to Daisy.

"Watch these?" I ask, Connor's hand still in mine.

She gives me a smile and a thumbs-up, her green sunglasses masking whatever pain she may be feeling. I'm literally seconds from asking our bodyguards to go make a drugstore run for us. I'd even leave and go make one with them.

"I have Advil!" Poppy shouts, weaving through the crowd with Ryke and Sam behind her. My tan older sister is more prepared for the luckiest day of the year than I am. Her long, straight hair splays over her green tunic, wooden bracelets decorating her forearm.

Poppy is "chill" in comparison to me, as Loren has said before. I'm not surprised. When I was younger, she always disappeared to our backyard to paint, finding quiet places away from our mother. She discovered calmness in her teens that she's carried to thirty.

I'm twenty-six, and calm has still evaded me, even boozed.

Maybe that's why I have Connor. Just as I think it, he finishes speaking with the bartender. I slide closer to him and scan his hands and the counter for my new drink. It's nowhere to be found.

"Have you just been talking with him this whole time?" I question, my feet aching. Not because of the shoe but because my muscles keep constricting.

My heels have *not* betrayed me.

Connor clasps my hips and pulls me against his body a little more, guiding me so that my back digs into the lip of the bar. I look over my shoulder, hoping to spot the bartender making my drink, but he's helping another girl.

"Rose." Connor forces my name and simultaneously grabs my attention. I focus on him, his deep-blue eyes almost eating me out. His gaze is as dirty as that sounds.

You love it, Rose.

I do, but there are onlookers . . .

He holds my face, possessing me with one strong move.

"I'm not ready . . ." The words prickle my skin. "I need another drink, Richard."

He lowers his head, his lips grazing mine before he whispers something in French. I can't translate it, not unless he speaks slower. The alcohol jumbles my thoughts, and he notices the confusion blanketing my face.

"Concentrate on me," he repeats.

I scrounge up a decent glare. "I am."

I expect him to kiss me now. *He's going to make out with you against the bar with everyone watching.* I wonder if he can feel my pulse race, my chest collapsing, half-anxious, half-wanting.

Very swiftly, he grasps my waist and lifts me onto the bar.

What the fuck.

What the fuck.

My ass hits the wooden surface, and cameras swing in our direction. My legs hang off, and I grip his forearms so hard that my nails must be leaving imprints.

"Connor . . ."

I expect him to kiss me *now.*

He doesn't.

Instead he effortlessly hoists himself onto the bar, and he kneels on either side of my thighs. He's straddling me. The crowd cheers, and I sweep his features: his grin lifting, his eyes only dead set on me, his fingers—his fingers *remove* his first layer of clothing . . . pulling his long-sleeve shirt over his head, now in the white buttondown and tie that he was wearing underneath.

He tosses the navy long-sleeve shirt aside.

The band dies down, leaving only chatter and this event on the bar, spotlighted by camera flashes. *Everyone* is watching him.

More him than me.

This fact begins to morph my anxiety into sexual awakening, a pulse mounting below. My brain tries to register what's happening, his fingers loosening his tie.

He clutches the back of my head with his other hand. And very slowly, so I understand, he whispers, "Get ready, darling." His breath heats my neck. "This may spin your head."

Thirty-one

Rose Cobalt

My body thrums, and he slyly fastens his tie around my wrists, binding them behind my back. The cheers inside the bar nearly pull me out of the moment, but Connor rests a hand on my cheek.

"Only look at me," he reminds me.

I nod, trusting him. Then he kisses me so powerfully, nipping my bottom lip with his teeth before he rises to his feet, no longer kneeling.

He *towers* above me, my head level with his crotch.

Oh God.

I cross my ankles, which hang off the bar, and glue my thighs together, the pulse starting to hurt. My body is screaming for him to ram inside of me, this *need* escalating while in a fully packed pub. This can't be happening.

But it is.

He strokes the top of my head with his hand, within arm's length of me, even standing. I look up at him, and he unbuttons his shirt with a heady, seductive gaze that nails me like a hard fuck between my legs.

"Take it off! Take it off!" so many people chant. Among them are my sisters and friends, crowded near the bar.

Connor tugs my ponytail, forcing my attention back to him and not my surroundings. *Focus*, his eyes say, loud and clear.

His fingers unbutton the last one, his shirt opening to reveal his infuriatingly defined set of abs. My husband is stripping on a bar, a show meant to stir the media, but also meant for me.

His confidence transforms what could be a silly, sloppy act into a commanding, stimulating experience that has undoubtedly roused my body. I am completely soaked. I'm thrumming for his cock. Not to mention, I'm horniest the few days before my period, and this is one of those days.

And his hand—his protective and possessive hand—on my head is doing a number on me.

He tosses his button-down aside, now shirtless.

"TAKE IT OFF!" The chants grow.

His pants . . . is he . . . ?

I instinctively want to use my hands to shield my mouth, which literally keeps falling open. My wrists jerk against the restraint, and Connor tugs my pony again, until my eyes meet his intimate gaze, which pushes right into me.

I take shallow, short breaths.

The corners of his lips begin to lift once more, especially as he unbuckles his belt, right near my face. *Fuck . . . me*. He steps closer so that my cheek is almost pressed up against his cock, an inch of space separating us. As he unbuttons his slacks, his knuckles brush my nose.

"TAKE IT OFF!"

The howls of approval sit far into the back of my head. My skin heats like we're having sex on the bar. Are we? This *feels* like he's fucking me, right here, right now. Everyone is watching.

He never falters. Never even balks. He acts as though it's just us here, as though this is the easiest adventure he's ever taken.

"Connor . . ." I say, not so much in warning, just in place of expletives and exclamation marks that blare inside my brain. He teasingly pulls down the hem of his pants, inch by inch, revealing the band of his navy boxer briefs.

I quickly steal a glance at my sisters, and they all have their fingers pressed to their wide smiles. Lily's eyes look ready to pop out of her head.

I internally experience all of that and a pulsating arousal that screams *fuck me, fuck me, fuck me!*

Connor switches hands on my head, holding me with his left one—for Connor, his left hand is his more dominant hand.

Loren comes behind Connor, and he pulls down his pants and boxer briefs enough to show off his bare ass. Connor is grinning at *me*. I must wear every emotion that pounds at my mind.

Lo pinches Connor's ass. "Happy St. Patty's Day, motherfuckers!" Everyone cheers and raises their pints and green cocktails. He lifts Connor's boxer briefs back, but I'm aware that Connor has my head entirely stationary, in line with his cock.

He thrusts against my cheek three times, my entire body combusting, and a strangled moan latches in my throat, the noise smothered by the euphoria around us.

I break through the tie restraint, and I grasp his thigh with one hand and a little higher with the other. His ass flexes beneath my palm.

I've frozen.

He lowers, kneeling on either side of me again, and while my head spins in a million different directions, his lips meet mine, the force—the power returns. Though it's never left. It just fills me orally, his tongue parting my lips, his arms pulling my chest into his body.

I can't keep up. I fall into wherever he directs me. Into the headiness that he supplies me. I just hold on to his biceps, and he slides off the bar, bringing me with him, setting me on my feet.

He's still kissing me, still wrapped up against me. *Yes*, I think. He manhandles me the way I love to be manhandled, and I accept him, every action, every flick of the tongue. My lips sting beneath his, my skin flushed, the alcohol not even coming close to the effect that Connor has on me.

"DO IT AGAIN, CONNOR COBALT!" The nearby shout breaks into my actions, and I squint at the harsh light of camera flashes, coming in waves once again. My husband is still shirtless, his belt unbuckled and pants unbuttoned, but his slacks rest in the proper place, covering his ass from view.

Connor holds my face caringly, his grin lifting higher and higher. "You liked that."

I smack his chest, still breathing heavy, and he's hardly even winded. He seizes my hand and kisses my knuckles. I realize I didn't even need to be on-the-floor wasted to accomplish a bigger public display than most people will ever commit to in their lifetimes.

He made me feel safe.

Comfortable. He's done this before, switching an event onto himself to ease me into it. His confidence has a way of seeping straight through me, and I love this person in front of me . . . a man that I *always* want to be with.

I splay my palms flat on his bare chest, and he hugs his arms around me, even if I don't really reciprocate it with my arms around him. I just keep my hands right here.

My tipsy self almost wants to tell him, *you're so hot. I want to bang you. You're bangable, you know? Your hair is perfect. Your lips even more so.* I keep opening my mouth, but even the thought of uttering an overly sweet compliment tastes strange and wrong.

So I land with this: "I hate you."

He grins more. "So much so that if I'd stayed up there for three minutes longer, you would've climaxed."

I scoff. "No . . ." I trail off, remembering the pulse of my body that was climbing towards a peak. *You would've orgasmed on a bar, Rose. In front of everyone.*

I believe it, but I just raise a hand to his face to shut him down.

He clasps my wrist, and he lowers his lips to my ear. "I'll take care of you tonight."

Translation: *keep drinking if you want.*

I do want.

And then I watch his eyes slip off me, and I follow them to Ryke. Everyone laughs around him. Even Daisy looks like she feels better with a brighter, more genuine smile. However, Ryke wears a dark, questioning glare, pinned on us.

It says: *why the fuck are they doing this? Did they lose a bet? It doesn't make fucking sense . . .*

What we can't reply: *we're doing this to draw attention off our kids and onto us.*

This might be the night where Ryke refuses vague excuses and fights for a real answer.

Thirty-two

Connor Cobalt

Daisy and Rose stumble down the hotel hallway together, drunkenly laughing and clutching onto each other for support. They both took tequila shots until the pub closed, and they've been singing "My Heart Will Go On" by Celine Dion, incredibly out of tune.

I'd enjoy the whole scenario more if Ryke weren't beside me, silently overthinking my striptease back in the pub. I can practically feel his mind at work as we walk behind the girls, and he steals reticent, cautious glances my way, hoping I'll meet his eyes and regurgitate every secret I have.

I'm not that easy to crack.

The girls trip over each other near our hotel door, and they collapse in a heap, *giggling*. I rub my lips, trying not to laugh since Rose never makes this noise. It's a rarity that I'll remember—it's one that I do adore.

I stop in front of them, staring down as they look up. "Girls," I say, passing Ryke the hotel keycard.

Daisy, with glazed eyes, says, "Rose wants a cupcake. Don't you, Rose?" She pets Rose's cheek.

Rose wears a pleased smile. "Yes . . . cupcakes, please." She holds out her hand, as though waiting for me to kiss her wedding ring or deliver her a treat.

"How about bed, darling?"

She makes a face at me like I offered her dirt in a bag. "That's a horrible present, Richard."

I clasp her forearm and help her up, but she staggers against me. It's easier for me to carry my wife, so I cradle her in my arms and kick open the door before it closes, then Ryke helps Daisy the same way.

"We've decided on a sleepover," Daisy declares behind me, her arms wrapped around Ryke's neck as he carries her into the room with one king-sized bed.

I set Rose on the hotel bed and she sprawls out and hugs a pillow. "No boys allowed," Rose adds as a requirement, which further leaves me alone with Ryke. We have *four* hotel rooms, and I'd hoped the girls would want to talk with each other for another hour and then let us split them apart.

Clearly that's not happening in my favor.

Ryke obliges and actually tosses Daisy on the bed beside her sister. She laughs, and Rose spreads out her arms as though she's suddenly at sea, sinking on the *Titanic*. Her hairband is lost in the depths of the white comforter.

I lean over my wife and comb her hair out of her face, and her eyes narrow at me; even glazed they still contain heat. Blood pools in my cock. I can always tell when she'll start her period because my body grows more primal, attracted to every physical move she makes.

She emits pheromones around this time, and the chemicals usually send me over until I fuck her—but tonight is different.

She looks closely at my lips. "Why do I love you?"

I rile her. "If you really want me to list all the reasons why, I'll be here all night."

She tries to cover my mouth with her hand, and she misses completely, swatting air beside my head. I laugh.

I notice Ryke sitting on the edge of the bed with Daisy lounging drunkenly across his lap. "Big bad wolf . . ." She reaches up to touch his hair, but her arm sags limply next to her. "Eat me."

It's a provocative, intoxicated statement that I do my best to block out.

Ryke lowers his head to her, kissing Daisy once . . . twice, and then he says, "Every fucking day, sweetheart."

"Where's Lily?" Rose asks me.

"Her hotel room with Lo." They're fucking, something I'd prefer to be doing with Rose, instead of sharing Ryke's company.

"Where's Poppy?"

"Her hotel room with Sam."

"Where is Willow . . . and where's her boyfriend?" Rose swats the air for answers. I clasp her hand.

"Lo's sister didn't want to go out," I remind Rose. Willow turned eighteen last week, but Lo said that she preferred to spend the night at her apartment and read a comic book. "And she doesn't have a boyfriend." I know Rose must be referring to Garrison.

Rose snorts and tries to wave me off, but I have possession of her hand. "I've seen them flirt," she says matter-of-factly, as though that's evidence enough.

"Your logic isn't sound, darling." I tug her dress down when it rides up her thighs. I'd let her be, but Ryke is on this bed too. "We flirted for years, and you never called me your boyfriend."

Her mouth falls and eyes flame. "What we did wasn't *flirting*."

I arch a brow. "When I was seventeen you said you wanted to perform an autopsy on me, to *crack* open my rib cage and squeeze my heart until it burst between your fingers." What is that—if not flirting?

She lifts her head off a pillow to near me, propping her elbows on the mattress. "That was me hating you, Richard. I dreamed of your *death*."

"You dreamed of clutching my heart," I rebut.

"Of *killing* you," she emphasizes.

I lean closer to her, our eyes locking. *"Vous m'aimiez."* You loved me.

She breathes shallowly and collapses back against the mattress, conceding early, mostly due to the alcohol. Her heavy-lidded eyes fight to stay open longer, just to glare at me.

When I turn to look at Ryke, he's staring between Rose and me with more suspicion than I'd like to meet. "You know," he says, "for so many years, I've never fucking understood why you both occasionally use '*vous*' instead of '*tu*.'"

My muscles still stay flexed, even if this a pointless topic for me.

Rose answers before I do. "It's formal." We're both not natives of France. Since we usually only converse with each other, we do what we want.

"You were fucking dating and now you're married," Ryke retorts. "Your relationship is informal."

"We weren't always dating and we weren't always married," I explain now, referring subtly to our days in prep school where we were competitors. "We began as formal and so now we switch between the two whenever we like. We're well aware of the rules. They just don't apply to us."

Rose is grinning from ear to ear.

She says she hates when I'm conceited, but I'm more than certain she takes pleasure in the real me, even if I'm an arrogant prick.

Ryke shakes his head like he wishes he hadn't asked, and then Daisy rolls off of him, closer to Rose, and the girls begin whispering together.

I stand off the bed the same time as Ryke, and we exchange a look of recognition.

We have to spend actual alone time together, beyond just passing each other in the morning and conversing sporadically for ten minutes. No Daisy. No Loren. Nothing that bridges us together.

Wonderful.

Thirty-three

Connor Cobalt

finish taking a shower after Ryke. We spoke a few words earlier that basically confirmed we'd be spending the night in this hotel room together. We don't hate each other enough to hassle the front desk at 4 a.m. for an extra room on St. Patrick's Day. And I'm not foolish to believe Ryke would just drop his suspicions if we separated.

He'll bring them up sometime, so he might as well let them out tonight.

After I brush my teeth and put on pajama pants, a light still floods beneath the door. I assume he stayed up to question me, and I never really thought he'd go to sleep without broaching the topic.

I quietly exit, passing a mirror-covered closet and entering the main portion of the modern hotel room: a desk, a chair and one king-sized bed, nothing more. Before Ryke sees me, I catch him on his side of the bed with his knees bent, something hidden behind them.

He's in gray cotton track pants, bare-chested, with a dark tattoo along his shoulder, rib and hip. When one of his knees falls, I spot his scar from the transplant surgery. It begins right below his sternum in the exact center of his chest, and it stops before his belly button, veering beneath his ribs, almost like the shape of the letter *L*.

It now accompanies the small scar on his eyebrow from the Paris riot.

I've never viewed people as physical canvases for their life, revealing time and memories outwardly like Ryke, whether by choice or by circumstance. I may be a blank slate, but not all people are.

I move closer, and he drops his other knee, his head rising. That's when I notice the book in his hand. *He's reading.* Strangely, I've never seen Ryke read before.

He stuffs the book behind his pillow. "I have to ask you something." He's trying to distract me.

My curiosity has escalated, and I'm not about to let it go. I head over to his side of the bed, and he immediately stands and blocks my passage to his pillow, his jaw hardening and features darkening.

I've never been intimidated by him.

"I have to seriously fucking talk to you."

I know. "Why are you so ashamed of what you're reading?" I question, knowing it's not about shame.

"Fuck off." He scowls. "I'm not ashamed of anything, so don't twist this your way."

I am twisting it my way, but I'm not done yet. "If you're not ashamed, then you shouldn't have any problem showing me the book."

His nose flares. "What does it matter to you if I read the back of a shampoo bottle or *Ulysses*?"

"I value intelligence," I say easily. "I find it agitating that you hide yours."

"Well, there you go." He gestures between my chest and his. "I don't rank people above or below me based on whether or not they can outscore me on a fucking math test."

That's how he sees me, then? I shake my head. "You've pegged me wrong. I'm not saying I look down on Lo or Lily because they're not as intelligent as me. They have other qualities that I admire and value and that I personally lack, but they don't hide these qualities from anyone."

"I'm not fucking hiding."

"Your book is literally sitting behind a pillow, hidden from view."

His jaw tenses. "And I'm saying that book isn't me. I could do this all fucking day, Cobalt."

"It's nighttime," I correct.

"You're so fucking annoying." He grimaces and sighs heavily. I don't move a muscle, and it irritates him enough that he reaches over and grabs the book. He shoves it into my chest.

I read the title in Spanish. *El cuento de la criada* by Margaret Atwood, a foreign edition of *The Handmaid's Tale*. "Have you read this before?" I ask. I've only read the English edition, but it's largely popular and actually one of Rose's favorites, a science fiction novel with feminist themes.

"Yes." He snatches it back. "I'm not having book club with you at four in the fucking morning—or ever." He returns the book to his backpack.

I wander over to the window, the maroon curtains open to a glittering view of Manhattan. "Your intelligence doesn't belong to your mother, you know," I say. "It's yours. You earned it. She didn't." I look over my shoulder, and he's standing stiffly by the bed, quiet. In the many years we've known each other, I can count on one hand our personal heart-to-hearts. I don't know why I bring it up now.

Maybe to prolong the discussion about my secret with Rose.

Maybe because I think he'll actually open up tonight.

The longer I look at him, the more I'm certain that I've hit the real reason why he shuts down so often. I can see it as he stares off, shaking his head.

"I did *everything* my parents asked growing up. Every fucking thing. I can't dissociate learning four languages from the rest of the shit my mom pushed me into."

I've gathered most of these facts through observation, but hearing the grit in his voice starts to churn my stomach. I lean my arm against the window, slightly uncomfortable, and I realize he's triggering empathy inside of me that only extends to people I care about.

He looks straight at me. "You want the truth. I went to college and I wanted to just be *me*. I had no fucking clue who that was, but I thought I'd figure it out." He lets out an angry breath. "I couldn't determine if I loved Spanish, Italian, French or Russian because she wanted me to love them or because I really did. I switched my majors *five* fucking times my freshman year, so you fucking laugh that I landed on a thing like journalism that I've never used, but I tried almost everything and nothing felt right."

I digest each of his words and the emotion behind them.

Before I can speak, he continues, "Look, she made it fucking harder for me to find my identity, but if I asked her permission to rock climb, even when she didn't really like it, she'd still let me. My mom and dad spun lies and I had to abide by them to protect their reputations. I used to be academic and athletic for their pride, not mine, but now I read for *me*. I run for *me*. I fucking speak for *me*. But I was conditioned so much that I know some things are just my parents in my head." He extends his arms. "So there are some languages that I'd like to forget."

"Which ones?" I question.

"Russian . . . French." That's why it's like pulling teeth trying to get him to speak French to me.

I walk over to the room's desk and lean against it, my hands on the wooden surface. "I don't think you've ever spoken this much to me," I say. ". . . I appreciate it, for whatever that's worth to you." My life was nothing like his.

I've never once struggled with my identity the way he did. But someone in our group did grow up as the yes kid, just like him. "You always saw yourself in Daisy, didn't you?"

He tenses and nods. "Yeah."

"Now we're back to one-word responses."

He sits on the edge of the bed. "Maybe you should tell me what the fuck you were doing tonight."

This is why I think he divulged more than normal. He thought I'd do the same in kind. "I've given Rose a lap dance in front of you all. This isn't different."

"You *stripped* in front of a fucking pub, not just the five of us, and that lap dance was part of a bet during the reality show." He adds, "It also never fucking aired on television. This was *live*."

It never aired because it would've shown the physical chemistry I have with Rose, and Scott was trying to edit the show to make it look like Rose was attracted to himself, not me.

"And?" I ask.

"And what the *fuck* was it for? I've been trying to make sense of everything that you two have been doing, but I can't . . ." He shakes his head. "I know something is going on, and I'm asking you as my friend to tell me."

"It's better if you don't know."

He gets off the bed, which forces me to stand. "I will fucking deck you."

"This is why I can't tell you," I say calmly, even as he edges closer, pissed. "You'd respond like you are now, and I need rational, levelheaded people on my side."

"I'm assuming Rose knows the truth. You think she's that fucking rational?"

My jaw twitches, and I rub my lips to hide my irritation. Rose isn't rational all the time, but she's far less aggravating than Ryke. They have a lot of similarities, and the things that make them different make me exponentially more compatible with her and exponentially less compatible with him.

I have one inch on Ryke, but we're still nearly level.

"You have no idea how badly I want to fucking punch you right now," Ryke growls. "You need to *stop* manipulating me, Connor. I can see every time you do it."

I let him share, thinking that I'd share in return.

I didn't.

What hits me out of everything he says—it's not the *I want to fucking punch you* or the *you need to stop* . . . it's his use of my name. He rarely calls me Connor and not Cobalt, and when he does, I can practically taste the severity of our friendship, trembling in the balance between broken and whole.

A real friendship is a two-way street. I've driven down it with Loren. I've given him vulnerable parts of myself, more of me, and he's let me see his weakness. Ryke might've been brick-walled in the beginning, but *I'm* the variable that makes this friendship sit at a standstill, not him.

"Take a step back and I'll tell you," I suddenly say. I don't want to manipulate my friends. I don't want to deceive him. I want something real.

Ryke hesitates. "Don't lie to me."

"I won't," I assure him. "I promise."

With this, he takes a couple steps away from me, putting about five feet between us. "Let me talk all the way through before you interject." My voice is impassive, holding no notes of irritation or defeat. I spend the next few minutes detailing what I've done with Rose, first to help Moffy and bury an article, then our test to see if we can redirect the spotlight off our children.

When I finish, I watch him run his hands repeatedly through his thick, brown hair. His eyes set on the carpet as he processes the complete truth. The first thing he says: "I could've fucking helped you."

If someone asked me to name the first two attributes of Ryke Meadows, "aggressive" wouldn't even be on the list. In the heart of his soul lies kindness, wrapped tightly in selflessness that shows in almost every action.

I recognize, unflinchingly, that I don't share his compassion with the world and with so many people, but a part of me longs to understand on a deeper, more human level.

"It was easier on me if you didn't help." I tell him the truth.

He exhales roughly. "That's *my* fucking brother and his kid. That rumor was partially about *me*. I could've done something so Rose didn't have to."

"Rose wanted to," I remind him. I'm a little concerned that he's going to share this information with Lo. "You can't tell him, Ryke. You realize this?" It'd send his brother to a dark place. Guilt weighs on Lo more than it *ever* hits me, so we have to keep secret anything that'd push him to drink.

Ryke sets his hands on his head and takes a couple deep breaths.

"Please confirm with me," I say, unable to read him past frustration and anger.

He drops his hands. "I won't ever fucking tell him. It'll always just stay between you, me and Rose." I hear Lo in the back of my head, joking about an *older kids' club*.

It exists during times like this.

"I want to fucking help," Ryke tells me, taking one step closer.

"You don't need to . . ." I see his fist tighten and then the angle of his body. *He's going to hit me.* I don't turn out of it.

He decks me in the jaw. My inner cheek digs into my teeth, and I taste iron from blood on my tongue. I don't touch my face, I just rotate to him once more while he settles down.

He's been waiting *years* to punch me. He's stopped himself short countless times before. His features relax, the hardness of his jaw less apparent. His face holds no malice, no aggravation anymore.

He's content.

Ryke nods to me. "Tomorrow you can tell the press I hit you and that we fucking hate each other or you can make up another story." He walks back to the bed, giving me a headline to stir the press away from my daughter.

I let out a laugh, stunned and amused. "This is your way of helping me?" I follow him, my jaw throbbing, but I don't complain. In my life, I've given Ryke more shit than any other person.

Because I knew he could take it.

Still, it added a thin layer of animosity over our friendship—jokes half in jest and half in irritation—and I just now feel that layer begin to slowly peel away.

"Yeah," he confirms. "I never had a better fucking reason to hit you until today." He climbs back on his side and slips under the covers.

He literally couldn't deck me unless it helped *me*. "How kind of you." I settle on my end of the bed.

"Just say the word, Cobalt, and I'll fucking punch you again." He turns off his lights.

I arch a brow. "And what word is that—'woof'?"

"Fuck off." His voice is lighter than before.

My lips rise and before I turn off my lamp, I feel pressed to say one more thing. He deserves this answer in its entirety. "During Christmas, I told you that I didn't celebrate Christmas because my mother didn't, but I never mentioned that I'd come to spend them at Faust."

He shifts onto his back, brows furrowing in confusion and surprise. "How many guys spent holidays there?"

"Not many, and to you it seems lonely—"

"How is that *not* fucking lonely?"

"I spent my time running towards goals and ambitions. I never wasted a moment to consider the loneliness around me, and to this day, all I see are the things I achieved, not the things I lost. So I can't relate to you, no matter if I took more time to try."

Ryke stares off, thinking about this for a second, and then he laughs in realization. "We must be oil and water."

I smile. "I assume I'm water in this scenario."

Ryke gives me the middle finger before he turns on his side again and mumbles, "Night, Cobalt."

With this, I shut off my lamp, blanketing us in darkness.

Ten minutes into sleep, my phone buzzes beside me. I squint at the illuminated screen and prop my body on an elbow.

Daisy had low segdeive does feed know this?!?$4—Rose

It's one of the worst drunk texts I've ever had to decipher from my wife. I sit up against the headboard as another messages comes in.

It takes her a long time to organs too did you knew—Rose

"What is it?" Ryke asks, sitting up with me. His voice isn't groggy since we shut off the lights only minutes ago.

"Rose is drunk texting me about Daisy." I can barely make sense of the first one, but the second one sounds like she's discussing orgasms. I pass the phone to Ryke.

He pinches the bridge of his nose the moment he reads them.

"Translate," I say, the word foreign from my lips.

"Daisy has a low sex drive." He tosses the phone back to me, about to go back to sleep.

With better context, I translate the text to: Daisy has a low sex drive, does Frederick know this? The girls must still be talking right now, and Rose is concerned that Frederick doesn't have all the information that's relevant to her health.

"Has she told her therapist?" I ask him.

He scrunches the pillow beneath his head. "Yeah."

I wonder if he's had an idea what's wrong with Daisy. "What do you know?"

"I'm not discussing my fucking girlfriend with you." He rolls onto his side, back towards me.

"She suffers from depression," I guess. Her low sex drive and struggle to orgasm point either to this or to the effects of the medication she's been taking. Maybe it's a combination of both.

He turns back to me, and I can see his brows furrowing, even in the dark. "Frederick told you?"

"No," I say. "I just guessed."

He rakes a hand through his hair and then shifts to his back, staring at the ceiling. "I think I've always known, and so has she— we just didn't ever call it that out loud." He lets out a heavy breath. "I just want her to feel happiness every fucking minute of her life, and each time I wake up, it's further out of reach."

"You just have to be patient and kind," I say calmly. "Do what you do now, and it'll be enough, even when it doesn't seem that way." I usually supply everyone with the right words, but there are no right ones in this instance. He understands that he can't fix Daisy, and all he has to give is himself, to be there throughout her life.

He nods and then rolls onto his side again, away from me. "Can you please stop fucking talking to me now?"

I slide back down and shut off my phone.

I value having details, but I never took into account the emotion behind them.

Thirty-four

Connor Cobalt

I squat on the other side of the kitchen, four towers of wooden blocks separating the distance from the two children and me.

"Daddy!" Jane calls, her blue eyes pinging inquisitively to each colored tower: red, blue, yellow and green.

"Knock over the blocks," I encourage, waving both kids towards me. I can barely piece together her next words, unintelligible noises that she shares with Maximoff. The little boy points to the red tower, as though constructing a plan with Jane.

On this particular Tuesday afternoon, I'm the designated nanny, and even though I'm swamped with paperwork from Cobalt Inc., I'm gladly using this day to play with my daughter and nephew. I'm always at the mercy of time, but I try not to let it steal precious, rare moments from me.

I set my knee on the floorboards. "Do you need me to show you?"

Jane looks curiously at me. I'm not sure she understands half of what I ask, but that never stops me from speaking to her like she does, like she will, one day.

I'm about to stand, but Moffy makes the first step. Steadier on two feet than Jane, he rushes out and charges into the red tower. He laughs as the blocks scatter the floor around him.

"Nice work, Moffy," I congratulate, my lips upturning. "Do you know what color those blocks are?" He picks up one of the wooden ones, the letter *E* carved on one side and an eagle on the other.

He mumbles a word that sounds very close to *eagle*.

I smile. "Almost."

Jane points at the yellow tower. "Daddy!"

"It's not moving, Jane," I tell her. "You have to reach it yourself. It's possible to walk there, honey. You just have to pick up your feet." I talk a little slower but in my usual tone, hoping she'll process the gist of what I say.

She smacks her lips, uncertain and confused. My phone buzzes in my pocket.

I check it once to see a text. Told you I could fucking help—Ryke

I don't look at Twitter, but I've seen the tweets from after St. Patrick's Day, the whole New York trip long passed. Most tabloids speculated that I had a fight with Ryke, and so our fans believed it too. In our own circle of friends, everyone but Rose thinks Ryke punched me from a heated argument. It's not an off-base assumption since we rarely talk cordially.

It was bound to happen, Lo told me that morning with the shake of his head. *Did you both get it out of your systems?*

We nodded, and that was that.

I look up right when Moffy darts to the blue tower in front of him, showering the floorboards with more blocks. He laughs and turns to look at his cousin, her brown hair reaching her ears and half in a high pony, tied with a blue bow. He mumbles what sounds like *Janie*, the name not perfectly clear off his lips.

Jane teeters with each step towards the yellow tower. I put my hand to my mouth, my throat closing. She's going to fall in a second, and instinct nearly springs me to my feet, to gather her in my arms before she hits the floor.

I force myself to stay motionless.

She can't be afraid to walk. There will be many, many days where she has to do it without either Rose or me present, and she needs to recognize that *she* holds the power to stand back up. We don't.

Just before she reaches the blocks, she rocks backwards, her weight shifting, and she lands on her bottom with a *thud*. Her chin quivers, searching for me with glassy blue eyes.

"I'm right here, Jane," I say.

She meets my comforting gaze and sniffs.

"You're okay, honey." I smile and nod to her. "If you can't stand back up, you can always crawl. Don't forget that."

She speaks to me incoherently. I nod as though I understand, but I have no idea what her string of noises truly means. And then Moffy carries a blue and a red block over to Jane. He bangs them together and speaks like her, babbling until Jane tries to pick herself off the floor.

She stands and runs into the yellow tower, her face breaking into a smile as the blocks collapse around her.

"Good job, Jane." I begin to clap just as my phone rings. I check the caller ID and my world seems to mute, deadened silence that's as easy to brave as a plastic bag tied around my head.

Henry Prinsloo.

Stanford graduate and also my old classmate from Faust.

He only ever calls me in dire situations, when an integral part of my life is at risk of decay. Before I answer, I immediately head over to Jane, and I realize she's crying.

She's fallen again, and this time tears collect, her cries starting to trigger Moffy. His eyes redden as he watches her, and his lips begin to tremble.

"Shh," I coo, lifting my daughter into my arms. I whisper in her ear, doing my best to calm her. Then I bend down, able to pick up Moffy in my other arm. I carry both of them hurriedly to the living room, my mind racing along several paths. I attempt to form conclusions from miniscule facts.

In the past, Henry's calls were most commonly about Loren or Lily. He's my contact inside major media outlets. He's the one who tipped me about the *Celebrity Crush* article before it went live—the article that would've cast doubt, that claimed Moffy's *real* paternity test was false.

Whatever he has to tell me, I can fix. Just like that article. I have the power to latch whatever has come undone. *I* have that power.

Me.

And I'll piece together whoever falls this time. One by one. We've all been through this before. We can survive it again and again. I just need to act quickly. Whatever this is, there's usually no margin for error.

My phone rings incessantly. I set Moffy and Jane in their playpen beside the Queen Anne chair, their tears only partially dried. "Keep playing." *Just keep playing.* I try to distract both babies with stuffed animals and multicolored balls strewn around the circular pen. "I'll be right back." I prop the door open between the kitchen and living room with a chair, able to hear them well.

On the final ring, I answer the phone. "Henry," I greet.

"I called as soon as I could," he says, no background noise on his end. "You have to believe me. All the news outlets have been really tight-lipped until a minute ago."

"Can you email me the article?" Henry can gain access to the tabloid's server and send me their scheduled draft. He's only a line producer at GBA News, but he has connections to every tabloid that I need.

"It's not just an article . . ."

I rack my brain for answers, heading down the most logical, sensible paths. "What photo is it?"

I can buy the photograph.

I've done it before.

Over a year ago, Henry tipped me about a photographer from

Paris Fashion Week. The man had just sold three pictures to a well-known tabloid. They were all of Daisy undressing backstage.

She was completely naked.

I bought them and destroyed them with Rose, almost immediately, and so they've never even been muttered of anywhere.

"It's not a photo," Henry says, having trouble delivering the news.

I stay calm, but I want more facts quickly. "Then what is it?" I ask. "A video, an article, a photograph, a fucking comic strip—tell me."

"It's everywhere," he says vaguely. I grip the edge of the bar counter, wishing he would tell me what the fuck I'm dealing with. "Some of the articles have turned into *videos*." His voice lowers. "GBA is headlining the story on their seven o'clock news tonight."

I check my watch. That's five hours away, plenty of time. "I'll call the—"

"It won't matter."

"Henry—"

"It's *everywhere*." He emphasizes this point. He still won't say what *it* is. "*Celebrity Crush* is running it in an hour. Other tabloids are talking about releasing it sooner than that. You don't have time to do anything."

He's wrong. "Send me the story."

"I can't. I don't have time either. GBA is holding a staff meeting in five minutes."

He won't say what it is.

If it centered on Lily or Loren, it would've been the first thing out of his mouth. Anyone else, he would've said the name by now. But if it was me—he'd choke.

So if I listen to the most rational part of my brain, it says that I'm about to be ripped to shreds. "Text me the names of every magazine and news station that plans to run this story." I hear

Frederick in my head: *You're not superhuman, Connor. The world will not change for you.*

I bend to the world if it won't bend for me, and yet, if this is *about* me, will I finally have to bend until I break?

"I'm texting you right now," Henry says.

A pit descends further in my stomach. "Tell me, Henry," I say, "what's the headline most are running with?" I almost don't want to hear the truth, not even when I need it most.

After a moment of silence, he utters, "They're all calling your marriage a sham."

I rub my lips. "What evidence . . ."

"They have sources about ex . . . boyfriends? Yours. Three of them, I'm almost eighty percent positive. GBA News filmed an interview with one. He's claiming you two had sex multiple times and that you're not straight. They're all saying the same thing— that you married Rose to hide your sexual orientation from the press."

We have a child.

We have sex tapes.

I repeat these as my defense, my muscles constricting in taut, immovable bands. My knuckles whiten. "I have to call my lawyers. Text me everyone who's running this," I remind him before hanging up. I spend the next fifteen minutes talking to three lawyers, spouting facts. Never once wasting time to ingest an unneeded emotion.

I tell them to send out cease and desist letters to every single fucking guy who's planning to break the nondisclosure agreement. I tell them to threaten lawsuits and fines so steep that they will leave each guy destitute. I tell them to work on filing temporary injunctions, to prevent the news stations and tabloids from running the stories.

"We won't be granted an injunction in enough time," my primary lawyer says. "The cease and desists are our best shot. We'll intimidate them as much as we can and keep you posted. Turn on the news. Don't take your eyes off it until we tell you it's handled."

I have forty-five minutes, maybe less. I rush into the living room and switch on the television to GBA News, muting the station, and I open my laptop to *Celebrity Crush*. The *clack-clack* of plastic balls, the babies playing, is the only true noise.

Fix this.

Forty-three minutes.

My lawyers will have a better time threatening these guys than me, but while they work on the injunction, I can call the stations and tabloids. I have no idea *how* this happened. Why some of these guys decided to speak all of a sudden. Who cracked and under what kind of pressure. But the *how* isn't important right now.

Concentrating on the *how* will ruin any chance I have at damage control.

On the couch, I scroll through Henry's text, which consists of twelve names. I call the first one; it's the second most affluent tabloid, right behind *Celebrity Crush*. "We're going to publish it with or without an injunction. *Celebrity Crush* will beat us to it, and so will multiple prime-time news outlets."

"You'll be severely fined," I say sternly, my voice cut-and-dried, not defensive.

"It's a price we're willing to pay. We'll make it up in subscribers."

I call the second name.

The third.

The fourth. "It's going live in thirty minutes."

The fifth and sixth. The seventh and eighth.

The ninth. "Your deal was to bury the headline about Moffy," Andrea DelaCorte from *Celebrity Crush* tells me. "You said nothing about protecting yourself, and I can't strike a deal with you when it's not an exclusive story. It's going to break in fifteen minutes by us or by someone else."

You're not superhuman, Connor. The world will not change for you.

I can't stop this.

I can't prevent a barrage of questioning and speculation. I don't call the tenth, eleventh and twelfth media outlets.

I clutch the phone firmly to my ear, but my heart pumps deeper, louder. As soon as the line clicks, I say, "Rose . . ." I lose my thoughts in her name. My throat sears, and I think—*I missed a link somewhere. Was it Theo? Was it Jonathan Hale? Was it Frederick?* I fucking block out the *how*. I have to, but I know the *how* is stampeding the real pain—the worse thoughts.

The ones that attempt to barrel into me.

Rose will be dragged into this by her ankles, suffocating beneath someone else's rising tide, and the best I can do is hold her while we go under. I've never imagined myself drowning before. Not like this. And I've never imagined I'd have these two choices: drown apart or drown together.

Together.

Always.

I would never let Rose suffer through this alone.

"Is Jane okay?" she asks off my silence, concern bleeding into her words. I hear the shuffle of papers. She's already standing, I'm sure.

"I need you to come home," I tell her. "Quickly." Paparazzi will swarm Hale Co., Rose's boutique, Superheroes & Scones, tracking down everyone close to me.

"What is it?"

"Drive safe," I say, stoic and resolute. My voice belongs to the man who needs a therapist to tell him how he feels.

"I'll be there in fifteen minutes." *She* hangs up on me, sensing the severity, even if my voice carries nearly nothing.

I dial the second number.

"Lo," I say. "I need you to come home." *I need you* is a phrase I almost never use with anyone, especially not him. He needs me. *Everyone* needs *me*.

"I have a meeting in ten minutes. Should I cancel or . . ."

"Can you rework your schedule? This is important."

He doesn't ask why. His loyalty stems from a real, honest and genuine friendship, the first one I ever truly had. And I know— without a shadow of a doubt—that my past is about to ruin it.

"Sure." I hear him begin to walk. "I just need to know if it's Lil."

"No," I tell him. "It's about me. I'll see you soon." I hang up, dialing the next number.

"Hey, Connor," Lily says over chatter that sounds like her employees at Superheroes & Scones. "I was just about to call! How's Moffy doing?"

"Can you come home?" I ask, knowing I have to explain a little more for her and a lot more for my next call. "Something's about to play on the news about me, and it's better if you're not in public when it happens."

"Okay . . ." Concern drapes her tone like curtains closing on a comedy show. "How long do I have?"

"You should leave now."

"On my way."

My last call. The line rings three times before it clicks. "Hey," Ryke answers in a heavy breath. He went on a run with Daisy and their husky, but a "run" for Ryke sometimes turns into an all-day affair, time passed leisurely and peacefully, which is why he texted me earlier.

"Where are you?" I ask, refreshing the *Celebrity Crush* site. No updates.

"Down the fucking street," he says. "Everything okay? Is it my brother?"

"No. It's not about Lo or Daisy. It's not Lily either." He has to know it's about me now, or Rose.

"I'll be at the house in less than two minutes." His sympathy surprises me but also awakens me. I've never, in my life, needed Ryke's concern. Not even for a moment.

I shut off the phone and wait for my lawyers to give me good news that I'm certain won't ever arrive. Moffy and Jane have fallen asleep on beanbags in their playpen. I lean back against the couch for the first time. I'm left alone with silence and my raging, turntable thoughts.

I'm attracted to people.

To the words they speak, to the actions they take, to their full-bodied mannerisms and soulful gaits. I am attracted to *people*. To impassioned hearts that beat out of sync, the ones that skip a measure, heard in hushed places and violent spaces—I am attracted to people.

There is no other truth I can yell as loud as this one. And it won't help. They'll want a label to understand me, and I've never truly defined myself with any.

Nothing will fix this but a lie.

It's not a lie to one person, which is easier to swallow. It's a declaration to millions of people. It's condemning a belief that I've lived by, one that makes me *me*.

So what the fuck do I do now?

The door swings open, and the white husky pants as she walks tiredly to the window nook and lies on her fleece pillow.

Ryke emerges from the foyer with Daisy. He tosses his backpack aside. "Are they asleep?" he asks quietly, gesturing to the playpen.

I nod once and refresh the computer, check my phone for texts. Nothing new yet. I think I have five minutes. The sky seems to darken outside—clouds rolling over the sun, most likely.

I stand as Ryke nears with Daisy. I open my mouth to explain, but I falter, my stomach turning.

"I'll get you some water," Daisy starts.

"No," I tell her.

Ryke runs his hand through his hair, slightly damp from his run. "Maybe you should take a fucking seat?"

Daisy nods in agreement, rocking on the balls of her feet.

I frown and scrutinize her overly concerned expression, which matches her boyfriend's, no shades of confusion. "Do you know me?" I wonder. It's a vague statement, but they're both intelligent enough to understand what I'm implying. They could've deduced what this was about if they had one single fact: I've slept with men before.

She nods once.

I don't understand . . . "Both of you sit down," I order.

They take a seat on the coffee table together, cautious and respectful of my feelings. I stay towering above them.

"Who told you?" I ask.

Daisy twists the bottom of her lime-green tank top, restless. "You did."

I cover my eyes with my hand. "No." She was sleepwalking. There was the smallest, barest chance that she'd remember the things I said when she woke up.

I drop my hand, my eyes burning. Maybe there was a place inside of me that wanted her to remember, and that's why I took the risk.

"I'm sorry," Daisy whispers, her face contorting in guilt. "It wasn't my secret to share, but it was weighing on me—and I knew Ryke could keep it too."

I dazedly sit back down on the couch, my eyes flitting up to meet Ryke's.

He knew this entire time that I'd slept with a guy before, and he never said a thing. He never changed around me. Never pressured me to explain or elaborate. Never felt uncomfortable. I think back to St. Patrick's Day. He shared a bed with me, and he never acted differently.

Daisy springs to her feet. "I'm going to let you two talk. I can take Moffy and Jane to their nurseries." Ryke watches her collect both tired babies from the playpen, and his normally hard eyes soften a fraction the longer they pin to his girlfriend.

He scratches his unshaven jaw and turns back to me when she disappears upstairs. "How'd this get out in the fucking media?" *How.*

"It hasn't yet . . ."

His brows jump. "So everything's okay?" He knows it's not. I wouldn't have called him if it were.

I shrug. "You tell me." I'm referring, of course, to his knowledge of my past. Sitting in this silence, with the weight of the truth, feels like a forty-ton pendulum swinging at my chest.

He holds my gaze. "I was fucking surprised when Daisy told me what you said to her, but that's all I was."

I have a hard time believing this, and I wear the doubt in the corners of my eyes.

Ryke notices, and he lets out a deep breath. "Look, I may speak harshly, we may disagree on more fucking things than we can ever agree on, but after years of, I don't know what to call it . . . I guess *shit* we've plowed through together . . . I've realized that you care about other people just as much as me. You can twist it how you want, but the truth is, half of what you've ever done has been to protect someone else. And you're good with words, so what's the definition of that, Connor?"

Selfless.

A trait I'd never claimed before. It's still hard to now.

He continues, "When Daisy told me that you'd slept with a guy before, I was *shocked* but I wasn't fucking disgusted; I wasn't repulsed. I didn't question your feelings towards my brother or me.

I can differentiate when someone fucking *cares* about a person and when someone's sexually attracted to them. I was just surprised."

I rub my lips, my eyes clouding. "I wish I could say I thought better of you all this time, but I sincerely thought you'd put a hundred-foot barrier between your brother and me." To protect Loren. From me.

It's something Jonathan Hale has tried to do, and maybe this is all his doing . . . maybe he'll finally succeed. Lo knows about me. He accepts me, but I imagine other people won't be as understanding, as comprehending, of my relationship with him anymore.

Ryke shakes his head and rests his forearms on his knees. "There was a time I didn't trust you, but *never* because I believed you were into him like that. You're manipulative as fuck, and he's . . . fragile."

"I know," I say. "It's why I was easy on Lo when you were hard on him."

Ryke nods, understanding how I only tried to brace Lo from falling over every time Ryke needed to push him. We'd been at odds with each other for so long, disagreeing on how to treat a recovering alcoholic. His brother. My best friend.

"So tell me," I say, "if you were in my position, what would you say to the media?"

"I would tell them to fuck off."

"Of course you would."

He almost smiles. "Come on, Cobalt, you don't take fucking advice from dogs." It's his attempt at cheering me up—because it's obvious to him that I'm knee-deep in quicksand and sinking fast.

"You are not a dog, my friend." I lean forward to refresh the *Celebrity Crush* site, my laptop sitting next to Ryke.

"Don't mess with the status quo."

The status quo has already been trampled over a hundred times in the past forty minutes, a fucking carcass of what it once was. Not even I can reverse time to put it back together again.

A brand-new headline appears on the landing page of *Celebrity*

Crush, and my world comes to a standstill, an unquantifiable moment with a stagnant heartbeat.

The headline: CONNOR COBALT HAS SLEPT WITH MEN! MARRIAGE TO ROSE CALLOWAY CALLED INTO QUESTION!

My phone rings incessantly, as though someone close to me has died. I imagine the calls belonging to board members of Cobalt Inc. and my father-in-law and every person who knows me, wanting a quote or an answer. The *why*s and the *how*s and the *who knew*s all tangled together.

Half of their headline is true. I can't deny my past, but they have warped it in a criminal way, invalidating the one thing that has meant the most to me.

I struggle to read the article, to accept the permanence of the situation. I breathe through my nose, my jaw tensing. *Read the fucking article, Connor.* I stare unblinkingly at the computer screen. I stare, faraway, disappearing beyond the words.

I need to read it, but I'm afraid.

Loving someone else isn't easy. It doubles pain. It doubles worry. It doubles sentiments that I dislike in one dose. Loving someone else is a complex web of emotions, trying to ensnare me.

And I've been caught before.

When Rose went into labor, I truly thought, *This may be the day where I lose everything*. Stuck on a freeway in my limo where her survival rested in my hands. I was terrified at the idea of losing love. *Love*—of all sentiments, of all things. It's a gut-wrenching, nearly debilitating idea, and I tried to push it away as I delivered our daughter and while Rose bore the pain.

People called me a hero, but I'd never felt more human.

I suddenly feel a hand slide on my shoulder and a body sinks beside me. I look to my left, and Rose curls her fingers around mine. I wear apologies in my eyes, but her inflamed, narrowed gaze pins to the laptop screen, prepared to battle things that I've let drive over me.

"Have you read it yet?" she asks, lifting the computer off my lap. I notice Ryke standing to greet Loren and Lily in the foyer.

"Not yet," I breathe.

"We'll read it together, then." Her voice trembles, her yellow-green eyes alight with destruction.

I hold her closer to my side, bracing her stiff frame to my body. I focus again on the article, and I graze over information Henry has already explained, exact names of my exes never written or mentioned. Just "a source" and "we'll reveal more as the story continues to break"—meaning this isn't the end.

I land on the words that surprise me the most. Rose inhales sharply, reading it too.

Sources claim that Connor Cobalt knew the truth would be exposed soon. It explains why—for the past four months—he's been amplifying any public displays of affection towards his wife. To name just a few: he went down on his wife in a parking lot back in November, visited a sex store in February, and performed a striptease in March.

It's all been an act to fool people.

What we believe: they're not in love. Their marriage is nothing more than a business arrangement. *Celebrity Crush* has reached out to the Calloways and Cobalts respective representatives, and neither has issued a statement yet, but we're certain someone will speak out soon. And when they do, we'll be here to report it. So stay tuned.

I shut the laptop violently, and I stand, clasping Rose's hand in mine before she can even speak. I lead her out of the living room, her rigid body moving mechanically, in the daze that I've been crawling through for the past five minutes.

I'm more awake now. They're spinning *our* game—everything we've done in the past four months to protect the babies—around on us. They flipped the script, yanking guns out of our hands and pointing them directly at our heads.

Our six-month plan just backfired.

I saw consequences and the risk. There was always a cost attached. I'm not foolish to believe it was ever infallible. By nature, tests are meant to fail or they're meant to succeed.

I just never believed it would fail like this.

There's not a forty-ton pendulum hitting me anymore. It's two hundred tons of cement, burying me beside my wife.

"Where are you going?" Lo asks as I pass him, Lily and Ryke to head upstairs, Rose in tow.

"We need a minute." Or five. Or an hour.

Rose is rooted to the center of my being, and I ache to scream— to yell at anyone attempting to dig her out, to hollow me. To leave me soulless and meaningless.

My defenses waver in my mind.

We have sex tapes.

Staged, they will say.

We have a child.

Business arrangement, they will argue.

I am hopelessly in love with her.

Who else can see this but you?

Thirty-five

Rose Cobalt

Connor shuts our bedroom door, my brain on fire. *I am on fire*, my arms shaking from something much greater and hotter than rage. My phone buzzes in my fist, and I ignore the calls and texts from my mother and father, setting the cell on the dresser.

Slowly I rotate to face my husband, ten feet separating us—tension entrenched within my solid bones. His eyes are bloodshot from restraining emotion, but he stands tall, all six-foot-four of him. His gaze holds acceptance of our fate, which I've only just hatefully consumed.

He studies my reaction, the way I rub my hands together and inhale short breaths.

"Lily has been in this situation before . . ." I remember how the media cast doubt about her relationship with Loren, and then three-way rumors surfaced with Loren, Lily and Ryke in the center. They made it out of that unscathed. So can we.

"And?" His deadened voice drums against my heart.

My nose flares, and I raise my chin. My efforts to instill confidence in myself feel more like an ill-fitting mask. "What other people think doesn't matter . . . because it's a little rumor." My voice betrays me, quaking with each syllable. "It's what I told her before . . . that people can say whatever they want, but you know the truth. You *love* him."

As the words leave my lips, he closes the space between us, clasping my wrist and pulling me into his chest. Our rigid bodies weld together, and he clutches me in a firm, comforting embrace, but I catch sight of his jaw muscles constricting. He submerges as many pained sentiments as me.

Very softly, he whispers, "I'm so sorry, Rose."

I choke out a breath. *Do not cry.* "You shouldn't apologize for this." I fist his button-down, my gaze piercing him between the eyes. He stares unflinchingly at me. We need battle armor. We need guns and cannons. We need to hit them like they've hit us. Revenge—bloodcurdling, soul-screaming *revenge*, blares in my charred brain.

Connor is more logical.

He values no part of revenge the way I do. We'll feel better once it happens, doesn't he see? They'll pay, whoever betrayed him, and we'll rise again.

He cups my face, his large hand cloaking me, and his deep-blue eyes pour roughly through me like an invisible riptide. "It matters," he says, shoveling the coldest truth in my direction, and a chill snakes icily across my neck. He's never been one for false hope, not towards me. "I'm sorry that it does. This isn't a baseless rumor like the ones with Lily, Loren and Ryke. The media has actual evidence that discredits us, our marriage and our love, and public perception will be overwhelmingly *against* us, unlike anything they faced." His thumb strokes my cheek. "This isn't close to the same caliber."

I swallow hard, my nose flaring again. *Do not cry.* "Our companies can handle the blows." Calloway Couture is now attached to Hale Co. It has an iron structure that'll support any crippling movement. Cobalt Inc. is usually sturdy, and previously led by Katarina Cobalt—I bet the board members are just as progressive as she was. Connor shouldn't be shunned by them.

"It's not our companies I'm worried about," he tells me.

Translation: *I care only about our future together.*

Jane . . . and all the kids we've thought to have along the way.

The other kids may never exist now, but we have Jane. It will affect her. I can't even begin to picture the type of ridicule and judgment she'll face from her peers. Everyone will believe she was born from a cold, heartless arrangement by robotic, unfeeling parents. I'll wrap her in my unbending arms, no matter how rigid I may be or how mechanic I may seem, and I'll shield her from this unjust storm the best I can.

I say to him, "You're worried about Jane."

"And you."

I press a hand to his chest, taking a single step back. "I can handle this, *just* as you can. We're equals."

"No." He clasps my wrists, stopping me from rubbing my hands again.

"No? What do you mean, *no?*"

"I don't want to be equals with you," he announces, his voice terribly flat.

My lips part, pain clawing at my lungs. "You don't mean that."

His eyes redden. "I mean everything I say to you."

Tears threaten to well. *Do not fucking cry, Rose.*

"I want you to be better than me," he declares, tugging me back to his body by my wrists. *We can handle this. We can handle this. We can handle this.* I'll repeat it until it becomes a truth and not a mocking sound in my head. He holds my cheek. "Look at me, Rose."

I've been avoiding his clarity, and he tries to pull me towards it.

When I meet his gaze, he says, "This is the worst."

A *King Lear* quote punctures my head: "The worst is not. So long as we can say, 'This is the worst.'"

He can't fix this.

We can't fix this.

"No." I try to push him off, but he holds me tighter, my wrist aching from one of his hands.

"*Yes*," he forces. "There is nothing we can do but bear it."

"I'll defend my love for you," I retort, fire scorching my heart.

"How?" he asks.

I think about *Princesses of Philly*, how the reality show helped justify Loren and Lily's romance. They needed a way to showcase and validate their relationship. The plan worked perfectly. The public fawned over them after *Princesses of Philly* aired. People rooted for them and championed their affection. Their desire was painstakingly clear within each frame.

Loren would pin my little sister against the kitchen counter, and they'd kiss as though breathing life into each other. She'd cling desperately to him, like she'd fall if not for his existence, and when she cried, he'd cling desperately to her—bracing her soul together while she braced his.

Their love is emotional.

Their love is outward and apparent.

I think of our time during *Princesses of Philly*. Connor wasn't well received by fans. More people liked me more with Scott Van Wright—a man I despised—than they did with the man I loved.

Our love is inward and intellectual.

It's of the mind and spirit.

Who else can see this but me?

I've never had to defend my relationship on this grand, massive scale, and Connor is repeatedly telling me that it's impossible. I recount the past four months. If we act like Lily and Loren, increasing our PDA again—we're faking it.

If we act like ourselves—we're stiff and detached.

So we just bear the criticism, then. Let it roll off our backs, no matter how much it burns and scars us? "When a volcano erupts, we don't stand beneath it, Connor."

"Where do you suggest we go?"

I don't know. I shake my head a few times. *I'm scared.*

I'm terrified of what our future looks like. My breathing staggers, and I hold up a finger so he'll give me a minute. My smothered emotions threaten to rise and take hold of me. "I'll be right back," I whisper. "I need to change . . . into something better." I smooth my dress.

"Rose." He says my name with worry, but I leave him and head for the closet. I just need a minute. I'll be okay afterwards. I'll withstand anything, just like him.

I walk quickly and tensely to the closet, and he stays behind, searching the room for something. Once inside, I shut the door and leave the lights off. In the pitch-black, I use my memory to find my fur coat, unhanging the soft garment.

My legs buckle the moment I clutch the coat to my body. My knees dig into the carpet, my chest tight and lungs bound. I can hear the television suddenly through the walls, the volume escalating. Connor must've been looking for the remote.

". . . they have a child together, but a source close to the Calloway family believes that Rose had a child *for* Connor—"

I scream into the coat, the violent, excruciating sounds muffled. My body vibrates in agony at the invalidation of my love and now *my* daughter, who I carried for nine months. Who I love more than anyone else can possibly see or know or even realize.

I scream again, my throat raw and inflamed.

". . . there are multiple accounts on *Princesses of Philly* where Rose states point-blank that she hates children. She's *never* liked kids, and her old friends from Dalton Academy have attested to this and spoken to GBA News."

People can change. People can grow. People can realize that the idea of something is more frightening than the reality.

Am I not allowed all of that? Am I just supposed to be identical to myself at eighteen and at twenty-two and twenty-six? Can I never decide differently or think in a new way? Why must I be the same?

An onslaught of maddened tears squeezes from my eyes, and I scream into a cry that originates in my core. I sense a crease of light in the closet, but it darkens to blackness once more, the door opening and gently shutting.

I can't cease the waterworks, even if I tried. I purge my emotions, the television faint in the background, and I feel Connor kneel behind me. His strong chest melds against my back, leaning forward along my curved spine to whisper, "*Vous êtes en sécurité avec moi.*" *You're safe with me.*

His arms slide around my hips, holding me with care that no one else will ever see, these moments kept in dark closets. I scream one last time, every gaping wound tearing open and tunneling through me.

His chest rises and falls deeper, and he clutches me tighter. I tremble, my throat burning, and he turns me towards his body. Our limbs lost in the pitch-black. I simply feel him pulling me onto his lap, my legs splayed to the side, one of his hands resting on my thighs. He guides my head to the crook of his shoulder, my silent tears dampening his shirt.

Our heavy breaths fill the quiet.

He kisses my forehead, his lips brushing my cheek. "I wouldn't trade our love for any other."

A tremor passes through my body, and I reach up and feel for him, my palm skimming his neck, his jaw . . .

He clasps his hand over mine, lifting my fingers higher to his cheek, where I want to be. I raise my head off his chest, sensing my lips nearing his in the dark.

I whisper, "I can hear our hearts breaking."

A tear wets my fingertips, his tears, and his other hand encases my face, the way mine does him. His lips nearly skim mine. "I'll shield your ears from the sound of heartbreak."

My chest swells. "And what happens when I ache to hear your voice?"

"I'll whisper beyond every anguished sound." He closes his lips over mine, once, before murmuring, "*Tu m'entendras toujours, où que je sois.*" *You will always hear me, no matter where I am.*

He has shaped my life, shaped *me*, so entirely, and I think about him in every action, in every extraordinary or commonplace thought. I wonder what he would do or what he would say. I'm independent, self-sufficient and singular—I'm all of those things while carrying and feeling and living out love.

"And can you still hear me?" I wonder, a breath between our lips.

"*Toujours.*" *Always.*

I brush the wetness on his cheek, the rarest tears my fingertips have ever felt, hidden in the confines of the dark. "I'm here for you," I remind him. "I will stand beside you, whatever you want to say to the press." It's his sexuality, his choice, and if he'd rather lie about his past or if he'd rather try to explain the truth—I'd support him equally and with wholehearted vigor.

He's quiet for a long moment, his thumb caressing my tear-streaked face. I worry that he thinks it'd be better to let me go. To disentangle himself from Jane and me and fight this alone.

The darkness conceals the answers in the creases of his face. I can only feel him against me, his muscles firm and his eyes wet.

So I ask, "Would you choose to drown with me beneath a river or burn with me in flames?"

"Neither," he whispers.

We're together in those choices, no matter which way we fail—we're together. I don't understand . . . "You have to choose one." A heavy, cold pain weighs against me.

His fingers disappear into my hair, clutching my face, his lips so very close. "I will die with you when we are old and withered and gray, and I'll live with you every day until then. *This* is what I'll always choose."

I nod, my shoulders relaxing, even if he can't see it. "You'll die *with me*, then," I breathe. It's a Shakespearean tragedy at its finest, and I can almost feel his lips rise, just by a fraction, in thought of this.

"Yes, darling. I will die with you." And he kisses me, powerfully and forcefully. He draws back to whisper, "But not today."

Still, I think we both recognize that this media uproar has begun to hurt us, much greater than anything has before.

Thirty-six

Connor Cobalt

D on't blink," Rose says, squirting drops in my eyes while I sit on our bed. I'd do it myself, but Jane is fast asleep in my arms, and every time I set her down, she wakes and cries.

"You're enjoying this," I mention, referring to her towering above me.

Her red lips never pull upwards. "I'm not."

I reach out and hold her by the waist, her body molded in a sleek black dress, her yellow-green eyes accentuated with mascara and liner. No one would expect that Rose cried an hour earlier—that my eyes have burned and leaked in accompaniment. Or that an uncomfortable, foreign pain still gnaws at me.

"Blink," she says.

I do, a few times, the drops soothing my raw eyes, and I rise with Jane in arm.

Rose touches Jane's tiny, delicate fingers, our daughter's lips parted with deep breaths. Her fragility, her purity, remind me that we're the only ones who can protect her during this time.

I never thought about sheltering a child from the pangs of reality. My mother never sheltered me in my early adolescence. *You're smarter for it*, she said. I learned to shut out my feelings. I lost all empathy for anyone other than myself. I needed Frederick to remind me that I'm human.

I'd rather Jane believe in fairies and magic than follow in my footsteps, I've realized. I'd rather she become more like her mother than like me.

I fear that cameramen will traumatize her. I fear that her innocence will be shattered faster than it ever should be. These fears sat in the back of my brain, even while we were enacting our six-month test. Now they've slammed to the front.

My two priorities are Rose and Jane. What happens to me in the process, I don't care nearly as much as I used to.

"Ready?" Rose asks. Everyone is waiting in the living room downstairs, our publicists, her father, her mother, her three sisters, Sam, Ryke, Loren and his son. Before I face the world, I have to face the people closest to us.

And the severity of the situation is clear with one fact: this has become an *extended* family affair.

"Wait," I tell Rose. I comb her hair over one shoulder.

She inhales strictly, her collarbone jutting out.

I kiss the nape of her neck, and she clutches onto my arms. I kiss the line of her jaw and the softness of her cheek. She may be tentative and rigid, but this woman in reality is the same woman in my fantasies. No one else may ever understand this, but many people won't ever come to understand me.

"I love you," I whisper before kissing her forehead, my free hand holding her face.

Her yellow-green eyes narrow, scorching a hole through me. The corners of my lips begin to rise.

"I can't cry again, Richard." She's afraid she might, and she just put on mascara.

I grin more. "Does love make you cry?"

"Not all love."

"Just ours," I say, as though pocketing a first-place prize.

She covers my lips with her palm. Rose never steps away from me. We draw closer, our daughter between us. When she drops her hand, I still wear an unrestrained grin.

"Why are you smiling like that?" Her gaze flits to my lips.

"Because I love all of you." *Now I'm ready.*

The minute we descend the stairs and round the corner, everyone rises off various pieces of furniture. I sometimes receive this royal treatment, my confidence propelling people to their feet. While I am fully poised—standing straight, expression composed, hand firmly in Rose's while cradling my daughter with the other—I recognize that this is more of a trial proceeding than a kingly salutation.

Rose and I say nothing. We sit on the vacant couch, and everyone else follows suit. Our two publicists are seated across from us on wooden chairs. The one on the left works for the Calloway family: Corbin Nery, midfifties, extremely focused and bold enough to be a shark in high-profile crises, but also paid to protect Greg and Samantha's reputation, even at the cost of mine.

The publicist on the right works for me: Naomi Ando, astoundingly diplomatic, rational and objective—all valuable assets.

Corbin and Naomi act like they're working in conjunction—friendly, side-by-side allies—but they're no more accomplices than I'd be to Jonathan Hale . . . who is suspiciously missing from this formal meeting.

Naomi clasps a folder. "We have a lot of ground to cover, Mr. Cobalt."

Corbin unfurls his legal pad. "First, we all need to know what we're dealing with here. Regardless of how we plan to approach the press, we need the truth."

I unbutton my suit jacket, my daughter asleep on my lap, and I look straight at my father-in-law, seated next to his wife in the two

Queen Anne chairs. In so many words, he's basically telling me that he wants the truth, using Corbin as his mouthpiece.

Greg Calloway may be quiet-spoken and benevolent, but he loves all of his daughters *above* the men they attach themselves to. He's only appreciated me for my business skills, my ability to kiss ass and paint a fake smile. He has no idea who I really am. I've been in the game of building relationships, not destroying them, and the truth will ruin everything.

Samantha touches her pearls once. "It has to be a lie." I sense her judgment before I even utter a word. My irritation almost translates to my expression, but I force back any facial movements, remaining impassive.

Rose is biting her tongue, ready to lash out, but she won't unleash this answer before me.

It's mine to set free.

"Be more specific," I finally speak. "What exactly am I acknowledging?"

Naomi says bluntly, "GBA News and eleven other outlets are suggesting you've been in sexual relationships with three men, two of which were former students at Faust Boarding School for Young Boys."

"Is this true or false?" Corbin asks.

In this room, there are a handful of people unaware of my past: Sam, Poppy, Samantha, Greg and maybe even Lily if Lo hasn't caught her up yet.

I choose to meet my father-in-law's stern gaze. I can't falter this time, not like I have with my friends. I want it to come out like it means nothing, even if it may change everything.

As easily as if I'm stating the temperature, I say, "True." My core tightens, but I'm the only one who feels this.

Greg turns his head, unable to look me in the eyes. He practically grinds his teeth. I think his hatred stems from a father trying to protect his daughter, so he must believe the whole story, then—that'd I create a business arrangement with Rose. If someone in our inner circle actually believes this dramatic elaboration of the truth, then we're as sincerely fucked as I thought we'd be.

"Rose," Samantha says in a scolding tone. "Did you know about this?"

"*Yes*," Rose says powerfully. "And I don't care. We all have past relationships . . ." She trails off, and I glance at her in my peripheral. She made a slip—since she's never been in a relationship before me.

I squeeze her hand in comfort, but her shoulders lock.

Samantha rocks forward, her trembling fingers pressed to her mouth. Greg is glaring at the wall, and I'm more concerned with how Rose is handling their reactions. While she's had many disagreements with her mother and sometimes even her father, none have been this serious.

I study her sharp breathing, about to move this conversation along, but Rose's older sister interjects.

"You're really comfortable with this, Rose?" Poppy asks as though trying to make sense of the truth.

Lo chimes in, "For Christ's sake, he slept with some guys—he didn't commit a fucking murder."

Corbin makes a check mark on his legal pad. "It'd be helpful if you stayed quiet, Loren," he says. "You're going to make this worse if you talk at all."

The bottom of my stomach sinks, but I'd been waiting for Lo to realize the shredder our friendship is about to be put through.

"What was that?" Lo sends a scathing glare at Corbin and then passes Moffy to Lily, his family of three cuddled on the love seat.

"It's one of our talking points," Corbin states. "We'll reach it in a minute. Let's not go out of order."

Lo clenches his teeth and turns to me for answers, his questioning, baffled look asking, *did you know we'd be a fucking talking point?*

Yes. I knew.

"Why wouldn't I be comfortable?" Rose suddenly spouts at her sister. "I'm *married* to him. We have a child together. Do you worry about all the people Sam has fucked in the past?"

"Whoa." Sam raises his hands in defense. "Please don't drag me into this."

"No," Poppy tells Rose, her tone calm. "I don't worry about his exes, but this is a little different, don't you think?"

My mother-in-law, Samantha, pipes in, "Why wouldn't you tell *me* if you knew this entire time? I'm your mother."

"I'm sorry, *Mother*," Rose retorts. "Have you told me everyone your husband used to bang before he slept with you?"

Greg yells, "It's not the same, Rose!" He rises to his feet.

"It should be!" Rose stands with the same ire. *It should be.* Maybe one day it will be, but right now, today, me having sex with a woman and me having sex with a man do not hold the same connotation to them the way they do to me, the way they do to Rose.

Yelling isn't the solution, even if I'd love to rise by her side and scream as loudly and as passionately. I clutch her hand, pulling her until she sits down again. I rub the small of her back and whisper, "Give them time to process."

She whips her head to me, eyes on fire. "I just want them to understand." Her low voice is only audible to me.

"Patience, darling."

She lets out a vexed breath.

Greg remains standing, hands on his waist, pacing to the window and back to his chair a couple times. He motions to Corbin to continue, unable to produce the words, unable to look me in the eye and ask me himself.

So I must speak to someone who works for him. I imagine myself laughing in frustration, glaring at the ceiling, shaking my head, every reaction that I can only internalize. I don't wear my antipathy or my outrage or my aggravation—but it fucking exists inside of me, scraping at my brain.

Corbin asks, "Did you marry Rose to hide your sexuality? And is this arrangement consensual between both parties?"

I can feel my jaw muscles try to contract. *Consensual.* As though I forced her into our marriage. "I married Rose because we love each other," I state plainly. They wait for an emotional downpour from me. It's not in me to kick and scream and drop to my knees. Rose thinks she may have a hard time convincing the world that she loves me, but I'm going to have a much harder time convincing her parents that I love their daughter. "We had no ulterior motives," I conclude.

"What if he manipulated her?" Greg suddenly asks his publicist. I frown, wondering if Jonathan has been muttering in his ear.

Naomi cuts off Corbin. "That's something for the legal team, and we shouldn't inspect a bullet when no one has pulled a trigger."

I rise with my daughter in my arm, and the room falls to silence. I manage to capture Greg's gaze, even if he aches to look away. "I'm not going to beg you to trust me," I say calmly. "What I can ask is that you acknowledge the intelligence of your own daughter. She hasn't been duped by me; in fact, she'd leave me at the hint of infidelity. I've shared more with her than I ever have with you, so know that she's not blind by any means."

I pause, more cautious as Samantha fixates on Jane in my grasp. I adjust my daughter, her eyes almost fluttering open from her nap.

Greg pinches the bridge of his nose. "I think we should focus on how to bury this, and not what we think of it right now."

Samantha's strict bun pulls the follicles of her hairline. "It might be best for Jane to stay with us in the meantime—"

"No, she's safe with us," I cut her off, my defenses and guards beginning to lift higher than before. I feel Rose boiling beside me, looking murderously at her mother for even suggesting to take our child away from us.

I sit again, and I pass Jane to Rose, who pulls our daughter protectively to her chest. Jane only stirs to hold on to Rose's arm like she's clutching a teddy bear.

Greg watches Jane. "Is she in a loving environment?" His doubt leeches each fucking word. I rub my lips, pissed, so pissed I could scream. I could drum my chest and stomp my feet, but no matter how much I want to do it, I see no logical point in the actions.

Rose's face twists, bouncing between rage and hurt. "How could you even ask that?"

"I'm a concerned grandfather. I love that little girl."

He's suggesting that his love outweighs ours. I remember how I delivered Jane with my own hands. How Rose held her every night she cried. How we've spent sleepless months without complaint. How we've tried to minimize Jane's exposure in the media, redirecting the heat on us. How we've treasured every milestone she's made.

How do you measure love?

Is it by the things we're willing to do? By the sacrifices we're willing to make? If it is—then I love my daughter madly, because I would cripple my world to give her something to stand on. I would implode Cobalt Inc. if I had to, the foolish choice. But a wise woman once said that love is worth every foolish choice we make.

Would Greg Calloway bulldoze Fizzle for his granddaughter? Not a chance.

Rose straightens even more. "Be a concerned *parent* first and trust me, your daughter."

"Please, Rose," Greg says, not one to raise his voice, even if he's already accomplished that once today.

I hug Rose closer to my side, and she exhales a couple times, trying to move past her father's doubt. There is no solution here.

I rotate to Naomi, ready to speed this beyond accusations and blame. "Our marriage is real and consensual. The sex tapes aren't fabricated"—she jots notes as quickly as I speak—"and we had a child to start a family together. The only truth is in the past."

Rose scoots to the edge of the couch, keeping her hand in mine. "What's our best defense?" she asks Naomi.

"A public statement from both of you," she says. "There's a lot of evidence that says your marriage is a ploy." She thumbs through her folder. "Mr. Cobalt, your Instagram is littered with photos specifically of your wife with you, but she's glaring at you in almost every one."

How I like it.

"They love each other," Lily interjects. She flushes when every eye pins to her. "That's what their love looks like."

Rose nearly smiles, tears beginning to collect. She mouths to Lily, *thank you.*

"Well," Corbin butts in, "it looks like hate."

"Fuck you," Ryke slings a curse from the window nook, Daisy sprawled on his lap.

My lips lift.

"I'm here to state what everyone in the public is thinking," Corbin reminds him.

"And I'm here to flip this around in a positive light," Naomi states. "Don't delete any of these photos, Mr. Cobalt. It admits guilt. Try to add a variety of images, maybe date nights, photos of your wedding rings, and yes, continue to post ones that you normally would. There's a fine line between justifying yourself and trying too hard to appear like something you're not."

The increase in PDA bit us in the ass for that last reason. I respect Naomi's counsel, so I ask, "Should we acknowledge the striptease or anything the media has spun around on us?" Normally I'd be more specific and say that I went down on Rose, but her father is in the room. He needs time to cool down, and I'd rather not make it harder for him to like me again.

"GBA News had a body language analyst dissect those photographs," she explains. "And they found reasonable doubt in Rose's stiff posture. In almost every frame where you're in public—where you kiss her, et cetera—she seems uncomfortable."

She hasn't been the best actress, but she tried, and we couldn't have known this was what it'd come to.

"Hey," Daisy chimes in, her husky curled beside Ryke, "that's not her fault. You know, not everyone enjoys kissing in public."

"But why these past four months more than ever before?" Corbin asks. "The media is going to latch on to the timing."

Rose pulls back her shoulders. "We were trying something new, to spice up our relationship since we've had a child."

We'll never utter the real truth: that we were enticing the media—on purpose. As far as Rose and I are concerned, the only one who will ever know our secret is Ryke Meadows.

Naomi nods. "It's a decent defense, and it's better than staying quiet. We'll add that to your written letter. It's not something you'd need to say at a press junket." She'll type the letter. We'll read it and approve. That's how this works. "I know you have some family pictures of Jane on your Instagram, but you two should post more. In addition, you both should work on tweeting about parenting. People like these comments. It makes you relatable."

"*Loving* comments," Corbin clarifies, "not sarcasm or anything that can be taken out of context."

Rose huffs. "I have no idea what you mean." She combs her fingers through Jane's hair affectionately. She does know, almost entirely. She hates talking about it. I've seen regret flash in her eyes at comments she's made before, taking a concept too far, not meaning the degree of what she says.

She speaks her mind often, and she's penalized for every single word, even the ones said in haste, the ones layered with fears, the ones bleeding with rage. I love all of her opinions, the passionate ones, the dramatic ones and everything in between.

"'At ConnorCobalt,'" Corbin reads Rose's old tweet off his legal pad. "'Every time the little gremlin wails, my ovaries kill an egg. I'm going to be barren soon.'"

The people that know Rose laugh. Her mother and father remain quiet.

"It was a joke," Rose says, her voice breaking at the end. She stares harshly at the ceiling, more upset than I thought she'd be. I can feel her confidence waning.

My smile fades. I massage her tense shoulder and lean closer to whisper, "It's not your fault, Rose." None of this is her fault. Everything is being distorted.

"She should be allowed to be herself," Ryke interjects, sitting up on the window nook. Daisy slides off his lap and pets their dog.

"Not at the cost of her reputation," Samantha says. "You wouldn't understand—"

"I understand. I fucking understand more than you even want to know—and this entire thing is about turning them into people they're not." He points at me. "Let them be whoever they want to fucking be—the end."

If only it was that easy, my friend.

"You live off a Hale Co. trust fund," Sam chimes in, reminding everyone about the money involved in my decision. "We're trying to protect *companies* that can be hurt by public perception. I don't think you have a say here."

"Fuck you," Ryke fumes, standing off the window nook.

Lo hesitates to block his brother from a physical altercation, but Ryke hasn't charged Sam yet.

Naomi takes advantage of the brief silence and reroutes the topic. "The sex tapes are a good form of defense, even if everyone is trying to brush them under the rug."

Corbin taps his pen to his legal pad. "They're not brushing them anywhere. Everyone believes that the tapes are just another stunt to cover Connor's tracks. And frankly, I'd buy into it too."

"Then you're an idiot," Loren interjects.

"No," Corbin says, "the public doesn't know Connor as intimately as all of you. They know what they see, and what they see alludes mostly to a well-coordinated stunt. *My* suggestion—to clean everything quickly and easily—you need to deny these claims against you."

Rose tenses even more beneath my hand. I can't speak right away, but Corbin isn't finished.

"You'll say that you've never had sex with a man before. You'll say that these guys were friends of yours and they just want a quick payout by tabloids. You'll say you're *heterosexual* and in a healthy, loving marriage with your wife."

To fix this, I must lie.

I already know this. I've thought a hundred steps ahead of them, and I wait for Naomi to offer me a different version of the same hurdle.

"Fuck all of you," Ryke says, words that I feel but can't articulate.

"If you don't have anything constructive to add, I think you should leave," Corbin tells him.

Lo shoots a withering glare his way. "You're our goddamn publicist, not the king of the castle, so stop acting like you have the authority to banish my brother to another room."

Naomi abruptly stands. "I have an alternative." She procures a paper from her folder and passes it to me. I graze over a long list of sexualities: bisexual, pansexual, polysexual, among other terms. "Pick one," she says.

As if it's as easy as ordering an appetizer off a menu.

The room deadens, all eyes shifting to me. The paper is heavier than they may realize. My entire twenty-seven years of existence

I've wedged myself into parameters that other people construct—to blend in, to *appease* men and women alike.

To me, these terms are just another parameter—and I've never enjoyed stepping into this box, to pretend to be someone else when what I *feel* is so simple, so rudimentary. I admire other people who can identify with these words, but it's not what *I* feel.

I'm attracted to people, to the all-encompassing *passion* of the soul, of the body and the mind.

And I shouldn't have to be labeled to make sense. My sexuality shouldn't be of priority to anyone but me. If I'd only slept with women, no one would care, but they've learned differently, and now they're bothered, incensed—confused, doubtful.

So to appease them, I have to step into that cramped box. To make sense to them, I have to declare something I don't feel.

I know who I fucking am, but very few people truly know me. Now I have to choose which Connor Cobalt millions of people will see.

The fake one: I'll give myself a label. I will be what they need me to be. In doing so, I make good with my father-in-law and eliminate doubt that shadows my love for Rose and her love for me.

The real one: I never say one way or the other. The public will be left to wonder. I destroy relationships with Greg and Samantha, possibly damage my friendship with Lo. My love for Rose and her love for me may always be questioned.

My nineteen-year-old self wouldn't have flinched at this ultimatum. I would've faked my way through the rest of my life, through the rest of my days, and I would've lost that last shred of humanity I'd let Rose keep safe for all those years.

Be real, Richard.

I placate people. I appease them. What happens when I stop, for a moment, to live in the comfort of my own skin? I may lose everything. But what if this is the sacrifice I have to make for Jane?

What if I'm supposed to abandon who I am, to live a lie, so that she may live in peace?

The variables, the costs, the benefits, the lingering what-ifs, lead me to confusion—to a head-on collision with fear.

I rub my forehead that begins to perspire.

"It shouldn't be this hard," Samantha says.

"Have you ever had to declare to the world that you're straight?" I ask her. "Has anyone looked at you differently for it?"

Her lips tighten.

"No, I didn't think so." I fold the paper into fourths, everyone watching me keenly. "Heterosexuality is the norm. Maybe when you have to stand at a podium, with cameras at your face, and say *one* word that will change the way people perceive you—you'll understand that this isn't easy, not even for me."

Rose squeezes my hand in support, and when I look at her, I detect the pride glowing beneath her yellow-green irises. She says she'd stand by me no matter what I'd choose, but Rose champions every part of me that makes me *me*.

This is no exception.

"Then tell everyone that you're straight," Samantha says, "and no one will look at you differently."

"Mother," Rose sneers.

"Don't chastise me, Rose. I'm saying what everyone is thinking. I understand that we all have our secrets, but there are some that shouldn't be mentioned aloud." I've changed in her eyes, and she'd probably cast me back into a closet if she could, plug her ears and reverse time, so that I'm the person she needs me to be all over again.

This is who I've always been, even if she couldn't see it.

Ryke steps towards the furniture, his gaze darkened, and Daisy clasps his wrist, to keep him stationary. "Yeah, he shouldn't tell the fucking truth because *you* can't handle it? He shouldn't be himself because it makes you squirm?"

This subject rouses him more than others. He hasn't ever needed to be an advocate for me before, but it's nice to see that he would. I'm grateful for it.

"Enough," Greg says. "I think we've all voiced our opinions, and Connor has the final say-so."

I pass the paper to Naomi. "You'll write the formal letter, stating that I love Rose—all that we've discussed here—but you'll leave out any acknowledgment of whether or not I've slept with the three men. I need time to decide what I want to say before we hold a press conference."

Corbin lets out an exasperated sigh. "Silence admits guilt."

"You can tease the press conference so people know I plan on speaking."

He checks his calendar. "We'll schedule it for April tenth."

That's in one week. "Mid-May," I rebut. *I need time.* "You don't realize, but these guys are holding nondisclosure agreements, and if I claim that I'm heterosexual and they show them to *anyone*, I've just moronically trapped myself. So I need time to sort out my legal affairs." I can't sue them for breaking the NDA, not unless I want to admit that I've slept with them. It's complicated.

Corbin looks to Greg, and my father-in-law nods in acceptance of this open-ended conclusion.

Naomi closes her folder, and Corbin clears his throat. "One last thing . . ." He spins his pen between two fingers and then points it at Lo. "We need to clear this up." He motions to me, then back to Lo.

"And what's that?" Lo grits his teeth.

Corbin glances at his notes. "You were videotaped kissing in Mexico last year—"

"It was a dare." Lo's voice is a serrated edge. "Everyone knows this."

"In March during St. Patrick's Day, you were photographed pinching his bare ass—"

"He's my *friend*."

"During *Princesses of Philly*, you two often made remarks about 'blow jobs' and 'masturbating' and 'coming' with each other, not with your respective girlfriends."

Lo sits on the very edge of his seat, pointing a threatening finger at Corbin. "And *no one* gave a shit back then, so stop trying to turn it into a problem now."

"I represent the mass majority of people outside this house, and they've already begun analyzing your friendship. If we don't squash this soon, they'll start claiming that you're sleeping with him and that Lily, your *wife*, is actually with Ryke, your *brother*, and that your son isn't really yours. All I'm trying to do is minimize the ramifications."

Lo stares, faraway, at the ground, eyes daggered like, *why? How could this even happen?*

It happened because there's a stigma that I can't even shake.

"My suggestion," Corbin says, "is that you two never cross paths in public. Don't talk. Don't touch. Don't tweet each other. Don't so much as look in the other's direction. It's probably best if Connor does the same with Ryke."

My stomach is unexpectedly in knots. I remove my suit jacket, uncomfortably hot all of a sudden.

"People view your friendship differently now, Loren, and you don't want them to get the wrong impression."

According to the Calloways' publicist, I'm not allowed to have straight male friends. Our jokes aren't held at the same standards any longer. Everything I ever say to Lo and Ryke will be riddled with questioning and doubt. *Are you attracted to them? Do you want to sleep with them?*

No.

But who will even believe me now?

Ryke rakes his hands through his hair, disheveling the thick strands. He's so incensed that he leaves the room, banging the door to the kitchen. I hear him say something like *nothing has fucking changed*. And yet, it all has.

Daisy and Nutty, their white husky, race after him.

"Lo," I breathe.

He raises his head barely to meet my expression, and I see how reddened his eyes have become. I've seen him at his lowest point in life. I've watched him get sober and watched him relapse. I've carried him, barely alive, in my arms. He's seen me shed tears after the birth of my daughter. I've seen him smile after the birth of his son. We've been through two weddings, five of his birthdays, even more holidays and trips around the world.

There is *never* a dull moment in the company of Loren Hale.

Altering the boundaries of our friendship makes it change shape, and I'm not sure if it'll ever be the same as it was.

"You need to do what's best for you," I tell Lo, trying to make it easier for him.

His jaw sharpens, restraining emotion. "And ignoring you every day outside of this house is what's best for me? Pretending like you don't even exist? Now we can't carpool to work. We won't be able to pick up our kids from kindergarten at the same time, or eat lunch at the same restaurant. I can't call you. I can't text you. I can't act like I care at all about you—it's ass-backwards."

I try to find better words for him. "Lo—"

"You've helped me for years." His brows pull hard. "Now it's time I help you, and I'm not acting like you're a leper because this guy tells me to. You may be fucking weird as hell when you and Rose start verbally sparring, but you're *my* weirdo best friend. That's not changing."

Before I can even accept his declaration, shoes clap along the hardwood. I didn't even hear the door shut, but Jonathan Hale stuffs his hands in his pockets, standing tall behind my couch. I immediately rise—the *how* part of this massive leak slapping me across the face. *How did those three guys become pressured to break their agreements?*

"It is changing, Loren," Jonathan says. "You protect your wife, your son and your company. You don't protect *him*."

There are only three people that could've fucked me over:

Jonathan.

Theo.

Frederick.

Hearing the spite in Jonathan's voice, I'd bet everything on him.

Thirty-seven

Rose Cobalt

Loren Hale's features could kill, his jaw a battle-ax and his eyes steel blades. "When the entire goddamn world thought you molested me, I didn't ignore you," he tells his father. "And guess what? They *still* believe that, and here you are and here I am."

"Our relationship has no effect on *your* family," Jonathan sneers. "This does. Don't be a fucking idiot, Loren."

About three people, including me, prepare to interject, but Lo beats us to it. "You don't get to speak to me like that—*ever*." He rises off the love seat and gives Lily a singular look like *take Moffy out of here.* She nods once before leaving for the kitchen.

Loren's self-respect is a beautiful sight amid treachery, which first began with the crisis management to-do list, tallied with lies and shame, and now ends with Jonathan's unwelcome appearance. I don't like how Connor studies him, each standing on either side of the couch with strict postures.

There are answers that no one wants to hear. We've handled disloyalty at a grander, nastier scale once before, and that person has been *shunned* from our group.

Ryke's mother, Sara Hale, leaked Lily's sex addiction to the press. I can barely imagine someone trying to repeat that mistake and the damage she caused.

Jane stirs in my arms, and I lift her a little, resting her head against my chest. She clutches onto my gold necklace.

"I'm helping you," Jonathan retorts, drawing my attention to him. "If you can't see that, then you need to open your . . ." He trails off at Lo's scathing glare. I'm sending one too, but it's not effective when Jonathan only concentrates on his son.

I can admit this: when I was a little girl, I was frightened of this man who crept into our house, bringing with him a kid that irked me to no end. Jonathan was always refined, dressed in thousand-dollar suits, tailor-made, with even more expensive liquor in hand. He had a tyrannical demeanor that crushed everyone in his wake.

He was the villain from classic James Bond films, but as I grew older I saw his flaws, the underbelly of the beast. Jonathan was so insecure, so tortured by the idea that his son would discover his rotten innards and then leave him. He'd do *anything* to keep Lo in arm's reach.

He'd even become sober for him.

So while I was scared of Jonathan *many* years ago, he seems more human, less like a two-dimensional criminal. He's frailer now. Not just in his age, sideburns graying and lines pulling by his eyes, but in his words, which are riddled with fear.

Loren crosses his arms. "Connor is my best friend, so you're telling me that you wouldn't help Greg if he needed it?" He points at my father, who stands beside the Queen Anne chair. "That's *your* best friend."

"If you were the cost, no. I'd let Greg burn."

Oh God.

My hand dazedly rises to my lips. My father has always been my buffer between Jonathan and Connor. If Jonathan hurt my husband, it'd mean he was hurting *me*, his best friend's daughter. What he's saying destroys that last piece of armor we had.

"What'd you do, Jonathan?" my father asks, his fingers gripping the top of my mother's chair.

"Lo is running my company now. I'm trying to guide him, and then I learn about this one"—he jabs a finger in Connor's direction—"the kind of things he's done."

Connor finally speaks. "*Done*, as in past tense. Your broad use of 'things' doesn't help plead your case, and since you can't articulate yourself, let me help you. I've had sex with men and women before I ever began dating Rose. I'd hope you at least know the anatomical difference of 'men,' so I won't clarify that for you."

We all hang on every precisely constructed word, and my pulse skips with each tight breath Connor releases between them.

"Now, this may be hard for you to understand," Connor continues without missing a beat, "but I personally practice monogamy. I also believe in the customs of marriage, the promise to be faithful. I realize this term holds no ground for you since you cheated multiple times on your ex-wife, but you shouldn't use your experiences as weight against me. It's illogical, fallible and frankly annoying."

Jonathan opens his mouth, but Connor never gives him room for an interjection.

"Bypassing your sheer ignorance, you know that I am exceptionally loyal to my *wife*, so on what basis would I ever try to fuck your son?"

Jonathan goes to speak.

"That was rhetorical," Connor cuts him off. "There are *no* rational grounds for what you've done. So when you tell me that you contacted these three guys from my past and pressured them to out me, you better believe that it was the stupidest decision you could've ever made. To put it plainly, you've just shot yourself in the fucking face."

I stand next to Connor, supporting Jane on my hip. My brain

fires synapses that say, *claw Jonathan's eyeballs, rip him to shreds.* I envision a heinous, bloody murder, but my legs are congealed magma, unable to move even a step towards him.

"*Je veux lui faire du mal,*" I whisper to Connor, my voice trembling with pain and rage. *I want to hurt him.* It frightens me how badly I want to hurt this man.

Connor slides his arm around my waist, his lips to my ear. "It solves nothing, Rose." He's so outwardly calm, and I can't for a second believe that's what lies inside. His speech was one of anger, even if his words held very sparse inflection.

"Jonathan?" my father repeats, disbelief in his voice.

"Dad?" Lo frowns. "Tell me you didn't do anything . . ."

He glares at Connor, never shifting his gaze to confront the people he never meant to wrong.

My mother stands all of a sudden. "Jonathan," she scolds. "We've put our neck out for you multiple times, and if you knew anything at all about Rose's husband, you had a duty to tell us first, not the press."

I'm not surprised by my mother's loyalty. She may be a lot of things, but when it comes to protecting the Calloway name, she takes a front-row seat. I may be Cobalt legally, but to the media, I will always be Rose Calloway.

I protectively keep a hand on Jane's head while she sleeps. "Do you even know what you've done?" I ask him.

Jonathan outstretches his arms. "I did what I felt was right." He looks to Lo. "You don't know what your friend is capable of, and if you weren't going to separate yourself from him, I had to find a way to do it for you."

His admittance makes me stagger back, but Connor holds me closer, his hand tightening as though he needs me by his side as much as I need him.

Guilt and pain shatters Loren's expression. "No . . ." Lo shakes his head.

My face heats, and my eyes burn and narrow to sharp points. I keep wanting to say: *If you ever come after my family* . . . or *if you ever try to hurt my daughter* . . . or *if you destroy the people I love* . . .

But these threats have already expired.

Jonathan gestures to Connor. "You keep staring at me like you think I'm a fucking idiot, but *you* didn't even stop this from happening." His tone is less hostile, and his eyes flicker to Greg, seeing hurt scrunch my father's face.

Jane is awake, and she lets out a high-pitched wail. I bounce her a little and stroke her head. I take a quick glance at Loren, his gaze haunted and plastered to the rug. I hear commotion from the kitchen, along with howls from a dog, and I can only guess that Daisy and Lily are trying to restrain Ryke from storming into the living room.

Connor watches that door as closely as he watches Loren as closely as he watches Jane and me. He's that idle river, but for the first time, this is about *him* more than anyone. It has to be eating at his core, even if he barely shows it.

"I work within the realm of the law," Connor tells Jonathan. "I don't cast threats against someone's livelihood or family—so when I face someone who plays a more immoral game than me, I'm not blind to the fact that I'm at a disadvantage. But it doesn't mean that I can't win."

I narrow my eyes again at Jonathan. "How'd you even know *who* Connor had been with?" Even the thought of Frederick willfully handing Jonathan this information curdles my stomach.

Coconut howls again, scraping at the door, equally displeased at today's events. I like that dog. She can smell the foul stench of disloyalty. From the kitchen, I hear cursing: a barrage of *fucking*s mixed with *calm down* and *wait*.

Jonathan scratches his jaw, a slight shadow from skipping a shave. "I had some time after my transplant surgery . . ." He looks to Loren and then to Greg again, the consequences hitting him better than my anger has. At least he's feeling something ugly. ". . . and I called Faust. The boarding school gave me a roster of everyone who attended while Connor was there. It cost me fifty grand . . ." I think he just now realizes that it cost him more than money.

Loren rubs his eyes, about to excuse himself as he nears the kitchen door.

"You called hundreds of names?" Connor asks. He went to all this trouble, just to see Lo and Connor separated?

"I had time on my hands, and you'd be surprised how many caved with a cash offer in the six digits. People piss on their non-disclosures as soon as you tell them you'll cover the fine. Remember that, Lor . . . en." His words falter at the sight of his son, who rubs his reddened eyes.

"You're sick," Poppy suddenly says. I turn to my sister, who's stayed quiet mostly, Sam near her side. She's slack-jawed in horror.

Jonathan touches his chest defensively. "When you're protecting your child, you'll do just about anything." He looks to me. "You'll see." I press my daughter closer to my chest, her cries at a minimum.

"None of us would ever do this," Lo declares. "We'd never even consider it for a second."

"Then you're weak—"

"No," Lo cuts him off, his face twisting with pain. "I'm twenty-five, Dad. I don't need you to hold my hand and tell me who to trust. I don't need you to speak for me or to degrade me. I need you to *love* me." His voice cracks. "And the saddest thing . . . I'm beginning to think you don't even know what real love is."

Jonathan reacts like a bullet passed slowly and excruciatingly through his brain. Like he shot himself in the face.

Connor was right. *By the surprise of no one,* he'd say.

I watch Loren head towards the kitchen while my father asks, "Why not tell me, Jonathan?"

Jonathan's throat bobs. He seems small and defenseless now. I've never seen Loren hold so much power over his dad, not until today. "Connor would've convinced you otherwise," Jonathan tells him.

"Not because I'm manipulative," Connor says easily, "but because I would've been right. It's impossible to reverse what you've done."

Jonathan shrugs his tense shoulders. "I had to try."

My blood still boils, my arms quaking. I need to leave with Loren, and I glance quickly to Connor to let him know. Instead of nodding, he tells Jonathan, "Leave."

"I'm going to wait for my son—"

"Which one?" Connor asks. "You see that door that Lo is about to open? On the other side is a man who gave his father part of his liver, with hopes that he'd be kind and a better person than he once was. This man also likes to use his fists on people who've wronged him. So if you're staying, you're going to be punched in the face. So leave."

Jonathan's brows furrow. "Don't you want to see me get punched?" Weirdly, he looks like he'd rather be hit than go home alone.

I cringe. I don't want to pity him. I want to *hate* him. I'd rather focus on Jonathan's two-dimensional villainous qualities than the parts that make him a troubled human being. It makes my hate feel justified, rational even.

"I've never had a father figure, nor do I particularly want one," Connor announces. "But I'm aware of what it means for a son to hit a father, and I don't take pleasure in seeing that. So if you're smart, you'll leave."

"I don't know how you do it," Jonathan says, almost beneath his breath. He actually heads to the foyer.

I ask since I know Connor won't, "Do what?"

His eyes land on my husband. "You make me feel like I lost

when I should've won, and you make it seem like you won when you lost."

He must've been planning a victory lap around my living room, ready to pump his fists in the air and exit with his son, safe and sound by his side.

Now he's leaving with his tail between his legs.

"We both lost," Connor says, and I pale.

He never admits this aloud, even when it's true. A cold blade drives through my abdomen, reality sweeping me back into a tempest.

You don't love your husband.

You don't love your child.

It's all a big game. It's all fake.

Fake, I mentally scoff.

Fake.

What about our pain and fury and grief? Are those fake too?

Thirty-eight

Connor Cobalt

t takes us a couple minutes to push through Lily and Daisy's kitchen barricade, table and chairs stacked together to bar Ryke from the living room. When Lo and I finally breach the doorway, Ryke attempts to charge past us. I seize his bicep and push him further back, to where Rose and Loren can slip around me.

"He's gone, Ryke," I say, as calmly as I'm able to. My throat constricts with the rest of my muscles. It's hard for me to concentrate on the future, past today, and stay fully upright. Never have I had this problem before. To trick myself, I just worry about the present and leave tomorrow out of my mind.

"He's not fucking gone," Ryke growls. "I hear him—I *fucking* hear him." He shoves me to reach the door, but I grab hold of his arms again.

"You hear Corbin, Samantha, Poppy and Sam." I told Naomi she could go, and then Greg left to talk to Jonathan, probably outside in the driveway. I'd never tell Ryke how close his father actually is.

Unfortunately, Jonathan is attached to almost all of us, so when he does something deplorable, nearly everyone is affected. Theo had only a thin strand tethered to Loren and Rose through Hale Co.

If my past had to be showcased at all, Theo vindictively outing me would've been better than what we face now.

"Did he really . . ." Ryke struggles to speak. In my peripheral, I notice Loren whispering to Lily by the microwave, his eyes misted, and then Daisy quickly lets her Siberian husky out the back door, the yard fenced in.

I don't see Rose anywhere, and I don't even have time to contemplate *where* she could be, my phone buzzing in my pocket. My mind is either fogged or rotating backwards and sideways.

"Connor." Ryke growls my name. "I have to know if it's fucking true." I assume he only heard fragments of our discussion through the wall.

I rest a hand on his shoulder, concerned that he may try to bolt past me again, and with the other, I retrieve my cell. "Yes, it's true." Before the guilt hits him, I add, "And if you blame yourself for this, you're past tragic, my friend. His actions aren't yours, in the same way that your mother's actions aren't yours."

Daisy swiftly slides between us, setting her hands on Ryke's chest. It enables me to let go of my grip on him. "Hey there," Daisy says.

Ryke lets out a tense breath. Unsurprisingly, he relaxes more in her company than in mine.

I check my phone.

You free? We need to talk.—Scott Van Wright

He's the last person I want to see, capping off one of the worst days I've ever experienced. Regardless of my personal feelings, I have to meet him. I can tell that he doesn't trust me one hundred percent yet. We haven't brought up our hatred of each other during the reality show. So how could he believe that I'm truly his friend all of a sudden? It's a conversation that has to happen.

I brace my arm on the bar counter, my body in knots.

"I feel sick to my stomach," Ryke says to Daisy.

"I can get you a water or a cupcake."

He almost smiles. "A fucking cupcake?"

She nods. "We have fucking cupcakes too. I hear they can cure all maladies."

"Is that a theory, Calloway?"

She shakes her head. "Nope, it's just true."

Before I text Scott back, I have to check on my wife. "Where's Rose?" I ask Daisy, her arms wrapped around Ryke's waist and his arms wrapped around her shoulders.

"The half bath." She points to the bathroom door beside the pantry.

I pocket my phone and hurry to find Rose.

When I enter the tiny half bath, I catch Rose vigorously scrubbing her hands, the faucet running. Jane sits near the toilet, shaking a bracelet.

"Rose . . ." I shut the door and slide behind my wife, more concerned than I try to let on.

"I changed Jane's diaper," she tells me, her voice tight. Usually she can change Jane, wash her hands once, and be done with the process and not obsess. The stress from today has thrown everything out of sync.

"And how long have you been washing your hands?"

"They still smell like baby wipes." She sniffs her palm and cringes before adding more soap.

I extend my arms on either side of her body and grip both of her wrists.

"Richard," she warns.

"Look at your hands, Rose."

Her eyes are bloodshot, and when I peek at myself in the mirror, I notice that mine are too. She finally absorbs her raw palms and reddened skin, one of her nails bleeding at the cuticle. She inhales and recoils backwards at the sight, knocking against my chest.

I grab a small towel and spin her around, so she faces me. Then

I gather her hands and encase them in the towel to dry, her yellow-green eyes locked on my blue.

"I didn't realize," she whispers.

"It's been a long day," I say. I'm ready for it to be over, but it's not yet.

She can tell there's more. I watch her collarbone protrude. "I'll handle the social media," she says. "It'll take some stress off you, and you can just think about what you want to say or not say at the press conference."

"That's not equal division of labor, hun. The social media should be split." I rub my thumb over her bottom lip, the truth wedged in my throat. *I have to see Scott.* A longer moment passes—and she waits patiently even if her eyes begin to burn holes into mine. "I have to see Scott."

"What?" Her face falls, and she frees her hands from the towel. "Today."

She slaps my thumb away. "He can wait."

"No, he can't, Rose."

She glances once at Jane, who's more interested rattling the bracelet than us right now. "You don't have to do this anymore, Connor."

"Yes, I do," I say. "I want him completely out of our lives as much as you, and this is the only way." I pause, already hearing her rebuttal in my head. *You can't handle it.* "The argument that you want to use isn't good enough, so don't even say it."

She clutches onto my shirt, fire returning to her gaze. I'm happy to see more of it, even for a moment. "You have no idea what I'm going to say."

"You're going to tell me that I can't stomach Scott and this media shit storm at the same time."

She raises her chin. "Or maybe that's just your conscience."

Or maybe Frederick is in my head. I've been ignoring his calls all day. He'll want to hash out my "feelings," which are stronger than usual.

"Emotions are just obstacles," I tell her. "They're not restraints unless I let them be." I can control them a little longer.

She looks frightened by my declaration, her knuckles whitening, still fisting my shirt.

"Rose," I murmur, "*n'ayez pas peur*." *Don't be afraid*. I draw her even closer, our bodies curving together. She's fearful I'll forget who I am—a man who can love and empathize—but I know she'll remind me. I'm counting on it.

She surprises me by kissing my neck.

I smile at her tentativeness, and I lift her head and kiss her more aggressively on the lips. The force pins her back against the sink. My mind almost drowns out the dozen other frequencies and white noise, leaving only her mouth and her heat.

Then the door swings open.

Ryke bolts for the toilet. Thankfully Jane sits out of the way, Ryke's abrupt presence distracting her from the bracelet.

He kneels. And he pukes.

Daisy is quick to appear by his side, rubbing his back.

"Already on your knees for me," I say, hoping the lighthearted quip will lessen the tension. My skin crawls at a grating realization. "I suppose that's the last joke I can make with you." It's not like he responds with anything more than a middle finger and a *fuck off*, but I'll miss those all the same.

He clutches onto the toilet bowl, breathing heavier, angrier. Before he responds, Lo slips into the half bath with Lily, Moffy on the crook of her hip. He shuts the door behind them, and I scan him from head to toe for signs that he's stable.

Ryke does the same from the ground, but he's more obvious about it than I am.

In my opinion—which should be trusted above everyone else's—they both seem equally distressed: skin pallid, eyes puffy and muscles flexed. They've put too many emotions into their father to take this news well.

"I'm okay," Lo tells his older brother. "You're the one who looks like shit."

Ryke flips him off and shifts to a sitting position, elbow on the toilet seat. He whispers something inaudible to Daisy, who nods and whispers back. It's easy to discern what goes on between Lily and Loren, but the other couple is too private to infer a faint conversation.

"I know it's hard to talk about . . ." Lily is the first to really speak to everyone. She sets down Moffy and the little boy walks over to Jane, plopping down beside her. "But while we're all together now, we should talk. It may help." She nods at this, probably remembering her own experience with the media's bashing.

Lo hugs her to his side. "That's a good idea, love."

Rose solidifies, my arm around her stiff waist while she leans against the sink. "Connor and I are taking care of it," she says tightly. "The four of you don't have to worry about anything." She doesn't want to saddle her sisters with a heavy burden any more than I want to saddle Ryke and Lo.

Ryke breathes through his nose and shakes his head a couple times. But he stays silent.

"What's 'taking care of it' exactly?" Lo asks, his voice edged.

I tilt my head. "I didn't call my publicist so she could entertain me for an hour with useless advice."

Daisy rests her chin on Ryke's shoulder. "I thought the whole point of being on social media was to be ourselves?"

"And clarify when the tabloids spread lies about us," Lo adds.

"And support each other," Lily chimes in, the biggest advocate for Ryke and Daisy's relationship online.

Daisy smiles. "And to always have fun."

Rose crosses her arms. "Then we'll have fun implementing Naomi's to-do list."

Lo glares. "Then I better see you smiling when you tweet things like 'my little angel sleeps so peacefully when I sing her a lullaby. Hashtag, I'm a lying liar.'"

Rose is too exhausted to retort anything of equal intensity. She supports most of her body weight against me and just shoots him a look like *stop talking.*

"I know it's hard for all of you to accept," I tell them, "but if we don't make at least a small effort, this won't blow over. We can't simply *be* who we are online if people keep twisting our relationship into something . . ." *Cold, loveless and empty.* The words hit me but I don't want to say them aloud.

"Why isn't this harder for you?" Lo asks me, his face contorting with more emotion. He gestures to both of us. "You're just standing there like it's a goddamn pothole that you can drive over." This is a crater with no alternate routes. I'm aware. "They're degrading your *marriage* . . . and everything you two are." Maybe he thinks we should be immobilized on the floor.

I recall Rose crying earlier in the closet, *screaming* into her coat so no one could hear. I could feel her pain grow, and I could feel mine burst. I let it out then, but it's not gone. It's sunken low so I can keep standing, so I don't become crippled and small.

"I don't know how to wallow," I tell him honestly. "Maybe that action isn't in me, but I assure you, *grief* is." I'm never going to be entirely expressive with my emotions, but the fact that I feel anything at all is what matters.

His brows furrow, as though trying to detect it, and then he notices Rose rubbing her hands together, her skin dry and peeling. I clasp her palm in mine, and she stops.

Lo nods a couple times to himself. "We know that you two love each other, so now we just have to make the whole world realize that *your* love is equal to the rest of ours."

It's not possible. "You can't make people see love. It's intangible. They can see affection, the actions between two people who are in love, but ours is less physical and more mental." Naomi's plan is the best, regardless of how much it shames the way that we love each other.

"I saw your love," Lily tells us.

Rose frowns. "What?"

Lily's eyes smile before her lips do. "The first time I ever saw you together, at my apartment with Lo. It looked like you two were fighting, but I always believed it was flirting."

I can feel my grin. *Flirting*—I told Rose so during St. Patrick's Day.

"And I also sensed a lot of . . . sexual tension." She reddens. "I can't be the only one who thought so. Right?" She turns to Lo. He was there that day, a long time ago.

"I thought they were weird," he admits. "But in hindsight, I guess, yeah, it was flirting." No one is convinced by him, least of all Rose.

She lets out a jailed breath. "We're going to do what Naomi says."

The room tenses, and Ryke finally speaks. "I fucking hate this."

"Not as much as people hate my tweets," Rose grumbles.

Ryke gives her a look. "They're fucking funny, Rose."

"Apparently they're insensitive."

"I've tweeted more insensitive shit and no one gets onto me," he rebuts.

Lo's brows rise. "He did once tweet that anyone who's praying for rain again needs to shut the fuck up."

Daisy smiles, the whole room brightening an extra degree. "And anyone who's performing a rain dance needs to sit the fuck down."

Lo laughs, but it fades among the proliferating stress.

Rose fills the silence. "It's a small sacrifice."

"I don't like when we have to sacrifice who we are . . ." Ryke trails off, his hard gaze drifting to the two babies, closest to him. Jane even smiles up at Ryke and babbles a string of noises that desire to be words.

Rose says, "I've never shied away from who I am, even when people asked me to be softer, quieter or warmer. I've proudly remained *me*. But I'm willing to appear as the person they want *for Jane*." She turns to me, and I read the look in her eye, which says *just as you'd be willing to make that sacrifice*.

If I lie to the world and pick a label, she doesn't want me to lift this burden alone.

Her loyalty is admirable, but her speech hits me in a new way, with a new realization.

I'd rather Rose teach Jane to *never* step down and cower, to never appear as something else, as I've always done.

To be real.

To be herself, to love every part of her own soul, no matter if it's what someone else desires or not.

That's the woman I love.

I don't want her to be anything less.

I open my mouth to combat her, but she says, "Just let me try. If Jane is heckled by her peers, I want to at least know that I did something to change the outcome."

"You teach Jane to never be afraid to speak her mind by never being afraid to speak yours," I whisper to Rose. "You give her the tools to defeat their words through confidence and self-respect."

"And you?" she asks me. "It's not fair that you have to carry this . . ." She rolls her eyes as they fill with tears. I wipe beneath them.

"I haven't made a choice yet." I can't tell her that I'm leaning towards the option that'll help Jane. The fake me. I'll sound like a hypocrite, and maybe I am in this instance. I would much rather protect Rose's spirit, even if it means barring her from protecting mine.

"I'll support you no matter what," Lily suddenly says to us.

Rose sniffs and then Daisy passes her a piece of toilet paper, and Rose dabs beneath her eyes.

"Me too," Daisy says. "Whatever you say, I'll stand behind." She gives me a smile, referring subtly to my choice and the press conference in May.

"I have to ignore you," Lo says. "Don't I?"

"It's up to you," I tell him.

"For how long?" he wonders.

"I don't know." It's the truth.

He shakes his head automatically. "No. I'm not doing it. I'm not going to give my dad what he wants. Then he'll just keep doing this shit over and over again, and goddammit, if *anyone* needs to learn a lesson, it's him."

My lips curve upwards.

Ryke nods in agreement, his jaw hardening. "I gave him part of my liver, and this is what he does?" His distraught eyes rise to me, for understanding, for anything that'll make it better.

I do have more knowledge than them, but it won't ease his pain. What no one but Rose may know and what Jonathan may not fully understand himself: he reacted today based off fear of abandonment. He can give reasons like *I'm trying to stop Connor from seducing my son* all he wants, but it's more than that.

It's about Jonathan feeling like I've taken his position in Lo's life. For guidance, for connections, for money—Lo comes to me. When I'm around, Jonathan is unneeded. There's nothing worse than being useless when you thrive off being useful.

He felt inferior and powerless, probably for the first time ever.

Greg, his best friend, is kindhearted and malleable. I'm calculated and stoic.

When I meet men like Jonathan, I usually step back and try to appear nonthreatening. I fake it because they can't put up with how I normally am, but I've never had reason to do this with Lo's father. He served no value to me. I didn't need anything from him. I didn't want him as a connection. If we were at odds, I thought it made no difference.

I didn't regard Jonathan Hale as a variable in my life. He was nothing. And the *nothing* I disregarded turned out to be the something that I should've paid more attention to.

That's why this happened. There is no other reason than this.

As I look at Ryke, I realize I have the opportunity to shed light on the situation, or I can leave it how it is. They can believe that their father is a bigot and an asshole—or I can show them that he's just utterly imperfect.

I don't like Jonathan. I hate him, in fact, but I pity him more—and maybe it's this pity that has won me over. Or maybe it's because I really see no point in revenge.

Either way, I begin to share my thoughts, which won't rid the hurt he's caused, but it'll at least put to rest the villain in their eyes.

Thirty-nine

Connor Cobalt

I casually suck on a cigarette, inhaling deeply. Scott watches the color of the smoke that leaves my lips: filmy, translucent gray rather than a plume of white.

He's constantly making sure I'm not playing him. I remember his extremely opinionated comment a month ago: *real men don't hold smoke in their mouths.* And I unfortunately have to abide by this.

"You realize there are two cameramen on the eastern balcony of that apartment complex." I tap ash into a tray and then sip my whiskey to drown the cigarette taste.

Scott takes a large swig of his bourbon, barely acknowledging the apartment complex that overlooks Saturn Bridges, a Philadelphia bar that's been flooded with people since we arrived at 1 a.m. He also chose to stand on the bar's deck, potted plants partially concealing our view of the street.

Scott wanted to meet in public, the same day that the news broke about me, further reminding me that he loves money only one degree above notoriety.

I'm aware that this isn't the best look for me: *Connor Cobalt is seen without his wife at a local bar the same day it's revealed that his marriage is a sham!* Rose plans on picking me up, so the "without wife" comment will disappear.

It doesn't help that the world believes Scott is Rose's ex-boyfriend. I'm not sure what the public will think about me meeting him. It'd make more sense if they knew the truth: he was the producer of *Princesses of Philly.*

"I'm secure in my sexuality," he reminds me for the second time. He puts his cigarette between his lips, and I rest my forearm on the iron railing, a fern brushing my hand. "So who was it that spread the lies?" he wonders.

This is why he asked me out today. Curiosity.

He also believes the accusations are entirely baseless. He's weaved enough false webs for the public that he must not take anything in the tabloids at face value.

With another sip, the liquor burns my throat. "Do you plan on giving them a handshake?" I ask with a growing smile, my voice lighthearted, even if it's not what I feel.

Scott shrugs with a smugger smile. *Go ahead and smile, you fool.* "I just never want to piss off whoever you did." He raises his glass in cheers to that. I do the same, and we drink in unison. Then he licks his lips and nods. "So . . . do I know him?"

I let the embers eat my cigarette. "No, and trust me, you don't want to be dragged into this mess." *Trust me* is a declaration that he'll cling to, waver over, until he asks—

"Why spend time with me?" He combs his fingers through his slick, dirty blond hair, doubt in his furrowed brows. "Why try to help me convince your friends to be a part of a season two?"

I suck on the cigarette again and blow smoke into the air, my posture more like Loren Hale—slumped and apathetic—than like me: domineering and overconfident. "I honestly thought you were into Rose," I begin my speech in an easygoing tone. "Like—really into her. I was jealous of what you had that I didn't, of what you could offer her that I couldn't. And there was a moment where I thought that she liked you *way* more than me, man." It's all a lie, obviously.

He sports an entitled smile, as though women are flocking to his side and feeding him grapes. "I could've told you that she wanted to fuck me on *day one*." He's attempting to piss all over me, but he's the idiot with opinions that don't match the facts.

Rose never wanted to fuck him, not even for a moment.

He chuckles into his next swig.

I always try to find another road before I put myself in this situation, but I need his trust and there's not another lane to go down. I see no other *legal* way to achieve my goal than this.

I laugh. "If you did tell me on day one, I would've hated you a million fucking times more." It's like we're reminiscing about our deep-seated loathing of one another—exactly what I want.

He laughs too and pats my arm. "I would've hated me too."

I blow out smoke again. "Look, I don't hold anything against you. After I figured out that you had no interest in Rose, I didn't give a shit."

"The sex tapes—"

"Genius," I tell him, my lips rising into a brighter grin. *If you have nothing real to say, Richard, then why speak at all?* I hear Rose's quick-tempered voice.

It has to be this way, I think before I speak again. "Those tapes gave me the exposure I needed to profit off a diamond corporation. *You* helped me, man." These words rip through me, and I know they're not going to be the worst ones. "Rose may be upset, but she doesn't matter." *That's complete bullshit, Richard.* My stomach twists unnaturally. "I had to hit you so she wouldn't throw a little tantrum about *why didn't you stick up for me?* afterwards, you know." I roll my eyes, as though everything Rose does irritates me. As though I struggle to put up with her every single day.

How do I know who the real Connor Cobalt is? she asks. *You're different around certain people.*

Don't ever leave my head, I think. I need these constant re-minders. I need to feel the guilt, remorse, every human sentiment that I used to abandon. When they leave, when I'm left hollow and detached, I've lost too much.

Scott's lips part in complete realization, as if I've given him the missing puzzle piece that forms the whole picture. "So if I'd asked you to help me plant the cameras for the tapes—"

"I would've helped you in a heartbeat, man," I say. "It was a great idea. Fuck, I wish I'd thought of it first." I nudge his arm playfully. *Shove him off the balcony, Richard.*

Patience, darling.

He laughs. "It was genius, wasn't it?" He finishes off his drink with a self-satisfied grin. "Had I known you were cool with it, I would've just asked you to put the cameras in there. It took my crew five tries to hardwire them in your room when you were gone."

I snuff the cigarette on the ashtray. "No shit?"

"It was a bitch," he says, "but you have the real bitch, don't you?" He watches my face, waiting for my lips to downturn, but I just smile again. The only thing that keeps me from breaking char-acter and publicly humiliating him among cell phone cameras and bar patrons is the idea of ruining him at the end of this.

"She's a handful," I tell him and then pat his chest. "Speaking of which, she's actually coming around to a season two, but she has a ton of requirements." No one can lie like I do.

He snorts under his breath. "Of course she does."

"I'll email them to you." I check my watch. She should be here . . . and then my phone buzzes.

Just parked. I'm coming in to claw your face off—the fake one, not the one I love.—Rose

I like when we work together, but I don't want her to see Scott or vice versa. I squeeze his shoulder in goodbye, triggering camera flashes. Scott almost laughs at them.

"I have to go," I say, "but thanks for this." I down the drink and set the glass on a wooden patio table.

"I knew you needed it." He actually shakes my hand—the first time he's offered this gesture. It's a friendlier handshake, pulling me to his chest. He pats my back. "Keep me posted about everyone?"

"Yeah, definitely." I have a better read on him than I ever used to. He has this nervous look in his eye whenever we leave, afraid I'm going to pull a switch on him and fuck him out of his deal with GBA. I hold more cards, and I just need Scott to trust that I wouldn't hurt him.

I predict that he'll test me sometime soon. One test. Just to see if I'm being truthful about everything I've ever said to him. We meet every weekend, and I'm sure he'll pick one sentence I told him, a phrase or comment, and try to see if I contradict myself.

If I pass that, he'll view me as a real friend.

exit the bar using the outside staircase with my bodyguard in tow, bypassing hordes of people, some journalists that I recognize from *Celebrity Crush*. Wendy Collins among them. When my soles hit the sidewalk, I can't blow past the paparazzi. Despite my bodyguard yelling warnings to *back up*, his arm outstretched, they press up against me, pushed nearer by other cameramen hugging too close.

"Have you slept with men, Connor?"

"Are you gay?"

"Do you love Rose?"

"Who's your partner and is Jane considered his child too?"

I stay silent and search for Rose at the entrance of the bar, the bouncers instructing everyone to remain in line and not flock me.

I dial a number and put my phone to my ear. "Where are you?!" I yell over the noise and try to push ahead.

"I'm stuck in the parking lot—*shoo, stay back*." The cacophony on her end is louder than mine. "Give me space or I will ram my five-inch heel into your asshole."

I barrel through the cameramen, unable to run, but I shove them aside, no longer slowly trudging through. A few fall over, careening into the pavement. My bodyguard rests a hand on my shoulder to keep up with my pace, and when I have enough space, I sprint around the brick building to the side parking lot.

As soon as I see the sheer volume of cameras and people surrounding Rose, I race as fast as I can towards her, all other insignificant thoughts disintegrating from my brain.

Vic, her bodyguard, tries to escort her through the masses, and her other bodyguard, Heidi, who she hired after Jane was born, flanks her left side.

"Rose!" I yell, tall enough to see over the droves of people.

She whips her head in my direction, but she can't see past the cameras. "Connor!"

I'm ten feet from her, about three people blocking me. I have to ditch my bodyguard to wedge between bodies, the questioning, the shouting increasing tenfold by my presence.

"Rose, I'm right here!" I yell as she cranes her neck. I reach a hand past someone's arm, trying to touch her.

"Is your marriage fake?!"

"Are you even in love?!"

Rose is finally able to clasp my hand, and she pulls me towards her, Heidi helping by gripping my wrist. They both tug, and I pass through the last row of cameras.

I hold Rose to my body and cup her face. The heat in her eyes hides panic, but her arms clutch me more securely, in fear that we'll split apart again.

I can feel my heart pumping vigorously in my chest, and I kiss her forehead, the cameras flashing wildly again.

"Why didn't you kiss on the mouth?!" someone yells.

Because you'd dissect her rigid posture and say it was a publicity stunt, like everyone has done before.

I whisper in her ear, "Ça va?" *Are you okay?*

"Just pissed at that one." She points at an older man with a full beard. He raises one hand off his camera in surrender when I meet his gaze. "Don't act innocent," she snaps, tucking her purse underneath her arm. "Everyone heard what you said!"

The other cameramen shift away from him, dissociating themselves from his behavior. I draw Rose closer to my chest, unsure of what he said. For her to be this upset over a comment, it must've been worse than all the others.

She takes a deep breath, and the shouting from paparazzi escalates around us. I lower my head to her lips so I can hear her speak.

"He said that social services should take our daughter away—"

A camera nearly clocks her in the head, but instead hits the Escalade. Alarm flickers in her eyes, and I pull her towards the driver's side. "We need to leave," I tell her.

She nods in agreement. "Heidi," she says loudly. "You can follow us with Vic and Stephen?" My bodyguard is already at the extra SUV with Vic.

Before she leaves, Heidi shouts, "We'll try to keep the paparazzi off your rear!"

I protectively stand behind Rose while she opens the driver's-side door. I wait for her to slide in. Lenses hit my back, paparazzi shoving each other in haste.

"Crawl in," she tells me. I open my mouth to refute, but she adds, "You've been drinking."

I forgot. The past ten minutes have pulverized any buzz I had. I put my lips to her ear again. "Stay close to me." I move around her, keeping an arm around her waist as long as I can. I have to crawl over the driver's seat and onto the passenger one, a feat much more difficult for someone of my height.

I manage well enough, quick as I can be, and by the time I sit,

Rose is already in her seat, slamming the door shut. She turns on the ignition and flicks on the light.

"I hope I blind them," she mutters.

I stretch my arm over the back of her headrest, watching as the paparazzi disperse to their cars, some still stationary and others putting the lenses to our side windows.

"Go slow," I tell her.

She's always been an aggressive driver, and these situations call for someone who straddles the line between careful and assertive.

"I think we should just run them over." She lays on the horn while letting out a frustrated growl.

"You failed defensive driving, I presume." My arm falls to her shoulders.

She relaxes a little, but her voice stays tight. "I *passed* with a perfect score."

I can hardly believe this. I'm positive she took the course. Rose likes safety classes and learning, more than anyone I know, but she becomes vexed when people go out of turn at a four-way stop. "Was it a pass-or-fail course?" I wonder.

She shoots me a glare before focusing on the road, inching forward until we reach the curb.

"By your silence, I'm assuming *yes*."

"Passing is a perfect score," she retorts.

I can't hide a grin. "Then the percentage of people who have perfect scores is high, and it loses all bragging rights."

She rolls her eyes dramatically. "It's a *personal* victory. My achievements don't have to be measured by everyone else's."

Mine usually are, I realize. I like competitions. I like being the best. I've always thrived off of it, but what she says makes sense— "Stop," I suddenly say, and she slams on the brakes.

A cameraman's sedan just pulled out in front of us. The Escalade jerks to a standstill at the curb, right before we reach the busy road.

Rose hits the steering wheel a couple times and growls again.

I roll down the window and ask a photographer with a Canon to help push back some of the men and women who stand too close. He obliges and clears the path. Some paparazzi know if they're kinder to us, we'll be kind in return.

Space opens, and Rose pulls onto the road, the SUV with our bodyguards tailing us. Without the extra noise, the car quiets, the only sounds from vehicles speeding down the street.

Rose's fingers tense around the steering wheel, and it reminds me where I just was, who I was talking to—everything I said.

"Tell me you at least didn't use the word 'dude'?" She cringes at the thought.

My lips rise again. "No 'dudes' this time."

Her eyes flit to me, softening just a little to ask *are you all right?* She doesn't have to say it aloud.

"You were with me tonight." My voice is almost a whisper.

"Did I tell you to castrate Scott with a dull steak knife?"

"No castration, but bodily harm was mentioned at least once."

"I must have been only partially with you, then. I always find ways to chop off his dick." She stops at a red light and then sniffs the air, frowning. She smells her dress, the lingering scent of cigarettes more on me . . . but I pressed against Rose, so there's a very slight possibility the odor is on her too.

"The light is green," I say.

She drives again, but she tries to focus on the road and me, her eyes narrowing with each glance back and each sniff. "Did you . . . you didn't . . . you *did*. Richard!"

I try not to laugh. "I did do many things. You're correct."

"Take your shirt off," she demands.

"Mmm." I feign contemplation. "No."

"I need to smell your shirt," she rephrases, waving her hand theatrically at me to relinquish my button-down, her yellow-green eyes plastered to the street.

"Is this a new fetish, darling?" My grin widens at her glare. "I can think of a few things worth smelling before my shirt," I say, my hand skimming the bareness of her neck. "My hair, my—"

"My car *reeks* of your ego."

"My ego smells like success, so go ahead and fumigate your car—I know you'll miss the scent."

She snorts. "And what does success smell like, Richard?"

I lean back, my hand caressing her neck and shoulders. Her body melts against the seat, and I watch her knees squeeze together. "Like newly pressed suits, leather belts and Oxfords, a hint of shaving cream and even more sandalwood." I don't dare restrain my grin. "You lie with me every night, Rose. I'd hope you know what I smell like."

And her neck heats beneath my palm. "The smell of success seems to be biased towards *you*."

This is a riddle that I know she's already solved but I state aloud even if she can't. "I *am* success, darling."

She turns her head to look at me, just once. "At least your arrogance is still intact." The seriousness of her tone tugs at a place deeper inside of me.

I stroke the back of her head. "You make me forget the worst parts of life."

She actually smiles, focused back on the street. "And what's the term for that?"

I think for a moment. A person who shrouds the painful moments, who conspires to make joyful ones. Who eliminates all the mundane shades in favor of ardent colors and keeps you burning alive. Is there a word for this rare person in someone's life?

I think there is.

"Soul mate," I say.

Her lips part in surprise. "What?"

"If you'd like other terms, I have those too: my wife, my

sometimes competitor, my always teammate, my friend, the mother of my child—"

"Rewind." She waves at me. "To the soul mate part."

I smile. "I love you, Rose."

She slackens completely, her shoulders drooped and fully relaxed. She opens her mouth, to compliment me, I think, but then she inhales the cigarette-scented air and her eyes narrow once more.

"You can take a shower with me when we get home." My hand slides down her arm and to her thigh. "I'll wash you slowly . . . every part of you." I dip my hand underneath her dress.

She clasps my wrist, stopping me from riding up between her legs. "It's been a long day," she says.

I frown. It has, and I just want to spend the rest of the night tangled with her, holding her—

"So I'd rather take a bath with you."

"I like that plan." I kiss her hand and place it back on the steering wheel. I'm not certain what's going to happen next in the long-term future or what I choose in May, but I remind myself that Rose keeps safe all the real pieces of me.

If I ever lose myself, I just need to find her.

"Rose!" A van cuts off our Escalade, narrowly missing a collision with our headlights. Instead of slamming on the brakes, she switches lanes quickly and speeds past the van.

Their windows are rolled down, cameras directed at our car.

"They're going to kill us," Rose says, fire smoldering her gaze, but panic returns to her tense shoulders, her breath heavy.

"We'll make it," I try to assure her, though the cold reality ices me.

This is day one of a shit storm. It only gets worse from here.

Forty

Connor Cobalt

Spotted! Loren Hale and Connor Cobalt grab lunch together. Could this mean they're declaring their relationship to the public? Perhaps it's much more than platonic. All we know is that LoCo is one HOT couple, even if they are cheating on their wives.

Lo holds up the phone in front of my face, letting me read the caption below the photo of us together at a restaurant eating tacos and acting civilized just ten minutes ago.

"It's fucking everywhere," Lo says in disbelief. "We were just there. Do these people not have a goddamn life?"

I raise my ankle to my knee and sit straighter on the leather chair. I followed Lo back to his office to discuss some financial contracts. He values my advice, especially since he knows the board members aren't all on his side. It's why he can't simply champion Rose's ideas and win them over. Business relationships take time to build.

"I told you this would happen," I remind him. There's no going back now.

His eyes flit to me. "And I don't care about it." His phone vibrates for the twelfth time since we arrived at his office. He groans under his breath. "Corbin keeps texting me, telling me how I fucked up." His jaw sharpens, and he starts texting back. "*Go choke on roadkill.* Send." He pushes a button and drops his phone to his glass desk, his eyes murderous. He's been shooting glares at every single person who so much as glances his way.

When his gaze returns to me, it hardly softens, but that's because he's been on edge all day.

"I can't believe you haven't even glared at a single person." He shakes his head. "Not even when they called you a . . ." He can't repeat the words. I haven't made a decision. I haven't spoken to the press or lied or told the truth. I'm silent, which some people believe is no better than admitting to the accusations. I'm fine with waiting for the press conference to make a speech. I need time.

"Your glares are far more effective, darling," I tell him with a smile.

He nods, returning it, even though there's a tense layer when I make the joke. We both know it's what's causing the outside friction.

Lo spins his wedding band, the giveaway that says he's craving alcohol. "Please tell me you at least screamed or cried or something."

I remember how I broke down while holding Rose in my arms, but I don't want to mention this. There's a large part of me that craves the way Lo looks at me. Immortal. Impervious. A god among men. That has only been altered a handful of times over the years, and today I don't want to add to the count. So I pivot the conversation. "How's Lily?"

He shakes his head once. I've poked at a sore spot.

"That bad?"

He rubs his temple, anxiety wounding through him. I'm causing this. *Me.* My past. The thought cages my breath for a second.

"Uh . . . shit. She wouldn't want me talking about her." He taps his fingers on the desk, obviously wanting to share. To get it off his chest.

"I won't tell."

"Rose?" he asks. "Because she'll probably feel the need to talk to Lily about it and then I'm fucked for telling you."

"I promise."

His shoulders fall and he stops twisting his wedding band. "She's really upset about the new fandom name the journalists made for her and Ryke. *Celebrity Crush* has been posting about it everywhere." Now that there are rumors of Lo and me together, the rumors of Lily and Ryke have resurfaced. "She said she's not upset about the *actual* rumors. It's just that she's been promoting freakin' 'Raisy' for the past year, and now they came up with 'Rily.' She said it makes her sick."

Lo looks crushed, the weight of Lily's pain pounding him. It's this type of love that scares me the most. Feeling that much empathy is crippling.

"Maybe it'll all pass in time," I say, letting a shred of hope float into the world. It may be false, but I choose to see it as real.

His eyes are reddened, and he lowers his head so people in the hallway can't see, his office mostly just glass walls.

"I'm sorry, Lo," I tell him. I've hurt him, whether he wants to believe it or not. Whether he wants to bury it with glares and *I don't give a fuck*s. The pain that he is going through is the result of my history.

He shakes his head. "It's not your fault. If anything, Lil and I should be apologizing to you. We're the ones who started this." He's talking about the fame. It all began with Lily and Lo. Their addictions and the salacious headlines.

"It's kind of you to take credit for this, but it's unneeded," I tell him. "We're all so far past the beginning that the end is no one's to claim."

He stares at me for a long moment before he says, "That's pretty fucking deep, love."

"I've been deeper."

The innuendo makes him laugh. His eyes trail past me to his door. "Speaking of where you've been," he says.

I follow his gaze, turning my head slightly. I see Rose approaching, a binder in her clutch. Beside her is someone I haven't seen in years. I know Lo isn't referring to Theo, seeing as how he has no knowledge that I've slept with the Hale Co. employee, but the irony isn't lost on me.

need to wash my mouth out with soap." Rose takes the seat across from me. "The words that came out of it were *vile*." Theo remains standing off to the side, holding a folder and waiting for Lo to acknowledge him.

Lo's concentration is on Rose. His brows knot together. "You didn't call anyone an ogre, did you?"

"Not to their face." She flattens her pencil skirt and places a binder carefully on the glass table. "But that's not what I said that makes my skin crawl."

I press my fingers to my lips, thinking, and simultaneously keeping an eye on my ex in the corner. He's quiet, perceptive, blending into the walls like he's made of transparent glass. Theo Balentine hasn't changed. I didn't need to see him to know this.

He wasn't the one who told the press about my past. That alone tells me he's still the same moral guy I met in boarding school.

Rose takes a large breath before explaining. "I had to tell the board that I *loved* the patterns of monkeys eating bananas." She gives me a look and mouths, *ew*. I smile. "And then there were the ones with bumblebees." She glowers at Loren like he inflicted this on her. "*Bumble. Bees.*"

"I assume everything went well, then," I say, knowing her ploy.

"They told me they're going to take some time and rethink the designs," she says, her lips rising. "That's when I called one of them an ogre."

Loren lets out an annoyed breath. "Great. Just great. You know, even I can hold my tongue in a boardroom."

"It was all for show, *Loren*."

Lo has been informed about her new strategy to pretend to like all the board members' ideas that she actually hates, and every time she agrees with them, they change their minds. She's guiding them towards her styles and designs without them realizing. So far her plan seems to have worked to her benefit.

Lo looks to Theo in the corner. "Do you have the alternate designs?"

"I do . . ." He coughs into his hand and pushes the folder on the table. He edges closer to me, his eyes flitting my way.

Lo looks between us. "You two know each other, right?"

"From boarding school," I say calmly. We both meet each other's gazes and I nod, not offering a handshake, never rising to my feet. I just don't care enough to.

My phone buzzes and I procure it from my pocket.

"From Faust." Theo nods, looking mildly uncomfortable.

"Was Connor just as fun back then as he is now?" Lo says with a half smile, more enjoyment from this scenario than I'm receiving.

When was your last period?—Frederick

I almost laugh. My therapist is off his A-game. I text: Let me guess, Cobalt and Calloway are far too close in your phone book or you just text us more than your other contacts?

I look up and Rose is giving me a weird look, a glare that's half contorted in curiosity and half in confusion.

I mouth, *later.*

She lets out a small huff, a lot more impatient for details than me, but I love the way she crosses her ankles and her arms, her breasts rising with a deep inhale.

Theo answers Lo, "It was interesting. Every time he caught me smoking, he'd tell me that my ambition was being asphyxiated."

"I wasn't wrong," I say, my first words to him in years. I glance at my phone when it buzzes.

Ignore that.—Frederick

I do ignore his texts since I have Theo frowning at me, and Lo lets out a long whistle at my statement, breaking a string of tension.

I meet Rose's fiery, incensed gaze for a moment and she mouths, *who?* She's hardly concerned about Theo, just my texts, since we've been working together to handle this mess with the media.

I'm mostly worried about her OCD flaring, so I pass her my phone.

She reads quickly and hands it back, her shoulders relaxed, probably thankful it's not Scott. Her eyes meet mine again, and they still possess that fire.

I remember the time I asked her what she thought of Theo. And she called him "a guppy in our ocean"—*our* ocean. I love Rose, and it's easy for me to be amiable towards Theo when he sits so far in my past, a past that I don't cradle like everyone else.

I let people go all the time, and he's one that has drifted a thousand leagues behind me. I don't care enough to go swim after him. I wouldn't. I won't. But I do wholeheartedly appreciate his morality. It's one of those values I admire but know I don't always own.

"I still have ambition. Don't you see where I am?" Theo tells me, pulling my gaze from my wife. Rose hardly seems to mind. We have so much confidence in our relationship that it'd be nearly impossible for a person to wedge themselves between us and cause doubt and friction in our marriage.

Don't you see where I am? His gray eyes repeat the statement.

He's in a Fortune 500 company. He's in a higher-paying job than most at Faust. He's climbing his way to the top.

"It's not what you wanted," I tell him. He dreamed of writing poetry, of living off the land with life's bare necessities. He dreamed of throwing his arms in the air, half-naked in the wilderness, where he'd commune with nature and learn great, untouched meanings.

Now he's in a suit, in the city, stuck within a high-rise where poetry has little use except within his own mind.

"Dreams change," Theo says, and I can see that he's accepted this new life now. Maybe it is what he wants.

Dreams change.

I think there's good change where we see our path diverge and we willingly follow the new road. And then there's forced change, where debris impedes us from our path and we're searching desperately for a route back to our planned destination.

The dream I've always desired—to grow a family with Rose—is being forced to change.

And I can't see any way around the debris.

Forty-one

Rose Cobalt

Jane cries bloody murder, focused on the bodies cramped against the windows of Connor's limo. I want to slaughter *every person* that is making her cry this way. I can't tell if we already parked in front of the pediatrician's building, but I'm antsy to reach our destination and bring Jane to her regular checkup on time.

Her first birthday is in June. I'd like to think this'll die down by then, but it's most likely wishful thinking on my part.

I hold Jane on my lap, wiping her tears quickly. "Mommy's going to drop-kick anyone that touches you."

"And Daddy's going to bail Mommy out of jail," Connor says, placing tiny blue earplugs in my palm.

I give him a look. "Mommy will be within her full *rights* to assassinate any vile creature that harms her baby."

He caresses my cheek with his knuckles, the pressure how I like. "Nothing will happen to our baby."

He's pacifying me. Connor can't predict the future. He knows this, and there is reasonable probability that *something* could go wrong.

"Anything can happen," I tell him. I almost wonder if we should turn back and reschedule her appointment. We tried to lose the paparazzi, but they've been camping outside our gated neighborhood for the past week, waiting for us to drive out. Our neighbors have already complained, and Connor thinks another house will be up for sale by the end of the month.

It's very likely the media's presence could increase by the beginning of May, so it's hard to return home, knowing that tomorrow and the next week and the next week after that could be worse or the same.

"I'm not leaving your side," Connor reminds me. We've formed a plan to barrel through the paparazzi without Jane being harmed or even breathed on the wrong way.

I nod, soaking in his confidence, and I fit the soft plugs into Jane's ears.

Gilligan, Connor's driver, cranes his neck over his shoulder. "We're here." I hardly noticed the limo stopping since we've been inching along.

"Where's Heidi?" I ask Connor.

He has his phone out, texting our bodyguards instructions. "All three of them just parked next to us."

I peek out his window, a camera lens literally pressed against the glass. "I don't see them." And just as I say the words, our bodyguards push aside the paparazzi, clearing space by Connor's door.

I tuck Jane to my hip, her cries escalating now that I've put a foreign object in her ear. Outside is too loud and caustic for me to remove them. "Shh," I whisper. "Be brave, my little gremlin, and I promise they'll all go away." Her tears sincerely do a number on me, my chest twisting. I splay a woolen teal blanket over part of my shoulder and her head, all the while rubbing her back.

She settles only a little.

I let out a tense breath. I never believed a baby could stir this type of emotion from me, but I channel her fear into motivation, prepared to bypass every lens and person that stands in our way.

You're a fucking category-five hurricane, Rose. They should all fear your destruction.

Damn right.

Connor clasps my free hand, threading his fingers with mine. "Ready?"

I raise my chin and nod.

He opens his door, the flashes exploding. The noises and bright shutters blind me for a millisecond, almost pummeling me backwards. I've never seen anything like this in my life, not even when the media first took interest in my family.

I orient myself about the same time that Connor slides out. I scoot along the seat, his hand never leaving mine, and I exit with him.

"Is your marriage fake?!"

"Did you know Connor has been with men?!"

"Are the sex tapes real?!"

Connor squeezes my hand, and I can't shut the door behind me. Vic takes care of that, staying back while Heidi and Stephen push forward. "Give them room!" our bodyguards keep shouting for us.

I hug close to Connor's back while he guides me forward, Jane protectively shielded between my chest and his six-foot-four towering body.

I'd like to cast threatening glares in every direction, more territorial over my baby than I've ever been before, but every time I look out, flashes burst and white lights flicker in my vision.

So I dip my head and concentrate on Jane. The brick building with a pediatric sign isn't far from here.

"Whose idea was the business arrangement?!"

"Connor, do you have a boyfriend?!"

"You should be ashamed!"

I almost falter at this last exclamation. I've heard it before, but it packs a harder punch than the others. It rouses parts of me that ache to *scream* in reply, verbally sparring until I lose my voice.

"A child needs love! A child needs love!" more than a few people chant. These aren't paparazzi but rather haters that like to picket *us*.

I grit my teeth. A few days ago outside Hale Co., I already screamed once: *who are you to determine whether or not I love my daughter? You don't know me!* I was called "vicious, bitchy and belligerent" for simply defending myself. I've yelled that I love Jane until I'm blue in the face, but no one wants my words.

It's the most frustrating, enraging battle I've ever been a part of. My natural instinct will always be to speak louder if they tell me to shut up.

Bodies pack against me. I press Jane harder to my chest, and I can feel her heart pitter-patter in quick succession.

I won't let anything happen to you. I won't.

And then a strong, painful force snags a chunk of my hair by my temple. I can't tell what I'm caught on: jewelry or camera equipment or a jacket's zipper . . . something that I loathe right now.

I take a step forward, and I'm not coming loose. It yanks me backwards, and I stagger in my heels.

Immediately, I let go of Connor's hand, afraid that if I fall while clutching him, he'll topple backwards and crush Jane. "Give me space!" I scream at everyone around me.

"Rose!" Connor calls. Two people already wedge between us, and we're pulled apart. "ROSE!" He fights to reach me while I struggle to free my hair with one hand. I can't get it loose, and I'm close to being swept back and pulled onto the cement.

I make a split-second decision.

I can't fall, not with Jane in my arms, not in the throngs of people with heavy cameras, so I inhale strongly, both arms wrapped around my baby, and I charge forward with an aggressive jerk. The pain sears my scalp and wells my eyes.

But I'm free.

Connor reaches me, his commanding arm swiftly hooking around my waist. He leads me faster to the building. I don't look back to see the chunk of hair that I left behind. I just remember what could've happened: a pileup of people, smothering Jane.

It didn't happen.

I still shake like it did. Then quiet hits me, and I realize that I'm inside the hallway of the office building, the cameramen shut outside.

"Rose," Connor forces my name, slapping my cheek lightly until I focus on him. "You're in shock . . ." He clutches the back of my head, protectively and in control, making the chaos feel manageable—like it won't overthrow us, even if it almost did.

"No . . ." I say, even though I know I am. ". . . how is she?" I check on Jane beneath her blanket, and she's no longer crying, her face pressed to my chest in contentment. She studies the shape of an orange tabby cat printed on her blanket.

"Where were you?!" Connor shouts at Vic without letting go of me. "You were supposed to be right behind her."

"I got stuck in the crowd."

Connor's jaw muscle noticeably contracts. "Before we leave, you need to have a path cleared for us, and I'm calling more security to help you since you can't manage on your own."

He nods and says a few apologies to both of us.

At this, I wake up. *Everyone is safe.* That's what matters.

"Let's go, Connor," I tell him, and his hand falls to my shoulder, partially guiding me into the pediatrician's office. My steps still feel a little dazed, but as soon as we enter the empty waiting room, I break apart from him and sit on a chair by a stack of magazines, crossing my ankles.

I feel safer now that we're here. Connor goes to sign Jane in at the receptionist's desk.

My temple throbs and scalds. A gust of cold air blows through the vent and stings my wound. I ignore the pain and set Jane on my thighs, tucking the blanket around her. She immediately tugs at my necklace . . . and then, of course, my hair.

I wince. "No, don't touch Mommy's hair." I peel her fingers from the strands and procure her stuffed lion out of my purse. My brain is somewhat fogged, barely believing that my fragile, delicate child went through that *hell*. I can't and won't lock her in a tower and remove her from society, just because no one can behave properly.

There have to be boundaries . . . because this is too much for any kid to live through.

"Lion . . ." she says clearly, the rest of her words unintelligible and accompanied by spittle. I wipe her mouth with the corner of the blanket.

My eyes burn. "I hope you never question how much I love you, Jane."

She blinks at me and then smiles, replying with a variety of noises that I accept as *I will always love you, Mommy.* Even if that's not the case—I don't really care. It's what I believe it is. And in this moment, I believe she will never doubt my love.

When I look up, I notice the receptionist passing an item to Connor, and his lips form a *thank you* before returning to me.

"Is the doctor ready?" I ask. We're late, but not by much.

"They said five minutes and the nurse will weigh her." He sits beside me, a foreign look in his eyes. "Turn your head to me, darling."

"What are you feeling?" I wonder, just as I rotate to face him.

He gently brushes my hair back and reaches into my purse for a band, tying my hair off into a low pony. "Concern," he says.

It must be on another level of existence then, so abundant that it darkens his blue eyes. "I did what I had to," I tell him. I hone in on a line of crooked chairs by the wall behind Connor, a television mounted in the corner. Out of eight chairs, three are too far forward, two tilted too far to the left—it's irritating. Can no one fix those chairs?

"Rose, look at me," Connor says.

"This waiting room is a mess." I turn my head to find a kiddie chair overturned and on its side. I itch to set it upright, and the longer it stays in disorder, the more my ribs bind my lungs.

Connor pinches my chin, forcing my gaze back to his, and the severity in his features takes my breath. "Concentrate on me, *please*," he forces the word. "You're in complete control with me. You're in the neatest room you've ever been in with the smartest man you've ever seen, and there is *nothing* we can't do. Repeat it."

I snort and let out a deeper breath at the same time. "You would want me to repeat that in its entirety, just to stroke your ego." I hang on to the first line though. *You're in complete control with me.*

I exhale another short breath. When my eyes flit up to his, I expect him to smile, to banter back, but he's not doing either.

I notice the white gauze in his hand, the mysterious item that the receptionist gave him. He cups one side of my face, holding me still.

You're in complete control with me.

"Can you scoot closer?" I actually ask. I ease more when I can sense his stoic, unbending presence, coming into contact with mine. He moves as far as the armrests of the chairs will allow, his other hand on my neck for a second or two while I clutch Jane.

I inhale the calmness of Connor, the quietness of the room, and I don't look around this time. I just focus on him.

"I'm going to apply pressure to your temple," he says softly. "Just keep taking deep breaths." With this, he presses the gauze to the raw skin, and I inhale sharply.

Oh God. That fucking hurts.

I hold Jane with one arm and grip Connor's bicep with the other. He checks beneath the gauze, and beneath his fortitude, I spot the glimmer of a pained reaction, lines creasing his forehead.

"It's bleeding?" I question. He wouldn't have *that* response unless there was blood. "Let me see." He reaches for my purse. He's literally the only man I will let dig through it, and it's not long before he finds my compact mirror, holding it up to me.

Slowly I inspect the damage. Blood already seeps through the gauze. Connor gradually removes it. Right by my temple hairline, two quarter-sized clumps are missing, leaving only a reddened, scalped mess. And as awful as it looks and for however long it'll take to heal, I know I'd do it again.

Connor watches me carefully, most likely worried I'll lose sleep over my hair, something I've always nurtured like a child, but it's not my child. It's just a building block that creates my orderly life, and even though it feels like knocking one out of place knocks the whole tower, I *have* to keep reminding myself that I'm in control.

This doesn't destroy everything. What's important is that she's safe.

You're in complete control with me.

"Hair grows back," I tell him.

Connor nods. "And you can style your hair to cover it if you need to." The thought should comfort me, but I realize something . . .

"No," I tell him as he snaps the mirror closed. "*Everyone* needs to see, then maybe they'll stop putting Jane in harm's way."

He kisses my forehead and murmurs in French, too inaudible for my thumping brain to translate. He kisses Jane's head next, and she smiles, at peace in the quiet waiting room.

Connor returns the gauze to my temple, caring for my war wound. I want to lessen the tension that pools between us. I'd like to travel towards a place where he grins arrogantly, and I roll my eyes, trying desperately to suppress a smile.

I raise my chin a little, showing him that I'm better, and I quiz him, "Which sixteenth-century scientist is often said to have 'stopped the sun and moved the earth'? You have thirty seconds, same stakes as the last time we played." I'll have to ignore him for twenty-four hours if he answers incorrectly.

I know he knows this one though.

He removes the gauze again, nearly all red, and my stomach overturns. He folds it to find a white space—there is none, but he carefully presses it back anyway. I catch anger, frustration, hurt in his eyes—a whirlpool of emotions that he rarely ever expresses so outwardly.

"Richard," I snap, wanting him to not worry and to focus on my quiz. "Ten seconds."

"Galileo," he answers . . . incorrectly.

My mouth falls. "What?" He knew this one. I *knew* that he knew this one. I wouldn't have tried to trick him, not now.

His eyes tighten in a cringe. "It's Copernicus." He pinches the bridge of his nose and shakes his head once. "I wasn't thinking."

"Clearly," I mutter. Wait . . . I can't speak to him now. Can I? I bite my gums. "Maybe there can be a stipulation or exception for . . . overwhelming events." I grimace and glare at the ceiling even as the words leave my lips.

Once we make an exception as big as *you don't lose when you're supposed to lose*, none of our stakes hold the same weight. The games aren't taken as seriously.

His brows rise. "You know we can't. What's a realistic amendment: you begin ignoring me when we're in the limo again, safely on our way home."

I nod in agreement, and my lips lift at a thought. "Are you prepared to be ignored by me?" I've done it before, when we're fighting about philosophy or scientific theories, and it drives him mad. Not a lot unnerves Connor, but the silent treatment always does.

"It's my least favorite kind of torture."

"You have a favorite kind of torture?" I question.

He smiles. "Are you going to be able to ignore me, darling?"

I shoot him a glare. "Please, I already tune out half of what you say." I'm not really being truthful. I listen to almost every word he speaks, unless I cover his mouth with my hand and bar them from exiting.

"Such lies," he tells me, his lips continuing to curve upwards. "You're forgetting how much we talk and text and speak to each other in a twenty-four-hour period."

Am I?

"Even when you claimed we were broken up in college, we still called each other," he reminds me.

We did. Every day. "Let me gloat at the image of you pouting for at least *five minutes* before you claim that I'll be pouting too."

He almost grins fully. "We'll see."

Yes, we will.

Forty-two

Rose Cobalt

Only four hours since arriving home and I keep unlocking my phone, a heartbeat away from texting Connor a Fuck, Marry, Kill game or a random thought that tosses around my brain.

It turns out his punishment is an annoying consequence for both of us. So he was right thinking it would be. I'm hiding my distress as best I can.

If he sees it, he'll just gloat.

And *he's* supposed to be the loser here, not me.

Losers can't gloat. This is my law.

"We should be able to tag you out with Connor," Lo says with a bitter half smile. He camps out on the bar stool, *watching* me roll pizza dough on the kitchen counter. Flour plumes each time I use the rolling pin, and I simultaneously wipe down my mess and flatten the dough. It has taken me an excruciatingly long time, but my mood can only handle clean, tidy places right now.

It's pizza night, and we drew three names out of a hat for the cooks. Unfortunately, I was paired with Loren and his older brother, neither of my sisters to keep me company.

And no one was more displeased to see my name than me. Except maybe Loren.

"Tag Connor in?" I snap. "I'm sorry, am I wrestling you, Loren?"

"Just being five feet across from you is like enduring a back-breaker, so yeah, it feels like it." He gives me another dry smile and then sips a Fizz Life. His daggered eyes almost soften when they hone in on my temple, bandaged with gauze.

"You'd make more progress if you stared at the pepperoni and not my face."

He pretends to take interest in slicing the pepperoni—only *two* pieces on his cutting board.

"You don't want to trade in Connor today," Ryke tells his brother, chopping bell peppers on the other side of the sink. "He's moody as fuck. I passed him in the hallway, and before I even opened my mouth, he told me to go bark to my owner."

Loren eats a piece of pepperoni off a slice. We're never going to finish this pizza. "Huh," he says. "I thought Connor was your owner."

Ryke tosses a bell pepper at him. *God, no.* I don't want to find random bits of food strewn along the floorboards.

"I'm serious," Lo says.

"Yeah, me fucking too. I don't know what's up with him . . . besides the shit storm." *The shit storm.* That's what we've offi-cially begun calling this round of media invasiveness.

Loren points at my face. "Could be that his wife's all battered and he wasn't able to stop it from happening."

I jab the rolling pin in Lo's direction. "It's *not* Connor's fault. He knows that." My husband thinks logically and he'd know that there was no conceivable way he could've changed the outcome. I consider it fate. He considers it a terrible circumstance, dictated by the people surrounding me.

"Regardless, he's probably still pissed at the paparazzi," Lo tells me.

I don't doubt that. I caught him on the phone in passing, and he seemed vexed. I suppose he's calling extra security and other avenues to lessen our risk when we step outside.

We both get cooped up indoors for too long. Not like Daisy and Ryke, who seek adventure through terrifying activities. Remove working at an office, and I like shopping, getting manicures, fine dining, and any reason to dress elegantly. Connor is always on the go with me, and when we slow down, it's usually to spend more time with our daughter, my sisters, Loren and Ryke.

Connor and I have managed to keep our lifestyles intact, even with the media, but it's becoming harder for us now. Taking our daughter to the pediatrician shouldn't be a petrifying experience. And that's *before* we even step through the fucking doors.

Ryke licks his finger and then touches another green bell pepper.

My eyes widen in horror. "Ryke!"

"What?" He looks around. "What happened?" He notices my glare. "What the fuck did *I* do?"

"Wash your hands," I say. He touches my little sister with *those* hands. *Don't think about where they travel to and from, Rose.* I shudder.

He rolls his eyes but doesn't protest like Loren would have. Since he's being nice and actually washing his hands beneath the faucet, I decide to shed light on their discussion.

"Connor is moody because I'm ignoring him," I explain.

Loren frowns. "Why are you ignoring him?"

I wipe the counter. "He lost a quiz."

Ryke shuts the faucet, both of them quiet.

"Wait, that's it?" Loren gapes. "You're serious?"

"Do I look like I'm joking?" I train my fiery eyes on him.

"You look like you have to take a shit."

I growl. "You're disgusting."

"You're confusing," he retorts. "I thought you two were the mature ones out of the six of us, and here you are, playing the *silent treatment* like ten-year-olds." He laughs. "I think I've aged up in power rankings."

"Hardly," I say. "You're still on the bottom."

He rests his elbows on the bar counter. "Technically . . . I am your boss."

I knew he was going to throw this into the universe one day. "You promised you would never say that if I came on board with Calloway Couture Babies."

"I also don't keep three-fourths of my promises, Rose." Obviously. He's not my husband.

I let out a breath, dusting my hands off for the umpteenth time. "I only have to ignore Connor for twenty-four hours. He'll survive."

Ryke gives me a look. "We don't think he's going to fucking die from it. He's just not himself." He shrugs. "He usually spends five fucking minutes trying to get me to hold a conversation and banter back, not shut me down before I even speak."

"Just text him," Loren combats.

"Focus on your pepperoni, Loren," I reply icily.

Ryke notices me scrubbing the counter *again*. "Let's trade." He sets down his knife and the pepper.

"I can do this just fine," I argue.

"I'm not saying that you can't, but at this rate, we're not going to be eating dinner until tomorrow morning and I'm fucking hungry."

It's hard surrendering a task, even something as simple as this. I'm still clinging to things I can achieve, control and master when the paparazzi have made that difficult for me.

Ryke says, "I'm not stomping on your territory. Just let me roll the fucking dough."

I hesitantly relinquish this job, cleaning my hands on a towel again. I'm not one of those people who can smear flour on an apron. Mine is too pretty for stains.

We switch places at the same time, and Lo says, "I have to ask you something." I think he might be speaking to his brother, but when I look up, his eyes are set on me.

His sharp cheekbones become more defined, guards lifting as though this is serious.

"And . . . ?" I wait for the bomb. *Don't let Lily be pregnant. Don't let Lily be pregnant.* I cannot imagine a pregnant sister in the media shit storm right now. I'll have a coronary every time we leave the house, worried that someone will bump into her too hard or knock her down. I'm sure her mental state won't be any better.

"The press keep questioning Willow at Superheroes & Scones," he says. "They think she's my cousin, so they're going after anyone remotely close to you and Connor for answers."

His half sister is accessible, or at least more so than the rest of us, who hide behind bodyguards and gates.

"Yesterday, she was followed back to her apartment," Loren adds.

My jaw unhinges. That's unacceptable. "By who?" I ask, ready to hunt them down with pitchforks. I may not be Willow's closest friend, but she's family by extension of Loren. I'd use every tool I have in my arsenal to protect her, just as I would him.

"You can put away your talons. I already tracked down the guy and threatened to have him arrested for stalking."

"*We*," Ryke clarifies. He was in on it too.

Lo nods. "I really don't think it's safe for her right now."

There's a clear solution. "We have three vacant guest rooms on the east wing. She can choose hers." We bought an eight-bedroom mansion for a reason—we knew these rooms would fill up. Maybe more so by our children, but when your half sister stops by, a room should always be available.

"Are you sure? You can think about it." He's being considerate because of my "battered" face and the stress of the media. Otherwise, I doubt he'd ask.

"She's your family. What is there to think about?" I cut the core out of the pepper and scrape the seeds into the trash bin.

"Thanks." He nods a couple times. "I'll ask her to move in tomorrow. I'm pretty sure she'll say yes this time." She chose not to live with him in the beginning, but she should be more comfortable now that she's gotten to know him and us.

I slice the pepper perfectly evenly. "I don't know why Lily calls us the hot-tempered triad," I tell them. "We're all really civil right now, especially since we're all armed."

Ryke raises his *empty* hands. He's wearing a sleeveless gray shirt, and his biceps flex at the motion.

"Your muscles are weapons," I retort. It sounds dumb, even if it's logical. He has a lean build from running and climbing, but his muscles are so defined that it's hard to imagine an ounce of body fat.

"Jesus Christ, don't compliment his muscles," Lo says. "He's unnatural."

Connor comes close, but his brains are sexier than anything else he has.

"I'm a fucking athlete," Ryke refutes. "And your wife made a lame name for us."

"Hey"—Loren points his knife at Ryke this time—"don't insult Lily."

"Hot-tempered . . . whatever the fuck. I can't even finish it."

"Don't be an ass," I tell Ryke.

He extends his arms at me. "You were just fucking agreeing with me, were you not?"

"I changed my mind," I say. "I'm allowed to do that." I will *always* side with my sisters . . . unless they're against my daughter. Then I will side with Jane, but she's too young to be a part of these matches.

I'm excited for the day when she discovers her own voice. I won't bar her from having opinions or choices—and I know it doesn't seem important, but I can't wait to see what kind of fashion she leans towards, to see if her tastes diverge from mine.

I think I'd love that, to see her grow into her own being without my constant influence. It's something my mother never liked from us.

I finish cutting the last pepper and hand Ryke the jar of marinara sauce. "Speaking of my sisters . . ."

He meets my eyes. "We were only talking about Lily, not all of your sisters." I'm about to retract the jar, but he yanks it out of my grasp and unscrews the lid.

I can't back down now. "How are you and Daisy?"

"We're fucking fine." He shrugs and searches for a spatula. It's that movement, the *shrug*, that has me crossing my arms.

"Just 'fine'?" I wonder. I could ask Daisy, but she always says the same thing.

He lets out a frustrated groan, banging a drawer closed. Then he runs his hands through his hair. When he exhales, he says, "The last time I talked about my relationship, I was given a twenty-minute lecture about taking a break from her. So yeah, I'm not too fucking chatty about it."

My gaze narrows. "Poppy?" I'm aware of my sister's protest to Daisy being with Ryke because of "timing"—she's told me.

He nods once.

Loren reaches across the bar and plucks out a spatula from the utensil holder. It's sitting right in front of Ryke. He passes it to his older brother. "What's her problem?" Lo asks.

"Apparently she took a yearlong break from Sam during their first year of college, and she said it helped her put into perspective what she fucking wanted out of life. Poppy wants me to give Daisy the chance to 'find herself' before committing to something serious." He spreads sauce over the dough. "The thing is: Daisy and I—we've both been alone more than *anyone* in this fucking house, and if I truly thought that was what Daisy wanted, I'd break up with her tomorrow so she could be happy. Even if I'd be fucking miserable."

"Rose was a virgin until she was twenty-three," Loren pipes in. "I think she beats you on the 'alone' thing, bro."

"He's not talking about sex, Loren."

Lo ignores me and focuses on his brother. "Are you sure she doesn't want a break?"

"I'm telling you, I keep asking her—to the point of annoyance—just to make sure, and she keeps saying no." Daisy hasn't discussed the topic with me, but I can't see my little sister lying to Ryke just to pacify him.

"What's Daisy annoyed look like?" Lo pops another pepperoni in his mouth. I've never seen that sentiment from my sister either.

"Frazzled. She'll try to distract me off topic, and then when she gives up, she'll say *please stop* in this really pained voice, like I'm crushing glass in her ears. It fucking sucks."

It reminds me that he's been with her for a year and a half. "You don't have to take a break just because my older sister tells you it's right," I say. "It was right for Poppy and Sam, but that doesn't make it right for you and Daisy. Every relationship is different."

It's easy to weigh personal experiences against other people's relationships, but we can't see the ins and outs and complexities of other couples the way that we understand and live through our own.

Ryke nods. "I know, but I want to marry that girl one day. And it just really fucking sucks—because I'd get down on one knee tomorrow if people in her family didn't hate us together."

I gape, my mouth falling further and further. *He wants to marry Daisy. He wants to marry my baby sister.* I haven't been sure whether he even values marriage because he never talks about it to anyone.

But his opinion makes sense to me now. I've never seen him so infatuated and head over heels in love with someone the way that he is with Daisy. And he craves familial companionship since he didn't have any growing up. So it's not hard to believe he'd want his own someday.

My cold heart thaws—that is, before Lo's voice freezes it back over.

"When have other people's opinions ever stopped you?" Lo asks. *That actually wasn't so bad.*

Ryke heads to the fridge. "Daisy cares, and if she cares, then I fucking care." He grabs a bag of mozzarella and returns to the pizza. "Weddings and proposals—those are supposed to be *happy* experiences. I don't want anyone's judgment ruining that. Daisy deserves one day that belongs to her without any drama, and I can't give her that yet." He shakes his head. "It's all just bad fucking timing. With everything."

Because of the shit storm.

He has no idea if he'll be able to propose, ever. "Fate will be in your favor," I tell him.

"Rose thinks she can predict the future now," Lo mocks.

"I just have hope, Loren," I say. "Where's yours?"

Lo smiles, not a bitter one this time. "If I can be sober and raise a kid, I think anything's possible."

Ryke motions to Lo's cutting board: only four thick pieces of pepperoni sliced. "What the fuck are you doing?"

"Taking my time," Lo says. "And in the spirit of bad timing, I think we need to call a house meeting. I have something else I need to discuss."

I frown. "Right now?"

"Since everyone seems so willing to share, yeah, right now." He raises his brows. "You need me to text your husband for you?"

I roll my eyes but don't answer him.

"I'll take your silence as a *yes, of course, I love you, Loren Hale.*"

"Don't make me use this knife on you." I wave it threateningly, but he's too preoccupied with his cell phone to make a snarky remark. Whatever he wants to talk about . . . I think it may be serious.

Forty-three

Rose Cobalt

Can you both put the weapons away before we start the meeting?" Lily bounces Moffy on her hip, her eyes darting between Lo and me.

I brace my knife less like a kitchen utensil and more like artillery. It doesn't help that Connor is here now, securing Jane in her high chair. I slyly look his way, expecting him to steal a glance at me in return.

He doesn't.

Ignoring him is taking more effort than I ever thought it would.

Coconut eats out of her bowl next to the breakfast table, and Daisy slides onto the stool beside Loren. We're all here, the pizza baking and infusing pepperoni and cheese flavors in the air. It takes Loren a long while to actually drop his knife, and I realize that my grip is just as tight as before.

Lily says, "You too, Rose."

Fine. I gently set the knife in its holder. Then I fetch Jane's food. I chopped kiwi earlier into cube-sized pieces, and so I collect that from the fridge and scoop some yogurt into a tiny bowl. The hard part is approaching Jane's high chair with Connor so close.

He looks over his shoulder at me, and I whip my head in the

other direction, just barely catching the quirk of his lips. I will not fail at ignoring him. *You can do this, Rose.*

I slide the kiwi and yogurt to Daisy. "Give this to Connor," I instruct. Then I add the perfunctory, "Please." Although my *pleases* never sound as soft and inviting as others.

Daisy hops off the bar stool without hesitation. "You're still ignoring him?" I let my sisters in on my business earlier today.

"Until ten a.m. tomorrow," I say.

"This is ridiculous," Loren pipes in, watching my little sister hand off Jane's food to my husband. When I glance at Connor again, his deep-blue eyes are pinned on me, his grin escalating *every* time we make contact. His expression says, *you can't look away, can you, Rose?*

I can.

Watch me. I focus on Loren and his sharp jawline and half grimace, which practically says, *ew, why the hell are you staring at me?*

"There have to be repercussions for losing," I tell my brother-in-law. "So no, it's not ridiculous, *Loren*. It's the price of failure."

Connor says, "It's hardly a failure when there were distractions."

I snort. "Loren, tell Richard that one wrong question still means he lost, and that he's the one who says 'distraction' is a word that 'losers' use to make themselves feel better." I have to keep my back to Connor, even if I ache to turn around and glare in his direction.

Loren opens his mouth, but Connor speaks before he can even reiterate.

"My wife being injured unquestionably ranks above a competitor sneezing during a quiz bowl tournament."

I can't argue this. Someone's seasonal allergies did fuck with my concentration during an academic bowl in college, and he'll never let me live it down.

I growl. "Loren, tell Connor that I know his overinflated ego can't handle the word 'failure,' but by its definition, it still applies."

"For Christ's sake," Lo interjects. "Both of you shut up."

I only comply because he lets out a heavy breath, and I remember that *he* called this meeting and gathered everyone together.

Lily secures Moffy in his high chair next to Jane, and from her expression alone, I can't discern whether she already knows about the topic at hand.

Lo rests his elbows on the counter, hunching forward. "The babies are almost going to be a year old, and we still haven't chosen godparents."

The air thins.

Godparents. I crave to look at Connor and see if his complacency cracks for a brief second.

"You want to do this now?" Ryke questions. I missed the part where Daisy jumped on the counter next to him, sitting by the microwave. She swings her legs and peels an orange while his arm subtly drapes across her shoulders.

"There's no better time," Lo says. "We all keep dodging the subject."

Lily nods. "We need to make a decision soon." So she did know what he was up to.

Lo adds, "The outside is insane. I never thought anyone could hurt *you*, of all people." He motions to me, his cheekbones like razors as he glances at my bandaged wound again.

My temple throbs. "If it happens again, someone will lose their fingers and toes, I assure you."

"It's not happening again," Connor proclaims, his stern voice prickling my neck. *Don't turn around, Rose.* I stand rigid in place.

Lo focuses on Connor. "Whether it's you two or Lily and me,

we need to think about the worst happening. I can't let Samantha or my father have custody of Moffy."

Silence sweeps the kitchen, and tension thickens the longer no one speaks. We've all sheltered our opinions about godparents, mostly since there will be hurt feelings in the process. None of us are entirely religious, but we view this decision solely as a guardianship. The godparents will be responsible for our children should something happen to us.

Coconut chows down on kibble, her munching filling the deadened air. Jane slurps her yogurt, and Moffy whacks his hands on his tray table.

"Who's fucking dying?" Ryke asks, hardly easing the strain.

"Unexpected, shitty things happen," Loren retorts. "I think we can all agree on that." His eyes flicker to Daisy's face, the long scar down her cheek. And then to mine.

Lily raises her hand. "I have something to add." She clears her throat. "I know that no one wants to say anything in fear of rejecting someone else. But can we all take our emotions out of it and make a decision right here. *Please*." Her "please" is heartbreakingly desperate, reminding me that I need to work on mine.

"Says one of the most emotional people in the fucking room," Ryke mutters under his breath.

I shoot him a scathing look.

"Hey," Lo snaps.

"Yeah, *hey*." Lily's face scrunches, attempting a glare.

Ryke cringes with remorse and runs a frustrated hand through his thick hair. "I'm emotional too, Lil. I didn't mean it like it sounded. Sorry."

Lily accepts the apology with a smile.

Daisy shares her orange with Ryke, splitting the slices in half. "Aren't Connor and Rose having a million kids?" she asks.

I accidentally glance at Connor again, his features unreadable as he studies me. We haven't talked about children since our test backfired, but by the parameters of our rules, I think we're both in agreement that Jane is all we can have.

Don't think about it, Rose.

I don't like thinking about this new future, ever.

"Just what the world needs, a Coballoway army," Loren says, his sarcasm unusually absent.

"We may only have Jane." I pull back my shoulders to try and accept this outcome, even when it feels off-kilter, like life is unbalanced.

Lo frowns deeply. "What? Since when?"

Lily looks morose. "Is this about what happened with the paparazzi?"

Only Ryke knows about our test, but the reason behind everything remains the same: how can we protect our children? They have no choice whether or not to be in magazines or stalked and traumatized by cameras.

"Yes," Connor answers. "It's about the media."

"If you want more kids," Lo says, "you should have more kids and not let some shitty fucking journalists dictate what you do." He nods to Ryke. "Same goes for you, bro. I better be seeing a mini-you one day because I know for a goddamn fact you want a kid."

Daisy smiles as she bites into an orange slice.

Ryke rolls his eyes. He's been in our camp since the beginning, afraid of bringing a kid in this environment.

Daisy eases the tension with a brighter smile. "Let's just assume that Rose and Connor may have more kids. How many were you planning?"

"Eight," I send the number into the void. When Connor first proposed the amount, I thought he was insane, but the longer we've bantered back and forth about *eight babies this* and *eight babies that*, it's become less of a crazed idea, spawned from a verbal battle and egotistical notions. Now it's become an endearing plan. A family of ten. *It sounds strong*, he told me.

It does.

But I suppose it's traveled back to being a fantastical idea once more.

Lily picks at her nails. "Eight?" She seems worried by the number, unsure if she can handle that many.

I find my knife and point it between my two sisters. "Whoever wants to be Jane's godmother has to make a blood pact with me."

They both exchange a look like they're considering volunteering *out* of the position.

I rest a hand on my hip. "Fine, the blood pact is optional. The godmother part is still mandatory."

"Ryke and Daisy should do it." It's not Lily who voices that opinion.

It's Loren.

"And why is that?" I ask, slightly crestfallen. Is this headed where I think? Lo and Lily will choose Ryke and Daisy as well. I know I'm not cuddly. I'm cold at first sight. I know the media thinks I don't love my own child. I've said things in my past that condemn me before my actions tell the real truth.

But I'd like to believe that Lily sees how much I love Jane and her son. I'd give him the world as I would my own child. I suppose, secretly, I've longed to be the godmother of Lily's kids. We've always been the closest among our sisters, and if Lily left the world with Lo, I'd want the remaining pieces of her as close to me as possible.

I'm not as fun or as daring as Daisy, but I would really, *really* try to be as compassionate and as loving as Lily—for her.

I stare down at my knife, avoiding everyone's eyes.

"Kids are stressful," Lo explains. "Eight sounds like a nightmare. I don't know if we could do that without . . ." *Relapsing*, the unspoken word lingers.

"It's understandable," Connor says. "Ryke and Daisy were our first choices anyway."

I glare at the wall. "Ryke, can you tell Connor that this piece of information was unnecessary to share with Loren and Lily?"

Ryke stares past my shoulder. "You fucking got that?" he asks my husband.

Before he can say anything, Lily throws her hands in the air. "We're not offended. Honestly I'm glad we've made one decision. Two more to go."

Daisy mock gasps. "Is Coconut on the menu? She could use some godparents. I'm proud to say, she's not a bed wetter." She cups her hands around her mouth and whispers, "But she snores."

Ryke messes Daisy's hair with a rough hand, and he murmurs in her ear, the words almost distinguishable as, *I love you, sweetheart.*

Loren shoots Lily a look. "A dog godparent?"

Lily nods. "We can't abandon her."

My stomach knots. *Don't think about Sadie.*

Ryke and Daisy quietly discuss their decision for no longer than a few seconds, and then their gazes pin to Loren and Lily. Daisy says, "We want you two to take care of her since you both like dogs more than Connor and Rose."

This is true.

And still, I'm the one feeling more left out. I should've known it'd be this way from the start. I may be more responsible than my sisters, but people want their kids with someone who hugs them, so affectionately, so warmly, that a smile crests their face.

I'm the one who will pick children up from school on time, who will write note cards at midnight so they can cram for a test, who will always remember to pack their lunches and tuck them into bed. I may hound them to brush their teeth. I may even remind them constantly to remove their dirty shoes before they enter the house. But I would champion them. I would fight for them.

I hope this counts.

"Meeting adjourned," I suddenly say, not wanting to hear them choose "Raisy." Yes, it's hypocritical since we weren't planning on choosing Lily and Lo. But I can't change my feelings.

I'm about to open the oven when Loren snaps, "We have a kid too. Or is Jane the special snowflake here?"

I inhale, my chest tight. "Just choose your brother, and let's be done with this."

He snorts into a dry, bitter laugh. "Of course you have to make this hard for me." He shakes his head. "If you end up raising Moffy, I hope he learns how to be tough from you."

My brows pinch. *What?* I look to Lily for confirmation. She has a dorky grin on her face, nodding rapidly. "Will you and Connor be Maximoff's godparents?"

Something wet runs down my cheek. *No, no, no.* I spin quickly, wiping underneath my traitorous eye. When I look up, I realize I've spun *towards* Connor.

His brow arches at me. I glare at the sight of his wide grin, and I want so badly to mouth *shut up*, but I can't speak to him. Hopefully my eyes convey the message. This better not be considered cheating.

Loren laughs behind me. "Did you just cry, Rose?"

"No, *Loren*," I retort, turning back around. "There was dust in my eye."

"Sure," he says, a smile attached to his voice. "It was just dust." He tilts his head at me. "You know you're a kick-ass mom, right?"

I think he's *trying* to make me cry.

"I'm pretty sure you would rip out your hair for my son too."

I have to wipe my eyes *again*. "I would," I whisper beneath my breath. *I would over and over again.*

Lily adds, "I know that you'd love Moffy as fiercely as you love Jane." She wipes her nose that drips with her tears. She sniffs. "And we'd be at peace knowing he's with you."

I have to dab my eyes with a paper towel. I say what's aching to come out. "Thank you."

I live my life confidently, but motherhood has always been "in progress" for me. After I had Jane, I've felt more self-assured, but it belongs in my heart. My growth remains empty in the eyes of others. Except these people, in this kitchen. They see me. And I realize that's all I needed.

The oven timer beeps, and I glance over my shoulder at Connor. We lock eyes again.

Silence is a cruel punishment between the people you love.

Never again, I think.

I can't imagine how this is going to work tonight. Ignoring each other. In bed.

Something tells me a pillow barricade won't restrain my ambitious husband from getting what he wants.

Regardless, I'm no cheater. And the rules still apply.

Forty-four

Rose Cobalt

I brush my teeth before bed and do my *very* best to ignore my husband's dominant presence. He seems to make a show of stretching slowly across the counter, just to reach for the fucking *toothpaste*.

It's unnerving. His height. His unfaltering posture. His sheer ability to vacuum all oxygen by grabbing an object alone. This type of confidence intoxicates the air, and I inhale the poisonous fumes with each shallow breath.

I collect my hair to my right shoulder, holding it back as I spit into the sink and rinse my mouth. I avoid the mirror, his gaze beckoning me to meet him, and I search for my hairbrush. I won't succumb to him that easily.

He lost.

There are consequences.

"Rose, you're lying down with your ass perfectly raised," he says deeply. I try not to tense. *Ignore him.* "One of my hands is wrapped around your neck." I sense him nearing me. One step. Two. "I forcefully roll your panties down your ass, down your legs, off your ankles." His hand rests beside mine on the counter, and I slam the drawer shut. *Ignore him, Rose.*

"You just collapsed on the bed," he says.

I did not, I almost retort. I literally bite my tongue.

"I haven't even slid my erection inside of you yet, but I plan to . . ." His voice seems to be nearer, like a husky whisper in the pit of my ear. "I plan to fill you so full, Rose. My cock all the way between your legs, right in . . . right there . . ." I keep waiting for his hands to touch me, right *there*. Even when they don't and I'm left with cold air, I clench. *Fuck me.*

No, Rose. I ditch the pursuit for my hairbrush, which has disappeared at the most inopportune moment. Then I turn my back to Connor. On my exit out of the bathroom, I flick *off* the lights, shrouding him in darkness, as though he doesn't exist at all.

I feel his frustration behind me, his body tightening and coiling at my lack of response.

Connor rarely simmers. Our back-and-forth banter releases his pent-up conceitedness, his narcissism, which *needs* to be fueled and acknowledged, and without my reply, his irritation pools and pools.

I'm afraid my vagina does not understand tonight's mission. *Ignore thy husband.*

I delicately set every decorative pillow in the middle of the bed. Already dressed in a black sultry chemise, a slit up my thigh, I'm prepared for se—*sleep.*

God. I cannot have sex tonight. *Get in the game, Rose.*

I think I'm tangled in the midst of it.

I climb underneath the puffy comforter about the same time Connor exits the bathroom, shirtless but still in black slacks. I try not to hone in on his body for long or his styled, wavy brown hair.

In my peripheral, I catch him inspecting the pillows along our bed with agitation and then he unbuckles his belt, his movements rough and controlled and extremely audible. The *clack* of the metal clasp. The *whisk* of the leather leaving his pant loops.

I press my cheek to my pillow and reach out to my end table, switching off my lamp. I dip my hand underneath the comforter, splaying my palm on my thigh. I ache to go a little higher, a little closer to my panties, for stimulation . . .

I listen to him too intently, hearing him step out of his slacks. In effect, I imagine Connor in his boxer briefs, his bulge noticeable, maybe even already hard beneath them.

My fingers stroke my bare thigh, diving beneath the silk of my chemise. I'm dying to touch my clit, but I fear that he'll hear. Even married, I still masturbate, but not as often and *never* while next to Connor. He's never even seen me do it. My skin heats the longer I tease myself, my hand so close to my panties . . .

The bed undulates with his weight, and I hear each pillow being tossed onto the floor. Normally I stack them *delicately* on the chaise in front of our four-poster bed. I can't even curse Connor out for maltreating my pillows.

I could crawl out of bed and put them in their proper place, but my squeezed thighs and the pulsing inside of me have carnal demands, not clean ones.

I'm literally too horny to move.

I fixate on the wall, my back turned to him, and I wait for his lamp to flicker off. An eternity must pass and I sincerely wonder if he's reading a book just to annoy me. It's 2 a.m.—we both need sleep. *Or sex.*

That too—but only I can quench my own arousal tonight.

Ignore thy husband.

With this in mind again, I slowly turn and realize that he is, in fact, propped against the headboard with a book in hand. Not to annoy me though. His brows are cinched in frustration as he flips the page, focusing on the text. Reading is his attempt to stimulate his brain in ways that I'm not.

It's not working either. He shuts the book roughly and then locks eyes with me, his lips beginning to rise. *"Venez à moi."* *Come to me.*

Oh no. Not happening. At least not how he wants. I plan to turn off his light for him. I break eye contact and then scoot closer, stretching over his lap to reach his end table. I inhale as he grasps my ass, his fingers dipping quickly between my thighs and skimming my panties.

I hurriedly shut off his lamp, bathing us in semidarkness, and I go to move back to my side of the bed.

Right as I pass, he clutches my face and kisses me forcefully, stealing all oxygen from my lungs. I ache and pulse and then wake up, pulling apart and pressing my hand over his mouth.

"There are rules," I pant, trying to catch my breath. "Don't fuck with them."

My eyes already orient to the lack of light. His displeasure crosses his features. I gave him an order. In bed, I never play this role. I don't like it, and while it's not ideal for either of us, we can't diminish the stakes of our games. He knows this.

He's just not used to failing.

I peel my hand off his lips, remove his wayward fingers from my panties, and then slide back to my end. I fluff my pillow, waiting for him to speak.

"Do you even know how wet you are right now?" he asks.

I freeze.

"Your panties are soaked, Rose."

I don't doubt it. I hope he notices my fiery glare, even if it's not plastered to his face. I lie on my back, scooting fully beneath the comforter with my arms disappeared beneath it. I'm a stiff board, mummified. If brazen enough, I can also be a satiated woman.

I shut my eyes to block out Connor from my peripheral, but his domineering aura still shadows me. I feel him in the same position: propped against the headboard, his knee bent. His mind is at constant work to find a solution in order to achieve his desires.

"I never said how you felt the first time I put my cock inside of you."

My chest collapses in a deep breath. He's trying to arouse me enough that I succumb to him and allow him to dominate every inch of my body.

I'm not that easy to crack.

It's a part of why he's with me. He loves the challenge, and he thinks I won't touch myself while lying next to him. But I'm as stubborn as he is dominant.

"When I slid into you, Rose, you were so tight that my cock swelled from the pressure."

The first time I had sex. I never asked if I was that tight, but hearing that it affected him increases the pulse. It hurts, screaming for a hard, fast entry. My left hand kneads my breast and my other descends down the front of my panties.

I hesitate only when I dive into my mind, wondering if he's watching or if he's concentrating on other things. *Like what, Rose, the ceiling, the floor?*

When he speaks again, it goads me to continue to my clit, thinking that he's more focused on his words. "You were used to toys but you weren't used to the warmth or length of my erection, which fit perfectly between your thighs. In and out . . . in and out."

I swallow, my fingers rubbing the sensitive bud. My toes already curl in anticipation, and the wetness creates easier friction.

I want him. *In and out . . . in and out.*

I buck my hips once and then freeze. The silence solidifies me. If he's not speaking, then he's watching. Is this a bad thing?

It's partially unsettling, partially arousing, partially I-don't-fucking-know-what.

I have to see what he's doing. I can't let my mind draw irrational conclusions, so I slowly turn my head. He's in the same sitting position against the headboard, arm resting on his bent knee, and *yes*, his gaze is locked on me.

I glare on instinct, fire returning to my hellish eyes. *Look away, Richard*, I speak through them.

"No." His singular word holds more weight than anyone else's could.

I have three options.

1. Go to bed horny.
2. Continue masturbating with Connor watching.
3. Succumb to my husband's wants *too* easily and let him fuck me.

The second option is the best one, even if it's difficult. I stare at the chandelier above our bed, and I quicken my fingers. *I want to come so fucking hard.* I try to remain still, but my legs quiver at the overwhelming sensations, my skin heating with sweat.

In and out . . . in and out, I imagine Connor pumping between my legs, spreading them wider—

The comforter is tossed off my body, revealing my source of pleasure, hand beneath my panties, chemise rolled to my breasts, my nipples exposed as the straps have fallen off my shoulders. I'm so close to coming.

"Richard," I half pant in want of him, right inside of me, and I half warn in threat of him right inside of me. I sit on two polar ends of *yes* and *no.* Too complicated for an ordinary man.

Thank God I have Connor, an intelligent one, who can handle my bipolar desires.

He cups my heat, right where my hand resides, and my eyes drill into him. He's quick. He slides behind me, his legs extending on either side of my body, and then he *lifts* me against him, my back to his chest.

His assured movements, every one of them, knocks the breath out of me. I tuck my knees together, silently not cooperating.

He grasps my leg and pulls it open again, stretching to meet his leg, which seems too far away. I fit between him, every limb touching his limbs. I can feel the shape of his hard cock against my back. I tremble.

"You're cheating." My raspy voice scratches my throat.

His lips graze my ear. "Ignore me, darling." The words sound full of sex. He nips my ear, bites my neck, his fingers pinching my nipple . . .

"Play . . . by the . . . rules . . . Richard," I breathe.

"Stop speaking to me, and I am." He slides my panties off and then guides my hands to his thighs, dictating my movements.

I hesitate, my brain not functioning properly to understand.

He notices, his hand encasing my face while his lips touch my cheek, my jaw, then to my ear, "I see an alternate path." I'm listening. "I see us abiding by the rules." Yes. "And me fucking you how we *both* want. So ignore me. Be silent. Stay still. Do nothing."

Do nothing.

He found a loophole by being technical with each word to our rules. I ignore him for twenty-four hours, a *silent* treatment. It doesn't mean that he has to ignore me, and if we can't stimulate each other mentally, at least we can physically.

He's going to get what he wants.

And I am too, I realize.

We both win.

Just as I think it, he lifts me by the hips and lowers me onto his dick, the fullness blinding my mind. *I'm going to come.* His low breath warms my ear. "Don't move, darling."

And then he bucks up—*oh, Connor.* The deep rhythm never ceases, the friction winding into a giant ball . . . and I combust.

A cry breaches my lips, a moan that causes him to increase his vigorous pace. My body tightens, and I clench around him, bursting again and again. I can't see Connor behind me, but I can feel the sweat of his skin, the ripple of his muscle, his strong hand encasing my face as my head begins to loll.

He whispers husky French, sex dripping off each syllable, and my brain is too fried to translate a single word. I glance down, his cock driving into me, fast. *In and out.* My nerves prick again, ready for another heady, mind-numbing experience with Connor at the helm.

I do nothing.

And in doing *nothing*, I feel *everything.*

Minutes fly and his fingers brush my clit. I gasp, constrict and my lips part, a pleasured noise strangled in my throat.

He spanks the side of my ass.

My back curves, and when he rams up into me, he hits his peak too, his low grunt vibrating my whole body.

He just came inside of me . . . and part of me wants to take a shower and maybe even change the sheets, a neurotic impulse. But I'm too physically tired to enact that plan.

As we both catch our breaths, he carefully lifts me off him and rests me on my side. My eyes flutter closed and I can't will them open. His body is much closer to mine now, his arm affectionately draped across my waist. His lips press on my neck—the last sensation I feel before I fall quickly into sleep.

I wake to fullness, to Connor thrusting into me. I moan softly into the sheets, still on my side. My body rocks each time he pounds, his cock driving deeper, his hand on the crook of my hip.

I love these impromptu sessions, spurned by his arousal. My knees are slightly bent, which must have allowed him access into me, even on my side with my thighs pressed together.

My eyes graze the clock. 9:59 a.m.

He let me sleep in, and I want to ask about Jane—if he took care of her earlier this morning, even though I'm sure he did. But his punishment still has one minute left—

His hand suddenly envelops my chin, jaw and mouth, pulling

my neck back until I meet his gaze. He's tangled in my damp hair, and the intensity of his blue eyes drills me as much as his erection. His hand lowers from my hip to my ass, squeezing my flesh.

I moan into his palm, the noise tickling my lips.

"First word that comes to you," he tests me, probably right at 10 a.m.—not a minute too late. He shifts his hand off my mouth, his body and mind meeting mine at once. "Rose."

"Love," I say in one breath.

He kisses me, upside down, while thrusting, and I break away first as my body reaches its tipping point. I clutch the sheets and practically scream into the mattress, my orgasm electric and more powerful. I can feel him milking his own climax, slowly pumping inside of me one last time.

When he pulls out, he rolls me onto my back. He's half sitting, his hand beside my shoulder as he stares down. "Good morning, darling."

I've had so many thoughts that I wanted to share with him in the past twenty-four hours, and they all traitorously flit away, leaving me with the present. I throb like he's still inside of me, even when he's gone.

I need a shower, wetness oozing down my inner thigh. "It's like you're trying to impregnate me." My yellow-green eyes pierce him. His sperm already defeated my birth control once. Part of me wants him to say: *I am.*

His eyes sweep my features. "I get off on toying with science—"

"Fate," I clarify. He gets off on playing Russian roulette with my ovaries.

"When my sperm works hard to reach your egg, it's called *reproduction*. Science."

"The possibility of your sperm reaching my egg right now is a chance happening. *Fate.*"

"Probabilities are also scientific."

Ugh. I growl in irritation, about to push him away from my

face, but he clasps my wrist. Seriousness pulls between us for a moment. I have to ask, "Do you see an alternate path to have more kids?"

His body solidifies, his features blanketing in a hard resolution I don't want to meet. And he says, "No."

It hurts. That one word. I recognize *how much* I want more. How much we both want them.

"*Ça ne peut pas être comment ça se termine.*" *This can't be how it ends.* It feels like a closing of our future. All I see is a massive door trying to swing shut on our dreams. The ones we've built together. Raising eight children *together*.

"*C'est vrai.*" *It is.*

Two more gut-wrenching words.

"Then maybe you should wear a condom next time."

His thumb brushes my bottom lip, but I notice his jaw tightening. He's not happy with this verdict. I expect he's going to say, *not yet*. I predict that he's not ready to accept this outcome.

He kisses me on the lips.

And he says, "I will."

Translation: *we're done having children together.*

Forty-five

Connor Cobalt

misjudged you back during *Princesses of Philly*," Scott Van Wright says. "You're actually cool, Connor."

I head to the door, nodding a couple times. "Same to you, man." I block out Rose's voice in my mind, unable to hear her truth and cope with what just took place in Scott's house an hour prior.

What happened was a price I had to pay to reach a greater benefit. It was a loss leader. There are no emotions in facts.

I turn around and shake his hand, pat his back and say goodbye.

"We should grab lunch tomorrow," Scott tells me as I skip the steps down his porch.

I casually wave to him like *sure thing*, and then he smiles, accepting our friendship wholeheartedly, no trace of doubt, no hesitance—*exactly* what I wanted. He shuts the door, and I walk along his driveway, my house diagonally across the street from his.

On my way back home, I call Frederick.

He answers on the second ring. "I'm not talking to you about Daisy." He won't ever share more information about her progress, but that's not why I called.

"Remind me, Rick, why do people choose to feel?" *Because, Richard, it's—* I shut out Rose's beliefs. They're not helpful anymore. I was able to pass Scott's test this afternoon *only* because I pushed her voice away. In my mind, she's restraining me from completing goals. She's making this more difficult than it has to be.

"You know why," he tells me.

"Emotions stifle me. It's a straitjacket that superior people *know* not to put on."

I hear papers rustle on his end, as though pushing them aside to concentrate. "What happened, Connor?"

"You don't have an answer, do you?" I realize. "Because you know I'm right."

"Emotions make you human."

"Then I'm more than human." I'm indestructible this way.

"No," he says. "When you don't feel, you're *less* than human."

I swallow distaste. "No. I accomplish more than they do."

"You love less."

"There is *pain* in love," I suddenly say, hurt flaring and swelling my chest. I submerge it all, feeling nothing. *Richard*—no, Rose. I can't hear her. I can't feel what she wants me to feel. "I don't want any part of it."

"Greater men would experience pain just to love."

I reach my mailbox, and my hand tightens around the phone. "Are you trying to incite me, Rick?"

"You feel, Connor. It's there, inside of you. You're just afraid."

"No." But I have no other defense than that one.

I'm scared.

I'm scared to feel agony tear through me, and I'd rather return to the time where my choices were driven by selfish pursuits, where my decisions never emotionally impacted me. Where I could wake up the next morning and never waver. I'd never *feel* my soul wither.

"I won today," I say. "I don't want to feel like I lost." *Not again.* I step onto my porch and unlock the front door.

"Concentrate on what you have . . ."

I tune out his voice as Rose rushes into the foyer, barefoot, no socks or clean heels that she'll usually wear indoors. Off my gaze, she says, "I was in Jane's nursery, and I saw you returning. How'd it go with the devil?"

I say a short goodbye to Frederick and hang up. "It was easy," I tell Rose, locking the door behind me. Then I pass her and head to the kitchen.

I have no problem being what other people need, being the level head, the calm in the face of a raging, undying storm. I like being needed, being useful. Rose knows this, but she also knows, as well as I do, that Scott is different.

I've never despised a human being quite like him, and to be anything else but enemies has been far from easy.

She follows me with a blistering stride. "Last week at the golf course, you said it was hard not calling him a twat and decking his head with the nine iron."

I open the fridge. "I was thinking irrationally last week." I glance over the water bottles and leftover Lucky's burgers. I don't know what I'm searching for.

"Richard," Rose snaps.

"Rose," I say calmly, shutting the fridge and turning to face her.

The longer she looks at me, the more her nose flares, her rabid, sweltering emotions bubbling to the surface. It's beautiful . . . just not something I personally want to share.

"What happened at his house?" she asks.

They're just words.

I should be able to say them without falter. I'm superior that way. "I knew he was going to see if I contradicted myself, to test me." I take a step near Rose, towering above her. She raises her chin to appear taller, even when she's not. "And he chose something I said at Saturn Bridges." The bar where Rose picked me up. "That night, I told him that I didn't care about the sex tapes but you did."

I'd never bad-mouthed Rose in my life, not to climb a social ladder, not to fake my way through the corporate world, and that night at Saturn Bridges was the first time I degraded her. The words I spoke today are worse. They're unforgivable, so heinous that I struggle to crawl back to an hour prior in Scott's house and remember them.

If I just focus on my goals, on what I achieved, and not stare into her eyes, then I can be free of these crippling emotions.

It's hard to avoid Rose, seething in front of me.

I do look at her, and her hot gaze burns holes right through me. *She's fine. I didn't hurt her.*

She sets her hands on her hips. "It wasn't easy for you to tell him that lie."

"How do you know?"

"I saw your face in the car that night, and you looked distraught."

Distraught? "No," I say flatly.

"*Yes,*" she sneers. "It was in the corners of your eyes."

I raise my brows at her. "The corners of my eyes?" I rub my lips, wondering if I want to laugh or if I want to scream. Maybe I'm just numb to everything. "And what's in the corners of my eyes now?" I wear the blankest face I have.

"Ugliness," she retorts.

"You're the only person on this earth that's ever called me ugly," I muse. "Do you know that, Rose?"

"Then you've fooled everyone but me." She stomps over to the breakfast table. I don't understand what she plans on doing, but she drags the wooden chair to the other side of the island counter where I stand.

"You're scratching the hardwood," I point out.

"I don't care about the floor," she retorts, positioning the chair across from me. And then she stands on it, gaining two inches on me for height advantage. It's comical if not entirely ridiculous.

"Feel better?" I ask.

"Cut the bullshit," she tells me. "I know you, and you may be arrogant, you may be wholly conceited and unabashed to the millionth degree, but you're *not* coldhearted. You're not unfeeling, so stop pretending to be."

"I can't be you," I remind her. "I can't stomp my feet and *scream* and shout. It gets me nowhere."

"I'm not asking you to do those things." Her yellow-green eyes push me towards the imprisoned parts of myself, and a forty-ton weight tries to descend on me. Why would anyone want to feel this? For years, I've watched secondhand as Lo's hurt affected Lily, and Lily's hurt affected Lo—never did I believe I'd reach my own tipping point with the pain of love.

Never did I believe it'd be too overwhelming for me.

I look at Rose. "Then what do you want?"

"The truth," she says. "Not just facts."

"You can't handle it, Rose."

She almost appears wounded. *She's fine.* Then her eyes flash hot, indignant again. She points a manicured nail into my chest. "*You* can't handle it, Richard. If you could, you'd tell me the full extent of what happened."

I don't want to confront her or tell her the truth. I'll see her pain. I'll feel it churn through me, and I won't—I *can't*—bear this weight. I'm stronger alone. "Let me live with this knowledge. You don't need it."

She fists my shirt. "I won't let you lie to yourself. I made you that promise, and I'm keeping it." She stares down at me, her forehead nearly pressed against mine. I match the rhythm of her heavy, vexed breath.

"Everyone except you loves this version of me, so maybe it's you who's wrong."

"Everyone loves the awful, cowardly, *fake* versions of you." Her eyes swell with passion. "They love the *lesser* you because they don't even know the real one."

My hand shakes. "Rose," I murmur, my chest blazing the longer I stare into her. She fuels the fire in my soul, the embers slowly dying, and she tries feverishly to awaken me.

I open my mouth to say the truth—what happened . . . the words stick to the back of my throat.

I place my hands on hers, the ones clutching my shirt, as though she's seconds from throttling me to her plane of existence—where the world is painted vibrantly in sadness, in rage and despair. I'm the one who lives in muted tones of impassivity and emptiness, needing other people to color my landscape for me.

Tears drip down her cheeks, but she never smothers the fervor in her gaze. "I'll wait until you have the strength to tell me."

Strength. It takes more power to confront emotions than it does to expel them.

I cup her slender jaw with one hand, brushing her tears with my thumb, and I use the other to hold her hip, drawing closer to her body until we're two vertical lines pressed together. She stands two inches above me.

She's crying silently.

She's far from impervious. And yet she is better than me.

I asked her to be, so when everything compounded on top of me, she'd lift me back to her height again. "Facts," I whisper.

"Truths," she counters, resilient and unbending.

My throat closes. What's the idiom—*the truth will set you free*? It's a buoyant phrase that inadequately describes the torment of speaking truly.

"I'll wait," she reminds me.

I shake my head once.

Strength.

I hold her tighter, and I reroute my mind and go back in time. Across the street. Scott's house. "He wanted to see if I really cared about the sex tapes . . . since I said I didn't." Instead of avoiding her gaze, I meet her head-on, doing this right. "He sat me on his couch, remote in hand—and that's when I knew what he planned to show me."

I watch her face begin to contort as she tries to comprehend the event.

"I had to shut you out of my head . . . I couldn't do what he needed of me with you there."

Her chest collapses. "He made you . . . did you . . . ?"

"He asked me to watch one of our sex tapes—with him." I pause. "And I did."

I wait for her to release my shirt and slap me, but she holds on with a tighter grip as though saying, *I'm not leaving you.* Her features ride a roller coaster of dark sentiments. An overpowering, foreign emotion claws at my organs, a battering ram coursing through vital, necessary places inside of me.

I hurt her.

I open my mouth to explain more . . . to say how it was a tape that hasn't been released yet. Where I tied Rose's wrists to our bed, and I kissed her—I made love to her, and I had to sit there, beside Scott Van Wright, a man I hate, and make a mockery of the woman I *adore.*

I had to be vulgar and callous—I had to say things that'd make her skin crawl, that'd make her scream until her throat became raw, that'd make her sick at the sight of me . . . that make *me* sick at the sight of me.

The act of viewing the tape with Scott carries its own desecrations, but my words won't stop haunting me.

"I would've repulsed you," I tell her. "The things I said . . ."

"No . . . *he* repulses me." She jostles my shirt when the guilt weighs my shoulders down. I travel through a scalding cycle of pain, almost unbearable.

Wetness slides down my cheeks, and she holds my face, which

keeps fracturing. I'm paralyzed from my actions, no matter how much I've accomplished, no matter how grand the achievement I've shelved—my love for Rose outweighs these victories.

"I forgive you," she breathes, fighting more tears. Her forgiveness should unburden me, but I feel the same. I feel disgusted and ashamed.

"I hate myself for what I just did," I whisper. I want to separate the man that spoke ill of his wife from the one who would drop to his knees before her—if I could just pull them apart, then I'd be free.

But I'm one person with one soul, and I'm wading in every malignant word I uttered and every heartless laugh I made. I'm wading in my spirit that I've defiled, and I've never felt so utterly *low*.

Her tears mix with mine. "You have to forgive yourself, Connor."

Forgive yourself. How can I forgive hurting someone who is more than an extension of me? Who I've spent years seeking out during our adolescence, just a few more minutes, just one more hour—just a little more time. She can forgive me, but she never heard what I said.

I won't ever repeat it.

I won't ever think it.

It's too much—even for me.

I grasp the back of her head, my fingers tangled in the thick of her hair. "I'm not positive I ever can, Rose." It's a weight that nearly knocks me backwards, crushing my rib cage against my heart.

With her small hands on either side of my jaw, she says, "You should never hate the better version of you, the one that *loves*, the one that *hurts*—because this man in front of me is *extraordinary*."

Her words flood me, choke me, grip me and *burn* me.

Her words light me in a lethal blaze, and I'm smothered in hot sentiments that pull at me and beg me to scream. I hold her harder, tighter, my forehead pressed against hers.

I'm on fire, every part of me.

I don't want to be less than human. Maybe it's this natural remorse that makes me like everyone else, and maybe it's our everlasting, cerebral love that makes me more.

My muscles scald, my breath locked tight, but I hold Rose right here, pain distancing my lips from hers, tension tearing at my flesh. It's overwhelming. It's horrible and blinding, and I clutch onto her as my own guilt and shame keeps pummeling me at breakneck speed.

"I'm not leaving you," she whispers in a broken voice, further compounding this gut-wrenching pain.

Kiss her. "*Je t'aime,*" I choke, grasping her slick cheek. *I love you.* "*Je t'aime. Je t'aime.*"

I'm burning alive.

She cries more audibly, and I kiss her, our lips together in a fervent, tortured kiss that lingers. I inhale with her, and I slow the movement, our tears dripping, and it becomes a soul-bearing, passionate kiss that awakens my mind.

I hug Rose to my body, taking her off the chair, my lips stinging with salt and urgency. I press Rose so close against me that her feet never hit the floor. Instead, we're eye level. At perfect, equal height.

I've been split open. I've been spilled bare. I've allowed her spirit to seep inside of me—to remind me, *remind me* . . . why I love.

I can barely catch my breath, blistering against her.

And she asks so quietly, "What else do you need?"

What do I need? No one has asked me this before. The answer hits me at once. "A break." I need more time away from everything.

"I'll make it happen," she assures me, her hands dropping to my chest. I stare into her yellow-green eyes, and I sense that she's feeling my heart pound against her palms.

"What would I be without you?" I blink and a single tear drips down my face. We both know the answer to this—we both recognize what she's doing for me. *Remind me. Burn me. Love me.*

I kiss her forehead, my chest alight with passion and pain.

"*Ensemble*," she whispers in French. *Together.*

"*Ensemble*," I murmur.

Together.

Forty-six

Rose Cobalt

> Please come to Sunday luncheon. I promise Jonathan won't be there, but we'd love to see you all and the babies.—Mom

I delete the fifth text she's sent this week. We've been skipping the Sunday family luncheons since the media shit storm. All conversations would've surrounded the press conference, which is now in nine days. I can just picture myself at the patio table, brandishing a fork at my mother or even my father for pressuring my husband to lie to millions of people and do what *they* want instead of what he wants.

"Is that Mom again?" Lily asks, hands braced on the steering wheel. She drives my Escalade while I give her directions. My car is filled to maximum occupancy. We've been switching seats every three hours since it's a long drive, but currently Connor sits in the back row, the babies on either side of him in rear-facing car seats. Loren and his half sister, Willow, are in the middle chairs, an aisle of space between them.

Willow moved into our house not long ago, and when I asked her to join our mini vacation, I was worried she'd decline. We're not the quietest group of people, and I thought she might need a break from *us* when, ironically, we needed a break from everyone else.

I was glad she said *yes*, especially during a twelve-hour car ride with Loren. He tones down his asshole comments when he's around her. I wonder how different he would've been if he had grown up with a little sister instead of meeting her later in life.

"Rose?" Lily asks, eyes flickering from the road to my cell phone.

"She wants us at next week's luncheon," I say, "which is *not* happening." We're on a weeklong secret trip, and we're excluding luncheons from the itinerary.

A white Ferrari drives parallel to us, Coconut's head sticking out of the open window. I can see Ryke's hand clasping the top of the window frame, sitting in the passenger seat.

Daisy must step hard on the gas. One second later, the Ferrari goes from forty miles per hour to about a hundred on the quiet, nearly deserted street.

They speed ahead of us.

"Uhh . . ." Lily gawks. "I'm not supposed to follow them, am I?"

I'm all for comradery, but I do *not* want to join their death brigade.

"No way," Lo tells his wife. "We're not driving off a cliff with Thelma and Louise."

Willow digs through her Jansport backpack and takes out a water bottle. "Do they know where they're going?"

"Nope," Lo says. "I hope he gets lost."

They were supposed to follow us so we wouldn't find them lifeless in a metal heap fifty miles ahead. We even went as far as denying them the address.

"Knowing Ryke and Daisy, I'm sure that's their goal," Connor chimes in.

I crane my neck over my shoulder, noticing Connor rattling a toy over Jane's car seat. I just barely spot her tiny hands reaching out. Connor smiles, more relaxed than he has been of late, and it causes my lips to rise as well, *hoping* that our destination will serve as a much-needed sanctuary.

"Christ," Lo says with a cringe. "I swear every time you smile like that a demon sprouts wings. It's unnatural."

Connor looks up and catches my partial smile before it morphs into a withering glare. My husband grins more, but I direct my hostility at Loren.

"Do you know what else is unnatural? Your *face*."

Lo looks more amused, and he turns to Connor. "Did you hear that, love? Your wife thinks I'm pretty."

I'd let out a growl, but the promise beneath this banter from Loren to Connor overpowers any irritation, a promise that says: *I'll always have your back. You're my best goddamn friend, and no one is going to keep that from changing.*

Connor rubs his lips, but I see his grin as well as everyone. "She wouldn't be wrong."

Lo rotates back to me and flashes a half smile.

I stretch my arm and raise my palm at him like *shut up*, but I struggle to reach, seeming nonthreatening.

"You want a high five, Rose?" Lo mocks.

I growl this time, about to flip him off, but my phone's GPS beeps. I hurriedly swivel back to focus on my primary task. "You have two miles and then you turn right," I instruct Lily.

The windy roads curve around mountains and create odd forks combined with all-way stops that have had Loren scratching his head. Lily is a better driver than him, so I have faith.

Birch and maple trees jut into the crystal blue sky, no other car driving along the road. When we're all quiet, we can almost hear the wind rustle the leaves. The stillness contrasts our normal city atmosphere and the chaotic media presence.

"It's so quiet." Lily says what travels through my mind.

"As long as we weren't followed," I mutter.

"We weren't," Connor assures me. His confidence reminds me that we've *both* worked together to ensure a paparazzi-less vacation. When we left our neighborhood, our bodyguards drove in one direction and we left in the other. Connor and I mapped out our pit stops, calculating the most obscure, non-crowded areas. We were only tailed for an hour outside of Philadelphia.

"Willow?" I ask.

She checks her cell phone. "No pictures of you on Instagram or Twitter since yesterday."

I asked her to keep track, wanting to include her into our group, even if Lo called me a *fun sucker.*

"There they are," Lily exclaims, slowing our Escalade at a lookout point on the mountainside, the Ferrari parked. Ryke and Daisy stand on the metal railing to view the sprawling green landscape, a massive drop on the other side. Their unleashed dog sniffs the grass beside them.

"Jesus," Loren curses.

I roll down my window the same time as Lo.

He beats me to the punch. "Hey!" he shouts. "Crazy Raisins!" Ryke and Daisy both look over at the same time.

Lily mutters under her breath, "Crazy for Raisy," to correct his misuse of their couple name. Her preciousness makes light of their rebellion. I'm all for self-expression, but I don't want to find my little sister in the hospital with her boyfriend. Ever.

Since they're still standing on the metal railing, I add, "Follow us, please! Daisy, you don't need to be driving in the dark!" She bought the Ferrari two weeks ago, her first car purchase.

"How many times has she driven a car?" Connor questions from the back seat, his tone even-tempered.

She never really drove before she received her motorcycle

license, and I can't recall a time where she ever sat behind a wheel. I lean further out the window. "Daisy, how many times have you driven any kind of car?!"

She hops off the railing with Ryke, and he hugs her around the waist, nuzzling her neck with his head. Something foreign wedges in my rib cage. Jealousy? No, not quite. Their love isn't as blinding as Lily and Lo's, but it's a bright ray of sugary-sweet sunshine that almost everyone can see.

Daisy says, "*Cuatro!*" She wags four fingers.

Oh God.

"Bro, why are you riding in the deathmobile?!" Lo shouts.

Ryke flips him off. "We're fucking fine!"

Daisy is smiling so wide that it's hard to say no to her or to question further. Maybe she's joking. I trust that Ryke knows the truth. Loren and I roll up the windows about the same time, having more faith that they'll stay close.

t could be bigger," Loren says in jest. The seven of us stare up at the four-story lake house, fifty miles off the beaten path, winding gravel and dirt roads leading us to this sanctuary. With two wraparound porches, the house sits in a thicket of gorgeously overgrown maple trees, shingles painted cherry red. Our Realtor (who only knows me by a fake name) said that when the seasons change, the leaves will match the hue of the house.

It's nestled close to a grassy bank, the house reflecting off the rippling lake, landscaped by the Great Smoky Mountains. From the naked eye, I can't spot a single cabin in the distance.

We all chipped in and didn't buy just this property. We invested in acres and acres of land surrounding it, ensuring that no one would build near us.

"It's purposefully big," I remind Lo, my hands on my hips in triumph. This will be a safe place for all of us, where we can escape when our lives become unmanageable and hectic. Jane and whoever else may need this as much as we do.

"Back to spawning eight babies, Fertile Myrtle?" Lo banters.

I shoot him a look. "Just Jane, *Loren*. And there are more families here besides Connor and me." I cross my arms. "Like you." After Maximoff, his views on children changed, and I realize that he's a little like me in that respect.

He was afraid he'd turn out to be his father.

I was afraid I'd be my mother.

We're both too aware of their flaws and too self-aware not to spot our own, and I suppose this is our downfall and our saving grace. It's made us fearful, but it's also enabled us to diverge from the paths our parents took and learn from their mistakes.

"Yeah, yeah," he says with a short laugh. His amber eyes glitter in the evening light, grazing the house as though imagining the expansion of his family of three. "Maybe someday."

Daisy and Ryke walk hand in hand to the side of the house, Coconut sprinting down the hill. Ryke stops at the top of the slope, in view of the long wooden dock, I presume. He wears an awed, overcome expression, one I've only seen when he's with Daisy and after he rock climbs. He returned to the sport in April with his doctor's approval.

We were all proud that he waited to climb until he received the okay.

Connor sidles next to me, supporting Jane, asleep in the crook of his shoulder. "It's perfect, darling." I lace my fingers with his free hand. He kisses my knuckles.

"It has a good energy," I say matter-of-factly.

"You packed candles, didn't you?" His brow arches.

I did think about cleansing the lake house of bad spirits, but that's not why I brought the candles. I may as well warn him. "I wanted to throw a coed slumber party, and there are certain traditions that can't be ignored."

"Like?"

"A séance, and light-as-a-feather-stiff-as-a-board, face masks, desserts and maybe even the Ouija board if Lily's not too frightened by then." Before he spouts his disbelief in ghosts, I add my reasoning: "Apparently when we were younger, we always forgot about Daisy during slumber parties. She was there, but we'd leave her out somehow."

It pains me even thinking that I *forgot* my sister, but I was so much closer to Lily, and the age gap just weakened my relationship with Daisy. I should've been more aware . . .

"She told you this?" Connor looks shocked.

"No." Daisy would never cause me pain from her hurt feelings. "Ryke mentioned it to me a few weeks ago." He knew that I'd want to make up for lost time with my sister.

Connor sighs. "Can we eliminate a spiritual event in favor of an intellectual one? It'd benefit greater society and *us*."

"I'll take your request into consideration and gladly ignore your slight at my slumber party," I say and his grin expands.

"So I have this theory . . ." Daisy spins towards us, hand still clasped in her boyfriend's. "If we buy a little mini pig and see which bear forms a friendship with him, we've discovered Winnie the Pooh." She extends her arms and bows theatrically.

I ask Connor, "Are you picturing the bear eating the pig?" The gory scene *almost* makes me want to root for the underdog to win, but a pygmy pig has zero chance of survival.

"Yes, but my image is probably less bloody than yours."

"Then it's incorrect."

"A bear would eat anything as small as she'd described in one bite," he retorts. "No blood, Rose."

I roll my eyes, accepting this defeat. He's right. I just unnecessarily constructed a grotesque butchery in my mind.

Loren looks at Daisy with an expression summed up simply as *what the fuck?* "Did you smoke a joint on the way up here?"

Daisy wags her brows. "Did I?" She spins to Ryke. "You can pat me down for contraband. I like to hide things in my—"

"Okay," Lo cuts her off. "I'm already sorry I asked."

Lily raises her hand, her other one bracing Moffy on her hip. "Is anyone else scared of bears?"

"Moose are scarier," Willow proclaims, pushing her glasses further up her nose.

"There are moose here?!" Lily's eyes grow to saucers. "Why didn't anyone tell me about the moose?! Lo, did you know about the moose?"

I can't take her seriously when she keeps repeating the word "moose" with her high-pitched voice.

"No, no," Willow says quickly, "I just meant in general. There were a lot of moose in Maine, but I've never been around here, so I wouldn't know."

"No moose," Connor clears this confusion.

Ryke groans. "Can we please fucking ban the word 'moose' from now on?"

"Agreed," I say.

"I like a good moose in the morning," Loren says, just to piss us off.

"But really," Lily interjects before I shout a retort at her husband, "there are bears . . . so no one is scared but me?" We're all quiet.

"Wha . . . really?" She frowns.

"I'll protect you," I tell Lily, confident about this.

Loren snorts. "By what? Kicking the bear in the balls?"

I glower. "I have a gun."

He blanches. "Wait . . . you're serious? I always thought you were joking when you said you had one." I've made a few offhand quips about shooting my gun, so I can see how he thought it was another exaggeration of mine.

"We obviously need to go over the fucking rules about bears,"

Ryke interjects. "Unless it's hunting season or the bear is attacking you, you can't shoot it."

"Says who?" I snap back. I turn to Connor to confirm, and he nods like it's more than just an arbitrary rule Ryke made.

"The fucking law," Ryke refutes. "I can't believe I camped with you, and we didn't talk about this." He was too busy fucking my sister in a tent. I bite my gums, refusing to unleash this and embarrass Daisy. "Look, I brought bear spray for everyone, so it's non-fucking-negotiable."

"Let's start unpacking before it gets dark." Connor cuts into the conversation, checking his watch and then the lowering sun.

"You guys should look at the house first," Willow proclaims. "I'll start unpacking."

"You're not here as manual labor," Loren says, softening the edge in his voice. "So you should explore the house with us."

Willow clears her throat uneasily. "I . . ." She glances at my Escalade . . . like she's hiding something.

I can't imagine what though, and I look to Connor for his thoughts. He's still studying her.

She takes a deep breath. "I was going to call my mom—I mean, *our* mom. Or . . . you know, whatever she is. I just needed a minute alone."

The air thickens, and we all look to Lo.

He nods without falter. "Yeah, I didn't realize you were in contact with her, but . . . definitely, as long as you don't tell her the location of where you are—"

"No way," she says. "I'd never do that."

"I just had to make sure," he says, scratching the back of his neck and then he points at me. "We need to talk about the gun thing. Where is it?"

I walk up the steps of the lake house and everyone joins me except Willow. "My glove compartment," I tell him. My phone vibrates as soon as I reach the porch.

We scheduled the plane for the end of the week, so we'll be there in a couple days. Don't have too much fun without us.—Poppy

My older sister, Sam and their eight-year-old daughter were invited to the lake house, but Maria has school, so they'll be here for the weekend.

"Is it in the glove compartment all the time or just here?" Lo asks.

"All the time," I tell him, walking around the porch to inspect the deck and view from above before I head inside. I pass multiple rocking chairs and an outdoor chess set.

Lo, Ryke, Daisy and her husky are the only ones who follow me. Connor and Lily go inside with the babies.

"Is there a no-guns-in-the-house policy?" Ryke asks his brother.

Lo spins on him with sharpened features. "You have a gun," he assumes. "*In* the house?"

"I didn't think you'd be bothered by it," Ryke says, looking genuinely sorry for not telling him. We reach the front of the deck, and they're too focused on each other to see the sprawling view of the lake. I've never been partial to nature, a city girl at heart, but I'm already in love with this.

"I wouldn't have been a year ago," Lo explains. "But there are two babies in that house. Please tell me you keep it locked in something."

"It's in a fucking safe, I promise," he says. "I can keep it in the car . . . if you *really* need me to." He glances towards Daisy, like he's checking to see if she's okay with the plan.

And I realize—that gun must be for her, to ease her mind when she's scared at night.

Daisy scratches Coconut behind the ears. "I'll be okay without it in the house, Ryke," she says, not dodging the topic like she usually does. Then she howls, which makes Coconut howl.

I hate when she does that, since I'm not that fond of dogs, but it's somewhat more endearing in the wilderness.

"All right, Calloway," he says with a nod.

"You can keep it in the safe," Loren suddenly declares. "I didn't know . . ." He glances quickly at Daisy. "Sorry . . ."

An apology from Loren Hale is hard to come by.

"It's okay," Daisy says quickly, not wanting to cause anyone remorse. "Honestly, Lo, we should've asked first."

I clap my hands together. "Let's unpack." Everyone focuses on me, slicing through the tension. I strut towards the sliding glass door, my heels *click-clack*ing across the deck.

"Yes, Your Majesty!" Lo calls as I slip inside.

We're here, no paparazzi, safe and away. It's supposed to be a time of sanctuary, but I have a feeling some of us may kill each other.

Forty-seven

Rose Cobalt

There are rules," I announce to the living room, a candle in hand and a box of matches in the other. Violent rain pelts the deck tonight, which seems fitting for our spooky slumber party. We've pushed the oversized leather furniture closer to the wide, floor-length window, the house rustic with cabin decor like quilts and red, bear-patterned rugs.

"Of course there are," Loren says, carrying bowls of popcorn with Ryke and Connor into the room. Lily, swaddled in the thickest quilt, unrolls her sleeping bag with Daisy and Willow.

I strike a match, hoping to appear more threatening. With a flame in possession, I certainly feel destructive. "Number one: you knock over a candle, you have twenty years of bad luck. So be aware of where they're placed."

Connor heads over to me. "I'd take stock in your rule if it weren't completely nonsensical."

I give him a side-eye, his grin pulling his lips. "You've never heard that if you break a mirror, you have seven years of bad luck? It's the same concept, Richard."

"I've heard that equally bogus saying, yes." He blows out my lit match.

I'm about to combat when I realize it was seconds from burning my fingers. Fine. "Two." I speak more to Connor than the rest of the room. "No mockery." I narrow my eyes. "Or you will be severely harmed by fire."

"That's too bad for you," he says.

I try to hold my ground, not appearing as perplexed as I feel. "In what way?"

"I'm too smart to burn alone, so you're going to be set on fire with me."

I think we've already been set on fire together . . .

Loren passes Connor and tosses popcorn at him. "You two done flirting?"

"We're not *flirting*, Loren." I scoff, sensing Connor's ego growing in diameter.

Connor's eyes soak through me, his attention one hundred percent mine. Your importance to Connor depends directly on the amount of time he gives you—and if I travel back in time, to our teenage years, I realize that I've always ranked near the top of his list.

He holds my gaze and then takes the matches from me, setting down the popcorn bowl. He begins to help light the remaining candles that circle the room. I catch his eyes flitting back to me, his smile still there.

I can feel my lips traitorously mimic his expression.

He grins more, but I strangely like the sight.

"Is that the last rule?" Daisy asks, tying her hair into a high bun.

I had more, but they seem superfluous. I just want everyone to have a good time. "That's it," I declare, taking a seat on my dark-blue sleeping bag just as Connor finishes lighting the last candle. And then a phone rings.

We all begin to check ours—

"It's me," Connor declares. I stiffen, watching him put the matches on the couch. He's going to take the call. I can't read his expression, so I worry it's . . .

"Is it Scott?" I ask him.

The entire room falls into a tense hush. They all know he's been trying to befriend Scott, but no one knows what that entails but me. Even without the details, everyone can see how much stress has piled on top of him. He may not show it in his features, but there's a quiet intensity that hangs above Connor that wasn't there before.

"No," he says, passing me. "It's Frederick." He flashes the phone's screen to me, just to ease my concern. "I'll be a couple minutes. You can start calling upon air particles without me."

"No one likes a skeptic," I retort.

"On the contrary, darling, everyone *loves* me." He smiles as though he's the exception. He is, in a lot of ways, though I won't ever admit it to him. He puts the phone to his ear, disappearing into the bathroom for privacy.

We're all in a wide circle, the sleeping bags cushioning the floor.

Lily hugs her popcorn bowl. "Is anyone else scared of ghosts?"

Lo's smile dimples his cheeks, and he swoops an arm over his wife's shoulders. "I'll protect you from the supernatural, love."

"What if Rose conjures a demon?" she combats.

"I'm not going to conjure a demon."

"Because she *is* the demon." Lo tries to whisper this to Lily, but his voice echoes off the vaulted ceiling.

"Return to hell, Loren," I rebut.

"Not if you're there."

I consider grabbing the bear spray and directing the nozzle at his face.

"What first?" Daisy interjects and thusly breaks our small argument, which could've escalated into a fight.

This slumber party is about rekindling old times together while bringing in new things, all of the guys and Willow.

"Light-as-a-feather first."

Daisy wags her brows at her boyfriend. "I think we should do Ryke first."

It comes off as a sexual innuendo.

"I'm rating this party G," Lo says, "for 'Gross.'" His voice is lighthearted like he doesn't mean the words as anything more than a joke.

Daisy smiles. "I give it a NC-eighteen-to-twenty-seven rating." She extends her arms theatrically. "NC means No Cake for any of us." She puts her hand to her forehead, feigning fainting. "The *horror*."

Everyone laughs, even me. When we quiet down, I motion to Ryke. "You need to lie in the middle of the circle." He does as instructed without complaint.

Lo eats popcorn out of Lily's bowl. "Good luck, bro. May your sacrifice bring us twenty days of good harvest."

Lily pokes his chest. "We're playing light-as-a-feather, not sacrificing him." Her head whips in my direction. "Right?"

In no way would I harm one of our own. "We're not sacrificing anyone," I declare.

"You girls may not be able to lift me," Ryke warns us.

I laugh shortly. *We will conquer.*

"We're the Calloway sisters," Daisy proclaims, nudging my arm and then Lily's. "We can do anything, right?"

"Definitely," Lily and I say together.

"Plus Willow," Daisy adds and raises her hand to the eighteen-year-old girl. Willow high-fives her with a growing smile, and I recognize now that Daisy is better at integrating people on the fringe of groups than maybe I am.

Lo shuts off the lights before returning to his popcorn.

"Are you going to participate?" I ask him.

"I'm going to casually observe my brother being picked up by a bunch of girls at a sleepover." He snickers like this is too good to pass up and eats more popcorn.

"I can fucking hear you giggling," Ryke tells Loren, about to turn his head, but I snap my fingers and he looks at the ceiling again.

"Is the sacrifice supposed to be talking?" Lo asks me.

I ignore Loren, and I sit on one side of Ryke with Willow, and then Lily and Daisy are on the other side of his body. After I give brief instruction, we each slide no more than two fingers beneath him. I'm near his shoulder blades.

I say first, "Light as a feather, stiff as a board." The girls then begin to repeat the chant with me.

"Light as a feather, stiff as a board."

"Light as a feather, stiff as a—"

"Cock." Lo causes Daisy to break out in a fit of laughter, ruining the concentration of the ritual. Lily is probably a new shade of red, but I can't even tell in the dark, the candles only adding a dim, orange glow to the room.

I wish we'd started with Lo in the middle—then I could've purposefully dropped him on his ass.

My glower should send Loren shrinking, but he just stares right at me, unaffected. "What?" he says. "You knew I was going to do it." When I had slumber parties with Lily and friends, he *always* crashed them, and whenever we reached this part, he'd make the same infantile comment.

"For some insane reason, I thought you would've matured past ten years old."

"I'm twenty-five. I am acting my age. My ten-year-old self was the one ahead of his time."

I wave my hand at him, silently telling him to shut up. My heart may be smiling though—if a heart can smile. It is like old times, but better . . . I look at Daisy. "Let's do this again."

Daisy gives me a thumbs-up, and Willow and Lily nod, ready.

We begin the chant in hushed whispers, "Light as a feather, stiff as a board."

"Light as a feather, stiff as a board." We begin slowly raising Ryke with only our fingers. His body feels more weightless as we go higher, transitioning from our knees to a crouch.

"Light as a feather, stiff as a board." It becomes easier, his body hovering off the ground with our teamwork and focus.

"Light as a feather, stiff as a board." We're standing, and he's now four feet off the ground.

"Light as a feather." Ryke is at my shoulders. "Stiff as a board." Our voices grow in octave and the chant picks up pace. He continues to rise higher and higher, past my neck, past my head.

"Holy shit," Lily curses in surprise.

Instantly, his body feels like a ton of weight, ready to snap my index finger into two. Lily gasps and lets go first, then Willow falters, and Ryke *crashes* downward.

Onto *me*.

My ass hits the floor hard, maybe karma for my evil thoughts towards Loren Hale. Ryke's left elbow digs into my ribs, his body weight crushing me. This is not ideal.

"Fuck," Ryke curses. "Rose, are you okay?" His sincerity and concern are greatly appreciated.

"This is a new game." Connor's voice electrocutes my insides. I can't see him past Ryke's large head. Ryke picks himself off me as quickly as he can and apologizes to *me*, not to Connor. Since I'm the one he body-slammed into the ground.

"Enrage a spirit already?" Connor says as he steps over bowls to reach me in the middle of the sleeping area. His eyes sweep me for signs of injury. I'm all in one piece, and my glare must calm him enough because he never mentions ice bags or trips to the hospital.

"No," I say, straightening my black pajama top.

Connor puts a foot on either side of my legs and he squats in front of me, the whole motion caked with dominance, and I freeze altogether. "Were we playing Twister without the mat?" he asks, and I notice the wineglass in his hand. I didn't see him slip out of the bathroom and into the kitchen, but if he did, he saw our game.

He's just being an ass. His lips rise as he takes a sip, intolerably slow. An infuriating, attractive ass.

"Light-as-a-feather-stiff-as-a-board," Lily answers. "We were lifting Ryke."

He knows, I want to say, but I'm having a stare-a-thon with my husband. I will not blink and lose.

"I can't believe it worked." Daisy beams, and Ryke messes her hair out of the bun. It's her first time playing an adolescent game. When she *finally* reached the "slumber party" age in her life, she was treated so much older than that. Our mother aged her with us, but in doing so, Daisy skipped these youthful, fun years.

"Yeah, it worked before Ryke crash-landed on Rose," Lo says. "It was literally like a scene from *The Wizard of Oz*."

I whip my head to him, about to have some choice words, but Connor clasps my hand. I lost the stare-a-thon. I sigh as he helps me to my feet.

I place a hand on his chest. "You're just in time."

"For what, darling?"

"The séance, or, as you call it, *speaking to air particles*." A funny taste is in my mouth even repeating those words.

"So we're not done playing pretend, then?"

"It's magic," Lily pipes in. "Not pretend."

"It's not magic," Connor says. "It's science. You evenly distributed yourselves around Ryke, and it becomes easier to lift *anyone* like that."

"What about the chanting?" she asks.

"It helps coordinate everyone, so your movements are in sync."

I'm married to the biggest disbeliever, and strangely, I wouldn't have it any other way. I sit down in the circle again with Connor by my side, sipping his wine. Maybe he prefers to be intoxicated for this.

"Ohhh." Lily gapes in realization. She frowns a little and then turns to Loren. I hear her whisper, "So we're not magic?"

"We're definitely magic," he whispers back with a nod.

"Then what are they?" Her eyes flicker to Connor and me, catching us watching them.

Lo purposefully raises his voice so we can hear. "An immortal god who married an immortal demon." He flashes a dry smile. "Match made in purgatory."

Oddly enough, I do feel in purgatory with Connor right now, our futures in flux with the press conference looming and Scott still nagging my husband for a season two.

"Speaking of purgatory . . ." I rise and collect some of the candles, placing them in the middle before I take my seat again.

"Oh, wait, this is happening now?" Lily clutches a baby monitor and then tosses her quilt overhead. Lo cocoons her in his arms.

He whispers, "Are you trying to blend in with all the other ghosts, love?"

"Uh-huh," she whispers back, frightened.

Daisy waves her hand through the flame, too quickly to be burned, so no one says anything. "Can we call upon Old Aunt Margot and ask her what she thought of Dad's first bottle of Fizz?"

"It must've tasted like shit," Lo says. "Didn't he make it in his basement?"

"Garage," I correct. He was a teenager with lofty ambitions, kind of like me, I suppose. Only he started from nothing. I started from the high platform that he gave me—more privileged than most.

The more I relate Fizzle to his dream and his dream to fear of losing it all—I can understand his stance on the press conference. I just wish we were on the same side this time.

"I didn't know you had aunts and uncles," Ryke says, a little surprised and hurt by this fact . . . maybe because Loren isn't shocked at all. He's as close to our extended family as we are.

"All of them are in different parts of the United States," Daisy tells him, "but Old Aunt Margot used to live with her sister, which is our dad's mom." Grandma Pearl is retired in Palm Beach, Florida, living in what she calls "paradise" thanks to her son's generosity.

Connor rubs his lips, slightly irritated, I can tell. "So she's Great-Aunt Margot?"

"*Old* Aunt Margot," all my sisters and I say in unison.

"When did 'great' and 'old' become synonymous?" He looks to me for an answer since clearly she is our great-aunt by relation.

"No one ever called her 'great' . . ." I trail off, realizing how upsetting this sounds. "She liked being called 'old.'" *Oh God, that's worse, isn't it?* "It was her choice." I end with that, which is as good as it gets.

"I wish I could've met her," Connor says with a smile. "She seems interesting."

I almost tell him that he's about to meet her, but Loren pipes in, "She smelled like rotten green olives, so consider yourself lucky."

I glower. "You're going to wish you didn't insult her."

"Did I offend her already? Where is she?" He looks over his shoulder mockingly.

"You just broke rule number two."

"And I'm still alive." He nods to Connor. "What do you call that, love?"

"Favoritism," he says.

I gag. "He's not my favorite *anything*."

Coconut suddenly howls from the kitchen, paws pitter-pattering on the floorboards. Daisy stiffens, and scans the room quickly. We all go quiet, and Ryke pulls Daisy closer to him, his lips by her ear as he whispers, most likely comforting words.

"Aunt Margot it is," I say, trying to draw attention off Daisy. "Let's all hold hands." I clasp Connor's and then Willow's. Daisy takes a deep breath, especially as Coconut settles down.

"Close your eyes," I instruct.

I wait for everyone, mostly Connor though, who stubbornly keeps both eyes open. He arches a brow. *After you*, he seems to say.

I trust that he'll shut his eyes too. So I close mine first. "Aunt Margot," I start . . . and I have to take a peek at Connor, to see if he's playing along. Even if it's not real to him, it's real to me.

His eyes are surprisingly shut.

I love him even more for it.

"We're calling you, Aunt Margot," I say. The rain thrashes more viciously than before, the wind whistling. "We miss your beautiful, lost soul. Please come to us."

Lo snickers first, and I can feel Connor try not to laugh.

Ignore them, Rose. "Fight through the barrier of the afterlife so that we may speak with you."

Craaaaaaccck!

Lily lets out a petrified squeal beneath her quilt.

"What the fuck was that?" Ryke asks. He looks only out the floor-length window, so I think he's actually worried about the structural damage from the storm.

"It's electrostatic discharge," Connor tells him. "Also known as lightning."

The lights flicker on and off until a bulb cracks and they all go out. The TV clock blinks with them, so we've lost power.

"OhmyGod," Lily slurs in panic.

"Old Aunt Margot?" Daisy calls out, the only one with her eyes still closed. "Can you hear us?" Despite her playful voice, I can tell that she's putting on a brave front, her collarbone protruding as she holds in a breath. She white-knuckles her knees, and I worry that the whole séance might've been a horrible idea.

Whhhaaaaap!

Lily shrieks at the new noise, the one emanating from upstairs. Coconut scampers into the living room with determination, actually checking the sliding door . . . the dog locks it back with a nudge of her nose.

I saw Ryke training the Siberian husky on the first day here, showing her the latches to the doors and all the exits, so I'm not surprised she has the talent to lock the door—I'm just alarmed that the door is unlocked to begin with.

"What was that noise?" Lily asks, unable to see Coconut's vigilant routine. "Connor?"

He's staring at the ceiling. "An object fell."

"By a ghost?"

Thuuump! is followed by a long, sharp groan . . . maybe a human groan. *No.* There's absolutely no way. We're in the middle of nowhere. No one else is here. I made sure of it.

Animals.

There are live animals upstairs.

I will butcher whatever rodent has decided to lodge in our house. Mice, I think. It's probably an infestation of them.

Ryke immediately rests a hand on Daisy's head, her forehead coated in sweat, her breath shallow, struggling to swallow air.

Ryke whistles, and I see Coconut's white fur round the corner. "Lie down, Dais." He helps my sister on her back to combat the start of a panic attack, and the dog curls onto Daisy's chest, the applied weight acting as deep pressure therapy—I've seen it help her once before.

Footsteps patter upstairs. I stand and grab my baby monitor, listening for Jane. I can hear her soft snores, which eases me a little, but I plan to check—

More footsteps. *It's not a person. It's an animal.*

Lily flings off the quilt. "Moffy," she says, bolting towards the staircase, baby monitor still in her clutch.

"Lily, wait—" Lo runs after her, and then Willow sprints in the complete opposite direction, through a darkened hallway.

Without second thought, I race after Willow, feeling Connor hot on my heels. When she hurriedly ascends another staircase, Connor beats my pace and passes me, brushing my shoulder with his hand like *it's okay*. He knows . . . something that I don't.

The second-floor hallway is pitch-black. I try to flick on the lights, but nothing happens. Connor takes out his cell phone and turns on the flashlight portion, a blue glow illuminating Willow as she tries to turn the knob of a certain door.

She bangs on the wood. "Are you okay?"

I rush to her a little after Connor reaches and asks, "Is he in there?"

Willow says quickly, "He didn't have anywhere else to go. I made sure to blindfold him here. I promise, he has *no* idea where this place is."

I raise my chin, in battle mode with Connor. I pull Willow back closer to me so he can open the door. When he does, he points the flashlight at the room, illuminating the quilted bed. An eighteen-year-old boy sits on the edge, a lamp shattered on the floor. He holds his bare foot, as though trying to check the sole . . . blood trickles—a piece of glass lodged in the bottom.

"Are you okay?" Willow tries to rush closer, but I yank her back to me.

"You're not wearing shoes either, Willow," I tell her.

He hangs his head in more guilt than pain, I think, his hair falling into his eyes. "I tried to turn the lamp back on. I ended up knocking it over and I . . ." *Stepped on the glass.* He winces, trying to pull out the shard in near darkness.

"Don't," Connor warns. "Rose, can you go get a first aid kit and check on Jane?"

"I'll be right back," I say.

Loren's half sister snuck her friend into the house. I'm sure she had a reason for this, but it doesn't assuage the fact that an eighteen-year-old little asshole has been camping out upstairs and my youngest sister is terrified downstairs.

And by the look on Connor's normally stoic face, he's not pleased either.

Forty-eight

Connor Cobalt

learn that Garrison has no phone on him. He gave his cell to Willow when he stowed away in the Escalade's trunk, wanting to show his friend that he had no plans of deception. When we first checked out the house, Willow stayed back and "called her mom" so she could sneak Garrison inside.

It's basically all I gather before Rose returns with the first aid kit, Jane in her arms and a pair of shoes. "I want to talk to Daisy and Lily," she tells me. Her eyes ping to Willow.

"I'm sorry, Rose—"

"I understand what it means to be loyal," Rose says, "but you shouldn't have kept this from us. If you wanted to bring your boyfriend along, we could've worked something out."

"Friend," Willow amends, paling and avoiding her "friend's" eyes.

Garrison looks at Rose. "Would it make it better if we were dating?"

I answer, "It would make it exponentially worse."

He shuts up and hangs his head again, beaten more by his own guilt.

Willow hesitates by the doorframe and focuses on Rose. "Can I explain? . . . I want to apologize to Daisy too . . ."

Rose nods. "Follow me." Both girls disappear.

Maybe a minute later, Loren enters the room with candles and Ryke comes in with a broom, already up-to-date thanks to Rose. Since all the girls want to be together, the three of us decide to take care of the mess upstairs.

Loren lights candles around the guest bedroom while Ryke sweeps the glass. I sit on the bed next to Garrison with the first aid kit.

"I can do that," he says while I take out the tweezers.

I pass them to him. "You need stitches, and the nearest hospital is more than two hours away."

Ryke sweeps harder, pissed off since Garrison scared Daisy for a second time, but he's not about to say: *I'm not fucking driving him.* He would drive Garrison. He'd drive anyone to the hospital because he cares too deeply about human lives.

I'm not that way with just anyone, but I appreciate when other people fill the role.

Garrison seems to grind his teeth back and forth, his eyes clouding, and he glances quickly at me. "Can you stop watching me?" His voice is as serrated as Loren Hale's.

"I could, but I'm waiting for you to answer me."

He nervously inspects his foot, the tweezers hovering above the glass. He says something under his breath that I can't hear.

"What was that?" I ask, easing the tone of my voice for him.

His nose flares and he shouts, "I'm not going to the hospital!" He jabs the tweezers towards the door. "I promised her I wouldn't ruin the relationships she's made with *any* of you—and if I go to the hospital, people will see you and take stupid pictures, and everyone will know whatever nowhere-ville state we're in. So *no*, I'm not going." He takes a strained breath and focuses back on his foot, jaw tight.

He has a heart. And maybe he has learned from his mistakes. Enough for me to forgive him for his past transgressions? It may take longer for me to *want* to spend my time on him, but I can forgive. I can give him that.

"Relax," Lo snaps. "We're not going to force you to do something you don't want, but I would like to know *why* you're here."

Ryke crouches to sweep the glass into a dustpan, his face darkening. "If he's here to get laid—"

"What?" Garrison cringes. "No." He recoils at Lo's glare. "Not that I don't like Willow."

Ryke joins in on glaring at him, so he turns to me for comfort. My face is welcoming among the hard and rough edges of Ryke Meadows and the sharp and jagged ones of Loren Hale.

Garrison says with bite, "Some starship trooper nerd asked her to prom, okay?"

"Declan," Lo says. "You know who he is. Lily told me that he stops by Superheroes & Scones at least four times a week."

"To try to talk to Willow," Garrison complains. "And what the fuck kind of name is Declan?"

"What the fuck kind of name is Garrison?" Lo retorts.

Garrison rolls his eyes and sighs heavily. "Whatever."

Garrison hid in a duffel bag in a trunk for twelve hours, and he doesn't seem the type to go to that length just for a girl. I cut in, "As amusing as all of this is, we're still no closer to answers, and I'd like them sometime in the next five minutes."

Ryke dumps the glass into a trash bag and then disappears into the bathroom. Lo kneels beside the bed and gestures for the tweezers from Garrison.

He hesitates and then relinquishes them to him.

"Is there anything we can use to sew up the cut in there?" Lo nods to the first aid kit.

Garrison relaxes further at the idea that we're not going to the hospital.

"We can find an alternative if that's what he really wants," I say. I'm sure we can suture the wound ourselves, but it's not going to be pretty.

Garrison nods. "That's what I want."

Ryke returns with a cup of water and hands it to Garrison. I pass him a packet of Advil, the best we have to stop the pain.

Garrison looks between us, and strangely he seems like he might cry, maybe just overwhelmed. "I thought you two hated each other?" He gestures from Ryke to me. Based off tabloids, it would appear that way.

Ryke answers before I do, "We're good friends." I'd label us in a similar manner. Not just friends, but a friend that I count on, rely on, a person that I need in my life.

Garrison grows quiet, eyes fixed on the carpet.

"What is it?" I ask, unable to read the sentiments beneath his features.

He shakes his head and tears open the packet. "I was just thinking . . . I don't even know where I find the kind of friendship that you three have. My friends are dicks." He lets out a short, pained laugh. "I'm one too . . ."

I glance at Ryke and Lo. Through *years* of ups and downs, fights and riffs between us, we've each become closer, and they've both taught me valuable things: how to be selfless and how to bear the pain in love.

I don't live for money or for titles or achievements like I used to.

I live for people.

There is nothing greater than that.

"We're all assholes," Lo tells Garrison. "But one day, you'll meet an asshole that pushes you to be a better person. Those are the ones that stick with you."

Garrison rubs his eyes once, trying to hide the movement from sight. Then he downs the pills with a swig of water.

"We're encroaching on my five-minute time limit," I tell him.

His throat bobs. "I needed a place to crash . . . I've been

sleeping in the break room at Superheroes & Scones for the past month. But I found out that Lily planned to install more video cameras in the store . . . I just . . . I don't know. I couldn't think of anywhere to go."

I've already compiled a list of five places that seemingly should outrank where he is now. "Your parents' house," I suggest.

He licks his chapped lips. "They think I'm at Faust. You went there, right?"

I nod. "And why aren't you there?" Lightning cracks outside the windowpane, the thunderstorm still raging on.

"I flunked out in April . . ." He tugs his hoodie's string harder. "Most of the senior classes are college-level, you know that?"

I nod again. *I know.*

"I failed so badly that they wouldn't let me take another exam or even attempt the finals in May." He pulls the hood over his head. "And, you know, it's my parent's fault." His bloodshot eyes meet mine. "Why'd they have to send me to a new school in the middle of the year? I know . . . I know I fucked up, but if I even want a high school diploma, I have to be *held back*. Do you even know what that feels like?"

No. "What about your friends? They have houses, I presume."

"You mean all my friends that broke into your house to scare you? Those ones?"

"No," I say, knowing what happened to them. Their court date passed in April, and they were all tried as adults. They were each sentenced to serve a year. "Your other friends."

"I don't have other friends," he says. "No one wants to be associated with the bad guy, not at Dalton and definitely not at Faust." He shrugs. "I had nowhere to go, okay? I had Superheroes & Scones and Willow, that's it."

If Lily and Lo hadn't been sympathetic towards him—where would he have gone then? I stepped into Loren's life with zero altruistic motives at first, but these small instances, where we touch another person's life when they need it most, can be the deciding factor in whether or not they choose to wake up the next morning.

"I burned the letter that Faust sent my parents before they got it—the one that said I flunked. And, you know . . ." He chokes up. "I've never been a good person. I don't even know what some of you see in me . . . because I'm shit."

If he can see his flaws and ache terribly at the sight of them, I think he's going to be okay, especially with someone like Lo on his side.

"You're *not* shit," Lo tells him, as forceful as Ryke would have. "You want this glass out of your foot?"

Broken souls are mended every day by mended souls that were once broken.

"Yeah." Garrison finally lets out a deeper breath. "Yeah, I want it out."

Forty-nine

Rose Cobalt

Poppy arrived this afternoon with her husband and daughter, missing the power outage, the surprise of Garrison and Daisy's small panic attack. I don't have the energy to share all of this, so Lily and I just act as though the trip has gone smoothly and listen to updates from our older sister.

"It's been chaotic," Poppy says, removing the whistling kettle from the stove. "There's always at least four cameramen following Maria to school, and I've resorted to escorting her in with three bodyguards."

Lily sets three teacups onto the counter. "It's not so different from before, is it?" This is Lily's attempt to rouse my spirits. I'm more pissed at paparazzi than sullen and guilt-ridden, but I understand that I'm to blame for the increase in media attention. The newsworthy story centers on Connor and me, but I'd rather plan revenge strategies—that will most likely never come to fruition—than mope.

"That's true. There used to be one or two cameramen hovering around us before." Poppy's wooden bangles clink on her forearm as she pours hot water into three cups.

Lily plops in the tea bags.

My joints feel stiff and useless as I stand in the middle of the kitchen. "Neither of you need to waste time cheering me up. I'm *never* cheerful to begin with." My voice is chilled. I decide to put in my diamond earrings. "Don't you remember? I'm made of thorns." When I was in prep school and being particularly prickly and cold, Poppy would often tell me pointedly, *not all of us are made of thorns, you know.*

Poppy gives me an apologetic look, considerate of my feelings even when I'm telling her I have *none.* I can wave a black heart in her face and she'd still say it beats like everyone else's.

"What's happening is awful," Poppy says, "and I don't mean to turn it around and victimize myself." She passes me a teacup, as a peace offering. "I've been trying to tell Mom, Dad, and even Sam to stay out of your business. This is between you and your husband, and none of us have a place to tell you what to do. If I was in your position with Sam, I'd expect the sa—"

A guttural scream from outside slices Poppy off midsentence. *Daisy.*

The teacup slips from my hand, and I barely hear it shatter as I rush to the sliding glass door, heaving it open. When I reach the deck railing, Poppy and Lily race up to me.

Below us near the lake, Daisy stands on the long wooden dock with Ryke by her side, their husky sitting at his feet. With her hands balled to fists by her sides, she simply *screams* into the air. The hairs on my arms rise, her shrilled, pained wail scorching the mountainside.

Ryke is careful not to touch his girlfriend, cautiously watching her expel whatever has burdened her. I force my feet to this place, wanting badly to aid my sister, but I won't disrupt them this quickly.

Give them twenty minutes, Rose. I wince. *Or ten.*

"What happened?" Lily asks softly.

"What *hasn't* happened?" My tight voice burns my throat. What if it is something new and not just her panic attack from the séance?

Poppy puts her fingers to her lips. "I think he broke up with her."

Lily's face scrunches in horror. "No." She shakes her head repeatedly.

I'd like to think I know Daisy, and I can't picture her *screaming* because a guy ended their relationship, even if that guy is Ryke. And if she did want to scream, she'd never do it standing next to him. What I can imagine: Ryke saying, *we're taking a break*, and then Daisy retreating to her room to cry alone.

And *why* in everything that's beautiful would Ryke stomp on my sister's heart during a trip? A trip that has a twelve-hour car ride *home*?

He wouldn't.

"He didn't break up with her," I tell them.

"Are you sure?" Poppy asks.

Lily looks like she might cry. I remember Ryke's declaration in the kitchen some time ago. About marriage. He wouldn't end things with her, but there is always the microscopic chance something happened—something I didn't see in their relationship. They're just so . . . private.

"Not one hundred percent, but I can't see him doing it, not *here*." I cross my arms, struggling to stay on the deck and not hurry to Daisy's aid.

"I can't see him doing it at all," Lily says. "He *loves* her."

Poppy twists one of her bangles anxiously. "Not long ago, I told Ryke how important my year break from Sam was for me. Maybe he considered this for Daisy."

I press my lips together, already knowing about her talk with Ryke. Poppy just finished saying how she wouldn't meddle in my relationship, but she's willing to interject herself in Ryke and Daisy's. I understand though that Poppy just has experience being young and in love, and she relates more to *their* relationship than mine.

I glance at Poppy. "Ryke told me about your conversation, and he was more pissed than anything."

Poppy frowns. "Are you sure?"

Daisy screams again, deep from her core, one that rattles her body. My neck pricks. *Don't cry, Rose.* I'm the stoic, severe sister that can carry them anywhere, and I *can't* be that sister by drowning in tears.

I try to let out a constricted breath. I'm familiar with Daisy's vibrating scream, only I prefer doing it into my coat. My mind rolls through my childhood and adolescence, and I keep hitting a roadblock that Daisy and I share: our mother, the one who likes to interfere with our relationships.

I slowly turn to Poppy. "Did you talk to anyone other than Ryke about this 'break' idea?"

Poppy opens and closes her mouth like a dying fish. "I did tell Mother and Father in passing and . . ."

My eyes flash hot. "And what?"

"She pointed out that I had barely any worldly experiences at eighteen, so it made sense that I'd want to be independent from Sam after prep school. But Daisy has traveled to nearly every continent since she was fourteen. I hadn't thought of that until she mentioned it."

I freeze. "She disagreed with you?"

Poppy nods. "A lot, actually. Ever since she threw Ryke in jail, she's felt guilty. And she felt a little *too* similar to Sara Hale for her taste, I think." Our mother hates Ryke's mother, so comparing them at all must send her into a fit of rage.

It's hard for me to believe that *I* agree with my mother on anything, but I'd much rather have her on my side than going rogue.

Lily sniffs, her nose running. "And Dad?"

"He said that they've been so committed to each other that it doesn't make sense for them to break up unless Daisy wants to go to college, but she doesn't."

Regardless of our parents, Daisy's opinion matters most. "Have you talked to Daisy yet?" I ask Poppy.

"No, I just keep forgetting every time I see her." Poppy covers her mouth, upset, and I hear her curse beneath her breath.

"You didn't influence him," I tell her.

"I don't see how you can be so sure," she whispers.

Lily stops biting her nails and answers first. "Ryke is one of the most independent thinkers I've ever met, and if he did this . . . then he did it on his own . . . right, Rose?" Tears well in Lily's eyes.

"Don't cry yet. It's like sobbing at the title screen of a film."

She sniffs and wipes her eyes. "You cried at the title screen of *Titanic*."

"I was pregnant and hormonal," I rebut and huff. "And I *knew* the tragedy that was about to ensue. We don't even know what this is about." These are my defenses to keep the waterworks at bay, and I share them with her as much as possible. Because if she starts bawling—it's going to create a domino effect between us all.

I straighten, focusing on the dock. I go utterly silent when Daisy staggers back in exhaustion, her last scream already leaving her lips. She breaks into a sob and her legs buckle beneath her.

Ryke catches Daisy around the waist, holding her securely to his chest, and he collapses on his knees with her wrapped in his arms. She cries into the crook of his shoulder, and his hand disappears in her hair, his lips to her ear as he whispers. His voice is inaudible, but I watch Daisy's body heave with each sob.

I clutch the railing to keep from bounding down there. And then his eyes flicker up to the deck, spotting my sisters and me. He gestures for us to come over.

This is why I like Ryke Meadows.

I walk quickly in my heels, careful not to fall down the stairs. I step off the last one and descend the hill, Lily wiping her splotchy cheeks hurriedly. Poppy lifts her bohemian skirt off the damp grass, and I lead the pack, despite one of my heels trying to wedge into the sodden turf.

Ryke peels away from Daisy, concern hardening his jaw. She has a difficult time supporting her heavy limbs, weighed by sadness, and I can tell he's struggling leaving her, even for a second. He crouches in front of Daisy and kisses the top of her head, says something out of earshot and stands straight up.

He heads towards us.

By the time we reach the dock, Ryke is a few feet away, fighting back his own tears. He squeezes past us and says in a hushed voice, "She needs her sisters."

Don't cry, Rose. I breathe through my nose.

Lily doesn't wait to hear what happened. Gangly legs and all, she awkwardly runs as fast as she can to our littlest sister.

"Are you two taking a break?" Poppy asks.

"What?" His brows bunch, and he looks dazed. "No. Fuck no." He rakes a hand through his hair.

I waver between lingering for more information and comforting my sister, but I know Lily has great hugs. Better than mine can ever be.

"What happened?" I ask, a pit lowering in my stomach with pitchforks and needles.

Ryke shakes his head. "I can't be the one to tell you. You have to hear it from her."

"Is it bad?" I ask.

He nods once.

"Let's go," Poppy says, slipping her hand in mine. We walk together to the end of the dock. Lily holds Daisy on her lap, and she rests her cheek on Lily's shoulder, tears pouring down both of their reddened faces. I meet Lily's gaze for answers, but she shakes her head, silently saying she has none yet. She's just severely empathetic.

Poppy sits beside them, and I take a seat in front of all three girls, closing the circle between us. The maple trees rustle with a gust of wind, the lake rippling beneath us in this serene, remote atmosphere. I lace my fingers with my little sister's, and Poppy strokes Daisy's brunette hair, combing the strands off her wet cheeks.

My mind isn't constructing drastic conclusions. I'm knee-deep in the present moment, watching her ragged breath slow to fuller inhales. She stares off at the wooden planks of the dock, lost in her head.

I squeeze her hand. For right now, all we can do is be here.

Minutes must pass before she finally speaks. "I have this theory . . . that if you love someone so much, so overwhelmingly, so terribly, then some force of nature will smite you for your terrible love and you'll never be the same." Her voice cracks, her chin trembling.

I swallow a lump. "I liked your pig-and-bear theory more."

She lets out a weak laugh that morphs into pain. Poppy wipes Daisy's cheeks with the cotton fabric of her skirt.

Then Daisy turns her head, her heavy-lidded eyes on me. "I've had irregular periods since I first got them, but you all know that."

Lily and Poppy nod. I can't unfreeze the muscles of my neck to do so.

"I was . . . never a healthy eater when I was modeling," she continues with a jagged breath. "And some other, older models didn't have periods at all because they ate so little, and it seemed normal. You know?" Tears slip out of her eyes.

I can't fathom the world she grew up in—the one where she believed it was customary to start her period at sixteen and have it twice a year. *I'm sorry*, I want to say, but what use is an apology now? The damage is done, and the best I can do is hold my sister together for as long as she needs me.

"Your periods were still irregular after modeling," I remember, a tremor undetectable in my voice.

Lily looks to me. "But they are *better* than they were. Daisy told me that."

"They are," Daisy says softly, "but I also mentioned how they're still irregular."

"The gynecologist said it was stress," I recall this memory well. This was around the time I was pregnant with Jane, and Daisy had horrible cramps. Her period was lasting too long, and so I told her that I'd take her to the doctor, just to ensure that everything was okay. I was *there* when the fucking doctor said *stress* was the cause, nothing else.

Please nothing else.

She opens her mouth to speak, but no words come out just yet. Poppy keeps combing her hair, which seems to relax Daisy into Lily's arms.

And then Daisy squeezes *my* hand, and I realize she's looking at me. I think I know the conclusion she's going to draw, and it's already crushing my soul because I know it must be crushing hers.

"I went off birth control for like a couple weeks in March," she explains to the sky and then looks back at me, "and it was so painful; I thought they were monster cramps or something." She laughs sadly before frowning deeply. "I told Frederick about my periods and the birth control stuff since it affects my moods, and he just said I needed an ultrasound immediately."

My throat burns. "Why didn't you say something?"

"You were going through so much with Connor, and Lily was at a good place—Poppy, you have your own family, I just didn't want to unload on any of you. I thought that it might not be anything, and if it wasn't anything, then I wouldn't worry you, but if it was something . . ." She chokes on her tears, and I scoot closer to clasp both of her hands.

"Did Ryke go with you at least?" No one wants to picture her alone.

She nods. "He's been really great." She pauses, her voice breaking every sentence. "I was too sad afterwards to ride my motorcycle home, so I went on his, and he drove me around the city for an hour. It made me feel better." She nods again, more to herself. "At the doctor's they didn't give me the full results. All they said was that I had some . . . cysts on both of my ovaries, which were causing me pain and messing with my cycles. They said they could be harmless, but they wanted to do some blood work before they determined what kind of cysts they are."

Both ovaries. I pick this out and solidify.

The wind whips the trees again, a bird chirping, which is so blasphemous. The world should be in mourning with the four of us, another downpour of lightning and thunder. Instead, the sun peeks through the rolling clouds, the earth moving along at leisure and peace.

"The doctor called me this morning," she says softly. "He told me that my results are back, and I need to come in." She lets out a heavy breath. "I pleaded with him to tell me now. I just . . . I didn't want to wait the rest of the trip without knowing."

I have to ask, "What kind of cysts?"

With another deep exhale, she says, "Endometrioma." She has endometriosis. It's not cancer, but it's not good either. "He said that due to the size of the cyst and the state of my left ovary and left tube, the best course of action is to remove both."

I've held it together up until this point. I blink and a cascade of tears washes my cheeks.

Daisy cries silently.

Lily hugs her tighter and her reddened eyes flit to me for solutions. "There have to be other options."

I nod, even though I feel helpless. I raise my chin and wipe my cheeks before holding Daisy's hands again. "Daisy," I say strongly. "We'll take you to other doctors for their advice. You need multiple opinions before a surgery like that."

Daisy nods, but her voice is as dejected as it was. "You should've seen their faces when they saw the sonogram . . . They knew what it was right then. I know they did."

"What about your right ovary?" I wonder. We're skirting around the real consequence of this and I run into it for her. "You can still have children with one ovary, Daisy."

"He said that . . . any minute the cyst could rupture and I'd need it taken out then. Laparoscopic surgery would help improve the ovary, but there's no assurance that it'll work or last." Her glassy eyes meet me. "It's more likely that I will never have babies than it's likely that I will."

In a nondescript time, I always imagined this dock, the one the four of us sit on, crowded with kids and teenagers, their laughs and shouts pitching the air.

And then there'd be Daisy's child, climbing the nearby maple tree, shimmying onto the twisted branch that juts out. There'd be Daisy's child, jumping wildly and splashing into the lake.

"Shh," Poppy coos, "it's okay, Daisy."

It's not okay. It's a bad set of cards, a darker fate than I ever wanted for my sister. *It can't end this way.*

"Being here has been hard," she tearfully confesses, her body shuddering. "I know what this lake house means to everyone, and it meant that to me too." She inhales sharply. "I wanted kids. I know . . . I know I'm young still, but someday, I wanted them. I wanted that experience, the beginning, the during, the after." She pauses. "And you know the really sad thing? I actually started imagining the future past tomorrow . . . dreaming up babies of my own."

"You'll have children of your own," I tell her assuredly.

She hangs her head with doubt. "I could go into surgery for the left ovary, and they could say the right one needs to be removed too."

I refuse to sit idly with this sadness, this bereft conclusion for my sister. I want to give her a better end to her story. I *will* give her one. I rattle her hands. "Look at me, Daisy."

When she raises her head, her eyes well with more tears. I blink and more fall from mine.

I lace both of my fingers with hers. "You *will* have babies. You can save your eggs, and if anything happens, I'll carry your child, as *many* as you want." We're all crying, and I cradle these promises. I know it's not the exact same as experiencing childbirth herself, but it's as close as I can give her. "They'll have your features. You'll hold them in your arms, and you'll watch them grow big and strong."

Daisy is somewhere between another sob and a fractured smile. "Are you sure, Rose?"

Poppy rubs her eyes. She won't have another child, not even as a surrogate. Her morning sickness put her in the hospital for a few weeks. After Maria, she said she'd never have another. Because of the adverse affects pregnancy has on Lily's addiction, Daisy wouldn't want Lily to carry a baby for her.

Even if I wasn't the only option, I'd be the first to volunteer.

"My uterus is all yours," I tell her. "Whenever you want one, I'm ready." I've always been good at sharing with my sisters. This is no different to me.

Daisy lets go of my hands and hugs me first. My shoulders and arms are still stiff, but I try to reciprocate the hug like Lily would.

"Thank you," she breathes.

"I love you," I say, running my fingers through her hair. Lily and Poppy join our hug, expressing the same sentiment, and very shortly, we're all piled together, tear-streaked, mascara running, the paths of our lives veering just a little to follow our sister. And never leave her alone.

Fifty

Rose Cobalt

We linger on the dock, sticking our feet into the water and chat about everything and anything. Daisy laughs when Lily describes snuggling with a can of bear spray after Loren rejected her bear-barricade idea.

Lily's eyes widen comically. "If a bear can bulldoze through a stack of chairs, then *none* of us are safe. Think about it."

"There's an ax in my room," I tell Lily. "I'd decapitate that motherfucking bear."

Daisy kicks her feet in the water, a smile lifting her lips. "There are two wolves in my room, so I'm safe."

Poppy raises her hands in surrender. "I'm not hurting the bear. If by bad luck one stumbles in my room, Sam would help me lure it out."

I scoff. "With what?"

"Honey," Daisy pipes in.

Lily nods. "Pooh." She reddens. "I mean Pooh Bear . . ." She scrunches her face. "Wait . . . I don't mean how that sounds. I mean—"

"We know." I cut off this train wreck. "Winnie the Pooh."

She nods again, more confidently. "Yes. Pooh Bear. He likes

honey, so if we leave jars thirty miles away, maybe they won't come near us."

I want to point out that *no one* has even seen a bear yet, but Poppy stretches to look at Daisy beside me. "Daisy?"

"Yeah?" Daisy gives her a smile, to show she's better. I can't tell how forced it is, but I'd like to think she's truly not as morose as before.

"Have you ever thought about taking a break . . . like I did with Sam?" she wonders. "I just wanted to know your thoughts on it."

Before Daisy speaks, I hear the *whoosh* of the sliding glass door. We all turn our heads at the same time, and our husbands and Daisy's boyfriend collect onto the second-story deck. Loren opens the grill, and none of them intrude yet, just cooking and talking among each other.

"I have imagined it," Daisy admits, "but it's not like you think." She splashes the lake with her feet. "Every time I picture being alone, I'm traveling backwards to where I once was. I wasn't happy back then."

"When were you happiest?" Poppy asks.

Daisy smiles fully as she thinks about it. "The moment I started filling my time with him. I no longer did these fun things by myself. He surfed with me. He snorkeled with me. He jumped off cliffs with me. I had a friend. A *real* friend. I've learned more about myself, about my likes and dislikes and my limitations and my expectations, in the company of Ryke, than I have all the years I spent alone. And I don't want to go back."

I wrap my arm around her waist. "There is nowhere that says once you have a friend, boyfriend or husband, you lose your independence. They're not mutually exclusive, and we should all be allowed to have both." No matter what age.

Poppy nods, more understanding of this notion. "I agree."

Daisy inhales deeply, staring at the sky. "Some days I can't even imagine being a year older, and then other days, all I see is the far off future."

"I better still have a sense of style in your future," I tell her. "If I'm wearing an oversized poncho, the world has really gone to hell."

Everyone laughs, and not long after, we all stand together. Daisy holds my hand while we head up the hill, the smell of burgers wafting towards us. We climb the deck steps and reach the top, where everyone has gathered. Willow and Garrison sit beside each other on rocking chairs, nursing cans of Fizz Life.

I'm about to approach them when Connor cuts off my stride, Jane on his hip. *"Ça a été?"* How did it go?

Ryke informed him, I presume. In the corner of my eye, I see Daisy and Ryke reuniting by the grill. He hugs her with a great deal of support and affection, his love for her so apparent.

Connor tries to remove my smudged mascara with his thumb. I focus back on him. "I'm going to have her baby if she can't carry one."

He's not at all surprised or reluctant of this idea. He agrees with the plan. I see it in his genuine smile. And he says, "You're a strong woman."

I've been dealt a fuller set of cards than the ones passed to Lily and Daisy. They're just as strong, if not stronger. I've always been here as extra reinforcement, and however old we become, however gray we are, that won't ever change.

Fifty-one

Rose Cobalt

R espirez profondément," Connor whispers in my ear. *Take deep breaths.*

I have imprisoned oxygen in my lungs. My brain is *highly* aware of what Connor's brain wants to do. We're leaving the lake house tomorrow, and so it's not crazy to believe that he wants to push a boundary of ours. I think out of all the trips we've ever taken together, we do something "out of the ordinary" near the end.

Like the Alps. I lost my virginity before we left.

Like our honeymoon in Bora Bora. We had sex in a beach cabana the day before our flight home.

And you loved both of those and all the others, Rose.

That knowledge barely extinguishes my anxiety.

I lie on my stomach, and he leans forward, collecting my damp hair off my shoulder and gaining access to the nape of my neck. He kisses my sensitive skin, my body thrumming from the hour of foreplay—already wet, already primed for another climax. I realize all of this, but . . . even having used plugs for weeks, I doubt whether Connor in my ass will be anything other than excruciating.

"Get out of your head, Rose." He spanks my ass, and I exhale a tighter breath. Then he picks his weight off me.

I look over my shoulder. Completely naked like me, he straddles my thighs, which are pressed together, my body supine like I'm just sleeping on my stomach, at peace. He fits a pillow beneath my hip bones, lifting up my bottom for his possession.

"Just relax."

Relax. It's not that easy for my high-strung, neurotic mind. I try to focus on him: his confidence, which consumes the room and says, *this will be pleasurable for you, Rose*; his carved biceps and infuriatingly defined abs, muscles pointing to his erect cock.

And his knees are on either side of *my* body—it's an image I masturbated to as a teenager. I can't deny this, but in my fantasy, there was no anal sex at play.

"Shh," he breathes, his lips rising.

"Shushing me isn't going to help, Richard," I mutter.

"*Je connais toutes les façons de vous aider. Croyez-moi.*" *I know all the ways to help you. Believe me.*

Believe him? Trust him? I watch as he rakes my body with his gaze and a slow, desirous hand, drawing the curve of my frame with his palm. My nerves spark beneath his touch, and my legs tremble a little.

I swallow some reservations, knowing that he'll pull out if I even momentarily show signs of struggle.

You're a fucking lioness, Rose. Let him mount you.

Something cold and delicate skims my ankles. I crane my neck further over my shoulder, about to turn onto my back and sit up. He places a firm hand on my ass, keeping me stationary. "Don't move," he orders.

"What are you doing?"

He turns to me, an item in his closed fist. I bet it's a duplicate of whatever is wrapped around my ankles. It's so thin that I think I can tug it off and raise it with my toes, all without shifting onto my back. However, the moment I lift a single foot, Connor seizes my leg, trapping me.

"You don't want to do that, Rose."

I glare. "Why not?"

And then he leans forward to reach my wrists. He pulls them higher, clasping them together with one strong grip. "Because if you move, you'll break this." He reveals a never-ending, tantalizing strand of diamonds, the necklace fragile and faint like a whisper in your ear. He carefully wraps it twice around my wrists before clipping the tiniest clasp.

I wonder if these are new products for Cobalt Diamonds. Even if they weren't, I'd hate to shatter jewelry—especially a piece that's my style, my taste, perfectly me.

"Are you bribing me?" I wonder.

"No," he says adamantly. "I need you to *not* squirm or bolt upright or spread your legs open. And you've grown too used to handcuffs."

I can still crane my neck over my shoulder to peek at him. He's in the same position, his hands on my lower back. "Close your eyes."

"No."

He spanks my ass. I shudder and bite my pillow, my body aching for more stimulation. His fingers comply, massaging my clit for two agonizing seconds.

"You need to be completely relaxed."

He's reminded me before that if I tense up, it'll cause me pain, so he's trying his hardest to calm me before he does anything.

"I'm going slow," he communicates, knowing I can't be left in the dark with this. "I won't enter you all at once, I promise."

Translation: *I know your body. I know your limitations. Trust me.*

I do. I close my eyes and rest my cheek on my soft pillow, attempting to relax. I feel a new temperature, cold but a little warm.

Lube, I assume. Not long after, Connor gradually pushes his way inside of me. Just when the expansion begins to pinch, his fingers dip and rub, creating hot friction.

My mind shadows the pain as higher, orgasmic sensations blink in Technicolor. I gasp into the pillow, my lips parting in a staggered breath. He removes his fingers and pushes further in and out, edging his way deeper inside. The fullness (full of him—*oh God*) is unlike anything . . .

When I've stretched to his size, he thrusts in every second, not too rough but assured pumps. The pulsing between my legs grows and seems to time with his movement in my ass.

I open my eyes and glance back at him. With hands firmly clasped to my love handles, his body flexes with each drive forward. I keep watching him. How he's kneeling, how he's thrusting into me, how his focus is on my being. The arousal in his deep blues spins me to another sweltering place.

"Connor," I gasp, my mouth unable to close. I moan into the sheets, resting my spinning head back on the pillow.

A groan sticks to his throat, and he leans back to unclasp the diamond strand from my ankles, never missing a beat. He suddenly seizes my ankle and lifts it higher while he continues to thrust, allowing for fuller, deeper penetration. "Stay still—"

He warns too late. The quick burst, his powerful force, causes me to shift my arm, to brace myself for better support. The diamond chain snaps in two. He never stops to let me fixate on what I did.

With my palm flat on the bed, he grips underneath my bent elbow with the other hand, holding me secure in a slightly altered position. He takes me harder from behind.

He has my limbs. In his grasp. And he never ends the rhythm. I'm so aware of his cock inside of me, more than ever. I'm full of Connor Cobalt, and it's . . .

My eyes roll back. My toes curl.

Mount the fuck out of me.

I can't believe I like this.

But then I can. I've liked many things that I never believed I would.

If Connor is a god during sex, then he's certainty a god afterwards. He's so attentive to my body's needs, to be handled with the strange mix of rough and tender care. He massages my raw and reddened skin, from being slapped, with warm, smooth lotion.

I can tell he enjoyed it as much as I did—his heavy breaths and grin are signs enough. He helps me to my feet and we take a shower together, then put on new pajamas, and I crawl back into clean sheets. I face him and he tucks a damp strand of hair behind my ear.

"You're going to say *I told you so* and that my limitations are all in my head," I predict. He was right. I liked it.

"No," he surprises me. "Everyone has limitations, and I'm certain that some of yours aren't just constructed by fear."

My mind is on a slow, tired descent, so I try to imagine what my limitations even are. "You're not sucking my toes," I note.

I feel his smile in the dark. "I won't."

What else is there?

I realize I've said the words aloud because he answers with, "Fisting."

I cringe. "No."

"I don't want to either," he whispers in the pit of my ear, pulling me closer. Sometimes we cuddle (such a soft word) after sex, and I let him hold me for a little while, drifting in the security of his strong arms.

Fifty-two

Rose Cobalt

I cup a mug of coffee in bed with Connor, Jane playing with a picture book between us. We brought a newspaper to the lake house, and I hold one end while Connor holds the other. My eyes glaze over some of the words, the weight of our last day here hanging in the back of my mind.

I have to broach the topic. "I'm going to speak after you at the press conference," I say. "So if you change your mind at last minute, I'll just go along with whatever you decide."

Connor tenses, and Jane taps a button on the book, the speakers letting out a sheep's *baaaa*. I hope he doesn't feel the irony. Fate is cruel. Why couldn't the book let out a lion's roar or a wolf's howl? No, it had to be a sheep.

He lowers his side of the newspaper. I lower mine and cup my mug with two hands.

"That's more than considerate, Rose," he says, "but I'm not going to let you go in there blind and be surprised with the rest of the world." He angles his body against the headboard so he's more turned towards me.

"So you've made a decision?" I take a sip of coffee.

His calm features never waver, even if his mind does. Connor brushes my bottom lip with his thumb, and I see his thoughts spinning.

So I ask, "To strip naked in front of a crowd or to speak a truth where no one understands you—"

"I'd strip naked," he chooses before I even finish.

I nod, my chest hurting for him.

"I'm leaning towards 'queer,'" he tells me. He plans to define himself then. "It's an all-encompassing, broad term that has positive connotations. I like how other people proudly identify as queer, and I think it's a safe middle ground for me."

Everything out of his mouth sounds practiced, as though he's been tossing the phrases around in his head for weeks. I hone in on the way he says, *people proudly identify*. He didn't say, *I identify*. He left himself out.

I straighten up. "If that's what you want, I'd be okay, and I want you to know that you can't hurt me either way. And you shouldn't worry about hurting my father or my mother or *anyone* with your decision."

He lifts my chin with two fingers. "Believe me, I've thought about every possible surface of this choice." His thumb sweeps my cheek. "I've weighed every cost, every benefit, and it's all pointing to this."

I stare right at him, my eyes churning hotter than I'd like. I want them to be soft for him. That's what he needs, isn't it? My voice isn't even velvety. It's harsh and icy. "On what scale do you weigh these?"

"My scale." He grins.

I roll my eyes. "Well, on *my* scale, the cost of your soul outweighs everything else."

"How selfish am I going to be, Rose?" he asks me.

Baaaaa! Jane hits the same button. She giggles, and Connor leans forward and flips the page to a frog on a lily pad.

"Fate says you should be as selfish as you want."

"I can't listen to your fate or lambs in children's books. I just have to listen to the facts."

"You can't listen to your heart?" I roll my eyes again at how banal it sounds.

"If I listened to my heart, it would only say to protect my girls, nothing more."

"If you listened to your heart, it would ask if you're alive," I combat. "After the press conference, will you truly be? And I'm not talking literally, Connor, so don't bring up anatomy and blood vessels."

A fraction of a smile appears and then falls back into deep contemplation. "I don't know, Rose."

I don't know. It's a phrase Connor rarely utters. Hearing it now pulls at me.

"Let's do the crossword," I say, setting my mug aside and gathering the newspaper. "I'll let you choose the topic."

He arches a brow. "You'll let me?" His grin almost returns, and it's enough to shove the press conference to the back of my mind, shelving it once more.

Fifty-three

Connor Cobalt

I help Lo clean out the lake house's fridge before we leave. We toss anything that might spoil into a black garbage bag. My mind is always at work, but it's been spinning faster today, roaming through hundreds of thoughts.

"You okay?" Lo asks again, chucking leftover scrambled eggs.

I wear this faraway look that I can't quite extinguish. "You remember your wedding?" I put an extra packet of hamburgers in the freezer.

"You're thinking about my wedding right now?"

I'm thinking about everything. "It's taking up a portion of my brain," I say easily. I officiated his wedding, so I had an opening speech prepared. I only shared it with Rose before I spoke that day, and the girl who rarely sheds tears started bawling in our bedroom. I knew it was right, but after everything I've personally been through recently, the meaning holds greater power for me.

"I can't forget my wedding day, not that I would ever try," he tells me with a smile, opening the trash bag wider as I chuck the milk.

I hold his gaze. "When I said that you and Lily were the strongest people I've ever had the honor to meet, I meant every word." I can't even imagine, for a moment, battling the type of demons that they have *every day* of their lives, where it affects the person they love, where it tears them down equally. It's torture that I can barely experience, and I am in awe that they came out alive, together.

Lo nods a couple times, watching me to find the origin of my thoughts. "You and Rose—you're pretty much superheroes in my world, you know? If anyone wins in the end, it's you."

I have trouble believing words I always thought to be true.

My doubt is new, but it's lingering softly. I know in a few days, I'll push it away. It's just the uncertainty, the gray-washed future with no detectable paths that clouds my usually sound and assured judgment.

"Lo!" Lily calls from the top of the staircase. "Did you already put Moffy's diaper bag in the car?!"

"Shit," he curses, hesitating to leave.

"Go," I tell him, taking his trash bag.

"Thanks, love," he says. "You always know how to finish strong."

I smile as he leaves. I spend a couple minutes tossing mostly empty and half-eaten items. We don't have enough room in the trunk to pack coolers and save perishable food. I grab the quarter-full carton of orange juice.

"Hey, don't fucking toss that." Ryke approaches and steals the carton from my hand. He unscrews the cap and chugs the juice. While he drinks, he shoves something hard in my chest.

I take hold of the item . . . a decent-sized *book*. The title and part of the cover are obscured by a sticky note. I make out his handwriting, which says, *Merry fucking Christmas*.

I can't hide my surprise, not today.

He wipes his mouth with the back of his hand. "I planned to give it to you next Christmas, but I couldn't wait." His voice is less rough than usual. He nods to me. "Page two-sixty."

I'm honestly speechless, but he doesn't linger for a reply. He trashes the now-empty carton of orange juice, leaving me alone.

I peel off the sticky note and skim the cover: orange-and-yellow hellfire blossoming around gargoyle creatures, like they're nestled in flowers made of flames.

It's the Penguin Classics edition of *Man and Superman*, a four-act drama by George Bernard Shaw. I've read it once before, but in no way can I recall what's on page 260 by memory. So I do as he instructed and turn to the precise location.

The play ends on 249, and Shaw's *Maxims for Revolutionists* begins. In a section titled "Reason," Ryke highlighted a quote in yellow.

I silently read the words:

The reasonable man adapts himself to the world: the unreasonable one persists in trying to adapt the world to himself. Therefore all progress depends on the unreasonable man.

I rest my forearm on the counter, and the trash bag falls out of my grasp. The passage hits me harder than I thought it could.

I've always been the reasonable man. It's easier. I tend to go after the harder challenges, but not when it's like beating my brains against a brick wall.

To be *unreasonable* for the first time in my life—can I even do it?

Fifty-four

Connor Cobalt

M r. and Mrs. Cobalt won't be taking questions from the press, so if you have any planned, we suggest you put them away," Naomi advises the collection of journalists and photographers that have gathered for the press conference. I stand backstage with Rose, our daughter and Rose's parents and our friends, waiting for my cue to greet the media.

Lily whispers, "It's already streaming live on GBA News." She has Lo's cell phone cupped in her hands, and she flashes the screen to us. Sure enough, my publicist stands behind a podium with about ten microphones attached, insignias of each news station printed on them.

In seconds, that'll be me.

I can't determine what I feel in this particular moment. I don't have time to call Frederick to ask. Rose lifts Jane higher on her hip, and Jane says, "Daddy!" Her exclamation echoes in the speakers of Lily's phone, which means the microphones caught her voice.

I rest a hand on Rose's back and then kiss Jane's cheek. She touches my jaw with a wider smile, and I say quietly so only Rose and Jane could possibly hear, "The only apology I will make today is to the two of you." What I decide affects them, more than anyone else backstage.

"It's unneeded," Rose tells me, her shoulders pulled back, chin raised, ready for war. I love her for it. "So pocket your unnecessary apology."

I smile at the passion in her voice. "My pockets are full, darling."

She rolls her eyes. "Of what?"

"Of love."

She presses her lips to stop from smiling, but she's doing a horrible job hiding it.

"She's smiling for me," I muse. "It's a standing ovation before the speech has even begun."

She controls her expression and it morphs into a glare.

I grin. "Rose, Rose, Rose"—I feign contemplation—"always making me work for the win." Just how I like.

"Richard, Richard, *Richard*." She practically smites my name. And then she pauses, her eyes drilling into me. "Go win."

It brings me back to the moment, and Naomi pads through the black curtain, entering backstage. "They're waiting for you," she tells me.

I kiss Rose's cheek and then Jane's again. I leave their side.

Corbin lingers by the stage entrance. "Where's your speech?" His eyes dance around my suit.

"In my head," I say easily.

He curses like this is going to go terribly.

"Do you know me?" I ask him. I never cower, not an inch of my six-foot-four build. With every ounce of confidence I possess, I remain upright, assured and tall.

He takes too long to answer, so I extend my hand to shake his, as though we're meeting for the first time. By the guile of my assertive demeanor, he does shake my hand.

"I'm Richard Connor Cobalt," I tell him. "The man whose IQ doubles yours. I would suggest scripts for yourself, maybe line by line and in large font, but I won't ever need one." I pat him on the shoulder. "I'd tell you to remember this, but I'm extremely hard to forget."

I push past his startled body and enter the main stage. Cameras flash in quick succession, journalists seated in about eight rows with tripods stationed around the parameter, filming the conference. I stand behind the glass podium.

No paper.

No teleprompter.

I haven't rehearsed a poignant speech for hours on end. I haven't recited anything to Rose or in the mirror. I construct what I need to say in the moment, and I trust myself wholeheartedly to accomplish this to my high, impossible standards.

I'm used to the bright flashes, and I hardly blink as they appear in waves. Every journalist sits erect, eager for answers: *Did you really sleep with those guys? Have you had sex with Loren? Do you really love Rose? How does Jane fit into all of this?*

When the cameras settle and I'm no longer bathed in blinding light, I finally speak. "There is nothing that the media could say to me that would justify the way they've acted. You can hound me. You can follow *me*, but in no way should you frighten those around me. To harm my *wife* and potentially harm my daughter—there is no excuse that could put any of you on the right side of morality."

The day where Rose almost fell in a hoard of cameramen floods me. Many news stations condemned the paparazzi for surrounding us, for causing Rose to rip out her hair just to protect our daughter, but not much has changed since then.

"Is she your wife only in the legal sense?!" a reporter yells. Security squeezes through the rows to escort him out, but he struggles to stay put, clinging to the frame of his plastic chair.

I don't acknowledge him. "I met Rose when I was fifteen and she was fourteen, and through what she would call fate and I'd call circumstance of our hobbies, we'd cross paths dozens of times over the course of a decade."

I'm unlocking a private history book for millions of people to read, and maybe they still won't understand the love I share with Rose, but they'll at least know how much I desire her.

"At seventeen, I attended the same national Model UN conference as Rose, and a delegate for Greenland locked us in a janitorial closet. He also stole our phones."

The journalists chuckle at the image.

"He had to beat us dishonorably because he couldn't beat us any other way." I stare around the room, at all of them, and they quiet at this statement. "Rose said being locked in a confined space with me was the worst two hours of her life."

They look bemused, brows furrowing. I can't help but smile.

"You're confused because you don't know whether she was exaggerating or whether she was being truthful. But the truth is that we are complex people with the ability to love to hate and to hate to love, and I wouldn't trade her for any other person."

They jot notes, the cameras flash again.

"So that day, stuck beside mops and dirtied towels, I could've picked the lock five minutes in and let her go. Instead, I purposefully spent two hours with a girl who wore passion like a dress made of diamonds and hair made of flames. Every day of my life, I am enamored. Every day of my life, I am bewitched. And every day of my life, I spend it with *her*."

My chest swells with more power, lifting me higher.

"I've slept with many different kinds of people, and yes, the three that spoke to the press are among them."

The flashes increase, along with mutterings, but I never waver.

"Rose is the only person I've ever loved, and through that love, we married and started a family. There is no other meaning behind this, and for you to conjure one is nothing less than a malicious attack against my marriage and my child."

I pause, and they all wait intently again. As though I'll slam the gavel right after I announce what I am. After I step into their box so they can better understand.

"*Anything* else has no relevance. I can't be what you need me to be. So you'll have to accept this version or waste your time questioning something that has no answer. I know acceptance isn't easy when you're unsure of what you're accepting, but all I can say is that you're accepting me as *me*."

They go from bewilderment to being aware that this may end with loose threads.

In my eyes, it's all tied up.

I rest my hands on either side of the podium. My eyes graze the journalists, the camera lenses, and I settle proudly and comfortably with the choice I've made.

I leave them with a quote from Sylvia Plath.

"'I took a deep breath and listened to the old brag of my heart.'" My lips pull higher, into a livelier smile. "'I am, I am, I am.'"

With this, I step away from the podium, and I exit to a cacophony of journalists shouting and asking me to clarify.

Adapt to me.

I'm satisfied, more than I even predicted.

Some people will rewind this conference on their television, to listen closely and try to understand me. I don't need their understanding, but my daughter will—and I hope the minds of her peers are wide open with vibrant hues of passion.

I hope they all paint the world with color.

Fifty-five

Rose Cobalt

t's 3 a.m. and I barely drove to Manhattan undetected. As I enter a wealthy apartment complex, I lift my oversized sunglasses to my head. They've been obscuring my vision in the dark of night, but I needed a decent disguise. Since Connor's poignant speech this afternoon, the media hasn't lost their rabid bite. They've tried to leech all of us for a clearer, more definitive answer.

I'm proud to say that no one is giving the press what they want. I couldn't discern my father's or my mother's reaction backstage, but they skirt around Connor's sexuality whenever they're asked.

My phone buzzes. Tell me when you get there safe.—Connor

He knows my plan, and if Jane weren't so fussy today, I know he'd have joined me. I'm here, I text back.

Along a carpeted hallway, I stop at a door and knock hard, not once but three times, hearing footsteps. It swings open, revealing my husband's therapist. Frederick rubs his tired eyes, only in a pair of blue boxers. "Rose?" He squints at the harsh light. "What are you doing here?"

"Is this really how you answer the door, Frederick?" I wonder.

He just notices his lack of clothes, but instead of covering himself, he leans out of the doorway, peering down the empty hall.

"Connor isn't with me," I announce. "And the complex's

security is horrendous. I told them my sick, decrepit grandmother lived here and they just let me in."

Frederick scratches his messy brown hair. "You're here for the cat," he assumes.

"I'm here for *my* cat," I validate. "Connor and I agree that it's time for her to come home."

I expect a fight. I'm ready for one, purse braced like a weapon on my arm.

He strangely swings the door wider open, inviting me inside. I try to smother my surprise, and I enter his bachelor pad: leather furniture, bland walls with no splash of color, silver kitchen appliances.

"Sadie!" I call. "I'm here to take you home." Her bell collar jingles, but I can't see her anywhere.

"I watched the press conference," Frederick says, sluggishly sliding onto his leather bar stool. He's not going to help me find her.

"And?" I rest my hip on his couch and dig through my purse for cat treats.

"It reminded me of how far he's come."

I freeze in place, not expecting this response either, and I lock eyes with Frederick. He's never really told me anything about Connor. I always thought their client-patient privileges prevented it, and maybe so did their friendship.

"I first met him when he was twelve," he explains, "and I thought he was brilliant. He spoke like he'd been living for decades, not twelve years. It took him some time to open up to me, but when he did, I realized that he lacked so much empathy for the human race. He thought of people as stepping-stones to greater achievements and nothing more. You see, a narcissist is incapable of love, and I never believed he would love a single soul, until he met you."

The declaration almost pushes me backwards. I know Connor loves me, but Frederick is a man who's seen Connor through many facets of his life. He knew him before I ever did. Hearing that *Frederick* believed Connor would come to love me—it holds greater meaning, more power and more truth.

"How did you know?" I ask.

"You didn't just fascinate him, Rose. You made him feel for more than just himself. He cared about you, and you had no larger purpose in his life other than existing." He shakes his head with a disbelieving smile. "I never would have thought that twelve-year-old boy would become this man. It's quite extraordinary."

It is. My heart pounds with pride for Connor. I glance back at Frederick, ignoring the fact that he's in saggy, wrinkled boxers. "I want to thank you," I tell him, "for everything you've done for my little sister so far." He's helped her find healthy methods to combat her PTSD and panic attacks, and he was the one who advised her to get an ultrasound.

It hasn't gone unnoticed by me.

Frederick smiles. "I'm happy that Daisy is letting me help her. I think we're all in agreement that she deserves some peace."

"Yes." I get choked up, my throat swelling. *Are you going to cry, Rose? In front of Frederick in his saggy, wrinkled boxers?* God, no. *Pull yourself together.* I continue digging in my purse and find the salmon-flavored treats.

I shake the plastic bag, and the orange tabby cat darts out from beneath the couch. I snatch her around the waist, and she surprisingly lets me hold her. I can feel her ribs. "She's underweight." I glare at him.

"She was overweight when Connor brought her."

I flip my hair off my shoulder. "She was perfect." I scratch behind her ears, and she lets out a large tractor purr. She still is perfect. "Do you have her carrier?" I'm afraid she'll pounce out of my arms if I try to cradle her to the car.

He nods and heads to the closet. "You and Connor make a good team."

I realize that Connor must have called Frederick in advance, not tonight, since he was surprised by my arrival, but maybe some time ago, and talked Frederick into returning Sadie to us. And I've come to add the final say-so and cart her home.

If only the rest of our problems had been easy fixes like this one. It reminds me of Scott. Of the media's constant, unyielding gaze on Jane. Of Jonathan Hale's absence from our lives for weeks on end. Of Loren and Connor being suffocated by paparazzi if they go outside together, in any fashion.

It's all a big pile of shit. A mess that may never be polished and spotless, but if we scrub a little harder, maybe it'll be clean enough.

Fifty-six

Connor Cobalt

Does Rose give better blow jobs after two-plus years or does she still suck?" Scott asks with a snide smile. "Pun not intended." He saw the first time she ever blew me—the first time she ever gave oral to anyone—since it was recorded in the bathroom.

Fry his dick.

Rose's hostile voice returns to my head.

I internally grin. I can have her again as my conscience and do this right. I'm certain of it now. "She's a fast learner" is all I say.

I watch him sloppily eat a bar burger in a dim booth of Saturn Bridges. We're shoved in the back corner where no one can see us, no fans or journalists lurking.

He licks his fingers. "Daisy could probably teach her a few tricks."

I wait for the perfunctory laugh, but it never arrives. He's serious.

I lean back and take a swig of beer, relaxed. Inside, my blood begins to boil, and I concentrate on loosening my grip from the bottle. "Experience?" I wonder with a lighthearted laugh. The game has shifted just slightly, and I remind myself to pivot my strategy later to accommodate it.

Scott grabs his burger again. "Let's put it this way, I would pay her ten grand to suck my cock right now, but her psychotic boyfriend would never let me near her." He takes a large bite.

Because Ryke values and respects women—he's psychotic. Lo called Scott a "human turd" yesterday, but I honestly think that's being too kind. "What about during *Princesses of Philly*?" I wonder. "Ryke wasn't with Daisy back then."

He chews and swigs his beer. "They were still together all the time. I wish he'd left her with me for ten minutes. I would've had that little blonde bitch on her knees so fast." He licks his fingers again.

I smile and stomach this lie. "I always thought she liked to suck cock." *Richard, ew.* I know, Rose. I might as well be gnawing on rotten meat, the distaste sliding down my throat.

He nods in agreement, and then points his burger at me, the lettuce falling out of the bun. "You should fire your PR person, by the way." He dunks his burger in mustard. "The fact that she told you to lie about sleeping with a bunch of men is fucking stupid. I can think of twenty different publicity stunts that'd top it."

He thinks Naomi advised me to say I've slept with the three guys but leave an open-ended conclusion, so I'd gain more attention. To me, the media attention was the adverse effect of my speech, a consequence that I knew would happen. To Scott, it's a benefit.

"I might," I lie, leaning back and taking another swig of a beer. "Do you have a publicist?"

Scott pops a fry in his mouth. "No, I don't need one." Rose growls in my head, *I hope he chokes on that fry.*

I feign concern, touching my lips, my brows cinching.

"What?" He chews slower.

"I stopped by GBA's offices yesterday to talk about advertising for Cobalt Inc.—nothing for *Princesses of Philly*." I did actually meet with advertising at GBA for Cobalt Inc. yesterday, on purpose just to cover my tracks. "I wouldn't go over your head with the production for season two."

"You better not, you dick," he jokes with a laugh. He wipes his mouth with a napkin and leans back like me, attention now mine. It's like hooking a fish in the throat. I watch him pick up his beer. "And?"

"I overheard some things." I didn't hear anything out of the ordinary, but hearsay is hardly verifiable one way or the other. I scratch my neck like this is hard for me to share. "I'm telling you this because I think it's in your best interest to know. Otherwise, I'd just shrug it off." I gesture my beer to him. "So *Princesses of Philly* came up offhand, and I asked if they knew you, since you were in charge of season one. The execs . . ." I cringe.

"What'd they say?" he snaps, his fist tightening around the bottle.

"They mockingly called you the *porn guy*, and they didn't seem to take you seriously."

Steam might as well be blowing out of his fucking ears, and I sincerely hope he grows fond of these sentiments. He's going to be asphyxiated with them in the next few weeks.

"I know you're looking at a high-level position at GBA if we sign to a season two of the reality show, and I have a lot of experience in the corporate world. Reputation can make or break you, and being the *porn guy* will make it difficult to acquire respect from people who matter. It's one thing for GBA to promise you twenty-year security in a job with high turnover, and it's another for you to have purpose there. They could put you in a cubicle and tell you to shut up."

He groans out a couple swear words and then glowers at the wall. He doesn't even question the validity of my statement. I'm probably his best friend in Philadelphia now, so why would he?

And then he points at me with his beer bottle. "What do you think I should do?"

What do you think I should do? I'd call him an idiot, but I'm more of a genius for placing a gun in the middle of a table and telling him to pick it up and shoot whoever I want. In this case, I'm going to tell him to turn it around on himself and pull the trigger.

"You need to distance yourself from the distribution of the sex tapes in some way." I leave it open-ended for Scott, so he'll feel like it's his idea, not mine. "Let me ask you this: what do you want more, to profit off the remaining undistributed sex tapes or to gain an executive position at GBA while being more useful than a stapler or a fax machine?"

I know which holds more importance to him, which is why he's going to give me what I want without a single hurt feeling.

This is how you never make enemies.

"GBA," he says. He lets out a vexed breath. "I'd have given Rose the sex tapes if she just fucking signed to the season two."

"She doesn't want to make a deal with you," I tell him. "But she's finding benefits in reviving the reality show. I convinced her that the exposure would help Calloway Couture Babies, so I think she'll come around within the next month." Not true. Everyone is still adamantly against a second season. It was never going to happen.

"I don't want to give the tapes away without something in return, and I don't want the press to keep stating *who* I fucking sold them to." *Celebrity Crush* likes to track the distribution of the sex tapes, and they always cite Scott Van Wright in the articles.

For once, *Celebrity Crush*'s tactless journalism may spin in our favor.

I wait for him to sort out different scenarios in his head, and I bite into my blue cheese burger. After a full minute, I feel his eyes set on me.

"Would you buy them off me?" he asks. "It'd be a silent transaction. That way I'd get some money, and you can get off to them or whatever the fuck you want."

I shrug, not at all eager. "It depends how much you want for them."

"I'd take fifty grand for the rest at this point." That's nothing. He's received over a million for just one sex tape before.

"How many undistributed tapes are left?" I wonder.

"I'll show you," he says. "I'll call my lawyer, you call yours, and I'll sell you all the rights back tomorrow." He's the eager one, ready to patch his sullied reputation before he's even officially begun working at GBA.

If all goes right, he'll never work there.

I nod a couple times. "Yeah," I say. "I think we can work something out."

Fifty-seven

Rose Cobalt

Scott Van Wright (douchebag motherfucker): 0—Rose and Connor Cobalt (brilliant): 1.

Using an iron poker, I stir the flames in our backyard fire pit, smoke billowing towards the star-canvassed sky. The fire and heat of May builds sweat beneath my blouse. But it's the best sweat of my life.

"I'm ready," I tell Connor, standing up and tossing the poker aside.

He holds a cardboard box filled with DVDs and flash drives, every device Scott recorded the tapes on. After their meeting this afternoon, with a financial transaction and contracts signed, Connor now owns the digital and film rights of *Princesses of Philly* footage. He said that he made sure the contract was specific. Connor *only* wanted ownership of footage containing appearances by himself and me—our bedroom activities.

Anything else still legally belongs to Scott, but we were only after the sex tapes, and now we have them.

Connor passes me a DVD case and sets the box at our feet. "Fifteen sex tapes," he says, still in slight disbelief that Scott could've profited fifteen more times off us.

I thought there were two left, at most.

This is a big win, and I recognize what it took Connor to reach it. I open my mouth to thank him, but he puts a finger to my lips, to hush me. "We did it together."

He said I was in his head again, keeping him grounded. I try not to smile at this proclamation, but surely he can feel my lips rise beneath his finger.

He grins and then nearly laughs as I plaster on a decent glare. His fingers drift to my chin.

I rest a hand on my hip. "You're distracting me from our liberation."

"We've already been liberated. Your fire is just ceremonial."

"*Our* fire," I amend.

His grin widens into a full-blown one. "Our fire," he agrees.

I pop open the plastic case, Sharpie scrawled over the DVD: *Rose's room. 4/23/13—tied to a chair, 43 minutes.* My stomach overturns. I immediately chuck it into the pit, a growl escaping as I do so.

I pause.

I listen for a moment to the satisfying crackle and the melting plastic, my spirit igniting with each burst of sparks, orange embers glittering like celebratory fireworks.

Finally. I'm destroying the things that Scott used to hurt us.

Connor's arm slides around my waist as the flames consume and eat these tapes.

"Now you." I hand him a DVD case, not wanting to look inside.

Without hesitation, he throws the case in, and in less than five minutes, we've added each item onto the sizzling pile, along with the cardboard for good measure.

I spread a fleece blanket on the grass, and we both sit on the soft fabric, watching the darkest portion of our lives burn to ash.

I understand that the ones online will never disappear, but we've reclaimed fifteen intimate moments and they'll forever be ours. I breathe cathartic breaths, expelling ugly grit that has clung to me for so long.

I exhale and exhale. Connor's strong arm fits across my shoulders like extra security and warmth. I find myself leaning into him, my legs knocking into his, and it's not long before we peel our gazes off the fire and onto each other.

Connor has always had these deep-blue, austere eyes that flit between serenity and cold truths. It's as though he contains the world's knowledge and history, the dark ages and the light ones. Behind his own entitlement lies all of these grim and wonderful facts about millennia of people: the first voyagers, the first philosophers, the very first scientists.

When I look into his eyes now, the millennia shrink to a pool of two people. Just us. The facts are swept with truths, and history is right now. Beside a fire.

He cups my jaw, his lungs expanding, his breath joining with my breath. "'Dreams are true while they last,'" he recites in a whisper, "'and do we not live in dreams?'"

I hear his heart beneath those words. "Tennyson," I answer with a strong inhale.

A flood of emotion courses through his normally inexpressive features, reddening his eyes, drawing lines above his cinched brows. He tugs me closer, and all the sentiments that accompany love pull me to him and him to me.

He recites, "'I can't go back to yesterday because I was a different person then.'"

"Lewis Carroll," I breathe, "*Alice's Adventures in Wonderland.*" I cling to his shoulders, my hot gaze never leaving him.

I do feel mad with him, so swept in love that I can't untangle my jumbled, encumbered thoughts.

His gaze journeys across my features, as though he'd like to extend his stay for one more minute, one more hour—anything that time will give him, he'd take. I touch his hand that holds my cheek, our lips aching to meet.

And he murmurs, "'My drops of tears I'll turn to sparks of fire.'"

Our clutch tightens to each other.

"Shakespeare," I reply. "*Henry VIII.*"

He leans me back, guiding me to the blanket. His body hovers above mine, his forearms on either side of my head, his lips so close to my lips. My core heats the longer the silence encases us, the longer the fire crackles and our mistakes burn.

Connor combs my hair back and leans close to whisper, "So long as I may be living, I live with you."

I lose it at this line, tears building and wetting my eyes. Not because it's from a favorite play or a favorite piece of literature, but because these words belong solely to him.

I stood in a wedding dress.

I stood right across from him, from that rising grin, and he whispered, *So long as I may be living, I live with you.* The strength of his vows beats inside my veins.

I reply what I replied nearly three years ago: "In spirit and in mind, I live with you."

He brushes my tears with his thumb, and, one kiss away from my lips, he breathes, "I live with you."

He threads his fingers with mine, his eyes glassing, and he kisses me so soulfully that my body rises to meet his.

The strength of *our* vows beats inside my veins.

He breaks only once, his lips trailing to my ear, and I stare up at the night sky, burning alive with this love. "Forever is not nearly long enough," he murmurs, another line that belongs to him.

Forever is not nearly long enough.

I wholeheartedly, undoubtedly agree.

Fifty-eight

Connor Cobalt

E very machine is occupied at the gym on a Saturday afternoon. We probably should've stayed at home, but Ryke and I were too cooped up in the house to work out in the basement. It didn't help that when we left our neighborhood, three carloads of paparazzi tailed us and advertised our location to the public.

"MARRY ME, RYKE MEADOWS!" can be heard through the glass walls. Other men around the weights shoot us disgruntled looks for the disruption.

Ryke tries to ignore it, doing push-ups in the free-weight area. Loren performs sit-ups next to him, and I stand on the tops of his shoes to keep him stationary.

I sip my water and spot the posters outside along with shrieking girls and guys. I count the *Team Ryke* ones. "Five proposals for marriage, three to breed, and one to fuck," I say. "Someone should inform them that dogs can't read."

Ryke takes a hand off the ground and gives me the middle finger for calling him an animal. Then he continues doing a one-handed push-up. I just finished a circuit workout, so I don't join Ryke on the concrete floor to one-up him.

I just tower above his lean frame.

"Down, boy," I quip.

The corners of his lips rise in a fraction of a smile. It's barely detectable, barely noticeable, and maybe I haven't seen beneath all of Ryke Meadows's layers, but I do know one thing: we're good friends. I'd do just about anything for him, and I'm certain he'd do the same for me.

Lo relaxes after one last sit-up, stretching his hands behind him. I step off his shoes but remain standing. I watch his smile fade to a more guilt-ridden expression, his brows pinched.

"What is it?" I ask.

He looks up with even worse remorse. He carries more than necessary, beating himself up before I will ever even think to harm him.

I arch a brow. "You couldn't have possibly replaced me with a more intelligent, witty and handsome human being—since none exist—so whatever you did won't upset me."

He lets out a heavy sigh. "I've been talking to my dad again. Just on the phone," he admits. "I'm so fucking conflicted because I feel like if I even *think* about him, I'm taking his side over yours. And it's not like that—what he did was wrong, but he's just messed up . . ."

Ryke stops mid-push-up and shifts to a sitting position. He's quiet, his breathing heavier, but I assume it's less from working out and more from the sudden change in topic.

"I don't mind," I answer truthfully. "Jonathan won't ever be my favorite person, but it's hard for me to hold a grudge against a man who made an idiotic mistake out of haste and out of fear and love." Malicious intent would give me pause, but I don't feel any from him. "So please," I tell Lo, "don't guilt yourself on my account."

Lo nods a couple times, processing this. He looks to his brother, who hasn't said anything.

"He needs to learn, Lo," Ryke reminds him. "You said that,

remember? You can't fucking run back to him this easily. It gives him the idea that he can do more shit like this to us in the future. Do you want Moffy around that? You have a fucking kid—"

"Okay," Lo cuts him off. "I get it." He lets out another deep sigh, his hands splayed flat behind him, and his gaze returns to me. "Get back on my feet, love."

"This isn't quite my favorite position, but I'll make an exception for you, darling."

I'm about to stand on his feet when a forty-something man at the weight rack coughs beneath his breath, "Homo."

If glares could kill, Loren Hale has just massacred the gym in point-two seconds. "What was that?" he snaps, not needing to shout since the man is literally ten feet from us.

The guy picks up a forty-pound dumbbell and simmers silently.

I have no guilt about my decision to tell the truth. That I slept with men in my past. I am proud of the choices I've made in life, and I won't let other people dig beneath my skin and make me feel ashamed of who I am.

There isn't a single bone in my body that cowers. I will always stand six feet and four inches tall.

"I can't stand people," Ryke mutters under his breath.

"Next time we'll go to the dog park," I banter.

"Fucking hil—"

Out of nowhere, the man just *drops* the forty-pound dumbbell on Loren's hand, the one splayed flat on the concrete. Lo lets out a choked, pained noise, and Ryke springs to his feet.

I crouch down to Lo on instinct, to check the damage to his hand.

"What the fuck is wrong with you?!" Ryke yells at the guy, who huffs with deep-seated rage.

"I'm okay," Lo tells me, clenching his teeth and favoring his right hand. Three of his knuckles are clearly crushed, and I suspect his other bones have fared about the same.

"No one *here* wants to see that!" The man gestures between Lo and me with disgust.

I've stood on Lo's feet for sit-ups in this exact gym before. We've joked without anyone complaining. It's still all changed based on what I've admitted, and I won't ever take it back. But I would've rather the man thrown the fucking weight at *me* than hurt my friend.

"Speak for yourself!" This doesn't come from Ryke. Or from me. Or Loren. It's a random guy on a weight bench.

"Yeah!" someone else across the room pipes in.

"We don't want *you* here, man!" The exclamation is directed at the dumbbell guy. Gym employees in red-collared shirts begin to make their way towards us.

"Are you serious?" the guy sneers. "They were *flirting*!"

"Booooo!" The noise comes from the treadmills.

Ryke cools down at the support from over half the gym, and he squats in front of his little brother, inspecting his quickly swelling hand. Lo looks up at me like, *can you believe this?* He's not talking about his injury. There is more surprise and awe in his eyes than pain.

I think I share some of that awe—proud that intolerance can be met with reactions like these. The gym employees speak quietly to the man.

"You're not kicking me out. I'm *leaving*," he sneers. "And I'm telling everyone I fucking know not to come to this fucking gym."

As soon as he heads to the door, almost everyone stops their workout and starts clapping at his departure, happy to see him go as much as we all are.

"I'd join, but . . ." Lo winces as he tries to close his hand.

"You need a fucking cast."

"I need a drink."

Ryke shoots him a glare.

Lo's brows rise. "Joking." He adds, "I promise."

Ryke nods, believing him, and I reach out for Lo's left hand and help him to his feet.

Lo winces again. "I want to go home first and ice it—"

"This isn't a fucking sprain," Ryke retorts.

I frown at Lo. "Usually it's your brother avoiding hospitals, not you."

"It'll be on the news the minute we park near the ER, and I'd rather go home, ice my hand for an hour and tell Lily. That way, she'll find out from me."

If I had to choose who has the highest pain tolerance of all of us, it'd be Loren Hale, without question.

Please, Lil. I'm okay. It's okay . . ." Lo tries to calm his wife with a hug, and she wipes her tears repeatedly, trying to be composed for him. He still favors his right hand, all of us joined together in the kitchen.

"I know—I just . . . I can tell it's hurting you." She rubs her splotchy cheeks, guilt-ridden that she's crying in the face of his injury.

I search the kitchen cabinets for any painkillers with Rose. And Daisy zips a plastic baggie with ice, passing it to Lily, who hands it to Lo.

I knock shoulders with Ryke as he heads to the fridge, and we both exchange a look that says *you were in my way first* before returning to our natural course.

"My hand barely hurts," Lo tells her, and he tries to close his fingers into a fist, but he struggles to move his joints.

"Don't do that!" Lily holds his arm still, her eyes big and wide. "You don't have to prove anything to me, Lo."

Lo nods once.

I really want to drive him to the hospital now. The logical part of me—which is almost all of me—combats with his decision to linger at the house.

Rose and I end up at the same lower cabinet, crouched and digging through plastic containers for anything that'll help him.

"I didn't want to interrupt your movie for this long," Lo exclaims. He turns to Willow who sits contemplatively on the bar stool, observing everything with respectful, shy glances. "You're having a shit day."

Willow pushes up her black-rimmed glasses. "Being dumped the day of prom isn't as bad as having your hand broken."

Lo's cheekbones sharpen as he grits his teeth. "It all just depends." For Lo, emotional hurt will always outweigh physical pain.

Rose passes me a new basket, and I quickly thumb through seasonal allergy medicine and decongestants, finding nothing stronger than Advil. Rose growls under her breath, and she glances back over her shoulder at Lo.

I do too.

"I'm driving him in twenty minutes," she says beneath her breath.

I'd comment that I'd drive him in ten, but the way Lily has her hand on his waist, silently guiding him towards the garage door—I think it'll be more like five minutes until he's heading to the hospital.

Rose and I stand up together with nothing more than an Advil bottle. I dole out a few pills and pass them to him. Daisy is quick to retrieve a glass of water.

"Can you all seriously stop freaking out?"

"I haven't said a word," I mention.

"Exactly," he retorts.

Ryke is busy making a turkey sandwich, putting lettuce on top of the meat, and I can't believe for a second this is a selfish act to feed his own hunger.

Daisy hops up on the counter next to him, swinging her legs. "Have you all watched *The Young Victoria* before?" she asks Ryke, Lo and me, an easy distraction to alleviate tension.

"That's what you're watching?" Lo asks with a cringe. He looks to Willow. "You let Rose talk you into a boring period film?"

My phone buzzes in my pocket.

"I don't know . . . comics made me think of Declan, so Rose suggested something different. I like it so far."

Lo's face sharpens, all severe lines. "Don't let him ruin comics for you, Willow. That's shit on his part. Okay?"

Willow nods but stares solemnly at the counter, and I can't ignore my phone any longer. I check the message.

You free? Come over in 5 min. Two of my friends from L.A. are here, and we're going to hang out—Scott

I have to say yes.

I look up and life is still moving at the same pace. Ryke cuts his sandwich in half with a butter knife, and he walks across the kitchen to give a half to Lo.

"Thanks, bro." Lo accepts the food with his left hand.

As Ryke returns, he cuts the remaining half of the sandwich once more and passes a quarter to Daisy. He climbs on the counter beside her, eating what remains. They often share food, but this gesture today reminds me how close they've become and how similar they are.

"Your phone," Rose tells me.

It buzzes again, and she sees the next text blink on the screen.

We're going to start without you—Scott

I'm not sure what "start" implies, but I know I have to be there. I may own the sex tapes, but I'm missing a certain overwhelming victory that sends Scott out of our lives, ensuring that we'll *never* have to see him again.

It's a delicate process that I think may come to a head today of all days. If his friends from L.A. are here, he may be willing to do something illegal to entertain them, and of course I'm invited.

I'm his best friend.

"I have to go," I whisper to her.

She nods, her shoulders pulled back and eyes flaming as though to combat Scott, who sits across the street, in a house so close to ours. *I have to go*, I think.

And I don't want to detach from her. I'd rather stay here and be set ablaze, but based on facts—based on his friends' arrival—I sense that this is *it*. The last time I have to stomach his presence.

"I'll be here for you," she says, telling me she'll be in this house.

She'll be so much closer than that. I have no doubt that she'll be in my head, right there with me, even when it hurts. It's what I need.

I walk through the foyer and then open the door. On my way down the street, I spot a familiar face hurrying this way. As he approaches, I notice the formal black slacks, the white button-down and a bouquet of spring flowers.

Garrison Abbey.

When we returned to Philadelphia after the lake house, we dropped Garrison off at his parents', so he had to confront flunking out of Faust. Willow said that he's going to enroll in Maybelwood Preparatory next year, an hour from this neighborhood and ironically the same school Ryke attended.

We abruptly meet at the curb of Scott's driveway, and he strangely lingers instead of passing me, as though waiting for me to tell him that he's making the correct choice.

"Where are you going?" I ask Garrison, though I'm one hundred percent sure of his destination and his plans. The flowers. The formal attire. The date. It all points to prom.

He combs his hand through his brown hair. "Some douchebag bailed on Willow, so I decided I'd ask her out . . ." He trails off, studying my blank face for a reaction.

I wear none. The sun is beginning to set. "You have a couple hours before prom starts."

Garrison points at me with his flowers, his features contorting in confusion. "You know . . . people still talk about you at Faust.

The upperclassmen said you had an answer for everything—that you were some kind of prodigy."

A prodigy. I almost laugh. I'm satisfied knowing that this immortal, godly version of me still floats around the dorm rooms and hallways of Faust. I'm even more satisfied knowing that the vulnerable man remains in the arms of Rose, my passionate, gorgeous wife.

"Here's my answer for you," I tell him. "Ask your friend to prom for no selfish reasons, no vain motives, nothing less than because you admire her and because you'd rather spend two minutes sitting beside her at a dance than five hours in the company of *anyone* else."

His brows pinch in contemplation, as though it clicks. *I like her a lot. I'm doing the right thing.*

Garrison and Willow would seemingly never be friends. She's sitting inside with faded overalls, a blue shirt printed with bats, and glasses crooked on her nose. She's introverted and bookish. He's rebellious and outcast.

Their unique interests may not align, but something in the core of their hearts does—and that makes the difference.

I'm running out of time, so I begin to head up the steep driveway.

"Where are you going?" Garrison wonders.

I look over my shoulder once. "To set things straight."

He nods to me. "Good luck."

I smile. "I appreciate the sentiment, but I don't need luck." I turn back around and walk unflinchingly to my destination.

Fuck luck. I've spent months preparing for this, to put myself in this position on the chessboard, and in one strike, I may finally knock down the most abhorrent opponent I've ever faced.

There is no luck in my final moves.

The credit belongs to me.

Fifty-nine

Connor Cobalt

I take a beer from Scott and sit on the couch next to Trent. He's a thirty-year-old trendy photographer from L.A., black suspenders and a handlebar mustache. I only know him by Scott's constant aggravating reminder that Trent had sex with Daisy after a photo shoot, years ago.

"Scott says you're cool," Trent tells me, chewing on the end of a toothpick.

"In what sense?" I take a swig of beer.

"You're game for anything—you don't take life too seriously, that kinda thing."

My life is serious to me. It matters. I'm sitting in a cage of buffoons, acting like one because I can't fathom Scott existing for unquantifiable time in my world. I'm giving him thirty more minutes, and then he's gone.

"Sounds like me," I say with a smile into my next swig.

Scott enters the living room with a remote in hand. "Is Simon still shitting?" he asks.

Trent's best friend has been puking in the bathroom since I arrived. "He snorted too much coke before the plane ride," Trent says. "I told him you had extra, but he was convinced he'd spend two days without it."

"Idiot." Scott plops down on the square, modern chair. He switches the television to an input that connects his computer to the TV screen. "Pick a number one through seven."

"Me or Connor?" Trent asks.

"Either or." He scrolls through a video playlist labeled with only single-digit numbers, and I watch his cursor light up each one in temptation.

1

2

3

4

5

6

7

And he starts at the beginning again, waiting for us to choose. I look to Trent, and he hardly seems perplexed by the videos. I assume he's watched some, if not all, before.

So I say, "You pick."

Trent squints at the numbers. ". . . I can't remember the video where he tells her to strip."

"She's naked in four through seven," Scott answers, the cursor lighting up these numbers.

4

5

6

7

I stretch my arm over the couch but clutch my phone tighter. I have an idea what this is now, and I have to make an unsuspicious excuse to leave quickly. I touch my lips with my phone in mock contemplation. "Do you two always do this in your free time?" I ask with a blasé smile.

I hoped their illegal activities would start and end with drugs. The answer that hammers my brain has rippling consequences, and if I misstep even once, this will blow up in my face.

"Dude, when you see what Scott has, you'll wish he showed you sooner," Trent tells me. "It doesn't beat the real thing though." He laughs and pats my shoulder while he drinks his beer, verifying that he actually fucked whoever is on these tapes.

Scott mutters, "Lucky bastard."

Daisy.

I'm ninety-nine percent certain. I was only twenty percent at Saturn Bridges when Scott brought her up in the context of oral sex, and I was seventy percent sure the minute he brought up the numbered videos. But now I know.

Daisy is on one through seven. There are so many reasons why I would *never* watch them. Why I can't. Why it makes me physically ill to even picture Scott, Trent and whoever else repeatedly viewing these.

5

6

"That one," Trent says.

I act like my phone buzzes. "Shit," I curse, scrolling through an old text and springing to my feet.

"What?" Scott stops the cursor on number six.

"Jane fell off her fucking high chair." I rake my hand through my hair, appearing distressed. "I'll be right back—you can start without me."

"She's probably fine," Scott says. "You don't want to miss this." He clicks into the video.

"How long is it?" I wonder.

"This one is a half hour," Scott says, waving the remote at me to come back and join them. I waver, to act like I really want to watch. My muscles pull taut, flexing as I force myself to linger in fake curiosity.

The basement of a town house blinks on-screen, a time stamp in the bottom right corner, affirming the date of when *Princesses of Philly* aired. The camera overlooks the small room with a bed and a wooden dresser. Daisy's ex-boyfriend sits on the edge while she's already half-undressed and begins to shimmy her panties down her legs.

Don't look.

It's too late.

My pulse jackhammers, nausea rising to my throat, and I check my phone again, acting like Rose keeps texting.

Scott said he destroyed the footage of Daisy, but clearly he kept some of what he filmed during *Princesses of Philly*. Like the rest of us, she had no idea cameras were in the bedrooms. So she undressed and she hooked up with her then-boyfriend without fear of being recorded.

Daisy was only seventeen at the time.

"Take it off, baby." Trent laughs and looks to me. "She sucks him off at fifteen minutes."

I try to appear what he wants me to be—excited but dejected that I have to go home and miss it. I glance at my phone and groan. "Shit."

"What?" Scott asks.

"Rose thinks Jane hurt her arm. I'll be right back." With this, I sprint out of the door, able to run without them questioning my motives.

As I race down the driveway, the facts hit me all at once—facts that I researched after Saturn Bridges, to reaffirm what I already knew.

Pennsylvania state law prohibits the photographing, filming, and videotaping of a sexual act involving a child under the age of eighteen.

I run faster across the street.

Pennsylvania law punishes the voluntary viewing or possession of child pornography within an individual's home.

I was so close to joining him in breaking the law, but it's not why I sprint, why when I reach the mailbox I increase my stride.

There's only a small window of opportunity to fuck Scott over. I can't chance waiting another hour or another day. This is it.

When I enter the house, I bolt up the stairs, not even paying attention to Lo, Garrison and Ryke in the living room. "Connor?!" Lo calls, worry in his tone.

I confidently head down the hallway, listening to a group of voices . . . in my room. I turn sharply and open the door to find the girls huddled around the vanity with Willow. In seconds I deduce that she agreed to go to prom with her friend, and Rose, Lily and Daisy have been helping her get ready.

All four heads whip towards me in unison.

"I need you and you," I order, pointing to Daisy and then Rose. I gesture for them to go to the bathroom.

"What's going on?" Lily asks, confused as to why I'd leave her out.

"Connor?" Rose stands and approaches me while Daisy hesitantly heads into the bathroom.

I clutch the back of Rose's head and whisper quickly in her ear, and I start explaining everything. I feel her entire body constrict and coil against mine.

"What the fuck is going on?" Ryke asks in the doorway, following me upstairs with Loren in tow. I hold out my hand, telling him to stay back for a second.

"He wants to talk to Daisy," Lily explains.

When I finish filling Rose in, she looks horrified for a single second before she layers on an enraged, hostile expression, venom pouring through her yellow-green eyes.

"We'll be five minutes," Rose says, taking my hand and following me into the bathroom.

"Cobalt!" Ryke shouts.

Rose shuts the bathroom door on him, and then Daisy hops up on the sink counter and swings her feet. "What's up, guys?"

I stand side by side with Rose, hand in hand, prepared to drop a grenade on a girl who has suffered through too many already. I usually always have the right words, but it's hard to express the weight of what I'm about to unleash—and what it means to her life.

Rose is quiet as well. How do you tell a young girl that she's been violated? I remember how I bought and destroyed pictures of her backstage undressing—from a photographer—to avoid this for Daisy, and with strange circularity, she's about to experience a version of that anyway.

"Guys?" Her smile wanes. "What's going on?"

A chill snakes down my back and arms. "I just found out that Scott still has footage of you from *Princesses of Philly*. In your bedroom."

Her face falls. "What . . . that's . . ."

"It's not online. It can't be." I try to ease her concern. "It's child pornography, Daisy. It's a felony for him to film it, let alone watch the footage."

She stares up at the ceiling, horrified like Rose had been.

"He's going to pay for this," Rose says adamantly. "Okay? He's *not* getting away with it, but we need your consent to call the cops."

She shakes her head in a daze. "Why do you need my consent? It's illegal . . ."

"Daisy . . ." Rose detaches from my hand and kneels in front of Daisy, collecting her sister's hands in hers. "He has footage of you, which will be the basis of the case against him. You may have to go to court and testify . . . or at least make a statement."

"He hurt *you*," Daisy says, tears rising, almost as pissed as her sister's. "He hurt *me*. Who else is he going to hurt?" She inhales strongly and then extends her hand to me.

I frown, not understanding this action.

"I want to call the cops."

I think two years ago, Daisy would've had a hard time standing up for herself, even in a situation as grotesque and abysmal as this one. She would have asked me to call the police. She would have asked her sister to finish the job. Anyone but her.

Rose stands up straight and motions for me to give Daisy the phone, and there is pride in Rose's eyes. She even hugs her sister to her side.

"How long will he go to jail for?" Daisy asks as I pass her the cell. For Rose, to put Scott in jail for eternity would've been easy. For me, it would've been a guiltless action. For someone like Daisy, it's difficult, but I hear no remorse in her voice.

She raises her chin like Rose, following her older sister's powerful, confident demeanor.

"Maybe five years," I tell her, "and he'll be registered as a sexual predator." He may also face federal charges, but right now, I'm looking at the state law, and that alone will ruin his life.

It's not blackmail. It's not unjust. Scott is going to jail for crimes that he's escaped and twisted for years. If I'd never become his friend, I would've never found out what he had in his house. He would've never even *thought* to show me or trust me with it.

I would've never reached this place.

Daisy puts the phone to her ear. "Hi, I'd like to report a crime . . ."

Sixty

Rose Cobalt

Two police cars hug the street curb, one beside Scott's house and one beside ours. My eyes drill holes into Scott's mailbox, waiting for his disgusting, wretched self to appear in cuffs.

"He's cooperating," the officer tells us. "We're taking his computer as evidence, and with what we've seen so far, we'll be able to get a warrant to search his house for anything else."

Perfect.

Connor stands at the end of our driveway with me, poised and collected, while I'm *fuming*, a shark with jaws wide open, a lioness crouched and ready to pounce with claws bared.

"If you need my cell phone records, you can have them," Connor says. "He texted me to come over there today, and when I saw what he was planning to watch, I immediately ran back to call the police."

The officer jots this down in his notebook. "That'd be helpful, thank you."

I perk up the minute I spot the other officer across the street, a bit diagonal to us. He escorts the three guys out of that house. Connor said two were named Trent and Simon, and of course I can distinguish Scott among them, no longer smiling with smug delight. He scowls at the cop car, all three men handcuffed behind their backs.

Turn around, I mentally command Scott, but his face is still pinned to the vehicle. They're out of earshot, and I watch Trent and Simon slide into the car, and the officer shuts the door on them. He sets a hand on Scott's shoulder and directs him to the police car in front of us.

"Excuse me," the police officer says, leaving our side to talk to his partner.

Scott Van Wright is handcuffed.

Scott Van Wright is going to jail.

Scott Van Wright is never obtaining *anything* he desires, ever again.

"There were so many days," I tell Connor, "where I thought he'd always walk free, travel in his *yacht*." I cringe in distaste. "Get a tan, get high and apparently watch my little sister . . ." I can't even finish that truth.

It's one thing to watch me, but to know, all this time, without our knowledge, he's been getting off to *Daisy*—it's past conscionable.

Connor wraps his arm around my waist. "Those days are gone," he announces, the best truth of all.

The two officers chat off to the side while they leave Scott by the car door, closer to us than to them. I hear the word "cocaine," so I assume he'll be booked for more than just filming and viewing child pornography.

Scott has largely kept his back to us, but he finally shifts, leaning his hip on the car door. His snide fury morphs his face into a repulsed snarl as he looks between my husband and me.

Connor laces his fingers through mine. I stand even taller with my husband, my five-inch heels mighty beneath my feet.

I have no trite jeers for Scott, no *how do those handcuffs feel?* or *have fun in hell.*

What he did was so vile, so gross, that there is *no* word in my vocabulary that is even worthy of attaching itself to him. I just let my glare puncture him tenfold.

Scott lets out a short, incensed laugh beneath his breath. "You fucking bitch—"

"No," Connor says, silencing Scott at this. "The next time you ever say anything derogatory about my wife or about any woman, it'll be in jail."

Inside I am doing victory laps around my driveway with fists raised, barefooted and howling at the sun. It's something my sisters would do. Something I'm proud to imagine, them here feeling the triumph with me.

Scott sets his murderous gaze on Connor. "You haven't been real with me at all, have you? It wasn't just this one thing that pushed you over. Or was it?"

In the most even-tempered voice, Connor says, "Do you know what an Aesculapian snake is? No." He looks to me. "Rose?"

I know where he's going with this. "A species of nonvenomous snake," I answer with my head held high.

"Among which is the rat snake." Connor focuses on Scott again. "Rat snakes are like ordinary snakes, except when held captive. When you trap a rat snake, it will attempt to swallow its own body and eventually self-cannibalize." Connor says, "*You* are the rat snake, and you've been slowly eating yourself to death ever since you moved across the street."

Scott's face—a twisted ball of shock, rage and terror—is priceless. He looks like he may puke, and he braces more of his body weight against the police car. He stares far away, as though adding up all the months Connor deceived him. The shots Connor took at me, at the only person he's ever loved. To accomplish what Connor did and still have a soul—it takes rare strength and power that no human being could ever match, not to this uncharted degree.

Scott slowly raises his gaze to my husband. "You're a psychopath."

"No," Connor says, "I just really fucking hate you."

Then the police officers begin to return to the car. Connor and I say a short goodbye to them and walk back up our driveway, distancing ourselves from Scott.

Connor kisses my hand. *"On a gagné."* *We've won.*

I hear the slam of the police car door. And I expel the *last* wounded breath that Scott imprisoned inside of me.

"On a gagné," I repeat with a rising smile.

We've won.

Sixty-one

Rose Cobalt

I thumb through the rack of baby clothes in one of the largest children's department stores. A-line pleated dresses, tulle skirts, Peter Pan collars—all in an array of pastel spring and summer colors. The boys' fashion line is nautical-inspired, with striped shirts, khakis and jean material.

My lips lift at the sight of a teal floral dress with a white collar. No zebra prints, no frogs licking flies or monkeys with bananas. The simplicity, the femininity, is all my style. I pluck the dress off the rack and inspect the tag.

There it is: *CCB* with a small inset *HC*.

Loren sidles next to me and hands me a lemonade. "Ew." Lo mock cringes and puts his hand up to his eyes. "The smile is back."

This particular department store is closed for a party, everyone from Hale Co. in attendance, and instead of schmoozing with men who'd rather do the opposite of everything I tell them, I just join the company of my ultimate reward.

These clothes. This fashion line. In a department store.

"Get used to it, Loren," I retort.

He tilts his head at me. "I already am." It's a small, actually *nice* moment between us, and I've realized that working with him isn't so bad after all. I mean—it's not ideal, but it's not horrible either. God, complimenting Lo will always be a feat.

He nods towards Mark and Theo and all the other employees who've gathered around the boy's clothes. "If you keep it up though, they're going to think you got what you wanted."

"I did get what I wanted," I say. "This is my victory lap." I set the hanger back. "Maybe in time I won't have to pretend to despise all the things I like in order to be heard."

"I want that for you too, you know."

"Is this your way of saying that you're *always* on my side?"

He lets out a short laugh. "Let's not push it, Angelica."

I narrow my eyes. "That comment alone makes you more Angelica than me," I note as always. He flashes a dry smile, not denying the truth. We both turn into bratty, hostile kids from time to time. I sip my glass of lemonade, avoiding work talk among my lovely coworkers.

"Have you checked Twitter recently?" Lo asks me.

"No. I've been logged off since the press conference." I didn't want anyone to ruin Connor's speech for me. He was brave, and having people say, *he doesn't love that bitch! They're using each other! This is all so fake!* would've tarnished something beautiful.

Lo suddenly reaches into my black handbag, and I whip away from him with wide, wild eyes.

"Excuse me?" I snap.

He gives me a sour look. "I'm trying to get your phone."

"You can't just go through a woman's purse." I press my lips together. He hasn't learned since Lily hates carrying purses.

He reaches for my handbag again, and I slap his fingers away. He leans closer and says beneath his breath, "You just *hit* your boss, Rose."

I poke his chest with my finger. "Oh, look, I accidentally *poked* my boss with my manicured nail."

"Your talon." He swats *my* hand away and then ends up taking his own phone and spinning it towards me.

I don't understand. "What's this?"

"What I've been trying to show you—holster the glare, 'gelica. Just read."

"Fine," I grumble and collect his phone. It's a tweet from Lily.

#RCC This is love.

RCC is my initials and Connor's. Lily attached a photograph to the tweet, one of Connor and me from Mexico last year. I'm pregnant, our yacht lounge chairs tucked close together. My yellow-green eyes are pierced on Connor, and his grin towards me is equally as prominent. Fire to water.

There are 4.8k retweets and 12k favorites. I scroll through Lily's feed and it's filled with similar pictures of my dynamics with Connor. Some candids that she snapped without us noticing. Like at the lake house slumber party, where Connor and I were staring at each other for a long, long moment to see who'd concede first.

She wrote: #RCC This is love. #nerdstars

My heart swells.

"She's been doing this for weeks," Loren explains. "Look at what's trending."

I click out of Lily's profile, and I see more tweets with a similar hashtag.

@morningside32: #RCCthisislove when intelligence is sexier than abs.

@heatherveronica: #RCCthisislove when you play chess with me, and we refuse to let each other win

@fashionpleeeaze: #RCCthisislove when you look at me like you love me, no matter what mood I'm in 😔

@neverneverland: #RCCthisislove when we share secrets behind a newspaper 🖤

@hearmeroar29: #RCCthisislove when I'd rip my hair out to protect my daughter & you'd shame the media for shaming us.

My fingers are frozen to my lips, overwhelmed. I'd question how all these people know some finer details of my relationship with Connor, if Lily hadn't taken so many photos of us. She posted so many honest moments with Connor and me—things I'd never think to capture, things I'd never think to share.

It makes me realize how much love my little sister sees between us, and now how much other people are beginning to see too.

The worldwide trending hashtag: #RCCthisislove.

"She's crazy," I say dazedly. "She's crazy and I love her."

Loren laughs. "I'll tell her you said so."

"I'll tell her," I say adamantly. I'd tell my sister that I love her a thousand times over. Before she made my love known to the world. And definitely after.

Sixty-two

Rose Cobalt

My mother air-kisses both of my cheeks the minute I step into the sunroom, something I've never seen her do. If this is her turning over a new leaf, I'll accept it.

"Hello, birthday girl," my mother says in a high-pitched voice, patting my daughter's head. I have a hard time picturing my mother acting this way with her own infant children, but maybe her grandkids are different. She feels more obligated to be overly sweet and less disciplinary. Then again, she wasn't this way with Poppy's daughter, so time could've been a factor too.

I adjust Jane in my arms, and she babbles back to her grandmother, the only recognizable words "hi" and "blue."

I don't know how "blue" ended up in her tiny vocabulary, but I don't question it that often. "Is that your favorite color now, Jane?" I ask her in my usual voice.

Jane just smiles as though the world has turned blue for her.

It's not blue. In fact, it's pink.

Pink pastries, pink roses, a pastel pink tablecloth. I set Jane on her feet and hold her hand while she curiously inspects the tablecloth, her stuffed lion in her clutch.

"This is pretty," I tell my mother, gesturing to the table setup. Morning sunlight streams through the windowpanes, and the fans spin languidly overhead. It's not too much at all. I thought she would've hired a string quartet and constructed a tea party outside.

I told my mother that one-year-olds won't remember their birthday and to save extravagant parties for when they know the difference between a backyard carnival and a ten-dollar bag of streamers from Party City.

"I went simple like you said," she tells me, and I watch her silently count the chairs at the long table.

"Everyone is coming," I assure her. Jane tugs on my dress, and I lift her back into my arms. She rests her cheek on my shoulder.

My mother lets out a soft breath. "You know, there was a minute where I thought you might not let me throw Jane a birthday party."

"Can you blame me?" I wonder. She no longer sat on my side during one of the most harrowing moments of my life. I needed her to support Connor and my love for him, even if she didn't fully understand it.

"No, I don't blame you." She touches her necklace, not her usual strand of pearls. This time, it's a silver locket. "I rushed to judgment . . . me and your father did." Before she can say anything more, the sunroom door opens and Connor and my father slip inside.

They both seem at ease, and Connor wears his usual complacent expression, not divulging much. He nears, tickling Jane's arm, and she giggles and squirms against my hip.

"Your father apologized," he explains, eyes flitting back to my dad.

My father nods repeatedly and clears his throat. "It's easy for me to go on the offense when I feel like my daughters and my company are being threatened at the same time. It wasn't right, but . . . I was just seeing red. I'm sorry."

It's nice to be back on these terms, and I sincerely hope it'll last. "I appreciate the apology," I say.

"Did you hear that Scott wasn't granted bond?" he asks both of us.

Before we can say yes, my mother chimes in, "He should get the maximum sentencing after what he's done." I spot the rage in her stiff posture. She can be a protective mother hen, I suppose. It just takes the right kind of bullet to head towards us before she grows horns and breathes fire like me.

"Connor doesn't think he'll go to trial," I tell them.

Scott is stuck in jail since the judge denied him bond, so he has to sit there and wait for what could potentially be months. He's being tried in federal court, so it's likely he'll try to worm his way out by a plea deal.

My mother looks horrified at the notion. "A jury needs to convict him."

"If he pleads guilty," Connor says, "and takes the deal, it probably won't be much better than a trial." Scott Van Wright is looking at five to ten years in prison.

And his name will *not* cloud the jubilant atmosphere of Jane's first birthday, so I decide to change the subject. "Mother says you're dieting," I tell my father, a clear digression, but I've never been subtle.

He laughs once into a smile. "My cholesterol is high."

"Where's the birthday bunny?! We come with presents!" Daisy exclaims before the door even opens. My parents turn to greet the large group of people, all squeezing into the sunroom, and I go near the other end of the table with Connor, settling in the head wicker chair with Jane on my lap. He sits adjacent to me.

I won the right to sit here after a thirty-minute game of Scrabble this morning. I only beat him by two points.

"Winners sit at the head of the table, Jane," I tell her.

She waves around her stuffed lion and looks up at me with big blue eyes. "Mommy . . ." I can't really understand anything else. Sometimes I think I can, but then I realize I just *want* to hear actual sentences, and it's my mind pretending her noises are intelligible words.

"You're glowing," Connor says. He has his finger to his jaw, his grin widening as I meet his eyes.

"I'm not pregnant, if that's what your oversized brain is thinking." The mention of pregnancy downturns my lips. *Jane is supposed to be an only child, Rose.* Whatever other babies I birth will belong to Daisy.

"I wasn't, but clearly you were," he says easily, as though the topic hardly plagues him. I don't see how it doesn't.

I think about our lost dream almost daily, and never once do I begin to smile.

Happy thoughts, Rose. It's Jane's first birthday, a momentous, joyful occasion on June 10. Being sad about not having more of my own children on my *actual* baby's birthday is downright mean and almost sacrilegious.

I try to be better. Maybe this is what life is always like.

Connor scoots his chair closer to me.

"Are you cheating, Richard?" He's trying to sit at the head of the table *with* me.

"Would you love me if I was a cheater?" he asks. In my peripheral, I notice our friends and family beginning to take their seats.

"Why do you ask me questions that you know the answers to?"

He steps over my comment. "You love me, so I couldn't possibly be a cheater."

Mind games. Riddles. Paradoxes. My head beats with them all. And I'm transported to us at sixteen and seventeen, when we were locked in a janitorial closet at Model UN together. I never knew he'd had the means to let us out, not until he admitted it at the press conference.

"You told everyone a memory of ours," I say, jumping to a new page of our book, and he follows me.

"I didn't think you'd mind."

"I don't," I say softly. "But you forgot to tell them the part where you leaned in to kiss me, and I pressed my hand to your face."

He gives me a look and shakes his head. "That's not how it went."

I glare. "Yes, it is. I have a *perfect* memory, Richard."

He scoots even closer. Until his shoulder bumps into mine. *"Moi aussi." So do I.* He lifts my chin with two fingers. "That day, you stared at me like you're staring at me now."

"And how's that?"

"With passion," he says with his own bout of passion. "You looked at my lips and I looked at yours."

He's already roped me in, and I draw nearer, our knees knocking.

"We never touched, but I made love to your mind. When you had enough, *that's* when you covered my mouth."

I made love to your mind. He's never uttered those words before, but I think I'm in love with them. "Hmm," I say.

His brows rise. "'Hmm'?"

"Your memory isn't terrible."

He laughs into another grin. "You do love me."

"And you love stating the obvious," I point out. I don't stare at him to see the full-blown grin that overtakes his face. I rarely agree that I love him to the extent that he claims, even if it's always true. Someone clinks a wineglass, and I redirect my attention to the filled table, every family member and friend seated.

We're all here, including Willow, Sam, Poppy . . . and Jonathan. He's positioned between my father and Sam, and his hair looks thinned on the sides, as though he's been battling stress.

I'm surprised that he stays quiet, and maybe he's a little guilt-ridden, like Connor has claimed.

Loren rises with chilled water in his left hand, his right hand in a black cast. As the table hushes, I take in the moment, the smiling faces of my three sisters, my parents with their hands clasped together beside a coffee cup, the quiet morning in my childhood home, Connor so close that his arm fits across my chair, and my daughter here, on my lap, hugging her lion.

"I know it's Janie's birthday, but after everything that has happened to you two"—he gestures with his water glass to Connor and me—"I have something to say."

This could go fairly bad or fairly well, but I have a lot more faith in Loren Hale to swing in a direction that won't cause World War III, me leading a platoon against him.

"I may always say that Rose is as cold as ice and Lily may always say that Connor must be a planetary alien," Lo begins, Lily nodding beside him while bouncing Maximoff on her knees, "but you both have astronomical-sized hearts, you know that?"

I look to Connor, and his fingers have returned to his jaw in contemplation. *We have hearts*. It's not an earth-shattering realization. I know I have a heart. I know Connor has one too, but for other people to acknowledge this is rare. Our hearts are submerged beneath the thickest, densest armor that we only let a select few through.

Loren continues, "You've both never judged me for being an addict, and even when tons of people judged you and questioned you—you *forgave* them." He shakes his head in disbelief at the notion, that we'd all congregate together peacefully in the end. "This table is full because of your compassion, and I want you to know that I can see it." He turns to my parents, his father, Sam and Poppy. "And everyone here sure as hell better see it too."

At this, my father rises with his mimosa, and then my mother follows suit in solidarity. When Jonathan rises, water in hand, the tension strangely untangles. He has a ways to go to repair his relationships with his sons, but being here without being an ass is a start.

I watch Poppy join them, then Sam and their daughter, Maria.

When Lily stands beside Lo, she clears her throat, already turning red. I watch her raise her chin triumphantly and then pull back her shoulders. *Go, Lily.* And she says with confidence, "I think if we can come together after everything that's happened, our kids are better for it." She nods in resolution.

I breathe through my nose, holding back emotion that swells my chest. I don't like the feeling of people towering over me, so I rise next with Jane on my hip. Connor is quick to follow.

Ryke and Daisy are the only two still seated, which isn't entirely surprising. Out of everyone, they've faced the most dissention from inside the family.

Ryke leans back and shakes his head. "Is this for real?" he has to ask. "Because I'm not standing up if in three months this side of the table"—he motions to our parents—"makes our lives hell because you believed a fucking tabloid rumor over *us*."

My father clears his throat and pauses, trying to find the right way to share his emotions. ". . . I know I've doubted a few of the men here with my daughters." His eyes ping from Sam to Ryke and lastly to Connor, a fresher doubt than the other two. "I can't apologize for caring about my girls, but I can apologize for putting a strain on your relationships and feeling as though you had to choose between the people you loved and your family." He pauses. "It's time for that to change."

Ryke's lips slowly part in disbelief. Over the course of a year, I knew my father has warmed to Ryke and Daisy's relationship, but I don't think he ever outwardly expressed this to Ryke.

My mother straightens, knowing half of Ryke's statement was directed at her. "You went through liver transplant surgery for your father, and you want to know what I told Jonathan—you'd never do it." Her hand loosens on her mimosa glass. It's a subtle acknowledgment that she's misjudged Ryke too. "I don't want to live like everyone is out to get my family, and it starts by trusting the people we *should* trust." She says, "And I trust you."

I freeze at the *much* larger declaration than I anticipated hearing. I'd think someone spiked everyone's drinks, but no one has taken a sip yet.

Ryke looks to Daisy, and tears crest her eyes. She whispers in his ear, and he nods.

They both stand together.

If someone asked me what makes me—a volcanic, fiery blaze of hell—shed tears and cry as though I'm a pathetic two-minute rainfall, I'd say my sisters growing up, my husband in his rare vulnerability, my baby at random immeasurable moments and the title screen of *Titanic*.

Somewhere between all of those, this singular part of time exists, and it hits me hard. With glasses raised in the air, with all of us unified around a decorated table, cake in the center, I accept a powerful, unbending realization as a warm, heartfelt truth.

All of our children will be raised without hatred. Bad blood will be washed away and feuds finally put aside. They'll have the sharpest, sturdiest tools to fight enemies that will *not* be in their own homes but miles and miles away.

Our children will have the best chance at life because we're standing together. Because we all have the capacity to love, no matter what form or shape it may come in. Because in the end, we each remain unbroken so their lives can begin.

I inhale powerfully, and Connor wraps his arm around my shoulder.

Loren raises his glass higher. "To Rose and Connor, for helping us realize the importance of family and the difference a good friend can make." It's not often that other people tell us this—that we've impacted them. I can't help but smile.

"To Rose and Connor," everyone says in unison.

Connor captures my gaze with his deep, glimmering blues, and together, we drink to us.

Sixty-three

Connor Cobalt

t was just a little fall, my gremlin." Rose squats in five-inch heels and blows on Jane's reddened palms. She tries to console our daughter, who cries in Claude Monet's garden, one of the most beautiful places I've ever visited in France. The lush, floral scenery is hardly tainted, in my mind, by Jane's tears. I watch as Rose wipes our daughter's rosy cheek, and Jane sniffs, realizing her stumble on the pavement didn't hurt as much as she thought it had.

Jane reaches out for Rose to pick her up, but then she whips her head, not noticing me towering above her. "Daddy!" She starts to cry again.

Rose rolls her eyes. "Your daddy is six feet and four inches of superiority, and his head is lost in the clouds."

I bend down next to Rose. "On the contrary, darling, my head is in the stars." Our daughter relaxes as soon as she sees me again.

Rose's yellow-green eyes bore straight through me, and my pulse pounds. "It's daylight."

"It's a meta—"

She covers my mouth with her palm, and my burgeoning grin peeks through her fingers. *I know what a metaphor is, Richard*, I read in her expression. She huffs, eyes blazing and flitting across my features, chest rising and falling. How someone can be so alive by words—it makes me come alive with her.

Jane mumbles a string of noises and we both break our gaze. I brush a tear streak from Jane's cheek, and she sniffs again.

Rose asks me, "Do you think we'll make it the whole day?" She fixes Jane's white sun hat, which fell off during her stumble.

"Maybe fifteen more minutes, and then she'll probably have had enough." We've been traveling around northern France most of the afternoon. It's June 22, so we plan to spend the rest of our anniversary at our hotel with Jane.

Rose lets go of Jane's fingers and asks her, "Who do you want to carry you?"

Our daughter stares between us before reaching out for her mom.

"Good choice," I tell Jane.

Rose's lips begin to rise as she collects Jane in her arms, and we both stand together. I hear the *snap-snap* of cameras, but I do my best to tune them out.

People stare. People take photographs, and our security team stands twenty feet behind us. I don't mind the constant, unwavering gaze from onlookers, as long as we can have a day like this—no fear of harassment or of being enclosed by paparazzi.

I rest a hand on Rose's lower back, and we leisurely walk towards the wooden bridge that oversees a lily pond. Purple wisteria blossoms drape and hang, roots twisting around the railing, and rich green plants crawl and canopy the bridge. It's like stepping into Monet's painting, experiencing a piece of art up close.

As we stop in the middle of the bridge, I spin Rose towards me, facing each other, our daughter between us. It's quiet here, the serenity filling my head with desires and clearing all doubts.

"Stop staring at me like that," she says, but she reflexively draws closer to me. I can feel her heart in her chest, beating against mine.

"It frightens you—what I'm going to say?" I question. She can't read my mind, but I must wear my wants across my face. And I want her and I want Jane. And I want many more children.

"What are you going to say?" she asks outright.

"When I look deeply into your eyes, I see more than just three years of our marriage," I profess. "I see ten, thirty, fifty, sixty years with you, and I see us returning to this place. I see us old and at the end of our lifelines, staring out at this water, on this bridge—as consumed by love as we're tragically consumed now."

Her hand grasps my bicep, half in threat, half to cover the fact that she's breathless.

"I see our children," I say. "Many more children, Rose."

"There are rules," she says pointedly. "We lost our game, and the media's invasiveness . . . You said there are no alternate paths." I haven't been blind to her disappointment. I meet it daily when she thinks about growing our family together. I bottle my own in the face of hers, but the defeat intensifies, an untouched dream trembling to be held.

I've never broken a game.

I've found loopholes, but this has none.

It's either we go against what we've planned or we live an *unfulfilled* life.

I'm not putting myself in any restraint. I'm tearing through every last one, even if it means taking a difficult plunge for both of us—one that has always felt like sliding down a mountainside with no traction and no way to climb back up. Even if it means that breaking the terms of what we set *one* time changes the way we play our games forever.

There has to be one exception. Always.

And this is it. "We can break our rules for our children," I tell her. "We've been under the notion that having more children would be selfish, but look around us, Rose—look at *her* and tell me what part of this world is so unbearable that we shouldn't give another child life?"

Rose watches Jane lean close to the purple wisteria, big blue eyes flooded with childlike wonder, and then our daughter points curiously at the fauna canopied above us. She babbles a string of noises that sounds like, *what is this?*

"It's a dream taking flight, Jane." I say the words to Rose, seizing her attention and gaze. She's not convinced one hundred percent that this is the best plan. "It's selfish for us to live by a rule that affects another life."

"The media though," she says. "How has that changed at all?" The real test wasn't our game that we constructed with the media. The real test was afterwards, how we handled the blowback with our daughter in our arms, and in my eyes, we've succeeded.

I explain, "Our love trumps any cost the media can inflict. Maybe this whole time, Rose, it's unconsciously been safe and it's taken *our* belief—that we can provide *love* to a child, that we *feel* with all our hearts—to finally see it ourselves."

She fights tears, and I pull her as close as she can go, my hand holding her jaw and my thumb stroking her cheek. Here I am, convincing Rose of love when she's spent so much time opening my mind to its true meaning. I will remind her every single day how much resides inside both of us.

"There is no more doubt," I say. "Whatever missteps our children take or mistakes we may make, their lives will be filled with love and *passion*—and our children, *ours*, will suck the marrow out of life and paint this gray fucking world with color." I stare deeply into those fierce yellow-green eyes, my heart drumming in sync with hers. "Our children will be unforgettable like us. You wait and see."

Rose's hand rises up to my shoulder. "This is the place where we've both gone mad." She turns her head just a fraction, to the lily pads idle in the water. "Who on earth would want to procreate with you? *Eight* times?" She meets my burgeoning, conceited grin. "I must be insane."

She's saying a resounding, earth-shifting *yes*.

I slide my arm around her waist. Winning and losing has always just been a state of mind, and I sense ours becoming sound again.

I rest my hand on her lower stomach, expecting her to slap it away, but she lets me touch her here without complaint. Her lips try to pull upwards, even when she hates to combat my grin with a smile.

Before Jane arrived, I loved seeing her pregnant, watching her body grow with our baby, a part of me and a part of her. Rose had numerous fears about motherhood, but she enjoyed the majority of carrying a child. If she'd hated it, she'd never consider another.

"We can't just have more on a whim," she reminds me. "I have to plan this out with Daisy in case she can't have a baby."

"I know." I'm assuming this means Ryke will be in the discussion as well. For every hurdle he's faced with Daisy, for every mountain they have figuratively and literally climbed, it'd be more likely they marry today than break up tomorrow.

Rose adjusts Jane, struggling to hold her weight for so long.

"I'll take her," I say.

Rose passes our daughter to me, and I easily hold her by the bottom, lifting her up towards my shoulder. Jane presses her cheek to my collar, her eyelids heavy.

I look to Rose. "How many more children do you want?" Eight has been my number. It's one she's grown accustomed to because I repeat it often, but it's not set in stone.

Rose takes Jane's crooked hat off and sets it in her Chanel diaper bag that looks more like a large purse. "I just want Jane to have a sister. We could have two kids and I'd be happy, or we could have ten, as long as there are two girls somewhere."

We can't plan the exact number, not when there are too many unforeseeable roadblocks, but we can try to achieve this.

Two Cobalt girls.

Sisters.

"Then as soon as you have another girl, *our* girl"—I have to preface—"we'll stop and that'll be the size of our family." I wait for this proclamation to sink into her features, and Rose's eyes widen. She almost rocks backwards, but I clutch her hip, keeping her near.

"Richard Connor Cobalt, you're leaving this up to fate." Her smile lights her eyes, filled with amusement. I'm more than satisfied to leave the number of our kids to science, and yes, to chance.

"Your fate will be kind to me," I tell her. "I can make anyone grow to love me in time."

Rose rolls her eyes. "*Your* fate is *my* fate." I believe it. "And they don't love you, Connor. They love the person you give them." She pauses and says, "I love *you*. I'm proud of *you*. And I can't imagine being anywhere but by *your* side."

Our pulses thrum again.

I lift her chin, her gaze burning all of these truths into me. There are rare people who will fuel the fire inside of you, who will awaken a dormant passion, who will challenge you, who will push you and better you. She alone is my rarity.

"I'm always whomever or whatever people need me to be," I say strongly, "but you were the only one who needed me to be me."

She nods with tears brimming her eyes. "I can hear your heart beating."

My lips pull higher, and I tuck a strand of hair behind her ear. "It beats in equal time with yours." I kiss the hollow of her neck and whisper, "*Toujours*."

Always.

Epilogue

Rose Cobalt

ONE MONTH LATER

T hey're in here somewhere," Lily says, hidden in the depths
of her walk-in closet. She keeps sliding hangers, expecting
to find two of my fur coats that she's commandeered over
the years.

I crouch beside the rack of shoes, pretending to hunt for them.
"You can keep the coats—"

"No," she says adamantly for the fifth time.

"I want you to have them," I repeat, also for the fifth time.

"I can't hear you," she lies and then disappears in the darkness of Loren Hale's black button-downs. She definitely can have
them if they've been traitorously making camp in between his shirts.

I let out a heavy sigh and look beneath a pile of clothes, tossing
her tank top aside and then a—*ew*. "Lily!" I shriek, bolting upright like a feral cat.

Lily's head pops out between the button-downs. "Whaa . . ."

I point to the stack of clothes on the floor, what appear to be
men's boxer briefs on top. "Is this dirty?"

She mumbles something that sounds like *maybe* and slips back
into darkness. Motherfucking *ew*—I just touched Loren Hale's

dirty underwear. I stomp out of the closet and enter the bathroom, scrubbing my hands vigorously in the sink.

I pump extra soap and lather my palms. Three minutes later, I dry my hands on a gray towel.

"Found them," Lily pants and holds up my two coats.

My face falls. I was sincerely hoping she wouldn't find them at all. "Are you sure you don't want them?" I ask.

"You wear them more than me," she expresses. "I want to make sure you have everything that makes you comfortable."

It's the last part of me in this house. I've been eradicated.

You chose this, Rose. I know. I'm moving down the street with Connor and Jane. We planned to wait longer, maybe years, before we actually packed our things and left Lily and Lo and Ryke and Daisy alone. But when we came home from France—with cameras hot on our faces, accusing us of incestuous relationships that were downright vile—I think we both knew the distance would help everyone.

It was time.

Moving on is a bittersweet feeling. It's saying goodbye to an era with my sisters and saying hello to an era with my husband. I'd never been ready or prepared to do this, but I am now.

I just wish little pieces of me were still left in my sister's closets. Like my coats. Like my high heels or a necklace I lent them. I don't want to be eradicated. I want to be remembered.

Off my silence, Lily says, "You're just moving down the street."

I roll my eyes. "It's the principle." I flip my hair off my shoulder and reluctantly collect the two coats, marching out of the room with her on my side.

"I'll keep one," she says. "Would you mind—"

"Which one?" I contain my smile, though I feel it grow inside of me.

"The brown one."

I pass her the soft coat and she hugs it to her chest. "I'll meet you outside!" She runs back down the hallway to put the coat in her room.

I descend the stairs into the living room, and I skim the back of the couch with my hand, as though saying goodbye. I stop right before the foyer and imprint this place in my mind. It's not empty.

It's just empty of me.

I've spent well over a year here, the first time I've ever lived with Daisy and Lily together. My daughter walked for the first time in the living room. She spoke her first word in the kitchen. Endings make me sentimental the way new beginnings do, and I suppose, if I look closely, they're one in the same.

Lily races down the stairs with her Wampa cap on, her shoulder-length brown hair looking washed. Her gangly legs move quickly beneath her, and I inhale strongly, pocketing my odd sappiness.

"Is that it?" Lily asks me, nodding to the coat.

"Yes," I say, "this is the last of me."

Lily frowns. "Don't say it like that. It makes me sad."

"This *is* sad. I'm still waiting for you to cry for me." I open the front door.

Lily tugs the flaps of her hat. "You said I shouldn't cry if you're not dying."

I don't doubt I said it. I would just like a *little* emotion today from someone other than me. I can't be the only one experiencing this bittersweet cocktail, can I?

"Beep beep!" Daisy does donuts in a golf cart at the end of the driveway, a lopsided smile brightening her face.

Yes, I am the only one in fucking mourning over myself.

Daisy whips the golf cart up to the front of the house and turns sharply like she's auditioning for a car commercial. "Hello there, pretty ladies. Want a ride in my vehicle?" She wags her brows and rubs the steering wheel.

Lily laughs and I roll my eyes, choosing to sit next to her while Lily plops in the back. We bought a golf cart about the same time we purchased the house down the street. It's just easier than jumping in a car—and walking, of course.

"Your hickey is showing," I tell her and fix my hair in the tiniest rearview mirror I've ever seen.

"It's a wolf bite." She chomps with her teeth and then smiles wider, a clear red mark on her neck. Besides the hickey, she wears Ryke's baseball cap backwards and a muscle shirt that says, *Whoa thar, pirate. I want ye treasure.*

"As long as you're happy with it, I'm happy," I say distantly, sitting back, and she swings the golf cart towards the road. I brace myself in case Daisy whips the golf cart again, and I check on Lily. She spiders the white cushion of her seat—in fear of being flung off.

Lily mouths to me, *I'm scared.*

We're going less than twenty miles an hour, but she saw Ryke accidentally fling off Loren this morning. He was also doing donuts.

But Daisy is driving in a straight line now.

Before Lily volunteers to walk to my new house, I reach out and hold her arm, silently telling her that she *will not* fall off. And if she does, I'll be falling with her.

"Hold your breath," Daisy says quickly, right as the golf cart rolls past a familiar mansion across the street, the caution tape and police cars absent. I immediately suck air back into my lungs, a habit that Daisy started once Scott was escorted from the neighborhood and movers packed his shit.

It's still on the market, but none of us will ever buy it, a dark aura practically circling the mansion.

We'll never have to see Scott Van Wright again. He pled guilty to avoid a harsher sentence. He knew the jury would've had all the evidence to find him guilty anyway. Major news outlets ran the story about how the *executive producer* (finally this was publicly announced) of *Princesses of Philly* faced federal charges for filming and viewing child pornography of Daisy Calloway.

The world views my little sister as an adventurous, free-spirited sweetheart, and for him to take advantage of her, in any way, illuminated his true form as the disgusting rat snake that he is. A vile creature who *deserves* to be in prison.

The judge agreed.

Scott took the deal of nine years in jail, following five more years on probation. Since it was a highly publicized case, the judge wanted to set an example out of him, and he went more harshly than expected.

We drive past the property and exhale together.

"Is Willow still working?" I ask Lily. Loren's sister wants to save up for college, and everyone keeps offering to pay for it, but she's avoiding a handout. I think she wants to prove that she's here not for money or notoriety, but to truly be a part of her brother's life. And the only way to do that is to be as self-sufficient as possible.

"Yeah," Lily says. "I tried to sneak extra in her paycheck, but she noticed and wouldn't accept anything more than the other employees."

Willow is noble, and she has a big support system here, in whatever she chooses to do. All I ask is that her "friend" treats her well. Garrison still works with her, but she said prom ended without a kiss or any promises of something more.

Lily holds on to my arm, which holds her. "So . . . what happens if I need to ask you about a book or a star constellation or . . . a funny character on television who looks like a president but I'm not sure which president it is—do I just . . . do I call you? Or do I go to your house or do I Google it—"

"You're *not* replacing me with Google." I glare.

Lily nods a couple times. "So I call you, then?"

"Or you can come over. I'll always stop by your house too."

Lily nods again, more assuredly. "Okay."

"We're here," Daisy announces, bumping up the curb and onto

the driveway. Pink tulip trees frame either side of the cement, the beauty not lost on me, no matter how many trips we take towards the house. We go quiet, listening to the gush of a regal fountain. When the last tulip tree passes, the fountain comes into view, sitting before the mansion as though to announce its queenly presence.

White siding, gorgeous molding, a stately double-door entrance—it's a home that I'd never thought would be for sale. The media uproar sent a widow packing, and we bought this ten-bedroom estate from her. It's only a little larger than the house we'd been living in before, and depending on fate, it may be too big, too small, or just right for the size of the Cobalt family.

Daisy drives around the fountain and parks in front. "Unmount."

I gather my fur coat and my purse, and we enter my new house. We're greeted first by the vaulted ceiling and crystal chandelier.

"I always feel like Cinderella when I walk in here," Lily whispers behind me.

"Why are you whispering?" I ask.

"It feels like one of those places you whisper in," she whispers and then turns red. "Right?"

"It's not a museum or a cemetery," I say, hoping she won't feel this way about my home for long.

"I guess it's just different," she says softly. "I never really visited you in college. You visited me, and when I did go to your house, I was living with you . . . so it was mine too."

This is the first time she's stepping foot into something we don't share.

She says, "You're right. I shouldn't whisper." She exhales a tight breath and then we both follow Daisy towards the large living room, suede furniture already moved in but plenty of cardboard boxes still left to unpack. Glass French doors lead to a pool and outdoor fireplace—

". . . I don't care if we never fucking do it." I catch Ryke's voice in midconversation.

"You forget how tight it is," Loren says casually. *How tight*—Loren. Ugh. They're talking about my sisters and sex, I suspect.

My heels clap against the hardwood and they both shut up the minute I breach the archway with Daisy and Lily.

"Fuck," Ryke curses, while Loren Hale doesn't even look marginally guilty. They lounge on the white rug, taking a break from moving heavy objects. Their cans of Fizz Life rest on cardboard boxes, and Moffy and Jane unsteadily chase each other around the new furniture.

Connor drinks wine and remains standing, supervising the children more than these two.

"Can you walk a little louder next time?" Lo asks with a half smile, his right hand still in a black cast. "Thanks."

"Maybe you shouldn't talk about anal sex behind our backs," I retort, able to deduce the subject of their conversation.

"Fine, I'll talk about it to your face," Lo challenges. "I hear you like it in the ass." He raises his can of Fizz Life to me. "Cheers."

I narrow my eyes at my husband. "Richard."

He looks as guiltless as Loren. "Rose," he says and then sips his wine with a smile.

Lily leans into me. "We just discussed anal thirty minutes ago." This is true. Daisy brought it up in casual conversation, and I admitted to trying it and, yes, to liking it.

So it's not any different for the guys to do the same. It's just *Loren* knowing this . . . I shudder, but he looks hardly excited by the knowledge. *Good.*

I splay my coat on the couch, noticing a sleeping husky on the cushions with an orange tabby cat curled on top of the dog's stomach. It's the most bizarre friendship of us all, we've concluded. Sadie and Coconut should be mortal enemies, but they were friends at first sight.

However, Sadie hasn't warmed to the kids, not entirely, but only Jane really tries to cuddle with her, even when the cat is being ornery. I always keep an eye on both of them to avoid any kind of scratching.

"Is that it?" Ryke asks, standing up with Loren. They both look at the coat, the last thing I needed.

I nod, knowing they're ready to go back home. Lo picks up Moffy and tosses him over his shoulder, the boy laughs full-bellied laughs. "Enjoy this flight, little man."

"What if I miss a period?" Lily suddenly asks me. The room quiets, and all the men exchange worried glances. "Hypothetically," she adds, turning bright red. "Do I call you or do I drive down here or do I—"

"You come see me." I hold her hand, and then I hold Daisy's, who has been suspiciously quiet ever since we entered the house. She's not smiling like she was on the golf cart.

"And what if . . . what if I'm having a bad day and I need you to walk into my room . . . and you do that thing where you open the curtains really fast and all the light floods in . . ." She bursts into tears.

It triggers Daisy, who begins to cry too.

And now I'm fucking crying. "Anyone can open your blinds."

"Not like you do." Lily's waterworks won't cease. Why did I ask for this? My eyes burn terribly, and no matter how many large inhales I take, a weight sinks on my chest. *This isn't goodbye, Rose.*

Daisy adds tearfully, "I'm going to miss the sound of your heels in the morning."

"And when you always put Pop-Tarts in the toaster for us, even though you hate Pop-Tarts," Lily cries.

We're all a mess. I squeeze their hands, but it only intensifies what remains between us, an underlying goodbye even if it's not a permanent, fixed one. This *is* goodbye of our lives in one house together.

"I love you both," I tell them strongly, "and I'll always be here if you need me."

"When," Daisy corrects. "*When* we need you."

Tears spill down my cheeks, and they hug me at the same time. I'm the oldest of them, but I consider Daisy and Lily wholly equal to myself, the sweeter and more lovable sides of a Calloway sister, while I'm the fierce quarter.

When we break apart, we all turn towards the men, all of them looking a little choked up. Loren has his son on his side now, no longer over his shoulder.

"She's not dying," Loren reminds Lily. "And I can put in a Pop-Tart for you."

"It's not the same thing." Lily sniffs, hesitantly leaving my side. "You like Pop-Tarts, and you'd eat mine."

He sighs, wishing he could fix her sadness, knowing he can't. The best he does is tuck Moffy to his chest, and then Lily springs onto his back, wrapping her legs around his waist. They head through the archway and towards the door like that.

Ryke looks about the same as Loren did, raking a hand through his thick hair. He patiently waits for Daisy to leave my side.

"Moffy!" Jane calls, not all that coherently though.

Connor scoops her up before she falls in pursuit of her cousin. He distracts her with his wineglass before finding a stuffed toy.

"Will you call me every day like you did before?" Daisy asks, her scar along her cheek more reddened since she's been crying. When I was in college away from everyone, I used to call her every day like I did Lily and Poppy. I made it a routine to keep in touch, even if I became a nuisance.

"I'll see you more than I call," I tell her. "I promise."

"Will you come to my doctor's appointments with me?" she wonders. It's the first time she's asked this aloud. "It's all really confusing, and . . . I think you'd understand the fertility treatments and all the options they keep bombarding me with."

I nod, restraining as many tears as possible. "Of course." I wipe her cheek. She's been postponing any kind of ovarian surgery until she has a better sense of the long-term effects.

"Okay, big sister," Daisy says with a heartfelt smile. "I'll see you tomorrow, then." We let go of our hands, and she approaches Ryke.

"Whoa thar, pirate," she says with half laughter, half tears, unable to contain her sadness like she usually can. She covers her face with her hands to hide it.

Ryke hugs her to his chest and kisses the top of her head. Daisy rubs her face and then whistles. Coconut leaps off the couch and sprints to her side. Then they all quietly leave, Ryke nodding to me in recognition on the way out.

The double doors slam shut.

I dazedly sit next to Sadie on the couch. "That was brutal," I tell her matter-of-factly.

She purrs in agreement before stretching—and then collapsing back in a sleep. The cushion undulates as Connor takes a seat beside me with Jane in arm. He passes me my own wineglass, and I kick off my heels and rest my feet on the couch.

He pulls me closer to him, until I lean my whole body weight against his side, and he sets his hand on my thigh. I sip my wine, and he combs his fingers through my hair.

"Is it quiet to you in here?" I ask.

"No, darling," he says.

"What do you hear?" I take another sip, and I reach my hand out so Jane can play with my bracelet on my wrist. She immediately takes interest in it.

"Alarm clocks beeping during school days, in multiple rooms," Connor tells me. "They keep ringing at different intervals."

I smile, imagining teenagers pressing the "snooze" button. "Who wakes them up, me or you?"

"We take turns." Of course we do.

"What else?"

"The slam of bathroom doors and the turn of faucets. Music from bedrooms and laughter—always laughter."

I rest my chin on his shoulder. "I must be laughing at your smile."

He immediately breaks into a full-blown grin.

"I wasn't joking, Richard." I glower.

"You don't *laugh* when I smile, you do this." He pinches my chin so that my head rises off his shoulder. I'm carving my name in his forehead with daggered eyes. "You do know what a laugh is?"

I give him a look of *zero* amusement. "I'm going to cut off your tongue."

His grin spreads. "Then the house will be literally and figuratively quiet."

I cover his mouth, and he kisses my hand . . . and then he kisses me, my breath caught in my throat and my wineglass almost slipping from my fingers.

His lips against mine, I kiss back.

And I hear alarm clocks beeping, laughter in the kitchen, yelling by the pool. I listen to the vigorous pulse of our future, roaring with life.

ACKNOWLEDGMENTS

This isn't goodbye, so no crying at this point. This is a thank-you. This book was spawned from your passion. It exists because of *you*. After we published *Kiss the Sky*, we had no plans to write more with Connor and Rose, but your fervor, your desire and your spirit encouraged us to pursue more of their story.

After *Hothouse Flower*, we made the leap and decided this book would come to fruition. So we began shaping this novel and the rest of the series with a vision in mind. A vision that Connor and Rose would banter together in French again one day, with glasses of wine in hand, with game boards spread over their four-poster bed, with those fiery yellow-green eyes pinned on that burgeoning, conceited grin.

And so came *Fuel the Fire*. A book spawned from passionate hearts.

Thanks to our family for teaching us the importance of never holding grudges and always moving forward. Our dad, for your constant support of our dreams—we love you.

Thanks to our mom, our very own Rose Calloway. You've taught us what it means to be strong, independent women and to be ourselves, no matter if we gravitate towards sneakers or your high heels. We love you tremendously, and this book wouldn't be nearly the same if we didn't grow up with a fierce role model like you.

Thanks to our translators Nieku and Ashley for not only helping us with the French and German but for being great friends. We're so happy fate aligned in college and we all met.

Thanks to Siiri—we know you're usually too sweet to take credit for this, but we have to give it to you here. You've championed Rose and Connor since their introduction, and somewhere in their journey, you coined the name "Coballoway." Thank you for breathing fire into this pair and into us. We'll always carry your friendship in our hearts.

And last is the loudest and mightiest thank-you, which will spread all around the world. Thank you to the Fizzle Force. We can't justly express our appreciation towards the Addicted series fandom—there really is no perfect word that describes what each and every one of you mean to us. You've changed our lives and given us the courage to write fiction that comes from the deepest parts of our hearts. *Fuel the Fire* was crafted with your love in mind, and we can't imagine the series without this final Connor and Rose novel. We truly love you, adore you and will always be here to support you, in whatever dreams you chase. So thank you, you impassioned spirits. Thank you for painting our world with color. It's immensely more beautiful now.

BONUS SCENE:

*Connor Cobalt and
the Day Before His
Twenty-Seventh Birthday*

Connor Cobalt

As soon as I step off the elevators in the corporate building of Cobalt Inc., my assistant hands me a coffee. I've already routed my course towards my office, and he skips to keep up with my assured stride. I never waver from my destination. I never cast doubtful or curious glances any other way.

I know where I'm going. I always do.

I wouldn't be able to say the same of all my employees. Some slack off in the hallway, their voices hushing once they spot me. I feel them. Their eyes roaming me, mouths parting with an audible breath.

Awed.

Stricken.

They shuffle towards the wall, granting me more space to pass through. I don't offer a greeting in return.

One time—before the death of my mother, as I climbed rung by rung up the proverbial corporate ladder—I would've stomached a banal *hello*. I would've rifled through copious facts for small talk. To appear personable. *How is your daughter? Is she doing well in Cambridge?*

Now that I'm CEO of Cobalt Inc., the falsities can be shelved.

Warmth does more harm than good. I don't need to be their friend. Just their assertive, dignified boss.

I must walk past a new intern because under her breath, she murmurs, "Whoa."

The corner of my lip rises.

My assistant *sprints* ahead and then blocks my office door with his five-foot-five frame. "I booked your flight to Hong Kong, Mr. Cobalt. It leaves tomorrow, just as you asked."

I blink once at him, not letting any emotion filter through. "Tomorrow *morning*?" I need to leave as early as possible on January 3. Rose always plans to "make this day special"—just for me. I always plan to not make this day anything other than it already is. Just a regular day.

We've been combatting one another on the topic for a long while.

Since I was sixteen.

She was fifteen. We attended a winter convention for all the prospective Ivy League scholars in the east. College recruits passed out pamphlets, hoping we'd go to their institution and empty our bank accounts for a piece of paper that says *you're very smart and capable, Mr. or Ms.*

I went to shake hands with almost everyone.

Rose went because her mother said she should, and she was still wavering between Princeton and the University of Pennsylvania. Even at fifteen, we both had these faraway futures built in our heads.

I found her first by her voice.

"I'm not going to a fashion institute, Mother." Rose crossed her arms over her chest, her hair slicked back in a glossy ponytail. She wore a high-collared black dress and matching heels. Of the times we would cross paths, I rarely saw her out of her Dalton Academy uniform.

I edged closer, and when an older man tried to introduce himself to me, I made an excuse to dip out of the conversation. If I sat longer, if I thought about it then, I would've realized that I only ever made extra time for Rose Calloway.

"The rep from Yale said that if fashion interests you, then there are better routes, Rose. You're starting Calloway Couture. You already know what you want to do."

Rose's fiery yellow-green eyes landed on the wall, thinking for a moment. She returned them to her mother. "I want to learn more than just fashion, even if Calloway Couture is my end goal. I need more, and these people"—she waved at the college reps—"they don't know me. They can't tell me what to do with my life off two minutes of time."

Her mother pursed her lips. "They're just advising you, Rose."

"And their advice isn't as good as the advice I'd give myself."

I began to grin.

"Just listen to Harvard and then we can go. Christopher Barnes is over by the snack table. It'd be nice if you said hello too. I'll be talking to his mother over there." At this, Rose's mother left to go socialize with the parents.

My own mother never came to these functions, not unless they benefited her in some way. None of them ever did.

Rose turned her head, and her piercing eyes met me.

I grinned more.

She glared, and then her heels clanked across the hardwood of Suite #157, a room inside the Conservatory of the Arts in Baltimore.

Two inches away from me, she stopped. "Richard."

"Rose."

She perched her hands on her hips, and I had so many things to say, so much to ask, but I would've rather listened to her. I wanted to know what she was thinking. What she saw inside of me. So I waited.

She perused my black tailored suit, my cuff links, my deep blue eyes and then my wavy brown hair. *You like my hair*—I bit the words on the edge of my tongue before they escaped.

Let her speak first, Connor.

"Where's your mother?"

I was surprised that she asked this first. Even more surprised when she began to scan the room for Katarina, thinking she'd be nearby.

I tried not to show it, my features composed, entirely unreadable. "Why do you want to meet my mother?" I arched a brow at her.

She snorted. "It's not like I want to ask her for your hand in marriage."

I grinned more.

She glared once again.

"You said it, Rose, not me."

Her cheeks formed a blush, just barely, but it could've also been from irritation. "I'm curious, especially since you just saw my mother for the first time." I opened my mouth, but she cut me off. "And don't say you didn't notice. You were spying on me." She raised her chin like she'd knocked over my rook.

"You're the only one who would call it *spying*."

"Then what would you call it?"

"Observation."

She growled a little bit.

I put my fists in my slacks. Still tall. I never cowered, and I could tell my height advantage was annoying her as much as my words. I'd grown another inch since the last time I'd seen her, but she'd never been able to surpass my height. Not even with heels.

"Whatever you were doing, it wasn't fair." She licked her lips in thought. "You can't know more about me than I know about you. Those are the rules."

I didn't ask, *the rules to what?* I wasn't dense. Beneath everything, we all were playing a game. Everyone in that room.

Everyone in the world. It just so happened that the game Rose and I chose to play meant we'd be fair. Equal. Until the end.

Until the end.

That was a future I hadn't built yet.

"My mother isn't here," I told her easily. "She didn't want to come."

Rose's brows furrowed in confusion, and her eyes swept my features for sadness, sorrow, hurt—but I felt none.

Fire returned to her gaze. "She just let her fifteen-year-old son go to Baltimore alone? Is your father here?"

"No father," I said quickly, before she began scrutinizing the crowds again. "And I'm not fifteen anymore."

Her shoulders slid back a little, and her brows jumped. "You're sixteen? When was your birthday?"

Today. January 3.

I wouldn't tell her until I was eighteen. I can give most facts easily, but this one, I knew she'd cling to. Like most people would. Birthdays have meaning for nearly everyone. Just not for me.

"What does it matter what age I am?" I began to tell her, letting her know exactly what I thought of the topic. "I'm competent enough to be here alone. I don't need my mother to help make decisions for me. I don't need her to hold my hand."

She rolled her eyes. "You're a minor. Whether you like it or not, Connor, the world will always see you that way."

"It's bullshit."

"It's life."

I almost let irritation cross my face. I relaxed my lips for a second and scanned the students my age and their parents who lingered around. "Life," I mused. *I can play that game.* I could play into society's constraints, but I wouldn't celebrate that day.

When she asked about my birthday, I told her that I stopped having parties when I went to boarding school. On purpose. I didn't find a point in it.

We spent fifteen minutes bickering about the meaning of birthdays and how you can take advantage of people doting on you. Every year, around the same time, we'd have the same conversation. When we were finally in a relationship, she tried to show me *why* on my birthday.

I dodged every party she attempted to throw.

It's become partly a competition, partly something soulful. I see how badly she wants me to love January 3, and that passion, every year, has been more of a gift than she'll ever know.

Back in the hallway of my office, my assistant shifts his weight, one foot to the other. I asked him if the flight is for tomorrow *morning*, but by his sweaty palms, I highly doubt it.

He says, "Your pilot cancelled. He has the flu. A replacement can bring you to Hong Kong, but not until after twelve thirty."

Wonderful. I hold in an annoyed breath. "Anything else?" I arch my brow.

He's guarding the door to my office—for what reason, I can't be certain without questioning. I'm not a mind reader, as much as Lily would like to believe.

I just know more than ninety-nine-point-nine-nine percent of the population.

I know more than you.

"Remember how you agreed to do an interview about your twenty-seventh birthday?" *To appease Samantha Calloway. Rose's mother.*

"Yes." I don't like where this is going.

"The interview . . . it wasn't something I could email you."

I put the pieces together. "A tabloid reporter is waiting in my office for an interview?"

He nods. "I meant to tell you earlier. I interpreted their email incorrectly. They showed up ten minutes ago, and I thought they asked for a time to *send* the questions."

I check my watch. "Order lunch for me and move back my

meeting at ten." I'll have to text Lo to cancel lunch. I was going to meet him at his office, only a block away.

"I will."

I don't waste time scolding him. He looks like he understands his misstep, which is what matters. I enter my office, rain pelting the wide floor-length window in downtown Philadelphia.

A young redheaded reporter rises from a leather couch. She stretches out her hand while clutching a notepad stuffed with papers in the other. "I'm Holly Marks." The minute I shake her hand, the notepad slips out.

She apologizes, and I help her collect it before we both take a seat. Her on the couch. Me across from her in a leather chair.

My desk sits on the other side of the room. Thankfully my computer is locked, and she wouldn't know the passcode. She should've been sitting in a waiting room, not alone in my office. I'll remind Douglas of this so he won't make the same mistake twice.

I wait for her to shuffle through her notes and say, "I only have five minutes."

"I-I understand." Holly clicks her pen. "All of my questions come from diehard fans." She taps at her notepad. "I'll just get right into it. What is your favorite memory of a past birthday?"

I lean back in my chair and rest my ankle on my knee. "I flew to Ontario last year. It was beautiful there." I didn't do anything out of the ordinary. I'd already been to Ontario before.

"What is the biggest adventure you've experienced in your life so far?"

I tilt my head, my lips upturning in thought. "Anytime I'm with Rose, and among that, being a father."

She mouths the answers as she writes down my responses. "Okay, um, can you describe your love for Rose in five words?"

"Brilliant. Passionate. *Unyielding*." I smile. "Devoted. Endless." I pause as she writes.

Then she questions, "If you were asked to speak to a graduating class, what would you say?"

"It would change depending on college or high school. Either way, if they were graduating, I'd congratulate both for achieving educational success. The paper they hold will be a key in bettering themselves. Whether they want to believe it holds that much weight or not."

"And if you had a time machine, what moment would you pick to go back and live again?"

I think for only a second:

The day I met Rose.

The day I married Rose.

The day Rose gave birth to Jane.

I've never been traditional in values, but I've felt more emotion on days that hold greater meaning to Rose. I understand these human concepts more and more. I feel them.

Still there's a part of me that doesn't want to reveal them. "I wouldn't go back in time. It's an impossible task for anyone."

"Right . . ." She flips a page. "If you had one wish, what would you wish for?"

"My daughter to grow up happy and healthy."

She nods a couple times and scribbles. "The fans will love that."

I smile again. "I'm glad my love for Jane can make the fans happy."

"So someone asked if there's only one antidote for a viral disease, who would you give it to, Rose or Jane, and why?"

I put my fingers to my lips.

It's a creative question, so I wouldn't fault its merit. I don't enjoy *what if* games where I'm forced to pick between Rose and Jane. It's a situation that I doubt will ever arise, so I haven't planned for it.

"I would choose Jane. Even if I gave the antidote to Rose, she'd refuse to take it and give it to our daughter." Rose would've liked this question.

"Let's say you are a real god for one day," Holly continues. "What negative force will you eradicate and why, and what positive thing will you let flourish and why?"

"I'd eradicate ignorance and let knowledge flourish. And if it's not self-explanatory, I suggest reading a little more."

I check my watch. "You have two minutes."

She speedily says, "If you had to choose between Lily and Daisy to accompany you to Mars, who would you choose and why?"

"Both would be horrible companions in a spacecraft, but mostly because I value my life. Lily would be frantic, and Daisy would wander off."

"What has been the strangest gift someone has given you?"

"Nothing is strange to me. Maybe unique, but not strange."

She nods and mouths my answer again, her pen scraping the pad quickly. "What would your ideal guys' night be like?"

"I'm interested in seeing other people's interests, so I'd do whatever Loren Hale wanted."

Holly smiles at her notepad when she writes down my response. "Okay, so this is the last question and then I have quick-fire ones. Do we have time for that?"

I nod without checking my watch.

"Using only one word or two if you have to, describe your relationship with Lily, Loren, Daisy, Ryke and Frederick."

I mentioned Frederick in *Princesses of Philly* a few times and on social media, so I'm not shocked he's on this list.

"Lily?" she asks.

Without missing a beat, I answer, "Friend." *And a girl I once tutored.*

"Loren?"

I grin. "Best friend." *First real friend.*

"Daisy?"

I pause. "Sister-in-law." *More and more like a little sister.*

"Ryke?"

"Our relationship is like a man and his dog. I'm the man, clearly."

Currently, our relationship is nearly *indescribable.* I don't know what we are other than complicated friends, but I don't tell this to Holly.

"And Frederick?"

"Advisor." *Loyal friend.*

She scribbles. "Quick-fire questions. On time or on point?"

"On time." On point could mean various things, so I can pass it, easily.

"Shakespeare or Sylvia Plath?"

Richard, I hear Rose in the back of my head, hostile, her heel tapping the hardwood. *Don't cheat.* I smile again as I say, "Shakespeare."

"History Channel or Discovery Channel?"

"History. Discovery has too many reality shows."

"Scientists or doctors?"

"Both." *Cheater.* I press my fingers to my lips to hide my burgeoning grin. My elbow on the armrest of my chair.

"Gold or silver?"

"Gold."

"Money or fame?"

"Money."

"No arms or no legs?"

"Did Lily ask this?" It sounds like a question she'd throw at me. Holly shakes her head. "Just a fan."

"No legs," I answer.

She nods and keeps jotting down everything. "Bald or long hair?"

"Long hair." I could pull it back.

"Black or blue suits?"

"Black."

"No fears or no regrets?"

Regrets are complicated. So are fears. If I thought longer and harder, I'd lean between both of them, but for now, I just say, "No fears."

"Reading comics with Lo or rock climbing with Ryke?"

"Reading comics with Lo," I say easily, and after she finishes writing my last word, she clicks her pen. "Finished?" I ask.

She nods, rising from her seat.

I join her and hold out her hand. "Thank you for the interview." The questions were tame—ones that I prefer over anything more invasive.

"Thanks for the time. The fans know how much it means to you." She almost drops a piece of paper, but I catch it and then slide it in her notepad. She gives me a sheepish goodbye wave.

I lead Holly out and open the door for her.

Before she goes, she says, "Happy birthday—for tomorrow, I mean. Do you have anything fun planned? Off the record, of course." Her voice is sincere.

"I'm going to Hong Kong."

The only person who can change the course of things—who believes I deserve something spectacular on January 3—will have to go to great lengths to win.

And Rose's odds—they're equal to mine.

Fifty-fifty.

BONUS: DAISY CALLOWAY'S BIRTHDAY LETTER FROM CONNOR COBALT

Daisy,

I'll keep this as short as possible. I'm not always a champion of brevity, but it serves its purpose now and then.

I understand what it takes to please people around you, but for many, many years I've seen you please people to your detriment. And then I've seen you overcome great odds and chase after something you've lost.

I want you to know that I've heard your voice. And by all that I know to this day, it's loud and strong and unwavering.

Happy twentieth birthday, Daisy. You are someone I dearly admire, and I'm positive many others truly admire you too.

Take care of yourself always.

Connor

BONUS:

Loren Hale's Twenty-Fifth Birthday Interview

*Note for the reader: Loren Hale's birthday takes place before the beginning of *Fuel the Fire*.

Here's what happened: Loren kept forgetting to fill out these fan questions, to Lily's horror. "We can't let our fandom down!" she declared, going into full-on panic mode the morning of Halloween (while they were in bed). She tried to fill out the questions for him, but he stole the laptop from her—finally agreeing. The power of Lily Calloway's love of fandoms won him over! Also: she peered over his shoulder while he was typing, and she wants everyone to know that she's not responsible for any asshole responses.

These are his results!

Q: What is your favorite memory of a past birthday?
A: This birthday because I'm in bed with my 'puff—and to Queen Rose out there, I didn't cheat. My birthday started at 12:01 a.m. (that is the past), so put your broomstick in the pantry.

Q: Now that you have a family of your own, are in a better place regarding your addiction and have taken over Hale Co., what kind of advice or words of encouragement would you give to the Loren Hale at rock bottom?
A: Stop fucking up. (Obviously I'm not good at giving goddamn advice.)

Q: Imagine an alternate universe where you and Ryke had grown up together in one household with the same parents. How do you imagine your relationship in that universe?

A: Perfect. We'd be dressing alike every day, skipping down sidewalks, telling each other bedtime stories. You wouldn't even be able to separate us. #bestfriends

Q: If you were told you had a terminal illness and had six months to live, what three things would be most important for you to do?

A: 1–3: CONVINCE RYKE MEADOWS TO NEVER WEAR THE FUCKING GREEN ARROW COSTUME EVER AGAIN.

Q: If you could commit any crime and get away with it, what would you do?

A: Murder. (Lily deleted who I want to murder—and she wants everyone to know that this is an exaggeration. I don't know why she's surprised. I'm sorted as a Slytherin, for Christ's sake.)

Q: If you had a time machine, what moment in time would you pick to go back to and live again?

A: The moment I first met Lily Calloway. I'd pinch her cheek again.

Q: What is the greatest thing Lily had given you so far?

A: Her love for me. And our son.

Q: What are your family goals?

A: Don't fuck up, and if I fuck up, don't let it fuck up my kid.

Q: If you had the chance to be a comic book character, which villain would you choose to play and why?

A: Hellion from X-Men is pretty much a villain at the start. And he's pretty much me.

Q: What is one quality you possess that you hope will pass on to your children?
A: My ability to see that *some* comics are inferior to literally everything else in this universe. Go back into your shitty cave, *you know who you are.* (Lily told me to "play nice" and take out the comics and specific superhero I'm referring to, but if you know, you know. And you're welcome, Lil.)

Q: Using only one word per person, how would you describe your relationship with Lily, Rose, Daisy, Connor and Ryke?
A:

Lily = soul mate

Rose = nemesis

Connor = BFF

Daisy = sister?

Ryke = family

Q: Any hints as to what/who you and Lily will be dressing up as for Halloween?
A: I've already given some throughout this thing. Another hint: she's in yellow. I'm in green. Anyone who can't figure this out, we can't be friends.

THIS OR THAT

Q: Long or short?
A: Lily thinks this means cock size. Long for Lil. (She's trying to delete this one too. I raised the laptop over her head. You're welcome, whoever's reading this.)

Q: Xavier or Magneto?

A: Depends at what point in time. Right now, Magneto.

Q: Captain America or Arrow?
A: Out of whatever loyalty, Captain America.

Q: Beetlejuice or Edward Scissorhands?
A: Beetlejuice. Lily likes Beetlejuice more—so I've seen it ten thousand times more.

Q: Freckles or dimples?
A: Dimples.

Q: Wolverine or Magneto?
A: Magneto for now.

Q: Chicken tacos or beef tacos?
A: Chicken tacos, no question.

Q: Lights on or lights off?
A: Dim lighting, not completely dark.

Q: Sansa Stark or Arya Stark?
A: Arya, every time.

Q: Pet-sit Coconut or Sadie?
A: Sadie doesn't like Lil, so always Nutcake.

Q: Understand multiple languages or read minds?
A: Read minds. Anyone can learn languages. No one can learn how to read minds—except for maybe Connor Cobalt.

BONUS: TEXT MESSAGE THREADS

AFTER THE EPILOGUE OF *FUEL THE FIRE*

LILY: I don't want to bother you while you're unpacking. Maybe this is a long shot. But do you have any sugar?

ROSE: Yes. For what?

LILY: Cookies.

LILY: No, cake!

LILY: Some sort of sweet thing. I haven't decided yet.

Rose: Why are you baking?

LILY: Just because.

ROSE: Since when have you ever baked "just because"? What's going on?

ROSE: It's a surprise party for someone, isn't it? Why wasn't I in on this?

ROSE: If it's for Connor, I can keep a secret from him.

LILY: There's no surprise party!

ROSE: That's what someone who's planning a surprise party would say.

LILY: The sugar is just an excuse. OK!

ROSE: What?

LILY: You moved out last week and I miss you and it's a normal neighborly thing to do to ask for sugar. So I asked for some sugar.

ROSE: Oh.

LILY: So . . .

ROSE: I miss you too. And you don't need to ask for sugar. Just stop by.

LILY: You make it sound so easy, but your mansion is intimidating.

ROSE: Then call beforehand and I'll meet you at the end of the driveway.

LILY: Really? 😳

ROSE: Really 🖤

. . .

ROSE: My mother just stopped by and gave me two shopping bags full of clothes for Jane. They're hideous.

CONNOR: That sounds like an exaggeration.

ROSE: They have frogs licking flies on them.

CONNOR: That is what frogs do, darling.

ROSE: You are not helping, Richard.

ROSE: I own a baby clothing line. Why would she give me baby clothes? It's a figurative slap in the face.

CONNOR: Passive aggression tends to be your mother's language, but there is a possibility she was trying to help.

ROSE: She said the new onesies for Calloway Couture Babies were "simple" and not in a complimentary way. She said it as an insult.

CONNOR: Do we care what she thinks?

ROSE: Of course not. I'm donating the clothes she gave me. Obviously. Could you take them with you on your way to work tomorrow? There's a donation box on your way.

CONNOR: I'd be happy to.

CONNOR: How's Jane?

ROSE: Perfect as always. She's helping me pick out swatches for the summer collection.

CONNOR: She's only one. You trust her judgment?

ROSE: Over yours. Yes.

CONNOR: Such lies.

ROSE: I think she's going to be an astronaut or pilot.

CONNOR: Such deflection.

ROSE: Her first word was "up" and that could very well be fate.

ROSE: And I'm not deflecting, I'm staying on topic. Unlike you.

CONNOR: Let's continue this topic when I get home. My meeting just got cancelled. I'll see you soon, darling.

. . .

LO: Would you tell your sister our house isn't haunted?

ROSE: She's your wife, Loren. Tell her yourself.

LO: I told her you haunted this place *while* you were living here. Now she thinks you left a "ghost" trail when you moved out.

ROSE: Have fun in that bed you made.

LO: She's searching for an EMF sensor to buy.

ROSE: Good. Maybe she'll realize you're the demon.

LO: See you in hell, Cruella.

ROSE: 🖕

LO: 🖕

BONUS: PLAYLIST

"Non, je ne regrette rien" by Édith Piaf

"Fire Meets Gasoline" by Sia

"This Time I Won't Forget" by Kongos

"When I Get My Hands On You" by The New Basement Tapes

"Don't Shy from the Light" by NEULORE

"Into Gold" by Matthew and the Atlas

"Terrible Love" by The National

"Every Night" by Josef Salvat

"I'm Only Joking" by Kongos

"Gold" by Chet Faker

"Drown" by Marika Hackman

"Common People" by Pulp

"Burn the Pages" by Sia

"Under Stars" by AURORA

"Saturn" by Sleeping At Last

Ryke Meadows

The longest blonde hair caught the wind, splayed wildly and fucking madly. I watched her grip onto the railing of a wooden ramp, suspended midair towards a bungee jump. She rocked back and forth like she was squeezing in early morning pull-ups for the day.

She wasn't. Doing pull-ups for the fucking day, I meant.

She just couldn't stop moving.

And I kept thinking, *this girl is off her fucking hinges*.

We stood near the back of the bungee line, and as she peered over the railing again, she lifted her hips onto it, hanging her head farther down.

Fucking A.

When everyone bailed on bungee jumping, all but Daisy, I didn't think she'd pretend to be a bird and crawl over the railing. I had no clue what sixteen-year-olds usually did, but for some fucking reason, I thought she would've complained about the long line or lack of cell phone reception.

I'd only known her for short spurts of time, and I was still trying to understand who she was at her core.

Six thirty a.m. in the tropical climate of a foreign country.

My first real time alone with Daisy Calloway. Without her sisters or my brother present.

And my fucking issue: in the back of my mind, while I watched her hang headfirst, I thought, *that looks like fucking fun.*

And then, *any farther over that railing and I'm grabbing her.*

I rebounded between wanting to protect her and wanting to do crazy shit with her. I tried to block out whatever thoughts continued to churn, and I just went on impulse.

"What the fuck are you doing, Calloway?" I sidled next to her and rested my hand on her shoulder, but I didn't pull her down. I leaned my waist against the wooden barrier and saw the answer in her green eyes.

She perused the landscape, as though appreciating the expansive view of Cancún, Mexico. The current location of my college spring break. Even though Daisy wasn't in college, she tagged along to spend time with her older sisters, who were all happy by her presence.

Daisy tucked a flyaway strand of hair behind her ear. "They're missing out."

"They won't fucking think so." Most of them didn't want to wake up this early, and Lily was too scared of heights to even contemplate the idea.

The line moved forward. "You coming with me?" I asked her, raking a hand through my unkempt brown hair.

She finally met my eyes, something devious behind hers. "Do a lot of girls come with you?" she asked.

My expression stayed in the same fucking darkened state. "If I'm with them," I said vaguely, treading the line between the sexual innuendo and the safer space.

Daisy set her feet on the ramp, and despite her flirty fucking question, there was true intrigue behind her eyes and some confusion that I couldn't read past. "So you've never had a girl not come with you?"

My head pounded, and I rubbed my lips. "Move, Daisy."

I was twenty-two.

She was sixteen.

I would've never—in a fucking million years—taken advantage of Daisy, but I always had a hard time shutting my mouth when someone asked me for advice in so many words, in so many fucking ways. This wouldn't have been the first time I talked to her about sex, but I worried that she would've started relating these conversations to me and concluded that I thought about her in a sexual way.

Daisy skipped up the ramp while she walked two of her fingers along the railing. "I was just curious." She glanced at me with a sincere apology on her face. "Sorry."

"You don't have to fucking apologize for asking me something."

We stopped again, the line at a standstill. Her hair flew in every direction, and she tilted her head, like she struggled to rephrase her first question. Daisy's expression could be summed up as pained confusion, and in my very fucking core, I wanted to help her. I just hoped I could.

"What's eating at you?" I asked.

"Mosquitoes." She wafted invisible bugs. She always tried to lighten the mood when she felt it going sour by her own hand.

My jaw hardened. "What's fucking *bothering* you?" I didn't fucking care about whether or not the air tensed or discomfort passed between us. I just cared about her.

"Nothing." *It's not nothing.*

I rubbed my eyes in annoyance. "Daisy—"

"It's not a big deal." She wore that uncertainty again.

"Yeah? Why do you look like you need to throw up?"

She crossed her arms in a very Rose Calloway fucking manner. "You're so pushy. You know that, right?" She'd reminded me of that before. "Are you like this with everyone?"

Only people I care about. "Look, I'm going to annoy the fuck out of you like you're annoying me right now, so you might as well do us both the favor and give it to me, Calloway." I waved her on.

Her lips lifted a fraction. "Do you want it hard or soft?"

"Hard as you want to fucking go."

A gust of wind whipped her hair in her face, blonde strands sticking to her mouth. She looked frustrated by her waist-length hair, and so I helped comb it back so she could see. She grunted in irritation at the tangled mess.

"Give me." I gestured to her hair tie.

She snapped it off her wrist, and I collected her fucking hair, putting it in the messiest bun. She said "Thanks" and sighed in relief before I even finished.

I stepped back one foot. "You asked me if I've ever had a girl *not* come with me. Why does that fucking matter to you?"

"It's not about you personally," she said quickly.

"I never thought it was."

Her brows scrunched, her expression fucking killing me. "I just wondered," she began, "if maybe there's something wrong with me." She took a long pause.

My jaw locked. *Nothing's fucking wrong with you*; the words sat like a pit in my throat.

"Or maybe," she continued, ". . . maybe there's something wrong with the guys I've been with." She then hiked herself on the railing, sitting and swinging her legs.

At six-three, my head was still higher than hers, so I stared down while she looked up at me. I would've sat next to her, but I wanted to meet her eyes.

"Some girls are hard to get off," I told her. "Some guys are fucking terrible at pleasing women. You're not going to know which category you fall into, sweetheart. Not until you find someone that you're fucking attracted to."

She nodded a few times, looking crestfallen and incredibly

fucking sad. When she sensed me staring, she gave me an *I'm okay* smile that I didn't believe.

There was nothing I could do to fix how she felt, and that was the hardest part of the entire thing.

"Have you been bungee jumping before?" she asked, changing the topic so I'd stop worrying.

"A few fucking times. What about you?"

"Mostly at theme parks." Daisy skimmed my features, her green eyes flitting over the carabiners on the belt loops of my jeans, rising up my green crewneck to my unshaven jaw, hardened gaze and thick, dark brown hair.

She wasn't discreet about the once-over, but she wasn't exactly being suggestive either. Just fucking curious.

She hopped back on the ramp, and we walked up the shortened line, tension winding between us.

"Can you say no?" I asked her suddenly.

She nodded and knotted the bottom of her loose-fitting white shirt, a neon-green bikini beneath. No shorts.

"What if I was just some guy and I tried to pull down your bathing suit, what would you fucking do?"

Daisy shrugged. "I don't know—a lot of factors would have to go into it, I think."

"It's not a fucking trick question," I retorted, pissed—not at her. I was pissed because I knew what made her think like that. She'd started modeling at fourteen. She'd been touched and man-handled and told to get dressed in front of people, treated like absolute fucking shit. I'd heard snippets of stories from her sisters, and their mom was forcing her to stand still when all this girl wanted to do was run.

Right now, she could barely even keep two feet in one place.

"Why does it matter to you?" she asked me what I'd asked her.

I shook my head, thinking about how much my mom silenced me, and it'd taken me a long time to find my voice. I wouldn't have wanted that rough road for anyone, but I started seeing pieces of my life inside of hers. And why the fuck were we the only two people here?

Why the fuck did I bungee alone all three other times in my life?

My head hammered again. *I care about you. I want you to be safe. Please don't fuck anyone that makes you uncomfortable. It's going to kill me if it kills you.*

Every word bled into my brain, but I fought myself from saying them out loud. I just kept shaking my head.

I rubbed my jaw and then noticed two twentysomething guys ahead of us. Staring at her ass. I ended up moving forward in the line. In front of her. I blocked them from view, and she spun around to face me once more.

She began to smile, understanding what I just did.

It was a better fucking smile. I liked those because I knew she was doing okay.

And then abruptly, I said, "You can ask me anything." The phrase was weighted. *Ask me anything.* I rarely shared personal facts with people. I barely opened up to my own brother beyond the subject of addiction. And I was letting her ask me anything.

If I dug deep enough, I would've realized that I wanted her to know me.

I felt so fucking compelled to strip a layer away, and I'd never been drawn to do it. I had no idea why. I didn't stand there and list out reasons on a diagram or chart like Connor Cobalt would've. I just followed my gut this time.

My stomach tightened as I waited for her to speak.

She wore confusion again. "I don't know what to ask."

Realization hit me in a second or two. She was still afraid of offending me or hurting my feelings if she asked the wrong thing.

We moved up the line again, and I said, "Maybe next time, Calloway."

"Didn't you hear?" She wagged her brows at me. "I may not be here tomorrow. Life could take me at any moment, and then *poof*, you'd be here again with another girl in another time and asking her to ask you anything." She said theatrically, "The unexpectedness of it all."

My gaze darkened and muscles constricted. "That's not fucking funny, sweetheart."

"You'd call her sweetheart too." Sadness lingered behind her fleeting smile. I saw it before. Flickering inside of her. Like she would've been all right with dying. Like she was searching for something more that kept slipping out of grasp.

I rushed to say the first thing in my fucking head. To make her feel better. To fix *this*. Something I doubted could be changed by my hand. *Light is dimming behind your eyes; do you fucking see that, Daisy?*

So I said the truth. "You know, you're the only girl I've ever called that."

I didn't tell her that it was the first term of endearment I'd ever used with anyone. I found "baby" and other pet names too fucking patronizing, but "sweetheart" fit Daisy completely and in a sort of nonromantic context. I would've never said it condescendingly or backhandedly. Always just kindly. How it should be used.

Her lips almost pulled up. "You think I'm sweet?"

"I think you're out of your fucking mind. And I'm going out of mine." At that, I focused on the line, but I felt her smiling fully beside me.

Good.

Only two guys were ahead of us, already harnessed and on the platform. About to take their turn. An employee reached us and asked, "Are you jumping together or separate?"

Daisy nudged my waist and joked, "If you're scared, I can jump with you. Lily said I'm a pretty good hand-holder."

I thought about everything she'd been telling me along the

ramp, and this underlying function inside of me said, *don't leave her alone*.

"We're jumping together," I told the employee.

Daisy's lips parted in shock. There was no way she could believe I was scared, and if she did, I didn't honestly care. After her surprise wore off, she rolled with the new plan.

The employee gave us instructions and helped Daisy with her harness. Maybe because I had carabiners on my belt loop or because I looked like I knew what I was fucking doing—he never hovered over me.

In the passing minute, Daisy and I repeatedly glanced at each other. I watched her smile gain more life, which actually pulled my lips upward too.

Over the screaming of guys who just jumped, Daisy retied her hair into a pony, and I wondered what she was thinking. If she was *overthinking* what I just fucking did.

I decided to be blunt since I requested to bungee tandem with her. "You know that I don't like you like that, Dais." The words were fucking static and actually hard to produce.

I thought it might hurt her, but she just gave me a knowing look—like she understood more than I gave her credit for. To lighten the mood, she said, "It's okay; you can admit it."

"What am I admitting?!" I had to raise my voice over the next guy's fucking screams.

We were ushered to the empty platform at that point, and two employees checked our harnesses, attaching more straps to our legs and clipping me to her. Face-to-face. They locked us together with another carabiner on our waists.

"That you're scared." She motioned to the descent, a playful look in her eyes.

"Cute."

"Cute because it's accurate." She wagged her brows again.

"Cute because it's fucking inaccurate." My hand slid to the

back of her head, and I felt her body react in a way that surprised her. I drew back only a fraction, my lips close to her ear. I whispered, "I'm not fucking scared of you." If she wanted to dive headfirst, I was going to dive right behind her.

She knew that was true.

She inhaled deeply, her chest rising against mine.

When the employees finished tethering us together, they instructed, "Hold on to each other. The tighter, the better, so your limbs won't smack into hers."

I wrapped my arms firmly around her shoulders, not hesitant about it. Hers slipped around my waist, not cautious either. Her heartbeat thudded against my chest. Racing with each passing second.

With Cancún as our landscape, we hugged each other in the sky. She rose and dropped on her tiptoes in crazed anticipation. I watched her focus descend, contemplating the distance between her feet and the ground.

So I pointed at the sun ascending in the horizon. Just as the darkened sky began to lighten. "Keep your eyes there."

Her green ones flickered to me before following my finger. Her pulse picked up speed. "And what happens when it disappears?"

I would've loved to tell her that it never would. That no matter where we were, the sun would always be present. But it wouldn't have been true.

The only thing we could count on was that the sun would rise again.

"Wait for it to return," I told her.

She gave me the saddest smile I'd ever fucking seen. "That's an awfully long time."

For some people, I knew a minute could seem like infinity. So maybe one night seemed like forever for Daisy.

"Hey, Calloway," I said softly, tucking a flyaway strand of hair behind her ear, one that escaped her pony.

"Hey," she whispered back.

"You ready to feel your fucking heart burst out of your chest?"

Her features illuminated tenfold. And she said quietly, "Yes."

I barely heard the instructor tell us to jump before we both charged off the platform together. Our bodies pressed close, my chest against hers, hers against mine. We sliced through air, and she hollered fucking happily. Like she was in the front seat of a roller coaster.

She laughed.

I smiled. *Fuck*—I was really smiling.

I never bungee jumped with another person, and doing it with Daisy had suddenly beat every fucking time I did it alone. As we slowed—hanging upside down, spinning some—we met each other's gaze.

She wore this honest smile that I hated to see leave. "Thank you," she panted, out of breath from excitement and adrenaline.

"For what?"

"For doing this with me," she said, "so I didn't have to be alone."

It was then. That I fucking knew how much I really understood her. How much I related to the loneliness in her eyes. I felt closer to her in a way that I couldn't articulate. It wasn't physical. Or mental. It was spiritual, something I couldn't shake.

I nodded a couple times, and she practically radiated. As though she felt the air shift, brighter and lighter.

I felt it too.

And I fucking thought, *thank God.*

Thank God the sun will rise again.

Krista and Becca Ritchie are *New York Times* and *USA Today* bestselling authors and identical twins—one a science nerd, the other a comic book geek—but with their shared passion for writing, they combined their mental powers as kids and have never stopped telling stories. They love superheroes, flawed characters and soul mate love.

VISIT KRISTA AND BECCA RITCHIE ONLINE

KBRitchie.com
KBMRitchie